QUINT ADLER, P.I.

QUINT ADLER BOOK #5

BRIAN O'SULLIVAN

This novel is dedicated to Time Magazine's Person of the Year in 2006.

This is a work of fiction. Names, characters, places, and incidents either are the product of the author's imagination or are used in a fictitious manner. Any resemblance to actual persons, living or dead, events, or locales is merely coincidental.

PART ONE: A TWENTY-YEAR-OLD MURDER

CHAPTER 1

The first time I ever laid eyes on Emmett Fisk, he was tumbling over the concrete slab in front of his handicapped parking spot.

It was before I'd taken his case. Before I knew his sordid family history. Before I learned about the murders. And before his case would drive me to the brink of insanity.

I wish I'd known his falling was the perfect precursor of what was to come. If ever I needed the gift of foresight, it would have been the day Emmett Fisk walked into my office.

In the moment, his fall wasn't at all surprising considering Emmett was a nonagenarian. That's the name for someone between the ages of ninety and one hundred.

That's another thing I found out later on.

He'd clipped his foot on the concrete block and went down. I saw it clearly from the waiting room of my brand new office. As I rushed outside, my initial thought, after making sure he was alright, was that Emmett Fisk shouldn't be driving. If you stumble over a four-inch piece of concrete, I'm probably not going to trust you with a two-ton automobile.

I extended my hand to give him a lift up but quickly realized that wouldn't be enough, so I grabbed him by his flanks and lifted him to his feet.

"Thank you, sir," he said, picking up his fedora off the ground and putting it back on his head.

Even his choice of hat was ancient.

"You're welcome," I said.

"Getting old sucks. Getting really old sucks even more. And at ninety-two, I'm probably more like really, really, really old."

I smiled.

"You look alright to me."

"That lie sounds convincing. Good. That's an advantage in your line of work."

"You must be here to see me."

"You're Quint Adler, correct?"

"I am."

"Then yes, it's you I'm here to see."

Emmett was wearing a beige trench coat and what looked like four other layers of clothing. It was early December and the weather had definitely become brisk, but we weren't exactly in Chicago or New York.

We were in Walnut Creek, twenty miles east of the bays and oceans of San Francisco, and generally about twenty degrees warmer than SF itself. It had its cold days, relatively speaking, and today was one of them. The mid-fifties was as warm as it was going to get. I'm sure no one in the Midwest was feeling too bad for us.

"Come on in," I said.

"By the way, I'm Emmett Fisk. And please, call me by my first name."

"Nice to meet you, Emmett."

"You too, Quint."

He walked into the office and I knew what he was going to say.

"I expected a bigger office," he said.

"I've only been here two weeks," I responded.

"A week for each square foot?"

I had a ninety-two-year-old comedian in my midst.

"Don't forget who helped you up," I said, immediately regretting it.

It didn't bother him. In fact, he laughed. My guess was that Emmett was a tough old SOB. Words weren't going to hurt him.

"Since you dragged me to my feet, it's like we're old friends now. So I can give you a hard time about this minuscule office. Or, bust your balls, as the young kids say these days."

It was safe to say, I liked Emmett right away.

"This way," I said, pointing down the hall.

"Like there's any other option," he said.

I led the sarcastic old fart down the tiny hall to my office. There was a tiny reception area with a couch, a ten-foot hallway, and my office. That was it.

I was located in a strip mall with a Starbucks, a 7-11, and some law firm. Mine was the smallest business by far.

I opened my office door. "Quint" had been etched into it earlier that morning. The engraver planned on adding "Adler, P.I." when he returned from lunch.

I extended my hand, pointing to one of the two leather executive chairs. The other was mine.

"Have a seat," I said.

"Better than the last seat I had," Emmett said, alluding to his fall.

The jokes continued.

"Are you always this funny?" I asked.

"It's only because I'm nervous about what I'm about to tell you. Over-compensating a bit," he said.

"Alright, let's get down to it. What brought you here?"

"My granddaughter."

"What did she do?"

"No, you dunce. She recommended you."

Being called a dunce by Emmett Fisk almost felt like a badge of honor. He said it with such gusto I felt like I'd won something.

"Do I know her?"

"Not exactly. Our family followed the Bay Area Butcher case and were impressed by your, shall we say, exploits."

I was flooded with frightening memories, including sprinting towards the Butcher before he had a chance to kill those children.

"I was grateful for the chance to do some good."

"You did a lot more than that. You saved a bunch of young lives. There's not an adjective strong enough for what you did."

"Thank you," I said.

"Anyway, my granddaughter heard through the grapevine that you'd started a private investigator practice. And since we were enthralled by your work on the Butcher case, I've decided to give you some business. You could certainly use it," he said, turning around and pretending to look for other clients.

"Keep looking, " I said.

"At least you're getting my jokes. That's a good start."

No one spoke for a few seconds.

"Alright, Emmett. Let's hear it. What do you need a private investi-gator for?"

He took a bandana out of his pocket and wiped his glasses with it. His eyes were starting to moisten. I think I'd heard the last of Emmett's jokes for a while.

"My grandson. Ronnie Fisk."

I thought this might be another missing person case like the one I'd just finished up in Las Vegas.

"Is he missing?" I asked.

"No. I wish."

My heart dropped.

"He's dead?"

"Yes. He was killed twenty years ago yesterday. December 5th of 2001."

Emmett took a picture out of his wallet. Ronnie Fisk looked like your all-American boy with a gap-toothed smile and long, wavy hair.

"How old was he?"

"He was fourteen years old at the time."

"I'm so sorry, Emmett."

"Thank you. I've never gotten over it. And I never will. But if we could somehow catch the guy who did it, it would give me a small measure of satisfaction in my waning years."

"Did the cops ever arrest anyone?"

"No. I'm not even sure they ever had a prime suspect."

"Where was he killed"

"In Berkeley. About twenty miles from where we now sit."

"His body was discovered?"

"Yes, two weeks later."

"I hate to ask, but how did he die?"

"He was strangled."

"Just horrible," I said, knowing no words would do it justice.

Emmett nodded.

"He washed up on the shore of the Bay, but the coroner concluded that he'd been dead well before he was dumped in the water."

"Which part of the Bay?"

"In Emeryville, about ten miles from where we think Ronnie was abducted."

"Think?"

"Well, he was on his way home from basketball practice, so it's hard to know exactly where he was abducted."

"How long was his walk home?"

"A little less than a mile."

"And no one saw anything?"

"No. He finished basketball practice, said goodbye to a few friends, and was never seen again."

"Jesus," I said.

"Yeah, Jesus. Although it's hard to be too religious after what my family went through."

I regretted using that particular exclamation.

"I'm sorry," I said.

"It's not your fault."

"I know you said the cops never officially suspected anyone, but how about you?"

"I suspected everyone. Truth be told, I was an asshole during that stretch. If a neighbor wasn't willing to help us walk the streets and look for Ronnie, I'd tear them a new you know what."

Although he liked to joke, I could tell Emmett Fisk was a tough guy. And that was as an old man. I have no doubt he was even more cantankerous in his younger years, especially after losing a grandchild.

"There wasn't one person you suspected more than others?"

"No. Trust me, I wanted to, but there was just so little to go on."

"No offense, Emmett, but this sounds like finding a needle in the haystack."

"It was that tough twenty years ago. Now, it's more like finding a singular grain of sand."

"And yet, you want to hire me?"

"Yes. What else am I going to spend my remaining money on? Viagra?"

I smiled in spite of myself.

"Do you have a case file or something for me to look at?"

"It sounds like you're leaning towards taking it."

"Possibly," I said.

"I don't have the case file myself, but I'm sending you to the person who does."

"Who would that be?" I asked.

"His name is Hank Tressel. He knows more about the case than anyone, myself included."

Hank Tressel was a well-known former police officer.

"I know who he is."

"Unlike me, an old man who is forgetting things, Hank is a young man of seventy-five."

I'd never felt younger in my life.

"A spring chicken," I said.

Emmett laughed.

"Along with the case file, he'll know all the details of Ronnie's case. And I don't want to misremember things and get your investigation off to a disjointed start."

"I understand. Wasn't Tressel a San Francisco cop, though?"

"Yes, he was. That's where he did his big cases. The Zodiac, Zebra Murders, and other non-Z-related cases. But he was an old friend of mine, so when he retired in 2001, the same year that Ronnie went missing, he decided to help look into the disappearance. And the case got ahold of him."

"And he's willing to talk to me?"

"Not solving this case is one of his big regrets. To answer your question, yes, he will talk to you. If you ever get anywhere on this case, he'll be almost as grateful as me."

"Looking forward to it," I said.

"So you're on board?" Emmett Fisk asked.

Considering I had zero cases, and liked and wanted to help Emmett Fisk, there really was no question.

"Yeah, I'm on board," I said. "Should we go through the monetary aspects first? I'd prefer to get that out of the way."

"Sure. I should tell you that I am not a wealthy man, Quint. You'd think I'd have accumulated more wealth in my ninety-plus years, but that's not the case. My grandkids make more in one year than I used to make in four. And yes, they've offered to help support me, but I won't take it."

I wasn't at the stage of my career where I could offer a case pro-bono, but he was making me feel guilty. I didn't want to take the last of his money.

My first two cases had been quite profitable, but half of the money was already gone. A new apartment, opening this office, and my old car had conked out, which I replaced with a newer model. I had to start making money again. Still, this guy was in his nineties...

"I'll tell you what," I said. "My rate is usually $1000 for a week."

"Usually?"

His point was obvious. My office was a ghost town.

"Don't be a smart ass, Emmett. I was about to offer you a deal."

"I can't help it sometimes. Continue."

"I'll give you the next seven days of my services for seven hundred bucks. A hundred bucks a day. And I'll pay for my own gas, food, copies, and any other residual costs that arise. Keep in mind, you're my only client at the moment, so your case will have my complete and total attention. It's the best I can offer."

"I'm not rich, but I'm not dead broke, either. I can rustle up seven hundred dollars."

"Alright then," I said and extended my hand.

Emmett Fisk shook it.

"You're hired," he said.

~

Twenty minutes later, I was walking back to my apartment in Walnut Creek. It was less than a mile from my thriving new business. Okay, thriving wasn't exactly the word, but I had secured my first client in my new digs. I was excited about that.

And yet, there was a shadow hanging over Emmett Fisk and his grandson. This wasn't going to be a pleasant case. I couldn't imagine many things worse than investigating the murder of a fourteen-year-old kid.

I'd be working, though, and there's something to be said for that.

～

I'd moved and now lived alone. Cara and I had tried to make a go of it once I returned from Las Vegas, but it didn't work out. We fought too often and were broken up half the time, so one day I just called it off. She didn't seem too dismayed about it.

I knew it was the end this time. We'd had a good run, but it was over. Last I'd heard, she'd moved up to Sacramento for a new teaching job she'd started in the fall.

My new apartment complex was known as 1716 Lofts and sat smack dab in the middle of Walnut Creek. I had coffee shops, bars, and restaurants all within a few hundred feet of the entrance to my complex. I liked living in the center of the city.

No, Walnut Creek wasn't the most exciting city in the world, but there was some good food, weather, and a few decent watering holes. Plus, I needed a place to settle down after cases in Hollywood and Las Vegas. My goal was to eventually spend a lot of time traveling from case to case, but I needed a home base to get my business off the ground.

I took the elevator up to the 5th floor of my complex and saw Rebecca, a pretty woman in her mid-thirties who I'd casually flirted with a few times. I wasn't looking for another relationship, that's for damn sure, but it didn't mean I couldn't flirt. Or, potentially, get lucky.

"Hey, Quint!"

"Hello, Rebecca. It's a little cold out there. Sure you don't need a jacket?"

"I'm hot-blooded," she said.

"Check it and see. I've got a fever of a hundred and three."

"Don't age yourself with old song lyrics."

I laughed.

"Guilty as charged."

Rebecca smiled and entered the elevator.

I continued to my apartment, which had a nice view of the restaurants and bars below, but calling it a loft might have been pushing it. I get why they named the complex 1716 Lofts. It evokes big apartments with high ceilings, but the reality wasn't quite as extravagant. I wasn't complaining, since it was a nice, clean, safe complex and I loved the location.

My cases figured to get grimy. I'm glad my apartment wasn't.

I'd bought an old-school record player and around ten vinyl albums. All classics. *Ziggy Stardust, OK Computer, Revolver, Physical Graffiti, Dark Side of the Moon,* and a few others.

On this day, I threw on Miles Davis's *Kind of Blue.* Jazz had long been my go-to music when I needed time to think.

The first note hit and I leaned back on my couch, closing my eyes.

A few questions quickly entered my mind.

How deranged must you be to grab a fourteen-year-old boy off the streets?

How could a family like the Fisks ever recover from a tragedy of this magnitude?

And finally, the big one...

Was the monster who killed Ronnie Fisk still out there?

CHAPTER 2

Detective Hank Tressel was a cause célèbre in the Bay Area.
He'd worked many famous murder cases and was never shy around a camera, nor did he lack opinions. Whether all his theories came true was almost irrelevant. The fact that he was willing to go out on a limb and voice his opinion made for good T.V.

A famous local police officer probably didn't happen as much these days, but the late '60s to the '90s were a different era. And from what I'd heard, Hank Tressel was the most famous police officer in San Francisco during that time.

He lived in Sausalito, a beautiful city in Marin County that sat on the San Francisco Bay. It was only five miles from the Golden Gate Bridge.

He answered the door and he looked quite fit for his seventy-five years. His face was a different story. It was a maze of diagonal lines, intersecting over skin that looked like it had spent a lifetime in the sun. Quite an accomplishment for having worked in the often clouded skies of San Francisco.

He was tall, right around my own height of 6'2", and that likely included shrinking a few inches over the years.

He'd have been an intimidating presence when he was an active police officer.

"You must be Quint," he said.

"I am. Thanks for meeting with me, Detective Tressel."

"Actually, in San Francisco, we were called Inspectors."

"I didn't know that."

"No problem, most people don't. I'd prefer if you called me Hank anyway," he said.

Emmett had insisted I call him by his first name as well. It's probably something we should adopt from our older generations. People can be too distant these days. Especially Generation Z or whatever they call today's youngsters.

"Why don't you come in?" he said.

We walked into his house and I was quickly greeted with the San Francisco Bay. His home sat on a slight bluff and had a fantastic view looking down on the Pacific Ocean. Or was the Bay not considered the ocean? I wasn't sure.

I would have been suspicious how he afforded this house on a former inspector's salary, but Tressel had written a few books, advised on a few Hollywood movies, and conducted countless interviews over the years. I'm sure the man had money.

"Can I get you a coffee?" he asked.

"Sure," I said. "Thanks."

"Why don't you take a seat out there on the deck and I'll join you in a few minutes?"

"Great," I said.

I walked out on the deck and took in more of the view below.

Hank returned a few minutes later with a cup of coffee for each of us. He sat on the other chair and we both took a few seconds enjoying our surroundings.

"So, what did you think of Emmett Fisk?" he finally asked.

"I liked him immediately. Models himself a stand-up comedian."

"That's something that has returned in his later years."

"Yeah?"

"Well, after Ronnie was killed, he didn't have much to smile or laugh about for years."

"Can't say I blame him," I said.

"He wasn't the only one. Tough time for his family. He may not seem it now, being in his nineties, but Emmett was a pretty intimidating guy back when his grandson first went missing. He didn't take shit from anyone and was quite demanding."

"I got that impression," I said. "The guy is still driving at ninety-two. I'm sure he doesn't suffer fools gladly."

"No, he doesn't. He wasn't intimidated by me, after all. Most are."

We both took a sip of our coffee.

"I'll be wary," I said.

He laughed.

"I'm not referring to a seventy-five-year-old me."

I laughed back.

"So, how did you first find out about the case? Was it through Emmett?" I asked.

"You're ready to get down to it?"

"Why not?"

Hank swiveled his chair from facing the Bay to facing me. I did the same.

"It was early December. December 5th, in fact. I'm sure Emmett told you the 20th anniversary was two days ago. I'd retired from the SFPD a few months prior. December was always a tough time of year in my former profession. The last thing we wanted to do as police officers was work on a missing person case around the holidays. Or worse yet, a murder case. Imagine having to go tell a loved one that they've lost a family member a few weeks before Christmas. Our job was never easy, but December was extra tough."

"I'm sure," I said.

"I was no longer officially a police officer, but Ronnie's case still hit me like a brick."

"I have no doubt. You were friends with Emmett after all. Is he the one who told you about Ronnie?"

"Initially, I heard it second hand from a friend of mine who worked for the Berkeley Police Department. He knew Emmett and I were friends. That was somewhere around 7:30 that night. He told me they'd received a report that Ronnie hadn't come home after school. I wanted to call Emmett immediately, but I was sure he had more than enough on his plate. Plus, I knew my reputation and people would have assumed I was hoping to be the center of attention, which was not the case at all. I just wanted Ronnie to be found."

"You were in a tough spot."

"I was. Finally, at around nine p.m., when Ronnie still had not been found, I called Grant Fisk's house, Emmett's son, knowing Emmett would be there. He asked me to come by their house ASAP. I got in my car two minutes later. Ronnie lived with his family on Oxford Street. It wasn't a bad area per se, but they were only a few blocks from Telegraph Avenue, where a lot of weirdos hung out. Lots of bums and street musicians. Despite all the riff-raff, not many murders took place in Berkeley. So, there was reason to hold out hope that Ronnie might be found alive. I quickly started to feel something was really wrong, though."

"How? Why?"

"Because everyone was so loving. It didn't seem like a family you'd run away from. And yes, I knew I was jumping to conclusions, but that's what you do in my line of work. Yours as well. I could tell just how worried the entire Fisk family was. They knew this wasn't a runaway."

"What happened those first few days?"

"Sadly, not much. These days, we've all been inundated with the idea that the first forty-eight hours are very important. And that's generally true, but not if you have nothing to go on. Ronnie didn't have a cell phone. That could have been a game-changer with the GPS, but in 2001 very few kids had cell phones. Many adults didn't even have them yet."

"Was there any forensic evidence?"

"Not really. Certainly no DNA. And no sighting of Ronnie getting into a car. Once he left the campus after basketball practice, he was never seen again. He just vanished."

I'd heard that phrase many times regarding Emmy Peters in Las Vegas. Sadly, Ronnie had suffered a different fate.

"Were any of the neighbors considered suspects? Or, at least, suspicious?" I asked.

"Due to proximity only. As I said, they had nothing concrete on anybody. The police asked the neighbors questions, obviously. Nothing raised any red flags. There were a few creepy ones, but that's not enough on its own to label someone a suspect."

"Especially in a town where being weird is an art form," I said.

"You can say that again," Hank said.

"How involved were you?"

"I was in Berkeley every day until they discovered the body of poor Ronnie, but I let the cops do their jobs. I tried to stay behind the scenes. The time I'd be out and about was when they did a neighborhood walk, looking for Ronnie or any evidence. Besides that, I laid low."

"I can't imagine how brutal those neighborhood walks must have been."

"You described it perfectly. Brutal. Just people walking through the streets, occasionally chanting Ronnie's name. Never to be answered."

We both took a moment.

"What were Ronnie's parents like?" I finally asked.

"His mother was a wreck and his father was mellow by nature. Grant always had a solemn look on his face, as if he knew this would end badly. He rarely raised his voice and almost never got emotional. The mother Patricia, on the other hand, was crying half the time. I can't say I blame her, but it doesn't help the psyche of the group. And trust me, that matters. It makes you work harder. In this case, it didn't bring the desired outcome, but the psyche of the family does matter."

He'd made his point and I saw no need to belabor it.

"Did you actually know Ronnie?"

"I'd met him several times, but I hardly knew him well."

"What impression did you get from him?"

"Seemed like your average kid. Liked to ride his bike around Berkeley and could be seen at local skate parks as well. Played basketball as you know, which was somewhat surprising."

"Why?"

"He was a slight kid. And short for his grade. Plus, he was good on his bike and his skateboard, but not so much on the basketball court. Just seemed like a random sport for him."

"Any idea why?"

"I think his parents probably preferred him playing a school-sponsored sport than hitting the skate ramps of Berkeley."

"That's understandable," I said.

"Yeah," Hank agreed.

"How about his personality?"

"He was a pretty street-smart kid. I think you almost have to be, growing up in Berkeley. It's not like being raised in the suburbs. You kind of always need to have your radar on, being suspicious of all the crazies that Berkeley brings."

"Did you ever suspect any of the people who lived or performed on the street?"

"It was similar to the neighbors. The police questioned them, but you couldn't label someone a suspect just because they were odd."

"Were you dealing with the Berkeley PD during the investigation?"

"Not officially, but I did have a few friends on the force and we talked."

"Any other information you'd like to give me?" I asked.

"How much time have you got?" Hank said rhetorically.

And then he stood up.

"Give me a second," he said and walked back into his house.

I watched the Bay breaking below us. I enjoyed where I lived, but part of me would always be jealous of people who lived on the water.

Hank returned a few minutes later with two huge boxes. He set one inside and brought the other one out to the deck.

"The police reports," he said and set them down next to me.

I was shocked by how much there was.

"Hey, you asked if I had any more information," Hank said.

The file for Emmy Peters had been a few inches. These boxes stacked together were probably six feet.

"Jeez," was all I could muster.

"It's a lot, isn't it. Which is kind of amazing considering just how little evidence there truly is."

"Then why?"

"Lots and lots of interviews."

"I should have guessed."

"Maybe you'll find a discrepancy in one of the interviews," Hank said, sounding like he didn't quite believe it himself.

"I'm guessing you would have found them after all these years."

"I'd like to think so too. Trust me, I'd be the first one in line to congratulate you if you find something I couldn't."

"I'll try my best," I said.

"I believe you will."

"And this is everything?"

"What, you want more?"

I smiled.

"No, I guess not," I said.

"And don't worry about replacing these files. Those are copies of my copies. I still have my own set."

"Thanks for this, Hank."

"You're welcome. There will be a few things that are redacted or marked up, but nothing that will prevent you from moving forward with your investigation."

"Emmett hired me for a week. I'm not even sure I could read all this in a week."

"You'll finish it today. Trust me, it reads like a true-crime book. Which, in essence, it is. You won't be able to put it down. My recommendation would be to start at the beginning and reread that section a few times. The further you get away from the day in question, the less good information there is."

Hank opened the top of "Box #1" and grabbed about ten pages that were stapled together.

"Here we go. This is the initial police report."

He set it on top of the box.

"Read this first."

There's one question I had to ask.

"Hank, I hate to bring this up, but did you ever think a member of Ronnie's family might be involved in his death?"

"I never did. That doesn't mean I loved every single Fisk. And there was a significant other I wasn't too fond of either."

"Who would that be?"

Hank stared at me and I wasn't sure why.

"Quint, I think it's better if I stop talking now."

"Why?" I asked.

"Emmett Fisk hired you to get some new eyes on this case. If I tell you about people that I was suspicious of, that will just warp your initial impression of them. I think it's better if you truly look at these case files with no prejudice built-in."

It was very smart on his end.

"I get it," I said.

"I'll be here if you have any questions, but let's let you form your own opinions first."

"I'm sure I'll have many questions."

"Good luck, Quint. I really hope you find something."

I only nodded, not wanting to promise something I was unlikely to deliver.

"Let's take these boxes to your car," he said.

Before I drove off, we shook hands with an agreement to talk again in a few days.

~

As much as I preferred reading in a cafe or a library, I didn't think going over police reports was all that appropriate in a public place.

So I drove back to 1716 Lofts, made a batch of coffee with my French Press, sat down on my couch, and started with the initial police report. The two huge boxes next to me looked insurmountable.

Three hours later, I took my first break. I'd finished the entire French Press and went the easy route the next time, using my Keurig to make my next few cups of coffee.

And then I read for two more hours.

At this point, I was on my sixth cup of coffee and my nerves were fried. Reading all the details of a teenager's murder didn't help much either.

I was coming close to finishing both boxes despite my brain running on fumes. I easily could have stopped reading, but decided to persevere. I wanted to get a fresh start the next morning, devoid of police reports and interviews.

Finally, at almost nine p.m., I'd read every single piece of paper in the case file. Some more than once.

I moved from my couch to my bedroom and laid back on my bed. I knew there was too much going on in my brain to fall asleep right away.

So I decided to go back over all I had learned.

~

Ronnie Fisk went missing on Wednesday, December 5th, 2001. He'd recently turned fourteen years old and was in the 8th grade. He was 5'3" and 110 pounds, smaller than most boys his age.

He was last seen at 4:50 p.m, right after the conclusion of basketball practice, and from all accounts never made it home. Their neighbor across the street, Ed Finney, said in a sworn affidavit that he was on his lawn from 4:40 until Ronnie's father came home around 5:45. He said he would have seen Ronnie walking into his house. Ronnie's sister, Evelyn, arrived home at five and also claimed that Ronnie never made it home.

The working theory was that Ronnie was abducted somewhere between Willard Middle School and his home. Most of the Berkeley Police Department believed it was likely closer to the school since none of Ronnie's neighbors saw him get within a half-mile of his house on the day in question.

Ronnie was the middle child with an older sister, Evelyn, and a younger sister, Maddie. Evelyn was seventeen and a senior in high school. Maddie was only eleven and still in grade school, which meant all three kids went to different schools.

From all accounts, Ronnie and Maddie were inseparable. Evelyn and Ronnie would butt heads from time to time, but at seventeen and four-teen, that's not all that surprising. Maddie was only eleven and I imagine it's easier to get along with a sibling who is that young. Once you become teenagers, as Ronnie and Evelyn were, problems tend to arise.

As I'd learned earlier, Ronnie's parents were Grant and Patricia Fisk. The police reports seem to indicate that Patricia was the more intense of the two parents, not usually what you'd expect in the case of a missing child. Grant Fisk was described as calm, measured, and in a few instances, detached.

That matched up with what Hank Tressel had told me.

Patricia Fisk was a bit of a firebrand, which most might consider a putdown, but to someone who had lost their son, I found it to be completely reasonable. Hank had said she was quite emotional, which I also found perfectly understandable.

Being detached, as some found Grant Fisk, was less comprehensible to me. Not that I was casting any suspicion on him. I was just trying to get a read on everyone in the Fisk family.

Evelyn was described as a hard-headed young woman. She was dating a man named Ty Mulholland, who although never officially a suspect, had been mentioned by more than one police officer. They said that Ty had bullied Ronnie. Apparently, Ty had been home on the day in question and no one could disprove his alibi.

I'd circle back to Ty Mulholland at some point in my investigation.

Was it possible that someone just snagged Ronnie off the street? Of course. It happens all the time. But so do family squabbles that end with someone dead. Sure, they usually aren't fourteen-year-olds, but who knew what went on behind the closed doors of the Fisk household.

The Fisks had too many neighbors to remember them all. The Andersons and the Belfours lived directly on the left and right of them. The Finneys, the husband of which testified that Ronnie never came home, lived across the street. I'd do a deep dive on the neighbors at some point, but getting to know the Fisk family was my first order of business.

Grant and Patricia divorced in 2004, three years after Ronnie died. I didn't know the stats, but I assumed many marriages ended in divorce once you lose a child, especially if the cause of death was murder.

Grant still lived in Berkeley and I'd surely be making his acquaintance in the coming days. I wondered if he was still close to Emmett? For some reason, I didn't get the feeling the family was all that tight anymore. My impression was that Emmett was doing this on his own, not at his family's behest.

Patricia had moved away from the Bay Area within a year of her divorce from Grant. This was where Hank Tressel's notes came in handy. The police reports and interviews mainly just dealt with Ronnie's disappearance and the months that followed. Hank's notes were able to keep me in the loop of what was happening in the present. Patricia lived in Portland and there was a contact number at which she could be reached.

Evelyn Fisk, Ronnie's older sister, was now thirty-seven years old. She was a doctor and worked at Stanford Medical Center, only about forty miles from Berkeley. I'd likely be meeting with Evelyn this week as well, assuming she wanted to talk. I could understand if after twenty years they didn't want old wounds to be reopened. I'd have to wait and see.

Maddie Fisk was only thirty-one years old, and she lived in New York working at a big advertising firm. That's all that Hank's notes said about her.

So, of Ronnie's nuclear family, two still lived locally, while two had moved away. I wondered if that meant that Grant and Evelyn were closer to each other than the other two.

It seemed like both daughters had become pretty successful. One a doctor, one in advertising. That was somewhat surprising considering all they must have gone through as young women. Especially Evelyn. The year before she goes off to college, her younger brother is murdered. I don't think I'd have been able to keep my mind on my studies.

Here I was, judging again.

Grant Fisk shouldn't have been detached.

Evelyn Fisk shouldn't have been able to study with a dead brother.

Although quite different from losing a teenager, I'd had to deal with my own tragedy. My father, Arthur, had been killed when I was thirty-nine years old. At the time, it looked like he had just been at the wrong place at the wrong time. Sadly, a year later, I found out that he had been targeted.

I did get my revenge out on the Pacific Ocean, but it didn't mean much. I'd gladly have changed that for another few days with my father.

I started to feel the tears coming. And I knew that as terrible as my father's death was, I got thirty-nine years with him and he got seventy years on earth. Losing a fourteen-year-old was much worse.

I couldn't imagine what Grant and Patricia Fisk went through.

I looked at my phone and it read 9:30. I'd been going over the case for hours upon hours.

It was time to formulate something of a plan and I figured it should start with Ronnie's father, Grant.

I looked down at Hank's notes and found his phone number. I dialed it.

"Hello?" a voice answered.

"Mr. Fisk, my name is Quint Adler."

"I know who you are."

That surprised me.

"Really?"

"My father called and said he'd hired you. When do you want to meet?"

"How about tomorrow?"

"Sure. What time?"

"The earlier the better," I said.

"I can see you at nine."

I got his address and was off the phone seconds later.

Minutes later, with my brain oversaturated and ready to turn off, I was asleep.

CHAPTER 3

U nlike Los Angeles, the Bay Area was not a sprawling metropolis. Almost everything was within an hour's reach. And while Marin had taken me fifty minutes the day before, Berkeley was only twenty minutes from my place and I arrived a few minutes before nine a.m., finding parking on the street.

Grant Fisk's current place was a dump. There was no other way to describe it.

He was on the top of a two-unit apartment complex, which sat feet from the main street. He was waiting on the stairs when I arrived. He had on a San Francisco Giants t-shirt and some long green cargo shorts. He wasn't dressed for winter, but then again, maybe his mind wasn't all that focused whenever early December rolled around.

There were several plants on his deck. Dead plants, actually. I'd say they needed some watering, but they were past the point of no return. Probably like a lot of things in Grant Fisk's life.

"Thanks for agreeing to see me," I said.

"Of course," Grant said.

"I'm sure this is tough, going through all of this again."

"Yes, it is. But if my father paid you to investigate Ronnie's death then I guess I should do my part."

It didn't sound like something he was too keen on.

"Do you mind if we talk inside?" I asked.

I didn't want to be rude, but it was cold outside, plus I didn't want to talk about his dead child within earshot of passersby.

"Sure. Come on in."

The apartment itself was cleaner than I expected. While the deck had been littered with dead plants, he had kept the inside presentable.

Maybe Grant wasn't as forlorn as I'd assumed.

To the left of the front door was a kitchen and to the right was a living room with a T.V. and an L-shaped beige couch. Beyond the front rooms was a hallway and I couldn't tell if there were one or two bedrooms.

"Do you live alone?" I asked.

"I've got a girlfriend, but she lives down near Stanford Hospital. When she comes out here, she stays with me. Besides that, I live alone."

"Your daughter works at Stanford Medical Center, correct?"

"Yes. My girlfriend was one of her patients, actually. I was there to see my daughter and started passing time in the waiting room. Sure enough, I started chatting to this woman next to me. Five minutes later, when my daughter walks out, we both stand up at once. Wendy, to enter her appointment. Me, to hug my daughter."

"That's a great way to meet. What type of doctor is your daughter?" I asked.

"She's an orthopedist."

I realized that I had read that in the case files. I had no doubt there were things I didn't absorb at the time. Blame it on six straight hours of studying.

"You must be proud. A doctor at one of the better hospitals in the United States."

He mustered a smile.

"Yeah, I'm proud of both daughters. Very, very proud. As time has passed on from Ronnie's death, I've been able to focus more on their success. As Evelyn was going through medical school and her residency, I don't think I fully embraced her career choice. Not that I didn't respect doctors, it's just that my whole world had crumbled when Ronnie was killed. It was hard to concentrate on my daughters' successes and I probably wasn't the best father during that time. I'm trying to make up for it now."

I was hard on him from the outward appearance of his apartment, and a few things I'd read, but Grant Fisk appeared to be a decent man. Probably a bit tortured after what happened to his son, but nonetheless, a good human being. My initial impression was that Grant had nothing to do with his son's death. It obviously still affected him to this day.

"I'm sure your daughters understood why your mind was elsewhere," I said.

"Thanks."

"Should we sit somewhere?" I asked.

It was the second time I had to suggest something to Grant. I wondered if his mind was permanently stuck in neutral.

"I'm sorry. This is all so odd, investigating my son's death again after all these years."

He motioned to the L-shaped couch and we sat a seat apart.

"Didn't Hank Tressel investigate over the years?"

"Yeah, Hank did. He's like part of the family, though. I'm referring to my father asking a PI to investigate this twenty years later. Seems like a wild goose chase to me."

"Sometimes it just takes a new set of eyes," I said, going with the lazy answer.

Was it true? Did having my new eyes on it really make it any more likely than if Hank kept investigating? I had my doubts. If anything, it would seem like he'd spot something incongruous much easier than I would.

"Nice stock answer," he said.

I smiled.

"You caught me."

He smiled back and Grant Fisk continued to come off as warmer than I'd first assumed.

"I guess it can't hurt," he said. "But look at it from my point of view. No matter what happens, you can't bring my Ronnie back."

"No, I can't," I conceded. "Maybe I can help find the killer, though. Wouldn't that make you feel good?"

I hated my choice of words.

"Not feel good, but at least get some closure," I added.

"A little, I guess. I apologize if I don't get my hopes up. Twenty years is twenty years."

I was parched but didn't want to interrupt the conversation.

"Can you tell me what happened on the day in question?" I asked. "From your end, obviously."

"Sure," he said. "Do you want a drink first?"

It's like he read my mind.

"I'd love a water if you've got one."

"Regular or sparkling?"

"What is this, a restaurant?" I asked.

Grant smiled.

"Regular water is fine," I said.

He rose from the couch and came back a minute later with water for me and a beer for him. I didn't judge people's drinking habits, but 9:15 in the morning certainly seemed a bit early for a beer. Then again, he was about to describe the day his son died. Maybe this wasn't an everyday occurrence.

He sat back on the couch.

"Ready to get this over with?"

It was hard to tell if he was talking about himself or yours truly.

"Whenever you are ready," I said.

He took a deep breath and started speaking.

"I woke up about seven that morning. It's funny. I probably couldn't tell you what I did yesterday morning, but I remember every single thing that happened that morning. I guess having to explain it so many times over the days that followed etched it into my mind forever. Anyway, I was up at seven, and my wife Patricia stayed asleep a little longer. We woke the kids up about 7:45 every morning so she probably wanted to get that little bit of extra sleep. Any mother with three kids certainly deserves it. I went downstairs. We had a small little home at the time, don't let the stairs fool you. I pulled out some cereal. I was hungry and didn't want to wait and eat with the kids. I sat there and ate, feeling like the luckiest guy in the world. I had a beautiful wife I loved, three awesome kids, and a job at a local bank with co-workers I enjoyed. How many people can honestly admit they have all three of those?"

He took a sip of his beer and I took a sip of my water.

"Patricia woke up right around 7:45, got the kids up, and quickly started putting breakfast together. She made some sausage, eggs, and bread. Some days she'd just have the kids make cereal or throw some Eggos in the toaster, but on this day she actually spent twenty minutes or so cooking. The kids came down and ate. Nothing seemed out of the ordinary. Obviously. It's not like any of us knew what was going to happen. Evelyn and Ronnie left for school about fifteen minutes later. We kissed them goodbye and told them we loved them as we did every morning."

I interrupted for the first time.

"Did your oldest drive?"

I knew that Ronnie walked to school on the day he went missing, but I wanted to find out if his schedule had changed at all.

"Evelyn had her driver's license, but their school was only a half-mile from our house. And we only had two cars. So she walked to school every day. If she drove, it was on weekends or at night."

"Ronnie always walked to school as well, correct?"

"Yes, unless my wife or I had the day off of work."

"And all three of your children went to different schools?"

I knew the answer but used it to move along the conversation.

"Yeah. Maddie, our youngest, was only in grade school. Patricia or I always dropped her off before we went to work. Evelyn went to Berkeley High School and walked with local friends. Ronnie went to Willard Middle School, which was grades 6-8. He also had friends he'd always walk with. I know what you're thinking," Grant said.

"What?" I said.

"That we were irresponsible parents allowing them to walk to school."

"I wasn't thinking that. I'm sure it's very tough when you both have to work."

"It was. We both needed to in order to pay the bills. And like I said, both Evelyn and Ronnie had friends they walked with."

"I'm not judging. I promise."

"Thank you," he said. "I know why my father did this, but it's just going to make things hard on me while you investigate."

"That's not what I'm here for. So, Ronnie had basketball practice on the day he went missing," I said, bringing us back to the conversation at hand.

I didn't want to say "the day he was killed," so I resorted to words like missing or abducted. Like they were any better.

"Yeah. And he didn't even like the sport. We just wanted him to do something at the school as opposed to roaming the city."

He looked like he was about to cry.

"Maybe if I hadn't forced him to play basketball, he'd still be alive."

I could tell that hurt him to say. And it pained me to hear it.

"You can't think that," I said.

"That's easier said than done."

"None of your kids had cell phones, correct?"

Another answer I knew the answer to, but it's the first thing that popped to mind. I couldn't let Grant keep wallowing in sadness if I wanted to get answers from him.

"No, not yet. Only a few kids around town had them back in 2001. They weren't everywhere like they would be a few years later. Another bad break for Ronnie."

Grant took a long sip of his beer.

"I know I barely know you," I said. "But you seem like a good father. Don't beat yourself up too much."

I didn't know if I was out of line or doing the right thing.

"Thanks," Grant said. "Sometimes I need to be reminded of that."

I was glad to see he'd taken it as I'd intended.

"What time did you arrive home?"

A third question I knew the answer to, but I wanted to hear it from the horse's mouth.

"Around 5:45. The bank closed at 5:00, but we had a few things to do.

And I always drove directly home. My wife got off about fifteen minutes later than me and she'd go pick up Maddie from daycare. They had one at her school. Maddie was too young to walk to and from school, so we always dropped her off and picked her up."

"And Evelyn was there when you arrived home, correct?"

"Yeah. She had cheerleading practice, which ended around the same time as Ronnie's basketball practice. So they'd usually both get home around 5:30 and I'd arrive shortly thereafter."

"Was Evelyn worried Ronnie hadn't arrived home yet?"

"No. He was only fifteen minutes late at that point."

"How long until you got worried?"

"Probably around 6:30. I started calling Ronnie's friends' parents at that point. And then I called the police at 7:00 after none of Ronnie's friends knew where he was. My wife was home at this point and she was starting to panic. Once I called the cops, I drove the route from our house to the school and left Patricia home to talk with the police."

"What did you see on your drive?"

It would probably amount to nothing, but I wanted to hear his answer.

"No signs of Ronnie, that's for sure. I saw a few friends of mine on the route and asked them if they'd seen him. None had. I stopped and talked to a few people who were facing the street Ronnie would have taken. Nothing. And then I got to the school and all the kids were gone. It was probably 7:30 p.m. at this point. I saw a teacher and asked her if she knew Ronnie. She did, but had no idea where he was."

"Then you came home?"

"Yeah. The cops were already there and my wife was hysterical."

For the umpteenth time, this conversation felt awkward.

"What happened next?"

"My father helped me set up a canvas to walk the neighborhood. I'd called him around 6:30 and he came right over. We got some neighbors to join and probably had twenty people walking from our house to Willard Middle School and back. We must have done it five or six times and were out till midnight. The police were as well. Although we didn't find Ronnie, it wasn't for a lack of looking."

"It sounds like your community rallied around you."

"For the most part, yeah. There were a few assholes that wouldn't help look for him."

"I heard your Dad was tough on a few of them," I said.

"I can't deny it. Just imagine what he was feeling, what all of us were feeling, really. His grandson was missing and these jerks wouldn't help. Plus, Dad, or Emmett as you know him, was always fiercer than me."

"Under the circumstances, no one can blame him."

"Most people went back to their homes around midnight. Not me. I was up until four a.m., walking the streets of Berkeley. I just knew the next street I walked down would be the one where Ronnie would run into my arms."

Grant paused.

"He never did," he said and wiped his eyes with his shirt.

I waited several seconds, letting Grant decide when he was ready.

What he said next was just as crushing.

"Not the next day. Or the next month. Or the next year. Or ever. I was looking for a ghost. I'm sure he was already dead at that point."

I was heartbroken. This conversation was too much for me.

"What happened the day after Ronnie went missing?" I asked, on the verge of tears myself.

"It was very much like the previous day, canvassing the neighborhood. In fact, the second day had even more searches since we started so early. All three of the local schools were shut down. I don't know if it was to help look for Ronnie or whether they were afraid a madman was on the loose. I didn't care. I was just happy to have the extra bodies. At least half of Ronnie's classmates helped search Berkeley. We searched up and down Telegraph Street, the Cal campus, even the neighboring suburbs. This time we had hundreds of people walking around different parts of Berkeley. There are some things I'm still pissed off about, but the reaction and outreach to Ronnie aren't one of them."

"What were some of the things you were pissed off about?"

"The bureaucracy of the police department. It was so hard to get an answer both right after Ronnie went missing and then a few weeks later when they found his body."

"Did they have any suspects in those first few days?"

"That's what I'm saying. I don't know. I couldn't get a straight answer out of any of the cops. Now, maybe they didn't have any suspects. That's fine, tell me that. Instead, they'd say things like 'We are following all leads,' and that type of bullshit."

"How about Hank?"

"He'd always been straight with us, but he was getting everything second hand, so he didn't know much, either."

Grant took another big sip of his beer, finishing it and setting it on the glass end table adjoining the couch.

"I promise I don't usually drink this early."

"You don't have to apologize to me," I said, not sure whether to believe him or not. "I won't take up too much more of your time, but can you describe the day they found Ronnie's body."

"It's hard to say which day was worse, the day he went missing or the day they found him. Probably the day they found him. There was no coming back from that. I woke up early that morning, like every day in the intervening two weeks, and I walked from our house to the middle school. Patricia and I had not gone back to work. How could we? We would have been worthless even if we'd tried. We were running low on money, but that hardly seemed to matter at the moment. I had done the walk to and from his school so many times, I could have named ninety percent of the people who lived in each respective house. On the day in question, I arrived back at our house after doing the walk one last time. There were two cop cars out front. For a brief moment, I let my mind think maybe, just maybe, he'd been found alive. That only lasted a split second. Once I saw the police officers' faces, I knew he was dead. And that's when it all kind of went black for me. It's odd, I told you earlier how I remember everything about the day he went missing. I remember very little of the day he was discovered. Once they told me he was dead, I remember Patricia walking out of our house, and just sobbing uncontrollably. And I know we went to the morgue where I identified him. At that point, I was already in a daze. And I literally can't remember a thing that happened after that. I was told later that we had something at our house and all our friends came over and tried, unsuccessfully, to comfort us."

"I can't imagine," I said.

"Don't try to. It won't do it justice anyway. It's a hundred times worse than you think."

I thought back to my father and whether to bring it up. I decided to.

"My father was murdered," I said. "And I realize how much tougher it would be to lose a child. Just thought you should know."

As he stared at me, I started to think maybe I shouldn't have mentioned it.

"I'm sorry about your father," Grant said.

"Thank you."

"How long ago?"

"It's been two and a half years."

And then something completely unexpected happened. Grant Fisk stood up, walked over, and put his arm on my shoulder.

"I'm sorry," he said.

It should have been me comforting him.

"And I'm sorry about Ronnie. I'm sure he was a great kid."

"The best," he said.

And then I uttered something I'd avoided saying to Hank.

"I'm going to catch his killer," I said.

~

I left Grant Fisk's house a few minutes after proclaiming I was going to find the man - or woman - responsible for Ronnie's death. I could have used some more time with him, but he'd agreed to meet me again.

Instead of driving back to the office immediately, I decided to do what Grant had done scores of times in the days after his son went missing. I walked the path that Ronnie took on what was hopefully his last day on earth. The idea that he was kept as a prisoner for a day or two before being killed was too awful to consider.

Besides the strangulation, there were no other abuses to Ronnie's body, so I was fairly certain this hadn't occurred. Thank God.

I was about to drive to the house the Fisks lived in at the time. I'd then walk from their house to the middle school.

I thought of a better idea. Ronnie would have been walking from the middle school to home on the day in question. I should take that route instead of the one from home to school.

It might have seemed like a small thing, but if I was going to do things right, then following his actual path was prudent.

I used my GPS and drove to Willard Middle School. It was .7 miles from their home. It was walkable in probably somewhere around ten to fifteen minutes.

I found a place to park and paid the exorbitant fee for an hour. That gave me a little extra time in case I struck up a conversation with some neighbors.

Willard Middle School was located in downtown Berkeley on Stuart Street. There was a brick facade that surrounded some of it and the front greeted you with "Willard Middle School" in white lettering on a concrete arch.

We were less than a hundred yards from Telegraph Ave., probably the most famous street in Berkeley and a place where you had to watch yourself. \

We were less than a mile from the campus of Cal-Berkeley so people on the street were just as likely to be college students heading to class as they were middle schoolers. Berkeley was a hodgepodge of many people and many things.

There were a few sketchy-looking people within yards of the school. I had liked Grant Fisk, but letting a fourteen-year-old walk home from here wouldn't have been my recommendation. Then again, both parents worked and Ronnie usually walked home with friends. It was also twenty years ago and maybe the area was safer in 2001.

I vowed not to second guess Grant Fisk. I was trying to catch a killer, not drag the parents through the mud.

Looking up towards Telegraph Avenue made me realize just how difficult my job was going to be. There were musicians, artists, bums, college, high school, and middle school students all middling around downtown Berkeley. I could be suspicious of thirty suspects on each city block.

As I walked across the street, I almost got run over by a biker going about thirty miles per hour. I told myself this wasn't the city to be looking down at my phone. It would be prudent to keep my eyes on the road.

I set the GPS to 2061 Oxford Street and started walking.

Was I sure that Ronnie didn't take side streets? No. Was I sure that Ronnie didn't stop at a friend's house? No. Was I sure that Ronnie wasn't picked up twenty feet from Willard? No.

And yet, I wanted to do this. Needed to. I had to get the feel of the walk Ronnie took every day. And it was still likely he was abducted somewhere along the path I was about to set out on.

Nothing of interest happened on the way to the Fisk home. Not that I expected anything. It took me fourteen minutes, and several of those minutes were waiting for lights to change. This wasn't a rural walk, that's for sure. Bars, restaurants, and tattoo parlors littered the streets. And the streets themselves were littered as well. If you know what I mean.

About four blocks from their house, it turned into a bit more of a family neighborhood, but you're so close to downtown that you'd hardly call it the suburbs.

I arrived at 2061 Oxford Street and stared at the home in front of me. It was a two-story, narrow home that was probably higher than it was wide. It seemed like a pleasant enough place, although the pale brown paint job could use a retouching.

"Do you have an interest in this house?" A voice said.

I couldn't tell where the voice was coming from at first, so I swiveled around and saw a man on the wrong side of sixty staring back at me.

"How long have you lived here?" I asked, breaking my mother's golden rule of never following up a question with another question.

"Your question has given you away. You must know it as the Fisk house."

He was perceptive.

I walked twenty feet to the other side of the street. The man was wearing sandals with long, colored tube socks, shorts, and a long-sleeved sweatshirt. None of the colors came close to matching. His hair looked like he'd put his finger in a light socket.

"You've got me pegged," I said.

"What do you want to know?"

"Since you're asking, how about who killed Ronnie Fisk?"

"Are you a true crime nut?"

"No, I was actually hired by the family."

This seemed to set his mind at ease.

"I'm Ed Finney. I lived next to the Fisks back then and, obviously, haven't moved since."

I knew who he was from the police reports.

"I'm Quint," I said.

"So they hired someone twenty years after the fact?"

I wondered if he knew it was exactly twenty years or just threw out a ballpark number.

"Yeah. I've got a feeling I'm Emmett Fisk's last shot."

"Oh, the old man hired you. He was always a tough, good man."

"You knew him?"

"Every neighbor did. It felt like he moved into his son Grant's house after Ronnie went missing. He was out talking to people every day, trying to find out if a neighbor could have been involved."

"Did he ever suspect anyone?"

"Not that I know of. Certainly not me. We got along pretty well, considering the circumstances."

"Were there some neighbors that Emmett, or Grant, didn't like?"

"Sure. The Dixons. The Scalas."

"Any particular reason?"

"Because they didn't come out and canvass the area every night like the rest of their neighbors. I don't think Emmett suspected them of having abducted Ronnie. He just had no time for people who weren't all-in on helping him find his grandson. Grant was a little more passive than his father. Emmett was full of piss and vinegar. Is he still the same?"

"Well, he's ninety-two years old now," I said.

"Yeah, I guess father time mellows out all of us in the end."

"From what I've gathered, it doesn't sound like there were ever any prime suspects," I half-asked, half-stated.

"It's tough in a neighborhood like this. You walk down a few blocks and you'll find ten people on the corner who look like they could kill a young kid."

He had confirmed my earlier opinion.

"How about you?"

"No, I wouldn't kill a young kid."

He'd meant it as a joke, but it wasn't exactly a laughing matter so I remained stone-faced.

"I'm sorry," I said. "That came out wrong. Did you have any suspects yourself?"

"I agreed with Emmett on the Dixons. Wanda Dixon was one of the weirdest women I've ever met."

"How so?"

"Her eyes just weren't all there. It's like she was staring right through you at all times. And she'd speak in these non-sequiturs all the time. We'd be talking about the weather and she'd say something like, 'Speaking of weather, I can't decide whether I'm going to have lasagna or steak tonight.'"

I couldn't help but laugh.

"She used the weather outside to segue to the old whether or not phrase? Which had nothing to do with each other."

"Exactly. She was an odd duck."

"And you thought she could have potentially done something to Ronnie?"

"I'm not sure I'd go that far, but if I had to choose a suspect from our neighbors, it would be her."

"Does she still live here?"

"No, she moved about five years ago. Right after her husband died. Rumor was she was shacking up with some other guy before her husband passed."

"Any idea if she still lives close?"

"Yeah, she's somewhere in the Bay Area. My wife, bless her heart, used to get the contact info of any neighbor who moved. She's still probably sending Wanda Dixon a Christmas card each year. My wife is almost as crazy as her."

And then he laughed.

"Can I get that information before I go?" I asked.

"Sure. Anything else you want to know?"

"What happened after Ronnie's body was found?"

"It was weirdly, and I know this is the wrong choice of words, anti-climatic. All the wind went out of the Fisks' sails. It's almost like they didn't care if they caught the killer at that point. Which, I guess I understand. Once you know your son is dead, it's not like you can get him back. I don't want to say they lost interest, but it certainly waned. And Emmett stopped coming around as much."

This surprised me.

"He doesn't seem like someone to give up. Shit, he hired me twenty years later."

"That's a fair point. And no, he doesn't seem like the kind to give up easily. Maybe he was talking to cops or working with a P.I. as opposed to going door to door."

My thoughts turned to Hank Tressel. Emmett had probably given him the reins.

"Maybe," I said.

Just then, a woman dressed even more shabbily than Ed Finney approached us, a scowl on her face.

"Who is this, Ed?"

"He's investigating the Fisk murder."

"Why? That was like a hundred years ago."

"Do you still have Wanda Dixon's address?" Ed asked his wife.

"I sure do."

"Great, we're coming inside."

"Lenore, this is Quint."

"Hey, Quinn," she said curtly.

"It's Quint," Ed said.

"Close enough," Lenore Finney said and waddled towards their house.

Ed smiled at me, ostensibly apologizing for his wife's behavior.

~

I received the address of Wanda Dixon - no phone number - from Lenore Finney, walked back to Willard Middle School, and started driving back toward Walnut Creek.

There was a bit of traffic around the Caldecott Tunnel, a few miles west of Berkeley, and it took me almost thirty minutes to arrive back at my office.

I parked my car in the space next to the handicapped spot where Emmett Fisk had taken a fall. I felt like I owed him a phone call.

I entered my shoebox of a business and walked back to my office. At some point, hopefully, sooner rather than later, I could hire a secretary and have them take calls from potential clients. Maybe hire another P.I. down the line and make an actual firm out of this.

It made me wonder why I actually rented an office this early in the game. When I was out on a job, the office just sat there, barren, slowly soaking up my money.

There was one message on the voicemail. I wasn't surprised one bit when it was an auto call. Not that it mattered anyway. I'd dedicated myself to Emmett Fisk for a week and couldn't take on another case at this point, anyway. Still, it would be nice to know that people knew who I was, and not just a ninety-two-year-old who heard about me from one of his granddaughters.

I decided the phone call to Emmett could wait. I wanted to talk to the other members of the Fisk family first. Maybe then I'd have more information to give him. I needed more than just a neighbor who thought a fellow neighbor used too many non-sequiturs.

I'd talked to Emmett and Grant. It was time to talk to the women of the Fisk family.

CHAPTER 4

"Hello?"

The voice was higher than I expected, even though I had no frame of reference.

"Patricia, my name is Quint and I've been hired by your former father-in-law to investigate the death of your son."

There was a pause and I was afraid she was about to hang up on me.

"Emmett?" she said instead. "He's still alive?"

She genuinely seemed to not know.

"He is."

"Guess I should have known that a guy like that wouldn't go easily."

"Everyone tells me that he was a tough SOB, but I've only met the ninety-two-year-old version," I said.

"I'm half-kidding. I was okay with Emmett. He had more of a backbone than his son...my husband."

I didn't want this to deteriorate into a conversation of her disparaging Grant Fisk.

"Emmett hired me, thinking it's his last shot," I said.

"Not surprised by that, either. He could never let it go."

"It doesn't seem like something you would want to let go of," I said.

"You wouldn't understand."

"Try me."

"Once Ronnie's body was discovered, I couldn't spend every waking minute thinking about him. Did I want them to catch the guy who killed him? Of course, but I couldn't spend twenty-four hours a day thinking about it. I knew if I did, I'd be a lousy mother to my two daughters. And my marriage probably wouldn't last either, which turned out to be the case anyway. My goal at that point was to be a good mother to my remaining children. I'd still think about Ronnie several times a day. I just couldn't make it the sole focus of my life. It would have driven me crazy."

"I can understand that," I said.

"Emmett had different ideas. It consumed him."

"I was told he wasn't around as much once they found Ronnie."

"That's true, but it's not because he'd lost interest. He was out hiring different P.I.s to try and find the killer. They were doing all the work. Well, them and Hank."

"Ever get anything promising?"

"Emmett would think he'd found something to go on, but it was never enough for the police. I'm pretty sure they looked down on investigators doing work they believed was meant for them."

"Hank wasn't a P.I."

"They liked Hank alright. Just not the other people that Emmett hired."

"Did you know Wanda Dixon?" I asked.

"Yeah, I knew that crazy old bat."

"Did you ever think she could have been involved?"

"She was nuts, but no, I don't think she was the killer. Don't tell me you've got something that implicates her."

"No, just a neighbor who told me to follow up on her."

"Well, feel free to do that, but I don't think she had anything to do with it. I'll bet that would make Emmett happy, though. He hated that lady."

"Because she wouldn't help look for Ronnie?"

"Sounds like you know quite a bit about this case, Mr. Quint."

"It's just Quint. That's my first name."

"What exactly is it that you want from me? I've recently turned sixty and my memory isn't so hot these days. I'm sure you have police reports that summarize the days surrounding Ronnie's disappearance better than I ever could."

"Is there any small tidbit you could tell me? Something you thought that maybe the police, or Hank, might have overlooked?"

"I always thought it was probably a serial killer."

There were very few references to that possibility and it was not the overwhelming opinion of the Berkeley Police Department. Most thought it was someone that Ronnie knew. Not necessarily a family member, however.

"I'm surprised more people don't seem to believe that," I said.

"Well, there had been a fair amount of kids going missing around that time, but the police told me that the MO of most killings were different.

They said that serial killers tend to kill in one way only. And there were stabbings, shootings, etc."

Hank's notes had contained a few pages on the other missing/dead kids around that time, but it had not been a priority for him.

"I read a little bit about some of the other missing or dead kids. Nothing stood out."

"The police would concur."

"Then why do you think it might be a serial killer?"

"To be honest, I'm not even sure that's what I think. But, to me, it was always better than the alternative."

"And what was that?" I asked.

"That Ronnie was killed by someone he knew."

There was a third possibility. Ronnie was killed by someone he didn't know, but it wasn't a serial killer. I found no reason to bring that up.

"I hate to ask this, but was there any family member, neighbor, or friend whose alibi didn't hold weight for you?"

"I won't even justify the family part of it with an answer. There was me, Grant, and our two daughters. We loved Ronnie with every part of our soul. Sure, my husband and I drifted apart after Ronnie died, but I can assure you he had nothing to do with his death. And yeah, Evelyn and Ronnie fought sometimes, but what siblings didn't? Finally, there was Emmett, and he loved Ronnie almost as much as we did."

I was going to ask why she and Grant got divorced, but the answer was obvious. The fallout from a dead son.

"How about neighbors or friends?" I asked.

"Listen, Quint. I know you are trying to do your job, but I didn't remember each and every person's alibi back then, and I certainly don't remember them now. I was a grieving mother and left the investigative part of it up to the police. Some good that did."

"I'm sorry for having to ask."

"It's alright. I just hope you realize how tough this is on me."

"Of course."

"Have you met with my ex-husband yet?"

"Yeah."

"And how's he taking it?"

"I think he'd have preferred if his father hadn't hired me."

"For once, we are in agreement."

"I haven't talked to your daughters yet. Do you think they will be willing to talk?"

"Probably. They like their grandfather and will probably do it for him."

"I will try to make my conversations with them as painless as I can," I said.

"I wish you wouldn't call them at all, but I guess that's an impossibility."

"I've got a job to do."

"So how is that cantankerous Emmett?"

I could tell she wanted to change the subject from her daughters.

"I've only met him one time thus far. He's still driving, I can tell you that. And I actually found him quite funny."

"He had a great sense of humor before Ronnie went missing."

I didn't want to go down this road again.

"I'll let you go soon," I said. "Is there anything else you can think of?"

"No, there's really not. As I've already said a few times, it's been twenty years and I wasn't one for details back then. It's highly unlikely I'll be remembering something new now."

"Okay."

"Have you talked to Hank yet?"

"Yes, I have."

"There's nothing I know about the case that you can't get from him," she said. And that was her way of telling me this conversation was coming to a close, as well as any future correspondence with her.

"I appreciate you talking to me."

"I hate to be the bearer of bad news, but nothing is going to come of this."

"You may be right," I admitted.

"Be gentle on my girls when you talk to them."

"I will," I said.

"Goodbye, Quint."

She hung up the phone immediately thereafter.

CHAPTER 5

"You must be Quint. I'm Aaron."

In the police reports, Aaron Everton was often mentioned as Ronnie's best friend. After a few texts back and forth, he'd agreed to meet with me.

He was a handsome man with brown hair that looked to be going prematurely gray. He would only have been thirty-four years of age, give or take a year.

His home was on a suburban street in Pleasanton, a city about a half-hour from both Berkeley and my place in Walnut Creek. From the outside, the house was nice, but not flashy.

"I am. Thanks for meeting with me."

"Of course. Come on in," Aaron said and led me into the house.

The first thing I saw was a large photograph of his family of four. He had an attractive wife with light blonde hair along with a young daughter and son to round it out.

There was a dark brown dining room table that Aaron motioned towards. I took a seat.

"I can't believe it's been twenty years," he said.

"Does it feel like a year or fifty years?" I asked.

"A little of both, I guess. Remembering what Ronnie was actually like is becoming tougher, and that makes me sad."

"Well, hopefully, our conversation will strike up some fond memories of him."

"I'd like that," he said.

Aaron Everton seemed to have a good aura about him. He struck me as someone who would see a glass as half full.

"My first question is what was Ronnie really like? It's hard to get that vibe relying solely on police reports and old interviews."

Aaron adjusted his chair ever so slightly to directly face me.

"What is anyone really like when they are fourteen years old?" he said rhetorically, but I got his point. "He was in love with life like I hope most young kids are."

I could have told him, correctly, that it's easy to find jaded kids these days.

"Was he mellow? Hell-on-wheels? A bully? The bully?"

"He certainly wasn't the bully. Ronnie was small for his grade. Our grade. As for his personality, he was mostly mellow. Not a wimp, though. He would skateboard over big jumps and ride his bike at breakneck speeds through Berkeley."

"I read a few reports that his sister Evelyn's boyfriend was a little rough on him."

"Yeah, Ty Mulholland was a jerk. And he was a senior in high school so Ronnie had no chance to stand up to him"

I remembered Hank saying something about not liking a certain significant other. I had a feeling he was referring to Ty Mulholland.

"What type of things would he do?"

"I didn't see much. It's not like Ty came from high school over to our middle school and waited for him. I heard stories that he was tough on him at the skate park from time to time. Not like beating him up, just bullying. I wasn't a skater, though, so I never saw it."

"I heard you and Ronnie were best friends."

"We were."

"But you guys didn't skate together?"

"Nope. We played basketball, we rode bikes, we played video games. Trust me, we had enough in common."

"Sorry, that's not how I meant it."

"No worries," Aaron said.

"Was Evelyn a good older sister to him?"

"Since she let Ty bully him, I'd have to say no."

"Did Ronnie ever tell you that he disliked his sister?"

"I knew they butted heads. He didn't have to tell me. He loved Maddie, though. He was bummed they weren't closer in age so they could go to the same school."

"Was it going to happen in high school?"

"Yeah, Ronnie was stoked about that. When he was a senior, Maddie would be a freshman. He'd say the wicked witch would be gone and he and Maddie could hang out all the time. Evelyn being the wicked witch."

I nodded.

"I got that. Did Ronnie get along with his parents?"

"For the most part. His father was a bit of a pushover so Ronnie could get away with a lot around him. His mother was stricter and he had to watch himself when she was around."

"What kind of things would he get in trouble for?"

"Going to the skate park too late. Being out and about in Berkeley after the sun went down. Oftentimes, it was he and I riding our bikes."

"I'd have to side with his parents on that one. Berkeley is no place for a fourteen-year-old at night."

"You're probably right. But we were young and carefree."

"I was young once. I get it."

"Ronnie will be young forever," Aaron said.

It was hard to tell whether he meant it as a good or bad thing.

"Did many of your friends walk home from school?" I asked.

"Some. If both of your parents worked, then yes. And both of Ronnie's did."

"Still, there were enough kids leaving basketball that he could have hitched a ride if he wanted."

"When you're that age and you go from school to basketball to home every day, it gets monotonous. If I could have walked home and avoided my parents for an extra half hour or more, I would have done it too."

"Your parents were a little more strict?"

"Well, my mother didn't work, so she picked me up every day from school or after sports ended. I didn't have much choice."

"Did your mother ever give Ronnie a ride home?"

"Sure. Pretty often actually, but not on the day in question," Aaron said and then bowed his head. "Obviously."

"Since we are stating the obvious, I've got one," I said. "No one is responsible for Ronnie's death except for the person who killed him."

"I know."

I needed to bring it back to the subject at hand.

"Didn't sound like Ronnie was much of a basketball player."

"No, he wasn't. Also, he played right field in little league. Does that answer your question?"

Usually, the most unathletic kid was thrown in right field.

"It does. Not much of an athlete?"

"I guess it's how you define it. No, he wasn't good at team sports. If you saw him on a skateboard or a bike, however, you'd say he was one hell of an athlete."

"I get your point. Those kids at the X-games are undoubtedly great athletes."

"They sure are," Aaron said.

"Did anything happen at basketball practice that was out of the ordinary?"

"Nothing. And the only reason I remember is that we were asked the same question after Ronnie disappeared. In fact, we'd won our game the day before so it was kind of a fun practice. The coach was happy with us. I remember telling the cops that."

"And do you know what happened to Ronnie after the practice ended?"

"I don't know for sure, but I always assumed he started walking home soon thereafter. A bunch of us gathered around the front of the school waiting for our parents to pick us up. And Ronnie wasn't there. That generally meant he just took off."

"Who did he usually walk home with?"

"I think he walked home alone that day because no one came forward and said they were with him."

"I know. I mean, in general. Maybe they would have an idea if Ronnie ever went off the beaten path."

"Not sure if you mean that literally or figuratively."

"Fair point," I said. "I'm trying to find out if Ronnie didn't walk straight home, where he would go."

"That was kind of the million-dollar question that day."

"What was your best guess?"

"I don't think he walked directly home. Or, at least never got too close."

"Why do you say that?"

"Because Ronnie would have known a lot of people on his route home. And no one saw him after he left Willard."

"Makes sense. However, I checked the weather for Berkeley in early December. And the sun is starting to set around 5:30. It's possible that people didn't see Ronnie because it was getting dark."

"That's true. Call it a gut instinct then. I don't think Ronnie got close to his house. He knew that area well, and if he was in trouble he would have known where to run."

"Unless he got into the car of someone he knew."

"I'd rather not entertain that possibility," Aaron said.

"I don't blame you. I'm just trying to explore all options."

There was a pause as we heard someone opening the front door.

The pretty blonde woman from the picture walked in. She was wearing a pantsuit and carrying a briefcase. If I had to guess her profession, I'd have gone with a lawyer.

"Hi, honey," she said towards Aaron.

"Hey, babe. This is Quint."

I stood up and shook her hand.

"Pleased to meet you," I said.

"Likewise. I'm Theresa."

She hugged her husband and took a seat at the table.

"So, what's up? I didn't know you were having a guest."

"Neither did I, until this morning," Aaron said.

"If I'm intruding, let me know," I said.

"Not at all," his wife said. "I just want to know what's going on. I'm getting a feeling it's something secretive."

Aaron took his hand and enveloped his wife's wrist. This was a weird dance the three of us were doing.

"Do you remember me telling you about my friend who was killed when we were young?"

"Of course. Ronnie, right?"

"Yeah. Well, Quint here has been hired by the family to take a look into it."

She looked at me. I think she was expecting an explanation.

"Ronnie's grandfather came to me on the day after the 20th anniversary of his death. He asked me to take one last look at the case."

"How terrible," Theresa said.

"Yeah, it hasn't been easy. Don't feel bad for me, though. Feel for Ronnie's family."

Aaron interjected.

"Have you met with his father yet?"

"Yeah. I think if he had his choice, he would just forget about it forever."

"I can't blame him," Theresa said.

She appeared the more dominant personality in the marriage.

"Me, neither," I said.

"Then why do you think the grandfather wants to?"

"He's ninety-two years old and was hoping for some closure before he goes."

"Well, I hope you give it to him," Theresa said. "Not that it's going to be easy."

"I compared it to a needle in a haystack."

"That seems easy in comparison," Aaron said, rejoining the conversation.

"So has Aaron been helpful?" Theresa asked.

"Yes," I said. "Not sure we cracked the case just yet, though."

They both smiled slightly, which had been my goal. Gallows humor for sure, but anything to break the doldrums of this case was fine by me.

"A few minutes with my husband and you haven't solved a decades-old murder? You must be one lousy P.I.," Theresa joked.

"Shit, I'd have figured you'd have caught the Lindbergh baby's abductor by now," Aaron said, piggybacking on his wife's joke.

"Or JonBenet Ramsey's killer," Theresa said, piggybacking on Aaron's piggyback.

We all looked at each other, realizing we'd taken it far enough.

"Sorry," Theresa said.

"Don't be," I responded. "I started it. Probably good for me, anyway."

"We're here to help," she said and smiled.

After a few more minutes of small talk, I said my goodbyes.

CHAPTER 6

I didn't scare easily.

Never really had. Especially after the last two cases I'd worked on, it would take a lot to rattle me.

That being said, I was a bit on guard when I saw the outside of Wanda Dixon's residence. It looked like something out of the Bayou. It would have fit more in rural Louisiana than in Northern California.

The weeds were overgrown, the front yard was littered with trash, two beaten-down pickup trucks were out front, and there was a sense of criminality in the air. Part of me felt like I was in the first season of *True Detective*.

From Aaron Everton's house, I'd headed directly to the address that Lenore Finney had given me. The difference between the two homes was startling.

I approached the front door, or what I believed it to be. Some overgrown vines had taken over from a neighboring lattice and were now almost fully covering the entrance.

They should have hired a landscaper to spend a half-hour trimming around the edge of the house to make it look presentable.

Somehow, I didn't think Wanda Dixon would approve of that.

She'd made this choice to live in squalor.

A little trepidatious, I knocked on the door.

A few seconds later, I heard someone approach.

The door opened and before me stood a woman who looked like she hadn't showered in weeks. She could have been anywhere from twenty to thirty-five years old. My guess was she was on the lower end and the dirt on her face and body just made her appear older.

"Who are you?" she said.

"My name is Quint. I was wondering if I could ask you a few questions."

"Me?"

"Are you the owner of this house?"

"No."

"Who is?"

"Why do you care?"

If I was being generous, I'd call the woman standoffish. Insolent was probably a more accurate word.

"Do you know a woman named Wanda Dixon?" I asked, ready to judge her reaction.

"I don't know no Wanda Dixon."

"That's a double negative, which in proper English means you do know her."

"Don't be a sarcastic asshole," she said. "I don't not know no Wanda Dixon. That's three negatives now, so shouldn't that mean I don't know her?"

I couldn't do anything but smile.

"You throw people off with all that dirt, don't you? You're a pretty smart cookie, I'm guessing."

"I always wondered why people used that phrase. I ain't never known no cookie who had intelligence."

She laughed and I was positive she'd used another triple negative on purpose.

"I'll ask again. Who owns the house?"

"Rudy."

"Can you go grab Rudy?"

"That would be hard since Rudy is dead."

I had so many questions, I didn't know where to start.

Who was Rudy? How did he die? Why did you take over the house? Why haven't you showered in 429 days? What do you have against pruning? Why are you pretending not to know Wanda Dixon?

"It's hard to own something when you're dead," I said.

"Not really. Until that paperwork gets transferred over to me, Rudy still owns it."

She had a point.

"Okay, I'll ask you a question then."

"Haven't you been doing that already?"

I hated to admit it, but this woman had me on my heels.

"Are you going to invite me in?" I asked.

"Figuring that you're not the law, probably not. Let me guess, a P.I.?"

This had become a battle of pointed questions being hurled back and forth. And I was losing.

"I'm just asking a few questions," I said.

"Don't insult my intelligence. You're a P.I."

There was no reason to lie. She had me pegged.

"I am," I admitted.

"And what exactly do you want?" she asked.

"I was actually here to talk to Wanda Dixon, but you've aroused my curiosity," I said, although my last word easily could have been suspicions.

"What did you want with Ms. Dixon?" she asked.

"Merely to talk to her. You do know who she is, don't you? And who is Rudy?"

"Wanda lived here with Rudy after she got divorced."

"Why did you deny knowing her?"

"I don't just spill my guts out to every private dick who appears on my doorstep."

This woman was wise beyond her years. She was a clear case of not judging a book by its cover. Its dirty, unshowered cover.

"That's fair, but now that you've met me, we aren't strangers. I'll ask again. Where is Wanda Dixon?"

"Then I'll ask again. What did you want with her?"

"Just to ask a few questions."

"That's a non-answer. Tell me what the fuck you want with Wanda or I'm slamming this door shut."

This was going nowhere so I didn't see the downside of telling the truth.

"I'm investigating the murder of a fourteen-year-old boy. Wanda was his neighbor."

"Did she kill him?"

"I don't think so," I said. "But I want to know if she has any guesses as to who did."

"Wanda is dead too."

"What?"

"Her and Rudy. Rudy and her. Killed together in a car crash about three months ago."

"Shit. I'm sorry."

"Don't be. As you can tell, I wasn't all that fond of Wanda."

"Were you fond of Rudy?"

She stared at me, contemplating whether to say any more.

"I'm Rudy's daughter. I'll leave it at that. And as I said, this house will be mine any day now."

Something was wrong with this woman. But unless my math was way off, she would have been too young to have anything to do with Ronnie's murder.

"Does the name Ronnie Fisk mean anything to you?" I asked.

"Never heard of him, but I'm guessing he was the little boy," she said.

"Yes, he was."

"Still never heard of him."

"How old are you?" I asked.

"After I answer this, I'm going to be calling the police if you don't leave. I'm twenty-six years old."

She would have been six when Ronnie Fisk went missing. Whatever stunk here, it wasn't related to his murder.

"Alright, I'm leaving," I said.

"Good."

"Last question."

She didn't respond.

"What's your name?" I asked.

"Nunya."

I knew what was coming next.

"Nunya fucking business!"

"Since you've been so polite," I said. "I'm going to pay for a gardener to do some pruning. Don't worry, it will be my treat."

"Fuck you, Mr. P.I."

And then she finally did slam the door on me.

CHAPTER 7

After my hair-raising interaction with Rudy's nameless daughter, I headed back to Walnut Creek. With nothing going on at my office, I went home and spent the next hour re-reading different parts of the case file.

Knowing I was going to meet with Evelyn Fisk that night, I concentrated on the sections involving her boyfriend, Ty Mulholland. Although there was never an official suspect, Ty came as close as anyone.

There were a few officers who felt he should have been arrested, although he never was. It was obvious that Hank Tressel was suspicious of him as well. Hopefully, Evelyn could answer some of the questions I had about Ty.

I looked at my phone and it was three p.m. It had already been an exhausting day and I decided to take a quick nap before heading off to the South Bay to meet up with Ronnie's sister.

~

"Nice to meet you, Quint," Evelyn Fisk said.

I'd arrived in the city of Palo Alto a few minutes early and was sitting outside of the Starbucks we'd agreed to meet at. I'm not sure if her father or grandfather had described me, but she knew who I was right away.

There had been a few pictures of Evelyn in the police reports, but they were faded and she was only a teenager. I didn't know what to expect. She was a very attractive woman. And more importantly, a very accomplished one.

"Thanks for meeting with me," I said.

Evelyn had light blue eyes and shoulder-length brown hair with a few blonde highlights thrown in. She was tall, I'd guess somewhere around 5'9". She had flawless, bordering on porcelain, skin.

She was wearing jeans and a loose-fitting orange sweatshirt. She'd obviously changed when she got off work.

We were meeting at a Starbucks in the heart of Palo Alto, a fun, bustling town most famous for housing Stanford University. The Stanford Medical Center that Evelyn worked at also resided in Palo Alto.

She was about to open the door of the Starbucks when she paused.

"I've had a long few days. What do you say we grab a drink instead?"

No, having drinks with someone central to my investigation probably wasn't a habit I should get in the habit of. On the other hand, it hadn't exactly been an easy week for me, either.

All the interviews. The never-ending talk of Ronnie's death. The brutal exchange earlier that day.

A cold beer was warranted.

"Sure," I said.

I followed Evelyn as we crossed the street and approached a bar by the name of Live your Best Life.

It was an odd name for a bar considering most barflies I knew probably weren't living their best lives. Then again, maybe drinking and laughing your way through life wasn't all that bad. They certainly seemed happier than some 9-5 stiffs I knew.

"Thanks for agreeing to this," Evelyn said. "I think you'll like it here."

"I'll be sure to let you know."

She smiled as we walked in. The bar was classy and clean. I'm not sure if the name had me expecting a dive, but Live your Best Life was a pleasant surprise. We passed by a couple that had what looked like a small bowl of risotto with short ribs on top. Hardly your average bar food.

Evelyn strolled past the bar and stopped at a table in the corner.

"This will give us some privacy," she said.

A server passed by and said, "Hi, Evelyn."

She waved back.

"Come here often?" I asked.

"Probably twice a month or so."

We took our seats.

"I'm impressed so far," I said.

"They have food to die for if you're hungry."

If I didn't know any better, this was starting to feel like a date.

"Not right now, but thanks."

"If you change your mind, let me know."

"Will do."

Evelyn looked out at the bar.

"I just finished three long days at work and could use a stiff drink right now."

"I've had a long few days myself," I said.

"Dealing with my family, I'm sure it was," she said.

It couldn't tell if she was being playful or sarcastic.

The same waitress approached.

"What can I get you, Evelyn?"

"I'll take a Jack and Coke. Thanks, Tracy."

"And you?" Tracy asked me.

As good as a drink sounded, I was driving.

"I'll just take a beer. You have Sierra Nevada?"

"We do. Draft or bottle?"

"Draft."

Tracy walked away.

"Alright, you ready to do this?" she asked.

"Sure. I appreciate you meeting me."

"It's alright. I know you are just doing your job. Guess I have my crazy grandfather to thank for that."

"Why do you call him crazy?"

"Because instead of enjoying his twilight years, he's still trying to find out who killed Ronnie."

"Maybe he thinks it would give him some solace he doesn't currently have."

"It would make me sleep easier as well. In the back of my mind, I'm always worried the guy is still out there."

"If he is, he's not coming after any of you. I can assure you of that."

"Yeah? What makes you so positive?"

"It's been twenty years, Evelyn. And they didn't pick Ronnie because he was a Fisk."

"Once again, what makes you so positive?"

Was she saying what I think she was saying?

"Do you really think Ronnie was chosen because he was a member of your family?"

It's something I hadn't even considered. Seemed unlikely, but it certainly wasn't impossible.

Grant worked at a bank. I really hoped I wouldn't be going back through his finances or his history at the bank.

Fuck!

This conversation had gotten off to a rotten start.

"Do I really think that?" Evelyn said rhetorically. "No, but it's not some crazy idea, either. Everyone always just assumed it was a madman. They never caught the guy, though. You'd think if it was a madman, he'd have made a mistake or two. Whoever did this to Ronnie didn't make any errors."

This was getting worse.

"I've read every piece of paper related to your brother's death. I've talked to Emmett, your mother, your father, Hank Tressel, and a few others. And none of them have mentioned that as a possibility."

"Does that mean it can't be the case?"

"No, Evelyn, it doesn't."

I was already imagining having to ask Grant Fisk if he owed anybody money or if he'd screwed over someone at the bank. For all intents and purposes, I'd be asking him if he was responsible for the death of Ronnie. I couldn't imagine many things worse.

"Listen, Quint. I'm not here to throw out random theories."

"You sure? That is kind of what you just did," I said.

"Well, that will be the only one. I just thought I should mention it since no one ever talked about its plausibility."

"If you don't mind, I'd like to concentrate on scenarios with a higher likelihood."

"That's fine."

The server brought the drinks over and set them down in front of us. We each grabbed our respective drinks and took a sip. Originally, I might have offered her a "Cheers," but not after the way our conversation had begun. I'd been thrown for a loop.

"So, what's next? Do you want to know what I remember from that day?"

"No," I said.

Evelyn looked surprised.

"No?"

"I've read all the police reports and talked to several people. I'm tired of hearing people describe the day in question."

"What then?"

"Had Ronnie ever bullied another student? Had he been bullied? Were there older kids who didn't like him? Was there a significant other who maybe didn't like him? A teacher who was tough on him? A coach?"

Evelyn went back for her second sip before answering.

"So you've heard of Ty Mulholland?"

There was no use in lying.

"Yes, I have."

"Very subtle way you sandwiched him among several other questions."

"Not that subtle if you figured it out."

She half-heartedly smiled at me.

"Was this the only reason you wanted to interrogate me?"

Our conversation had been combative from the start and it wasn't getting much better.

"I'm not interrogating, just asking a few questions."

"There's a difference?" she asked.

"Point taken. And no, that's not the only reason. But if I don't bring him up when talking to you, then I'm not doing my job."

"True. That doesn't mean I have to like hearing it."

"No, it doesn't. If it makes you feel any better, I didn't like asking it."

Another halfhearted smile from Evelyn.

"Ty did not like Ronnie. That's true. But Ty didn't like many kids in the neighborhood and they didn't all end up dead."

"All those other kids weren't the brother of the girl Ty was dating."

"Yeah, that's fair. Before we go any further, I'll just say that no, I don't think Ty killed Ronnie. I didn't at the time. I don't now. And at no point in the intervening twenty years did I think so. That doesn't mean that Ty was some saint. He wasn't a good guy back then and I often wonder why I dated him."

"I'm sure many girls of that age have made the same mistake," I said, trying to get Evelyn back on my good side.

She smiled, this time more fully.

"Thanks."

"You're welcome."

She grabbed a sip of her drink and I did the same with my beer.

"Ty did bully Ronnie. And I didn't say anything. Probably because I thought Ronnie was a pain in the ass. Another thing that many seventeen-year-old girls thought about their fourteen-year-old brothers. Ronnie would tell my parents if he saw Ty and me kissing. He'd tell them that I wasn't going to a friend's, but to Ty's."

"What did you do?"

"I didn't do anything, per se. But I did allow Ty to intimidate him, so I did something by not doing anything. Does that make sense?"

"Yes," I said.

"And I regret it every day of my life. Not that Ty had anything to do with his death, but I wish I could tell Ronnie that I was just a mixed-up teenage girl. I'd give anything to hug him again."

Every member of the Fisk family had regrets of some sort. Maybe it was like that with any family that lost a child.

"I'm not here to recreate your pain, Evelyn. I'm sorry."

"I believe you. Although I think that's inevitable with all the questions you'll have to ask of my family. Speaking of which, have you talked to anyone besides my father?"

"Your mother."

"Really? I'm surprised she was willing to."

"Why?"

"She would rather just forget it ever happened. She's similar to my father in that regard."

"Are you different?"

"I'd like to think so, despite how I've acted towards you thus far. I want to find out who did this as much as Grandpa Emmett does. And yet, I also understand my parents' perspective that no matter what happens, Ronnie won't be coming back."

"What does your sister think?"

"I wouldn't know. I don't talk to her."

"I'm sorry. Neither one of your parents mentioned that."

"Not exactly something you brag about to a stranger."

I nodded.

"Can I ask why you guys don't talk?"

"It has nothing to do with Ronnie's murder if that's what you mean," she said.

I wanted to pry, but if it had nothing to do with Ronnie, then it should be off-limits for me.

"I won't push it. I do have a few more questions about Ty."

"Okay."

"The police reports say he was at home on the day Ronnie went missing. Is there any reason not to believe him?"

"No. As I said, I don't think he had anything to do with Ronnie's death."

"From the little I've read about Ty, he doesn't seem like a homebody. Was it normal for him to be home between say five-thirty and six p.m.?"

"Sure, Ty was a social guy. His mother worked two jobs and wouldn't get home till late, so he'd hit the skate park a lot. That doesn't mean he wasn't at home on the day in question."

"Was his father around?"

"Only occasionally. His father didn't live with his mother. Thankfully. He was an asshole and much more of a real bully than Ty."

It sounded like Ty Mulholland had a pretty lousy home life.

"So, despite the fact that Ty hung out at the skate park a lot, you believe him when he said he was home the night Ronnie went missing?"

"He was my boyfriend, and he may have been an asshole, but I trusted him. So yes, I believed him then and I believe him now."

I could tell she didn't like this line of questioning. Who would?

"I realize how hard this is."

"You keep saying that, but the questions don't stop."

It was the first time I'd sensed genuine anger. Or was it sadness? It was hard to tell.

"I only have a few more questions about Ty."

"Okay. Let's get this over with."

"How long did you continue dating him after Ronnie died?"

"A few months."

"Who broke up with whom?"

"He broke up with me. But it wasn't because he killed Ronnie. It's because I was a ghost. A shadow of myself."

"Where is Ty now?"

"Maybe jail. Maybe dead. I have no idea. I lost track of him many moons ago. He's not the kind of ex-boyfriend you go on Facebook to find."

"Thank you," I said, knowing none of that had been easy for her.

"The toughest part was losing Ronnie, of course," Evelyn said. "The second toughest thing was that people kept mentioning Ty after Ronnie died. Not the police, per se, but my friends, my classmates, etc. There was always Ty looming over the investigation which put me in the toughest position imaginable. I was grieving for my brother while having to defend my boyfriend as well. That's why talking about Ty brings out the worst in me. I'm sorry."

"Don't be."

I saw Tracy the server take a brief glance at us. She could tell that we were in a serious conversation and chose not to approach us.

"I'm going to say one last thing that's going to piss you off," I said.

"This should be good."

"The only person I've found who feels like a potential suspect has been Ty."

"Then you're not digging deep enough," Evelyn said, which surprised me.

"What do you mean exactly?"

"There were other creepy neighbors that some people suspected. Wanda Dixon. Alma Jones."

"I went to see Wanda Dixon earlier today."

"And?"

"And she's dead. Died in a car accident a few months ago."

Considering my source, I told myself to make sure and double-check.

"Really? Wow. I guess it's going to be tough to confirm or rule her out as a suspect now."

"Exactly. If the killer is dead, how am I ever going to figure this puzzle out?"

"Hey, you took the case."

Evelyn smiled partially as she said it. She was starting to loosen up a bit.

"Yup. I'm the idiot for doing that."

"If it makes you feel any better, I don't think you're going to catch the killer even if he or she is still alive."

"Lucky me. Who is Alma Jones?" I asked.

"She was an old lady and a real bitch. Everyone hated her."

"I know Ronnie was slight for his age, but do you really think an old lady could have subdued him if push came to shove."

Evelyn pondered my question.

"You may be right about Alma. She was quite frail. Wanda versus Ronnie would have been a fair fight. Jeez, this is a terrible conversation."

I nodded.

"I feel like the skateboarders I see are naturally pretty strong."

"Generally, I'd say yes, but Ronnie was just starting to go through puberty. He was five foot nothing and a hundred pounds and nothing. If he'd lived a year longer, he probably would have been getting muscular and had a deepening voice. But someone took that from him."

For my own sanity, I needed to steer the conversation away from Ronnie's death.

"Give me some good Ronnie memories. I know you two didn't always see eye-to-eye, but there must have been some."

"Oh, we had plenty. I still laugh when I see a plate of bad food. From about ten to twelve years old, Ronnie would try to make breakfast for the family once a month or so. It was the worst combination you could imagine. He'd throw Cocoa Puffs on top of half-cooked eggs with a side of raw bacon."

I laughed at the visual.

"That's cute," I said.

"Our mother would always have to go back and finish off the eggs and the bacon. But, as the saying goes, it's the thought that counts."

"You said he only did that from ten to twelve or so?"

"I think once you become a teenager, cooking isn't something you pride yourself on. Especially boys."

"Was he trying to be a tough guy?"

"Not really. Ronnie was always a pretty sweet kid. It's just that when you are fourteen, you don't go bragging to your friends about cooking breakfast for your family."

I smiled.

"Yeah, probably not."

"It was fun while it lasted," Evelyn said.

"Anything else? I value these stories," I said. "It's tough focusing on the death over and over. I'd like to get a feeling for the real Ronnie."

"Trust me, I get it."

"So, you got another story?"

Evelyn looked at me as she pondered which one to tell.

"One of our favorite childhood games was something we could only do when our parents were gone. Usually, Ronnie and I would do it on school days before our parents got home. And we'd do it some weekends with Maddie. She loved it."

"What was it?"

"Hold your horses," Evelyn said.

The tone of our conversation had changed and I was grateful for it.

"So we lived in a small house, but it had two stories," she continued. "Ronnie would collect all the pillows from our beds upstairs and put them flush against the wall near the bottom of the stairs. And he had this big sheet of cardboard that he hid in his room. He'd bust it out once my parents left. And him, me, and occasionally Maddie would take turns riding the cardboard down the stairs, and then we'd slam into the pillows that were up against the wall."

"Sounds dangerous," I said. "But also something I would have loved as a kid."

"We all adored it. Maddie most of all. We'd have to remind her not to bring it up around our parents. You should have seen her little face light up when she was about to go down the stairs. The proverbial kid in a candy store."

This story was warming my heart.

"Thank you, Evelyn. This means more than you know."

"To me, too. I haven't told that story in years. It feels good."

"Did you guys ever hit the staircase on the way down?"

"Oh, yeah. We'd have to lie to our parents and say we bruised our bodies some other way."

I laughed.

"And your parents never caught on?"

"No, Ronnie hid that cardboard like it was the Holy Grail. There were a few times we heard our parents pulling in and we'd all be running the pillows back up the stairs."

"I love it," I said.

Evelyn let out a big smile.

"It was a great time. It's too bad you can't stay that age forever."

I was reminded of Aaron Everton stating that Ronnie would be young forever.

"You're a doctor. You've done well for yourself," I said.

"Thanks."

Evelyn was not wearing a wedding ring and Hank's notes had never mentioned her being married. It wasn't really my business, but I was curious. I decided against asking, however.

"Were you the one who suggested me to Emmett? He said it was his granddaughter, but didn't say if it was you or Maddie."

"He does have other grandchildren from his daughter, but yes, it was me."

"He said you heard I'd become a P.I. through the grapevine. What does that mean? I'm only curious because I haven't run any ads or anything."

"Oh, but you have."

I was perplexed.

"What do you mean?"

"You posted it on Facebook."

"Well, that's not really an ad."

"I think you're being a little naive," she said.

"Maybe," I admitted. "So we have a mutual friend who told you?"

"You got it."

"Who might that be?"

"Gilly Barber."

Gilly was a friend that I used to get drinks with when I was still dating Cara. He'd moved down near Palo Alto a few years back.

"Ah, you know Gilly. He's a maniac."

"A wild man if there ever was one," Evelyn said.

"How did he know to tell you that?"

"It came up in passing. I'd told him how my father, grandfather, and I had bonded over the Bay Area Butcher case. He said he knew you."

"No offense, but it seems an odd thinking to bond over," I said.

"You wouldn't understand, but every time there's a serial killer in the public eye, the three of us get very interested. I don't think it's because we think it might be Ronnie's killer. It's more just a morbid fascination brought about by the events of twenty years ago."

"That makes sense," I said, not sure I'd ever truly understand how their family was affected.

"I realize it's an oddball thing to bond over, but trust me, we do. Even old Emmett."

"I'm glad my case brought you guys a little closer together," I said, half-joking, half-serious.

"So anyway, I brought that up to Gilly and once he saw your post on Facebook about starting a P.I. firm, he let me know about it."

"Now it makes sense. And then you told Emmett?"

"I did. In passing, just because we'd been impressed with what you'd accomplished."

Tracy must have noticed that we were in better spirits because she approached the table once more.

"Drinks?" she asked.

"I'll have another," Evelyn said.

"And you?" Tracy asked.

"One more beer and then I have to go," I said.

"Got it," Tracy said and walked away.

"What I didn't know," Evelyn said, getting back to our conversation, "was that Emmett was going to locate you and ask you to investigate Ronnie's death."

"Would you have told Emmett about me opening up a P.I. firm if you knew he'd do just that?"

"It's a firm? Sounded more like it was just you from what he said."

She smiled.

"You sound exactly like Emmett right there," I said. "In fact, I think he made that same joke."

We both laughed. I appreciated these lighter moments. Both with the Everton's and now with Evelyn.

"As for your question, I don't know if I still would have told him. I guess it remains to be seen."

"If I find new evidence, then it was worth it?"

"Something like that."

Our drinks arrived.

"I really do have to go after this," I said. "I'm not sure having drinks with your family is the best idea."

"My father said you guys had drinks together."

"Not exactly. He had a beer, I had water."

"Ah. That makes more sense."

"I'll tell you what. When my part of the investigation ends, I'll meet up with you and Gilly, sans my car, and we can get rip-roaring drunk."

"I look forward to it."

Evelyn was not flirting with me, but she'd certainly come around and wasn't nearly as combative as earlier in our conversation.

I asked her a few more questions about Ronnie while nursing that last beer. At one point, I realized we were just talking in circles, so I stopped.

The rest of our conversation morphed into talking about Bay Area sports and our mutual friend, Gilly. I promised to keep Evelyn in the loop about my investigation and she thanked me for what I was doing for her family.

It had been an up and down conversation, but we'd undoubtedly ended on a high note and I felt we left as friends.

"Take care, Evelyn," I said as I was headed towards the door.

"You too, Quint. Be safe. You never know who is out there watching."

It was an odd thing to say, but it made sense looking back at our conversation. Evelyn, whether rightly or wrongly, still thought her brother's killer was out there.

CHAPTER 8

It turned out Ty Mulholland was not only alive, but living in the Bay Area.

It was the morning after my meeting with Evelyn and talking to Ty was my number one priority.

In Hank's notes, there was an old cell phone number for Ty that was no longer active. His last known address had been in Boulder, Colorado, but that had been three years ago.

It was time to do my own research.

I googled "Ty Mulholland."

It wasn't a very common first or last name and I was able to find Ty in a matter of minutes. He now lived in San Lorenzo, about thirty minutes from Walnut Creek, and worked at a Home Depot a few miles away in Hayward.

It was truly scary how much you can find out about a person in a few short minutes.

I was surprised that Hank hadn't kept up on Ty's whereabouts, especially since he'd had suspicions about him. I'd be sure to update him.

I decided to confront Ty at his workplace. Or, introduce myself, if that sounds any better. There was a high probability that Ty was going to be a combative interviewee, so I didn't want to risk being told to 'Fuck off' at his house. It would be tougher for him to do so while at work.

I called ahead and Home Depot confirmed Ty was already on and would be working till two p.m.

I left Walnut Creek immediately and arrived at the Home Depot in

Hayward, CA almost an hour later. Hayward was a blue-collar town that had long lived in Oakland's shadow. There was quite a bit of crime in Hayward, something they shared in common with their more famous neighbor.

I parked my car and entered the massive warehouse, approaching the first employee I saw.

"What section does Ty Mulholland work in?"

"Back left corner. The Garden Center."

"Thanks."

I was a bit surprised. I was expecting him to work with power tools or something.

I wanted to hit myself for continuing to jump to conclusions. And it was all based on police reports from two decades ago.

I was reminded of when Hank told me to approach this case with a fresh start. I was doing the polar opposite, pigeonholing people before I'd even met them.

I told myself to clean it up as I started traversing the gigantic Home Depot.

I made my way to the Garden Center which looked to continue outside, surely where flowers and plants were sold. I saw someone behind the counter who was probably in his late thirties and as I got closer, I saw his name tag said, Ty.

"Can I help you?" he asked.

I suddenly felt guilty. Was I just going to start asking him questions about a dead kid from twenty years ago? I'm sure his boss wouldn't take too kindly to that.

As had become standard in this case, I hadn't really thought ahead.

"Do you have a break coming up?" I asked.

He eyed me with suspicion.

"Do I know you?"

"No."

"Then why do you want to know when I have a break?"

Honesty was the best policy at this point.

"I'm a P.I. and investigating the disappearance of Ronnie Fisk. I talked to Evelyn last night and I'm trying to talk to everyone involved. And I thought it would be better to discuss it on your break than out here in front of other people."

"I'll talk to you, but don't claim I was involved. I had nothing to do with Ronnie ending up dead."

"I'm sorry. I didn't mean involved in that sense."

"Why don't you wait outside that door over there," he said, pointing to his left. "I'll be out there in thirty minutes."

"Thank you," I said.

"Did Evelyn send you?" he asked.

"No. She has no idea you're still in the Bay Area."

He nodded and from behind me, I could hear a customer approaching. I got out of the way and headed towards the door. Part of me feared that Ty would ditch work and flee, afraid of this mysterious private investigator who showed up unannounced.

I was wrong and Ty approached me almost exactly thirty minutes later.

"Let's walk away from the store if you don't mind. Thanks," he said.

His left arm was a sleeve, tattooed from his shoulder down to his wrist. He looked tough and didn't appear to be someone who smiled easily. Not that he'd had any reason to since I'd introduced myself. Call it a hunch. I didn't get the vibe Ty was the jovial type.

And yet, considering the circumstances, he'd been polite and seemed genuine.

His looks and his actions were at odds with each other.

I followed him as we headed into the abyss that was a Home Depot parking lot.

After about forty-five seconds of walking in silence, he abruptly stopped and turned to face me.

"Alright, what do you want to know? Not sure how helpful I can actually be."

It was a busy parking lot, but we were standing next to a light pole and were not in the traffic lane.

"I'd just like to hear your recollection of the day Ronnie went missing."

I'd told Evelyn I was tired of asking that question, and truthfully, I was. However, Ty was as close as I had to a suspect. It had to be asked of him.

"I was dating Evelyn. And I admit it, I was kind of an asshole to Ronnie. I was seventeen or eighteen and a bully. What can I say? I didn't freaking kill the kid, though."

"I didn't ask that. I just asked what you remember about the day in question."

"You don't need to humor me. I know what you are asking."

"As of right now, all I'm asking is your recollections of the day Ronnie went missing. You'll know if I'm accusing you of something."

Ty looked at me and seemed to relax.

"Alright, that's fair. What is your endgame here?"

"I'm trying to find out who killed Ronnie."

"No offense, but that seems pretty damn unlikely."

"You're not the first person who has told me that."

"Maybe you should listen," Ty said.

"I don't have much of a choice. I was hired to investigate."

"By who?"

I wasn't sure I was supposed to be divulging Emmett Fisk's name, but it was too late now. Everyone else knew why I'd been hired.

"Emmett Fisk."

"He's still alive? Shit, he was old twenty years ago."

"He's in his nineties now."

I saw Ty let out a brief smile.

"He hated me. Told Evelyn she should break up with me. Like he was the father. Busybody of a grandfather if you ask me."

That Emmett could be a busybody, or worse, seemed to be the prevailing opinion.

"He's just trying to find out what happened to his grandson," I said.

Ty looked on with compassion.

"I felt terrible, obviously. And I was in a tough spot because I'd been such a jerk to Ronnie. I knew that some people thought I might have been mixed up in his disappearance."

"Were you ever named a suspect by the police?"

I knew the answer but wanted to see his reaction to the question. It was a strategy I used often.

"No. Not officially. That doesn't mean the neighbors didn't have their suspicions, which found its way down to their kids."

"What do you mean exactly?" I asked.

Someone was moving towards us with a huge shopping cart and we kept quiet until he passed.

"What I mean is that some parents told their kids to be wary of me. That led to people in high school accusing me of being involved. I got into probably four fights in the weeks after Ronnie went missing. It also cost me my relationship with Evelyn so this was a pretty tough time for me too."

"Why exactly did you two break up?"

"You talked to her, what did she say?"

"She said she was a shell of herself. A ghost, I believe was her exact quote."

"That's true, but I would have stayed with her."

"Then why did you guys break up?"

"I think it was just a combination of everything. To start, there was the pressure of Ronnie's disappearance. And then the sadness when they found him. Plus, that cloud looming over everything, that I was potentially involved. Finally, her family never really liked me and if she was ever going to break up with me, that was the time. And so she did."

This was all new to me. Evelyn had said it was Ty who had broken up with her.

"She broke up with you?"

"That's how I remember it, yeah."

Before I could ask a follow-up question, Ty spoke again.

"I think. Everything was so muddled at that time. Plus, it was twenty years ago. I can't be the only one who doesn't remember everything to a tee."

Although inevitable, people telling me they couldn't remember things was starting to grate on me.

"Where were you on the day in question?" I asked, circling back to my original question.

"I went to school and to the skate park after."

"You did? Evelyn said you were at home. So did the police reports, in fact."

Ty stared at me. Was he genuinely puzzled or had I caught him in a lie? My gut told me it was the latter.

"Jesus, I don't fucking know," he said. "I always went to the skate park. I just assumed I did that day too."

"This must have been a big deal in the days that followed," I said. "I would think you'd remember."

"I was smoking a lot of pot in high school and would occasionally drop LSD. That continued after they found Ronnie's body and I kept doing that shit all through my teenage years and my twenties. I'm sorry if I don't remember what happened twenty years ago. Maybe part of me has been trying to forget it."

I wasn't done with that line of questioning but abandoned it for the moment. I tried to lay a trap to test his memory. I think it was better than he led on.

"Besides yourself, who did other people suspect? I don't mean the cops, I mean the people around the neighborhood."

"Some people thought the family was involved. The family assumed it was a serial killer. And anyone who had argued with Ronnie at some point had become a suspect. I do seem to remember one that stood out. His name was Drake Benoit. I think he was a freshman or sophomore in high school. I know he was older than Ronnie. Regardless, he'd be at the skate park a lot. His last name was pronounced Ben-Wa. I think it was French. And Ronnie, who could be pretty feisty at times, kept calling him Ben-oit, like it's spelled. It blew up one day. Drake told Ronnie his name was pronounced Ben-Wa. Ronnie calls him Benoit. And it ends in a fight. Ronnie gets his butt kicked. He was tough for his size, but he was an eighth-grader and slightly built. Drake was older and bigger."

He'd fallen for my trap in the biggest way possible. I didn't realize he'd go so in-depth about a seemingly random event.

"Can I be honest, Ty?"

"Sure."

"I find it odd that you can remember a fight between Ronnie and some other kid, but can't remember what you were doing on the day he went missing. Ok, that's not exactly true. I don't find it odd. I find it unbelievable."

Ty leered at me, surely harkening back to his bully days. It wasn't going to work with me. I was two inches taller and twenty pounds heavier. Maybe he was a menace in high school, but not anymore. It wasn't going to come to it, but if need be, I was confident I could take Ty in a fight.

"As I said, I've done a lot of drugs."

"I want to believe you, Ty. I feel like you've been honest with me for the most part, but I'm not buying your bullshit about not remembering the day in question. Try one more time."

"Are you just going to forget about Drake Benoit?"

"I'll be following up on that. But for now, you're in front of me and I'd like a straight answer."

Ty pulled his phone out and looked at the time.

"You've only got a few more minutes with me and then I'm going back to work."

"I'm going to ask you one last time, Ty. Where were you the day Ronnie went missing?" I asked vehemently.

It was my turn to put on the bully face. It seemed to work. Ty looked a little sheepish. He was hiding something. I knew it.

"My father was almost never around," he said. "He and my mother were broken up about ninety percent of the time. But occasionally, he'd stop by. And whenever he found out that I'd been smoking grass and hanging around at the skate park, he'd beat me. Badly. He happened to come over to our house on the night Ronnie went missing. And he was there when the cops started asking me questions later that evening."

I knew where this was going. Ty looked like he wanted to cry. He no longer looked like a bully, but a teenager who was scared of his father.

"If I'd told the officers I'd been at the skate park, my father would have beaten me. He knew what I did there. And it would have been a bad one, considering all the drama going on with Ronnie missing. Shit, he might have even suspected me of the murder. So I lied and told the cops I'd come straight home after school."

"Didn't the police follow up?"

"If I'd actually skated, then a bunch of people would have seen me. All I did was smoke a little weed with my buddy, Gib. We were on the outskirts of where people skated and no one else saw us."

"And you trusted Gib to not say anything?"

"Not exactly. I went over to his house after the cops left and asked him not to say anything. He barely knew Ronnie and I don't think the cops ever got around to interviewing him. If they did, he didn't mention me, because it never came out that I was around the skate park."

"How long were you there?"

"Twenty minutes max. Just enough to smoke some weed before I went home. And I didn't see anything, you have to believe me. The only reason I lied was to avoid a beating."

I hated that Ty had been lying for twenty years, but in that moment with his father looking on, I understood why he chose to lie.

"You didn't see Ronnie on your walk home?"

"No. If I'd seen anything suspicious, I would have come forward."

"Even if it would have ended in a beating?"

"Of course. I'm not an animal. I thought I was just telling a half-truth. I mean, I arrived home twenty minutes later. I swear on my life that I have no idea what happened to Ronnie."

Against my better judgment, I continued to want to believe Ty. He looked at his watch again.

"I have to go. Honestly, my boss will be pissed."

I hated to admit it, but I felt bad for Ty. At least, this older, more mellow version. He appeared to be a lost soul.

As for the seventeen-year-old version? I probably would have despised him. I'd always been disgusted by bullies.

"One last question," I said.

"What is it?"

"Who do you think killed Ronnie?"

"I kind of always assumed it was someone close to him. I never heard about a serial killer. Could it have been some random person who just killed one kid? I guess, but that seemed unlikely. So I guess by default I think it was a fellow family member."

I hated myself for what I asked next.

"Which family member would you suspect?"

"Not one of his sisters, that's for sure. Maddie was way too young and Evelyn wasn't strong enough. Even Ronnie's Mom was really skinny. I doubt she could have done anything either. So I guess by default, it would have to be Grant, their father."

I thought that was the worst of it. I was wrong.

"Unless it was that crazy grandfather who hired you," Ty said.

∼

I arrived home, still a bit shook from my conversation with Ty Mulholland. I told myself that he was just casting aspersions on the Fisks, trying to distract from the fact that he'd lied for twenty years.

And while that was feasible, I did have to entertain the possibility Ronnie Fisk had been killed by a family member. It certainly wasn't beyond the realm of possibility. I may have hated pondering it, but I couldn't avoid it altogether.

I'd met with Emmett, Grant, and Evelyn Fisk. I'd talked to Patricia Fisk on the phone and hoped to do the same with Maddie Fisk soon. Parts of them were broken, but I'd found things to like about each one.

To think that one of them had something to do with Ronnie's murder made me sick to my stomach.

I couldn't completely discount Ty's point of view, but I thought he was mistaken. Ronnie was not killed by a family member.

Maybe I was burying the lead, which should have been Ty's confession of lying.

On the other hand, if Ty had killed Ronnie, why would he admit to me he'd been lying all these years?

That would make no sense.

What I thought more likely was that Ty had nothing to do with Ronnie's murder, but felt guilty after all these years of lying. He'd been blindsided by me showing up, and without time to think it through, he instinctively confessed to something that had been bothering him for two decades. He was getting a burden off of his shoulders.

That made more sense to me.

Despite his admission of lying, I'd found Ty to be trustworthy. That may seem incongruous, but not to me. His admitting to a twenty-year-old lie actually put him in my good graces.

Gun to my head, I didn't think Ty had anything to do with Ronnie's death.

And I didn't believe his allegations against the Fisk family either.

Unfortunately, none of them could completely be ruled out.

My goal had been to eliminate suspects as I made my way through this investigation.

The opposite appeared to be coming true.

CHAPTER 9

I'd waited too long to call Maddie Fisk.

I knew why. Maddie was so young when Ronnie died. She obviously had nothing to do with the death of her brother. And I didn't think she could possibly add anything to what I'd learned. Even if she claimed to, it would be hard to trust the memory of a child that young.

Mostly, I didn't want to open old wounds from the youngest member of the Fisk family. It had been hard enough doing so with her older sister and parents.

Despite all my excuses, I had to make the call. I wasn't covering all the bases if I didn't.

I called her at eight p.m. that night. I'd texted her earlier in the day and she said she wouldn't be free until eleven EST.

I sat on my couch, fully expecting an uncomfortable upcoming ten or so minutes.

"Hello, this is Maddie."

Her given name had been Madeline and part of me expected her to have reverted back to the more grown-up-sounding name. I was pleasantly surprised she still went by Maddie. I can't say why exactly. Maybe I wanted Maddie to still be child-like since her childhood had been shattered.

"Hi Maddie, this is Quint. I told you I'd be calling tonight."

"What's taken you so long?"

"Excuse me?" I asked.

"I heard you talked to everyone else in the family days ago. What am I, chopped liver?"

While her words seemed antagonistic, her tone was playful.

"Saving the best for last," I said, saying what quickly popped into my head.

"Good answer. You're off my shit list."

Considering we'd soon be talking about her dead sibling, it was a pleasant, unforeseen start to our conversation. The opposite of her sister's.

"The real reason I've waited so long is that you were only eleven years old when Ronnie went missing."

"That's true, but I was the closest one to him in the family."

I felt like an idiot. More so, an incompetent idiot. Ronnie could easily have told Maddie some secret that Evelyn or her parents didn't know.

"I've heard you two were inseparable."

"We were. Ronnie was the perfect older brother, looking after me all the time."

"I'm not sure Evelyn would say he was the perfect younger brother."

"No, probably not. Although, from my vantage point, it was more that Evelyn was a lousy older sister than Ronnie a bad younger brother."

"I know all about the friction. I even talked to Ty."

"Shit, you even talked to non-family members before you talked to me."

I decided to roll with the playful tone.

"Many. Ty, Hank, Aaron Everton, Ed Finney. Probably some others I can't think of at the moment. You were way down the list."

"Well, this conversation is more light-hearted than I would have expected."

"Agreed."

"This will probably put an end to the joyful segment of the conversation, but I have to ask. How is Evelyn?"

"Our conversation got off to a rough start. She told me about you guys not getting along and I had quite a few pointed questions about Ty. By the end, we were fine, but there were a few bumps along the way."

"That's nice. We only had the bumps."

Maddie seemed more willing to talk about their relationship than Evelyn had.

"Why did you two have a falling out? If you don't mind me asking."

"I don't mind. I wouldn't characterize it as a falling out. That infers we were close at some point. After Ronnie died, I think she had a lot of regrets. Most of them involved Ty's bullying, but Evelyn could be pretty mean to Ronnie as well. I think that ate at her. And since I was only eleven, and Ronnie and I got along so great, everyone always hugged me first and possibly gave Evelyn a little stink eye. I'm not saying they suspected her, but some suspected Ty, and that made people think poorly of Evelyn."

"That's too bad."

"It is. But I was only eleven years old. What was I supposed to do? Stand up every time people came over and yell that Evelyn was a great older sister? Well, she wasn't. Plus, I was too young to realize just how tough Ronnie's death was on Evelyn. I mean, it was hard on everyone, obviously, but my parents and I just had to grieve. Evelyn had to grieve and defend herself. Does that make sense?"

"Yes. Completely. She basically said the same."

"So as we got older I think she started to blame me for what she went through. I was the lovable, pint-sized eleven-year-old whom everyone fawned over. She resented that."

"Did you guys ever make up?"

"She went to college a year later and we didn't have much bonding time before she left. Our family was a mess, as you probably guessed. Dad started drinking too much. Mom started taking too much of an interest in Evelyn and me. Every A on the report card was cause for a parade. Every minor accomplishment had to be shared with everyone on the block. The reason was obvious. She was going all-in on her two remaining kids. I think Evelyn was happy to get out. I guess I can't blame her. A lot of people asked how she did so well in college a year after Ronnie's death. I think it was partly because she was afraid of having to move back home. So she excelled. And she rarely came back, even though she was going to college in Southern California. We never really had time to talk out our differences. Then, when she graduated college, I was in high school, but she'd started medical school and was always busy. At least, that's what she told us. Part of it was her just not wanting to come home. And then once she finished Med School and started her residency, I came to the east coast for college."

"Two ships in the night," I said.

"Basically. Especially if one of the ships doesn't want to be near the other ship."

"I'm sorry, Maddie. It sounds like your relationship was another by-product of Ronnie's death."

"It certainly didn't help, although I'm not sure we were ever going to be that close. She's more domineering. I'm more mellow. We were like oil and water."

Did any of this bring me closer to Ronnie's murderer? No, but I was fascinated by the family dynamic that his death caused.

"Thanks for telling me all of this. I know it couldn't have been easy."

"Actually, I'm glad we were able to talk about it. Neither my mother nor father want to hear about it. So it's nice to get some things off my chest."

"Do you mind if we get back to the reason I called?"

"Wait, you didn't call to hear about a sibling rivalry?"

I laughed.

"Alright, are you ready?" I asked.

"Sure."

"What can you tell me about Ronnie that no one else would know?"

"He loved to skateboard."

"C'mon, obviously I know that."

"He didn't like basketball."

"I know that as well."

"He was scared of our mother more than our father."

"Aaron Everton alluded to that."

"Okay, allow me to turn this towards you," Maddie said. "What do you not know that you think I might?"

It was an interesting question.

"To be honest, I didn't expect a whole lot of new information from you. And then as we started talking, I hoped maybe Ronnie told you some important secret."

"He told me many secrets. None that had anything to do with his murder. Sorry. That's something I definitely would have remembered, even at eleven." Maddie said.

"Was Ronnie scared or nervous leading up to the day he went missing?"

"Not that I noticed."

"Would you have?"

"I think so. Sure, I was young, but you can still sense when someone isn't themselves."

"I'd agree. How about going back to the weeks leading up to it. Anything different?"

"He was a fourteen-year-old, so of course he had ups and downs. He was never scared of anybody or thought something bad might happen. He would have told me."

These were the answers I expected. I didn't think Ronnie's abduction was something that had been planned ahead so he couldn't have known about it.

"I've asked this of everybody I've met. What is your best guess as to what happened?"

"I always thought it was some random creep who happened to see Ronnie walking that night. A crime of opportunity, I think it's called. I never thought it was anyone we knew. Ty included."

"I tend to agree with you. Other people have put forth their theories, but mine aligns pretty closely to yours."

"Pretty closely?"

"I'm not sure the person was completely random."

"What do you mean exactly?"

"I'll get to that. Could Ronnie have been talked into the car of a stranger?"

"No, probably not. He was a smart kid. He was small, though, and I guess he could have been overpowered and forced into a car."

I heard Maddie's voice start to crack. It was the first time my questions had gotten to her.

"I don't think he was overpowered or dragged into a car," I said.

"Why?"

"Because most of the streets from Willard Middle School to your family's house are pretty out in the open. It's true the sun was starting to set, but if someone tried to grab Ronnie, there would at least have been a struggle. And no one saw anything. Now, if it was someone he recognized, and he got in willingly, there'd be no struggle and nothing for anybody to see."

"So you think it was someone he knew?"

"Yes, but not well. My current working hypothesis is that he got into the car of someone he'd met, but not a friend, family member, or well-known neighbor. It's obviously still a guess at this point. I'd say I deserve one after working this case endlessly for the last several days."

"No one else has solved the case. You deserve a guess as much as anyone. Except maybe Hank. He's put in his hours. His days. His decades," Maddie said.

"I bet it eats at him every day."

"It eats at all of us every day."

"I didn't mean Hank took it worse than your family," I said.

"I know."

There was a pause where neither of us said anything.

"When was the last time you were in the Bay Area, Maddie?"

"It's been several years. I still talk to my father. In fact, he's been updating me on everyone you've talked to. And I do plan to visit him at some point."

"He loves you and Evelyn. He's proud of both of your accomplishments."

"I know. Listen, no offense, but can we not talk anymore about our family dynamic? I didn't mind dishing the dirt on Evelyn and myself, because we never really got along. It cuts deeper with my parents."

"Sure. No more," I said.

Ronnie's death had so many long-lasting aftershocks on this family. Maddie had been polite, funny, and receptive to my questions. And still, there was an underlying sadness that was never going to go away.

"Is there anything else?" she asked.

"Not right now," I said. "Can I call you back at some point?"

"You can, but please only call if it's something you really think I can help with. Conversations about Ronnie always leave me with a sour taste in my mouth. Even though I always put on a brave face."

"I apologize, Maddie."

"I'm not mad at you. You're being as diplomatic as you can and honestly, we had a nice back and forth. I really hope you catch the guy. I'm sure you've been told a million times that you're on a wild goose chase, so I won't bother repeating it."

"You kind of just did," I said.

Maddie laughed.

"Guilty as charged."

I tried to think if there was anything else I should ask. Nothing immediately came to mind.

"I think that's about it, Maddie. Thanks for your time."

"You're welcome. And good luck."

"I'll need it."

"Yes, you will."

I hung up the phone with Maddie and, for the tenth time over the last several days, I regretted taking this job.

I felt for her. I felt for Evelyn. I felt for their parents. I felt for Hank. I even felt for Ty.

Whoever this killer was, he'd killed a lot more than a fourteen-year-old boy. He'd basically killed the entire Fisk family dynamic. Once again, I was assuming it was a male.

I began thinking about what I'd do if I ever found the killer.

I envisioned myself inflicting severe damage on him.

It brought me comfort and made me uncomfortable at the same time.

This case was driving me bonkers.

CHAPTER 10

I woke up the next morning and realized the days since Emmett Fisk arrived at my office had been a blur. I couldn't believe it had already been five days. That said, I'd also learned more about the case than I ever thought possible.

It was similar in some regards to Ronnie's death. To the family, it seemed like it happened both fifty years ago and last week. That's the feeling I had about my time investigating. It had sailed by and yet I still felt like I'd been on the case for months.

What was next for me?

I'd now talked to everyone in the immediate Fisk family. Outside the family, I'd spoken to several people as well.

It was time to take stock of all I'd learned. And most importantly, examine how and why people thought Ronnie had been killed.

Patricia Fisk seemed to think it was a serial killer. Evelyn suggested Ronnie might have been killed because he was a Fisk. Although he hadn't come out and said it, I thought Hank Tressel suspected Ty was involved. Maddie thought it was a random occurrence. A crime of opportunity.

I thought Evelyn's was the least likely scenario. I hadn't seen or heard anything that suggested Ronnie was killed for that reason. I also put a little less stock in her opinion. Part of me thought she was still trying to deflect from Ty being a suspect. Which ironically, she didn't have to do with me, because I did not think he was involved.

A serial killer or a random from off the street seemed the most likely to me. And those two were not necessarily mutually exclusive.

With only two days left on the case, I had to formulate a plan. My final meeting with Emmett was going to be here before I knew it.

I decided to go see Hank Tressel. It had been several days since I'd talked to him. I had much to tell him. And much to ask.

He agreed to meet me that afternoon.

~

Hank was waiting for me outside of his house when I arrived.

He was wearing a heavy-duty parka and the hood was covering his head.

I'd noticed the weather getting worse as I made my way from the East Bay to the North Bay.

I looked up to see the trees swaying back and forth and I knew it was only going to get worse along the water.

"Hey, Quint!" Hank yelled, above the rustling of the trees.

I walked closer.

"Hello, Hank. Cold day out here."

"We can't all live in the perfect weather that is Walnut Creek."

I almost asked how he knew where I lived, but obviously, Emmett had told him.

"We can't all live with a deck sitting along the Bay," I retorted.

"Touché, Quint. Touché."

He held the door open for me and I walked inside. I looked towards the aforementioned deck and some mist from the Bay was being sprayed up against the window. We wouldn't be sitting outside on this day.

"Have a seat anywhere," he said.

There were two different couches in the family room and I chose one. Hank sat opposite me in the other.

"It's good to see you again," he said.

"You too."

"Have you been busy?"

"You have no idea."

"I've worked this case on and off for twenty years. I've got some idea."

"Maybe it's me who had no idea what I was getting into. I didn't expect so many moving parts. So many people to interview. So much paperwork."

"Yes on all counts," Hank said.

"And, I hate admitting this, I don't think I've made any true progress towards catching the potential killer. And that's even with having pretty good knowledge of the case at this point."

"Those seem to go hand in hand. The more I learned about the case over the years, the more I realized I didn't know anything."

"Well said."

"Do you want to fill me in on everything you've done?"

"Sure," I said.

I spent the next fifteen minutes telling Hank about my conversations with Grant Fisk, Ed Finney, Patricia Fisk, Evelyn Fisk, Maddie Fisk, Ty Mulholland, Aaron and Theresa Everton, Nunya Fucking Business, and how I found out Wanda Dixon was dead.

I hoped I wasn't leaving anyone out, but it truly had been a whirlwind.

Hank seemed fascinated by it all, which was pretty amazing considering he must have known almost everything I'd discovered on my own, with the exception of Wanda Dixon.

He never interrupted, letting me have the floor right up until I finished.

"I've got a few questions, obviously," he said.

"Fire away."

"Did you believe Ty when he said he had nothing to do with it?"

"I did. And I realize that's not a very popular opinion."

"That's alright. You'd be a shitty P.I. if all you did was agree with what you'd read or heard."

"A few times he tried to show his bullying side, but mostly I just saw him as kind of a sad guy in his late thirties."

"That's fine. Just remember that we are investigating seventeen-year-old Ty, not the pathetic man he's become."

"I didn't say pathetic," I said. "He's just, I don't know, scared."

"Scared of what? Being found out?"

"I'd say no since he spilled the beans to me. And I really don't think someone who was guilty of Ronnie's murder would go around confessing to lies which would bring attention to himself."

"I'd agree with you there."

"You asked me to come into this with fresh eyes and ears. And those eyes and ears are telling me that Ty had nothing to do with Ronnie's death."

"Alright. I never liked that guy, and yes, at times I did suspect him, but I never came out and said he killed Ronnie. I was never close to being that confident."

"If I learn more, I know where to find him. So I'm not necessarily done with Ty just yet."

"Maybe I was right to be suspicious of him, considering he lied about where he was on the day in question."

"I wouldn't blame you," I said.

"There's so much more to this case. I'm done asking about Ty for now."

"Alright. What's next?"

"Was there anything that stuck out when you did the walk from Willard Middle School to the Fisks' old house?"

"How open it was. There were very few places to run and hide. And, at least when I walked it, there seemed to be a lot of neighbors out and about."

"Does that change your opinion on anything?"

I was going to be repeating what I'd told Maddie, but Hank hadn't heard it.

"I know the sun was setting, but I think the streets were too open for someone to have grabbed Ronnie off the street. Sure, he was small, but he wasn't a weakling. He would have yelled and punched and kicked and anything else he could think to do. I think he would have been heard."

"So you don't think he was abducted off the street?"

"Not by someone using force. Coercion? Now that's a different story."

"Like offering him candy?"

I couldn't tell if he was kidding or being serious.

"No, more like the abductor saying something like, 'Remember me' or 'It's good to see you again. I'll drive you home.' That's what my gut is telling me."

"Quint, you said you're not any closer to catching the killer. I'm not sure that's the case. Sure, you have no idea who did this, but you do have an opinion on what happened. That is not nothing."

"Thanks. Assuming I'm not way off."

"I'm learning to trust your judgment."

"Thanks. Does Wanda Dixon being dead mean anything to this case?" I asked, changing the subject slightly.

"Only if you thought Wanda was a suspect and I didn't."

"Neither did I, but Ed Finney did."

"Well, Ed was a bit of a loon himself."

I laughed.

"You should have seen the outfit he was wearing."

"I can only imagine."

"His wife seemed a little wacky as well."

"Like we mentioned when we first met, Berkeley is full of them."

"I've got a few questions about the case. You'll be breaking your rule of giving me your opinion, but I'm five days into a seven-day assignment and I'm not going to get to everything."

"I'll answer your questions. You've interviewed all of the main characters, anyway. It's time I came on stage."

"You make it sound like a play."

"Sometimes it feels like one, just playing out before my eyes. A tragedy, no doubt, but a play nonetheless."

It was an interesting perspective and I understood what he meant. Everything was happening in plain sight right in front of us, and yet we had no bearing on its outcome.

"Alright, first question," I said. "What was Ronnie's basketball coach like? Was he ever a suspect?"

"His name was Benjamin Gill. He wasn't much older than those kids. I think he was only like twenty-one."

"I noticed you said very little about him in your notes."

I paused, realizing that Hank had talked about him in the past tense.

"Wait, is he dead?" I asked.

"Yes. He was killed in a car crash about three months after Ronnie was found dead. And he was never a suspect. The kids, and the parents, all loved Benjamin. And there were about five witnesses that testified he stayed at the gym long after Ronnie had left. It wasn't him."

"Did you include all that in your notes? I don't remember seeing it."

"His death was in the police notes somewhere."

"Jeez. I don't remember reading it."

"You read five hundred pages or whatever there is. I'm sure you missed a few things along the way. Just like anyone would."

"And the team didn't have an assistant coach, right?"

"No. This wasn't exactly varsity basketball. Eighth-grade basketball is pretty simplistic. Teach them man-to-man and zone defense and maybe a few offensive plays. One guy can handle it."

"Alright, so there's nothing to the basketball angle?"

"No. Benjamin Gill was in the gym when Ronnie went missing. Sorry."

"Okay. My next question is kind of random."

"Good. We need some outside-of-the-box thinking."

Just then, a huge gust of wind hit, and ocean water pelted the sliding glass door.

"Jeez, that was loud," I said.

"And this isn't even the worst of it. We've got a big storm coming next week. The biggest in years, they say."

"Stay safe on this bluff," I said.

Hank smiled.

"I will not be venturing out on the deck. And that door stays locked."

"Good thinking."

"Alright, Quint. What's your out-of-the-box question?"

"Let me preface this by saying that dozens of people worked on this investigation. Some people were interrogated four and five times. And yet, no one was ever labeled a suspect. Sure, Ty was considered, but he was never officially labeled one."

"I get all that. What are you leading to?"

"What if the killer was just passing through town? If it truly was a friend or family member, I find it unlikely they wouldn't have been caught or, at least, come under suspicion."

"Is there a question in there?"

"I asked it. What if the killer was just passing through town? What if he was a painter? Or a contractor? On the path from Willard Middle School to Ronnie's home, were there any temporary workers lined along that road? Shit, maybe the circus or a carnival was in town and they were staying on that route that Ronnie walked."

"That's a lot to digest. First, no circus or carnival was in town. Ronnie wasn't taken by Bozo the clown."

Once again, I couldn't tell if Hank was angry or being comical, so to be safe, I didn't laugh.

"As far as things like painters or contractors, I'm not quite sure myself. I don't remember any being mentioned in the initial police reports."

"None were," I said. "I've read that initial report at least three times."

"I'm not discounting this theory, but it has a major flaw."

"What's that?" I asked.

"You should know. You've contradicted yourself."

It took me a few seconds until I realized what he meant.

"Ah, I get it. You're saying those people would be unknown to Ronnie and he'd put up a fight?"

"Exactly. And you said you don't think that happened."

"I get your point, but I've got a counter."

"I'm all ears."

"If someone was painting a house along Ronnie's walk, there's a chance Ronnie had interacted with them before. If that were the case, then it fits into my theory that Ronnie knew his abductor, just not very well."

"It's not the worst theory, Quint. However, as you said, no temporary workers were mentioned in the police reports."

"Probably not something we could find out twenty years later."

"I highly doubt it," Hank said.

"Fuck this case," I exclaimed.

"You can say that again."

I sighed.

"I really wish I could have worked on this from day one," I said.

"You'd be a jaded old fool by now. Be glad you weren't here from the beginning."

"You're right. But still."

"There were many great detectives who worked this case, Quint. Don't think you would have been special and solved the case."

"That's not what I meant."

"It kind of is," Hank said.

I laughed.

"Yeah, I guess so."

"What else you got? Any more questions?"

"Do you put much significance into where Ronnie's body was discovered? Because it's barely come up."

"I put almost zero significance to it. It was only a few miles from where he was abducted. Anyone with a car could have driven there at night and dumped him into the Bay."

"How about the fact that Ronnie's body was found two weeks later?" I asked.

"Also, very little. The coroner said the body had likely been in the water almost the full two weeks. Sometimes it just takes a while for a body to pop up on shore."

"Do they think his body was dropped away from the shore? In a boat, maybe?"

"They're not sure. It's all dependent on the tides, so they couldn't determine where the body was originally placed."

"That's depressing. Thinking of his dead body floating out there for days on end."

"Yeah, it's a shitty visual."

We didn't say anything for several seconds.

"I've got just a few more questions if you don't mind," I said.

"Fire away."

"Was Ty the significant other you didn't trust?"

"Yes."

"Alright, that was easy. Here's a question out of left field. What would you do next if you were me?"

"You don't think any of the Fisks killed Ronnie?"

"Correct."

"You don't think Ty killed him?"

"Correct."

"And you don't think Ronnie was killed by a neighbor?"

"Correct."

"You are basically at a total standstill and aren't any closer to finding Ronnie's killer than you were when you started?"

"A little rough, but also correct."

"Then I think there's only one thing for you to do."

I had no idea what Hank was going to say. For a second I thought he was going to tell me to quit.

"And what's that?" I asked.

"I'd reread the addendum I added."

"Which one?"

"There was only one addendum."

I tried to think. Hank had added his notes to the end of each set of police reports, but I guess those weren't technically addenda. And then it hit me what he was talking about.

"You're referring to the other missing or dead kids, aren't you?"

"I am."

"You don't think this will lead to anything, do you?"

"It doesn't matter what I think. This is your part of the investigation. I wouldn't tell you to spend your last two days investigating things or people you don't think were involved. Quint, you've done better work than I ever could have expected. But from what I gather, your investigation has solely been with the Fisk family, their neighbors, and their friends. It's time to branch out your investigation. And just maybe you can find something that ties another one of these murders or missing kids to Ronnie's death."

"How many other deaths were there?" I asked. "I'll be honest, I might have speed read that section."

"In the six months both before and after Ronnie's death, I included about fifteen boys that died or went missing. I went from June of 2001 to June of 2002. In a place as vast as the Bay Area, obviously many more kids go missing than that in a year's span. So I had to narrow it down. I didn't include San Francisco, because there were just too many cases. And I didn't go any further east than your city, Walnut Creek. There was no scientific reason I stopped at those two cities. It was just going to be too many to sift through if I didn't stop somewhere. There were also scores of runaways around that time, but if I was confident it was just a runaway, I didn't include them. Again, there would just be too many. I didn't include girls either because most of those cases involved sexual assault and that wasn't the case with Ronnie. I know my methodology isn't perfect, but it's the best I could do under the circumstances."

I was getting dizzy just thinking about delving into this new part of the investigation.

"Thanks. Hopefully, it will lead to something."

"Even if I think it's a dead-end, any knowledge helps. You might be able to eliminate one of the other murders as being connected to Ronnie. That might not seem like much, but any little tidbit will help. You may be off this case in a few days, Quint, but I won't be done until I die. And all the evidence I've collected is ever-changing. So if you find something new on any one of these other cases, even if it doesn't lead to Ronnie's killer, well, it still brings us new knowledge. That can't hurt."

"Why did I ask you what I should do next? I should have kept my mouth shut."

Hank smiled.

"As they say, 'Be careful what you ask for.'"

"On that note, I think I'll head home. I've got a new reading assignment.'"

We both rose from our respective couches and shook hands. I had just opened the door when I heard Hank call to me.

"You've had this case for five days, Quint. In the limited time you've had, there's no question you've done a bang-up job. I mean that with all my heart. We both know it's extremely unlikely you break the case over the next two days, but I don't want you to feel like you failed. You've done fantastic work."

"Thank you, Hank."

We nodded at each other and I opened the door to the brisk December air.

CHAPTER 11

I spent that night going over all the examples Hank believed to be close enough to Ronnie's death. They spanned from June of 2001 to June of 2002. That gave me a full six months on either side.

If Ronnie's murder was the work of a serial killer, maybe I'd find some connection. Hank didn't think so, but as much as I appreciated all he'd done, he hadn't identified the killer after twenty years. His viewpoint was hardly gospel.

Hank had typed up a few paragraphs on each teenager to go along with the initial police reports. I was never less than impressed by all the work he had done. Even on cases that more than likely had nothing to do with Ronnie's murder.

I wanted to have all the information on one page as opposed to having to flip through the files, so I grabbed my laptop and started typing. I listed the names, ages, dates, and the cause of death.

Jacob Hosmer. Age 16. Went missing on June 27th, 2001. Found two days later. Killed by stabbing.

Paul Inge. Age 15. Went missing on August 2nd, 2001. Never found.

Travis Hoffman. Age 15. Went missing on September 19th, 2001. Killed by gunshot.

Eddie Young. Age 13. Went missing on November 21st, 2001. Death by strangulation.

Adam Williams. Age 14. Went missing on November 28th, 2001. Found dead in a local river a few days later. Strangulation was the cause of death.

Michael Yost. Age 13. Went missing on December 12th, 2001. Body found in a rarely used park, months later. Cause of death undetermined.

Jordan Ziele. Age 14. Went missing on December 26th, 2001. Body never found.

Christian Yount. Age 13. Went missing on January 9th, 2002. Body found in San Pablo Dam Reservoir. Cause of death undetermined.

Todd Zobrist. Age 14. Went missing on January 16th, 2002. Body found in the Bay. Likely strangulation.

Henry Penn. Age 14. Went missing on January 18th, 2002. Body never found.

Zachary Chavez. Age 14. Went missing on January 23rd, 2002. Found a month later in a rural park. Cause of death undetermined.

Billy Warren. Age 13. Went missing on February 6th, 2002. Found a week later in a lake. Cause of death undetermined.

Stephen Snider. Age 14. Went missing on February 20th, 2002. Body never found.

Jim Kostoryz. Age 15. Went missing on April 12th, 2002. Drowned in the Bay. Investigators were not sure if it was suicide, accident, or homicide.

Nolan Rose. Age 15. Went missing on June 3rd, 2002. Death by gunshot.

And finally, Ronnie Fisk. Age 14. Went missing on December 5th, 2001. Strangled to death.

Those were the fifteen deaths that Hank had found to be close enough in both proximity and timeframe to possibly be related to Ronnie's death.

I paid closer attention when the cause of death was strangulation, three besides Ronniel, but not at the expense of ignoring the others. I know the common perception was that serial killers get used to one way of killing and stick to that, but I didn't necessarily subscribe to that.

I could see a scenario where the killer was trying to strangle one of these kids but had a gun or knife just in case things got out of control. Shooting him if necessary. Stabbing him if necessary. I hated the visual that came with these, but I couldn't avoid it. Part of my job as a P.I. was imagining different possibilities, as unpleasant as they may be.

I noticed all of the ages were between thirteen and sixteen. Had Hank deemed twelve too young and seventeen too old? He hadn't told me the reason.

Maybe there would have been too many. That was the reason he'd stopped at San Francisco or anything east of Walnut Creek.

I looked at the pictures of each kid, hoping to see any similarities to Ronnie. Truth be told, a lot of kids look alike at that age. Especially when the pictures are from twenty years ago. The tint of the pictures causes them to resemble each other.

Looking at their faces brought me to a place of sadness. So young, with their whole lives ahead of them. Brought to an end unnecessarily. And unmercifully.

I wanted to scream "These were kids!" at the top of my lungs.

Three others besides Ronnie had played basketball. Four out of sixteen hardly seemed enough to form a hunch.

The eastern Bay Area was a big place, and a year is a long time, but four potential strangulations over the course of a year seemed like a lot.

I spent the next few hours looking for similarities between Ronnie and the other kids. Age. Interests. Build (their heights and weights were listed in the police reports). Hair and eye color.

On the whole, it seemed that the majority of the kids had been small for their grades. But there were three kids who were over six feet and a couple who were almost two hundred pounds. I thought about eliminating the bigger kids as potential matches but decided against it. Hank had found enough similarities to include them, so I couldn't eliminate any just yet.

I wrote down some stats of the missing/dead kids as a whole.

Five of the sixteen had parents who were divorced. Ten were either blonde or had light brown hair. Six were shorter than Ronnie and eight weighed less than him. All sixteen kids were either white or a mix of white and Hispanic. No Asian, Indian, or African-Americans or kids of full Hispanic descent were listed. This was undoubtedly done at Hank's discretion.

Everything I discovered held at least a little interest for me. Nothing, however, was a game-changer. If I'd seen thirteen of the fifteen were in a chess club, that would have raised a red flag. There was no mic drop moment, however.

One thing that surprised me was that I'd rarely - if ever - seen these kids mentioned in the Berkeley Police Department's reports. Were they that positive it wasn't a serial killer? What was I missing?

I could tell my mind was starting to lose some of its acuity. I don't know if it was the last five hours or the last five days, but my brain was starting to wander. I was having trouble concentrating.

I flipped off my laptop and put the top back on Box #2.

It was time to get some sleep.

I made my way from the couch to my bed. This night might have been the toughest stretch of the entire investigation. While before it had only been the death of one child, now I had spent time with fifteen other children whose lives had been snuffed out well before their time. Sure, it's possible one or two of the missing kids were still alive, but I highly doubted it.

I closed my eyes, knowing I needed the rejuvenation that a good night of sleep brings. On one hand, I feared it wouldn't come easily. On the other hand, I was dreading the nightmares that might greet me upon falling asleep.

I was in a no-win situation.

CHAPTER 12

I woke up on Sunday, my last full day of investigating for Emmett Fisk. I didn't remember having any nightmares and took it as a good sign for the day to come.

I had to give Emmett credit, he'd been very hands-off since he'd hired me. If I were in his shoes, I'd probably be calling every day for an update. Maybe time doesn't seem all that important when you are ninety-two years old.

Shouldn't it mean more?

I'd talked to him briefly on Wednesday. I owed him another call.

I hoped 8:30 wasn't too early as I dialed his number.

"Hello?"

"Emmett, this is Quint."

"Hold on one second, Madam. Let me put my hearing aids in."

He came back to the phone about forty-five seconds later.

"Who is this?"

"This is Quint. Not a Madam."

I heard him laugh.

"Oh, hello, Quint. I'm sorry. I can't hear shit without my hearing aids in. How is the investigation coming?"

"That's why I called. Today is my last official day and I figured I should give you an update."

"Why don't you wait? We can meet tomorrow and go over everything you've learned so far. Who knows, maybe today is the day you catch that big break."

"With all due respect, Emmett, I think that's pretty unlikely."

"The doctors told me I was unlikely to live more than five years. That was ten years ago. I can live with unlikely. Literally."

I smiled. There was no denying it, Emmett Fisk entertained me. He may have been the hard-headed fool some had described him as, but the ninety-two-year-old version was one funny dude.

"Alright, that's fine, we can wait till tomorrow. What time do you want to meet?"

"How about nine a.m.?"

"Sure. Is my office okay?"

"That will work."

"Drive safe and slow, Emmett. You're no spring chicken."

"No, I'm certainly not. I'll drive ten miles an hour with my blinkers on the whole time."

I laughed again.

This case had been pulling at my heartstrings for the majority of it, but there had been some light-hearted moments thrown in. I was grateful for that.

"Goodbye, Emmett."

"See you tomorrow, Quint."

~

I opened my laptop up and went back over my notes from the night before.

There were a few cases that most closely resembled Ronnie's, but the case of Todd Zobrist stood out. He was also fourteen years old, went missing while out walking, and had been strangled. Just like Ronnie. The difference was that Zobrist had been found in a local lake, not the Bay. Still, it was a body of water, and I counted that more as a similarity than a difference.

I was a bit surprised Hank hadn't singled this one out. It sounded eerily similar to the death of Ronnie.

I grabbed Hank's notes and read them again.

There were some differences.

Todd Zobrist went missing in San Ramon, a rich, suburban area that differed greatly from the bohemian lifestyle that Berkeley prided itself on. He came from a wealthy family and his father was a Vice-President at Chevron Oil. He didn't play basketball or skate.

One big problem in trying to connect the two murders was that Berkeley and San Ramon were a good thirty-five or forty minutes from each other. Not that a serial killer couldn't traverse city and county lines. It just made it a little less likely.

Despite these reservations, the case of Todd Zobrist intrigued me more than any of the others.

Call it intuition.

I decided there was only one way to find out.

I used my laptop to google the information I was looking for and then picked up my phone.

"Hello, you've reached the San Ramon Police department," a woman's voice said.

"I was curious if you have any officers who have worked at your department for twenty plus years."

"That's not a question we hear every day. Let me think. Yeah, we've got a few."

"Will any of them be in the office today?"

"Yeah, Randall Picker is here."

"And he'll be there for the next few hours?"

"He works in the office," she said. And then her voice went up an octave when she said, "He's too old to go out and work the beat."

I was certain that was meant for Randall Picker's benefit.

"Thanks. I'll come to see him soon."

"I'm quite curious what this is about."

"You'll find out soon enough," I said and hung up my phone.

I headed south on Interstate 680 and arrived fifteen minutes later. Walnut Creek was closer to San Ramon than Berkeley was.

There were gray pillars and some cursive writing that said "City of San Ramon." It barely looked like a police station and I knew the reason why.

San Ramon was a small, safe town and I can't imagine they had much of a police force. It wouldn't have shocked me if Todd Zobrist was the last murder the city had experienced.

I entered the police department and saw a woman and a man seated at their respective desks. I didn't need any spidey senses to tell me who these people were.

I looked in the direction of the woman. She was around thirty years of age with dark brown hair in a bun. She obviously hadn't been on the force anywhere near twenty years.

"I believe I talked to you about twenty minutes ago."

"Twenty must be your number. Twenty minutes ago. Looking for people with twenty years on the force."

I laughed.

"Very true," I said.

The man rose from his seat. He wasn't nearly as old as I'd imagined, probably only in his late forties, possibly fifty. He had a salt and pepper goatee and his hair was slicked back with some serious product. It looked like it would shatter like porcelain if you touched it.

"I guess you're here to see me."

"You must be Randall Picker."

"That's what they say."

"Nice to meet you, officer. Where do we talk?" I asked.

"Right here is fine. Fiona knows all my secrets anyway."

Fiona laughed.

"And some you don't know that I know."

"You can come back this way," Officer Picker said.

He held open a swinging little gate that separated the officers from the people like me. I walked towards him and Fiona.

In my time as a crime reporter for *The Walnut Creek Times*, I'd been in many police stations around the East Bay, but never San Ramon. It had the most laid-back atmosphere I'd encountered. And possibly, the smallest square footage. It was tiny.

I took my seat and Randall Picker his. I saw Fiona shuffle a little closer.

"So, what could you possibly want to know that's twenty years old."

"The murder of Todd Zobrist," I said.

Picker nodded.

"I should have known. Our only non-domestic murder since I got on the force twenty-three years ago."

"Can you tell me what you recollect about it?"

"I think you owe me an explanation first."

"Of course. I'm a P.I. who was hired to investigate the murder of a four-teen-year-old boy. It occurred in Berkeley twenty years ago. I'm trying to see if the two cases are perhaps related."

"Can you show me your P.I.'s license?"

I showed him.

"You're a newbie," he said.

"I am. Used to be a crime reporter."

Picker didn't seem all that impressed.

"What was your victim's name?" he asked.

"Ronnie Fisk."

"It doesn't ring a bell. I remember we were trying to find similarities between other missing children in the area. I probably knew about the Ronnie Fisk case at the time."

"He was taken on his way home from school. His body was found two weeks later in the Bay. He'd been strangled."

"I think it rings a bell, but maybe that's just my imagination playing tricks on me. Todd had been strangled as well."

I noticed him using the first name of the dead boy. I wondered if you started seeing them almost as a friend or a family member.

"Yeah, that's the reason I'm here. It was the case most similar to Ronnie's."

I realized we were no different. I'd called Ronnie Fisk by his first name as well. I'd probably been doing it all week.

"What else, besides the cause of death?"

"The age obviously. They were both in eighth grade and fourteen years old."

"True. Anything else? I'm not trying to be rude, but San Ramon and Berkeley are pretty far apart."

"There are enough similarities to pique my interest."

He looked on, unconvinced.

"What is your working theory on the case? Do you have one?"

"I hadn't until recently. I had just been taking in all the information as it came. Now, I think Ronnie may have been abducted by someone he knew, but didn't know well."

"Not a total stranger?"

"I don't think so," I said. "Did you guys have a working theory on yours?"

"We really didn't. Todd went out for a walk one afternoon and never came home. And no one saw a thing."

"That's similar to ours. No one on the street saw Ronnie being abducted or a struggle ensue. That's why I don't think it was a total stranger."

"That's somewhat comparable to ours. The difference is that the houses are pretty big here and there's often a big separation between them. A struggle could easily go unseen here. It's not like Berkeley with condensed housing."

His words made it sound like San Ramon housing was superior to Berkeley, but that wasn't the tone he was using. He was just pointing out the differences.

"I've only been working the case for seven days," I said. "Some people think it's a family member. Some thought it was a family friend, a neighbor, or both. A few said a serial killer. I've got the theory I just shared with you, but who freaking knows if that's right? I'm sure it will continue eating at me."

"Welcome to the club. I still think of Todd's death and it's been twenty years."

"Is the case still active?"

"Technically, yes, but we haven't received any new information in probably eighteen or nineteen years."

"Did you have any suspects?"

"It's like your case in that regard. Neighbors, friends, family. Everyone was a suspect. And no one was a suspect. Do you know what I mean?"

"I know exactly what you mean."

My peripheral vision could tell me that Fiona had inched closer and was listening in. I can't say I blamed her. The only non-domestic murder in twenty-plus years. It had to be a talking point around the office.

"How much longer are you on the case?"

"Technically, I'm done tomorrow. But like I said earlier, I don't think this case will just leave my psyche because I'm no longer officially on the case."

"It could be worse. You could have been wallowing in it for twenty years like me."

Our discussion, while interesting, really hadn't brought me any closer to tying together Ronnie and Todd's murders.

"Is there any evidence that might not have made it to us?" I asked.

"Who is us, exactly?"

"Have you heard of Hank Tressel?"

"Every Bay Area cop has heard of Hank."

"He's a friend of the Fisk family and he's been updating all the evidence over the last twenty years."

"And he has a section on Todd Zobrist?"

"And fourteen other kids who went missing or wound up dead around that time. Fifteen if you include Ronnie."

Randall Picker sat up in his chair. That obviously had gotten his attention.

"Really?"

"Yeah, it's pretty insane just how much documentation he's assembled. Less on the outlying cases like Todd, but you wouldn't believe all the info he has on Ronnie's death."

Even I had taken to calling Todd by his first name.

"Jeez. I guess Hank Tressel's reputation as a hard worker is well earned."

"It is."

"And does he think these other fifteen kids are related to your murder in Berkeley?"

"No. He is most decidedly against the idea of it being a serial killer. He's just doing his due diligence."

"You're disagreeing with the great Hank Tressel?"

I laughed.

"I'm open to the possibility of it being a serial killer."

I hated the way the phrase came out.

"Enough similarities and possibilities and noncommittal terms like those. I'm going to ask you point-blank. Do you think Todd was killed by the same man?"

"I'm not trying to avoid your question. I just don't know. I'm not saying it's the same killer. I'm not saying it's not, either."

"Not good enough. I want an answer."

"If I'm only given two options, I would say yes, I think they were."

"Thank you for answering," Officer Picker said.

There was a long break where no one talked as my statement hung in the air.

"I'm going to go back over our case file in the coming days," he finally said.

"Will you call me if you find anything that grabs your attention?"

"Yes. Do you have a card?"

I handed him one.

"I will likely be off the case."

"Only officially," he said, reiterating our earlier point that these never really leave you.

"I have one last question."

"Sure."

"Did Todd play any sports? Basketball, specifically."

"If I remember correctly, Todd didn't play a single sport. He was kind of a little runt."

"Ronnie was small as well."

"I guess it's not all that surprising. If some scumbag murderer is going to grab a kid off the street, he's not going to pick a fully grown one. I have a fifteen-year-old. Believe me, he's not that far off from taking me. You wouldn't want to try and abduct him off the street."

"So you think they were chosen because of their size? Or, lack thereof?"

"I'd say that's a safe assumption."

We were once again silent for several seconds.

"If you get any new information that ties these two cases together, I'll be here. And in the meantime, I'll take a new look at Todd's file."

"Can I call you in a few days?"

He smiled shrewdly.

"I thought you were going to be off the case."

I had no response.

"Thanks for your time, Officer Picker."

"Stay in touch, you hear."

"I will."

I said my goodbye to Fiona as well and walked out of the San Ramon Police Department.

~

I arrived at my car, not sure if the last fifteen minutes had moved the needle on my investigation. I had admitted that I thought the two cases might well be related. That had to mean something. Right?

During my upcoming meeting with Emmett Fisk, I'd be able to regale him with stories of talking to police, neighbors, potential suspects, and his own family members. I walked the same road that Ronnie did on the day he died. I read everything that Hank had accumulated over the years.

But could I tell him anything that moved the investigation forward? Was there a single fact I'd found which was going to help me catch Ronnie's killer?

I didn't think so.

And stating that I thought Todd Zobrist's murder might be related, without any actual evidence, wasn't going to cut it.

People love to say that 'less is more.' For me, it was the opposite. I'd accumulated a wealth of knowledge about the case but had gained nothing by it. More is less was "more" apropos.

I started up my car and started driving, with no idea where I was going next.

~

Since becoming a P.I., the one piece of advice I'd been given more than any other - and I agreed with - was for me to go with my gut.

After all, I'd entered this business because I had a good bullshit detector. I was also a good problem solver who could decipher things with relative ease. If someone said I understood the human condition more than most, I'd have agreed. I had those intangible qualities.

Then fucking use them!

My internal monologue was fired up.

I took the Interstate 680 North entrance and headed back toward Walnut Creek. I started asking myself a series of questions.

Do you think Grant Fisk killed Ronnie?

No.

Do you think Patricia Fisk killed Ronnie?

No.

Do you think Evelyn Fisk killed Ronnie?

No.

Do you think Maddie Fisk killed Ronnie?

No.

Do you think Emmett Fisk killed Ronnie?

No.

Do you think Ty Mulholland killed Ronnie?

No.

Do you think Wanda Dixon or any other neighbor killed Ronnie?

No.

So what do you think?

I think he was abducted by a stranger!

A total stranger?

No. Merely someone Ronnie didn't know well.

Who could that be? A teacher? An administrator? An older teenager? An adult he'd met around town?

And that's when my internal discourse ended.

I didn't have an answer to that question.

I arrived back at 1716 Lofts, made my way to the couch, and quickly called Hank Tressel.

"Hello, Quint. How are you?"

My time was running too short for pleasantries.

"I wanted to know what Ronnie did in the few days before he was abducted."

"It's in the file."

"I've read it. I want more."

"I'm not sure what you mean."

"I want to know who he might have interacted with in the few days before his abduction."

"Well, surely not many strangers on the day he was abducted. He woke up at home, walked to school, went to class, and then to basketball practice. A pretty normal day where he probably didn't meet anyone new."

"How about the previous day?"

"The first few things were the same, but as you know, he had a basketball game that day."

"How many people go to these games?"

"Not many. It's 8th-grade basketball, not the Golden State Warriors."

"So what are we talking, fifty people?"

"That sounds right. Maybe a few more, considering you've already got thirty people with the players, coaches, kids keeping stats, scoreboard operator, etc. And then all the parents. Probably more like seventy people."

"What team did they play?"

"I think it was a middle school from Emeryville. Shit, even I'd have to look at the notes to verify that one."

"I'll check," I said. "And they went to a pizza place after the game to celebrate, correct?"

"Yup. A place in Berkeley called Zachary's Chicago Pizza."

"I remember now. I've eaten there before. And how many people were there?"

"Players, coaches, and family probably made up twenty-five people. And then everyone else not affiliated with Willard Middle School."

"One quick thing. You've said coaches twice now. Didn't you say there was just the one head coach?"

"Yeah. Sorry, that was a figure of speech. They only had the one coach who passed away."

"Did you interview anyone at Zachary's? Find out if anyone was paying particular attention to Ronnie?"

"Before I answer, I just want to say, you seem invigorated. I haven't heard you this fired up about the case."

"Maybe because I see my deadline fast approaching. So, did you talk to anyone?"

"No. Like I've told you, I was trying to let the Berkeley police department do their thing."

"Did they interview people?"

"Yes, but nothing came of it. It's probably only one paragraph in the entire case file. Nothing suspicious happened at Zachary's. At least, according to the police."

"Alright, we've done Wednesday and Tuesday. How about Monday?"

"School. Basketball. Home."

"Ok, how about the weekend?"

"I know he went shopping with his mother on Sunday. They went to the outlets in Emeryville."

"Did Patricia mention any weird guy approaching them?"

"No."

"Anything else on Sunday?"

"Nothing that made an impression. I think he went and played with some friends, including your new friend Aaron Everton."

"How about Saturday?"

"Now you're going back four days from the day he was abducted. My memory is a little hazy and I'd have to look at the notes. I can tell you one thing, though. Once again, nothing dubious happened."

"Is there anything else you can tell me about those four or five days before Ronnie died?"

"There's really not, Quint."

"I'll be in touch soon," I said and hung up the phone.

I'd been too brief with Hank, but he'd understand.

I went on the internet and found the number I was looking for.

"Zachary's Pizza. Will this be for takeout or delivery?" a male voice said.

"I've got an odd question. Do you have any employees who have been there for twenty years?"

"Highly unlikely. We've got a lot of college-aged employees who shuffle in and out every year or two."

"Would you mind asking a manager? It may not seem like it, but it's important."

"Hold on," he gruffly said, not very happy with me.

The voice returned thirty seconds later.

"No. I'm sorry. I just talked to the manager. She's been here eight years and says no one has been here longer than her."

"Alright, thanks."

"What could this possibly be abo…"

I'd hung up before he finished saying "about."

I was like a chicken with my head cut off. Constantly moving, but with no consideration of what I was doing.

I headed to Berkeley and spent the afternoon talking to local businesses along Ronnie's walk home. There were six businesses that had been around back in 2001, but none of them remembered hearing anything about seeing Ronnie on the day in question.

I asked each of them if they had any cameras back then. Only two did and they'd turned them into the police at the time. There was no footage of Ronnie on either.

I knocked on a few doors and upset a few more people.

'It was twenty years ago!'

'Give it a rest.'

'We're trying to move on.'

'You were just here a few days ago. C'mon man!'

After I left Berkeley, I drove directly to Emeryville Middle School. It was late in the afternoon at this point and a Sunday to boot. I figured they'd still have someone on campus, but who knew?

The school itself was locked down so I approached the first person I saw outside of the gates. It turned out to be a teacher, a woman in her forties, who told me she was just picking up stuff from her classroom.

"We're closed today for any outsiders," she said.

It didn't sound very polite, but she was right, after all. I was an outsider.

"Is there any way I could get ahold of the basketball coach from twenty years ago?" I asked, feeling silly as I asked it.

"I'm a teacher who's been here a grand total of five years. I have no idea."

"Do you know the name of your Athletic Director instead?"

"This isn't Michigan or USC, my friend. We are seventh and eighth grade only. We don't need, or have, an athletic director."

I'd been reprimanded on both questions and learned a grand total of nothing.

∼

Next on my list of things-that-would-probably-not-move-this-case-forward was heading to Grant Fisk's house. I should have dropped in when I'd been in Berkeley earlier, but it hadn't crossed my mind.

Emeryville was only a few miles from Berkeley so it's not like it was too far out of the way. I double-backed, deciding against calling Grant, thinking it might be better if I surprise him. It was Sunday so there was a pretty good shot he was home.

I arrived and instantly noticed he'd gotten rid of all the dead plants on his patio.

Was that because Emmett and I had reopened the case on Ronnie? Had it given Grant the kick in the butt to get his life in order?

Maybe. Maybe not. But I liked the notion of it.

I walked up the steps and knocked on the door.

He arrived in a few seconds and opened it.

"How are you, Quint?"

"The patio looks nice."

"Thanks. After having beers at 9 a.m., I had a little talk with myself."

"I've been having some internal monologues as well," I said.

Grant smiled.

"Come on in."

The inside had been presentable when I first met him, but he'd cleaned it up as well. We took a seat. There was not a beer in sight.

"This is your last day, isn't it?" he asked.

"Yup. For better or worse."

"I think everyone in the family is impressed with your work. While also all agreeing this isn't going anywhere."

"Maybe you're right."

"Maddie called me the other day and that doesn't happen all that often. My father stopped by as well. I'd originally thought that you investigating this case would open up old wounds, but I was wrong. Those wounds have never been sewed up. And maybe, just maybe, you'll help bring this family a little closer. Like we were so many moons ago."

I was floored. It was the single most gratifying thing I'd heard since taking the case.

"Thank you, Grant. That means more than you will ever know."

"You're welcome. You're one of us after all since you lost your father."

I wanted to reiterate what I'd already told him, that losing a son was much worse. It was such a nice moment, I didn't bother.

"I'm just happy the family is conversing a little more."

"It's not perfect. Patricia and I probably won't talk. And I doubt Evelyn and Maddie ever will. But, who knows, right?"

"Maybe I should stay on the case longer until everyone is talking."

Grant laughed.

"Slow down," he said.

I smiled.

"So what brought you here, Quint?"

I hated going from our hopeful conversation to asking about Ronnie. Not that I had much choice.

"I wanted to ask about the days leading up to Ronnie's disappearance. The basketball game. The trip to the outlets."

"To be honest, Patricia would be the better one to talk to. I worked at a bank and couldn't take time off to make the basketball games. They started around four and only lasted for approximately an hour. My wife's schedule was more adaptable and she'd try to attend at least every other game."

The last thing I wanted to do was talk to Patricia again. She'd been firm that I should only contact her if completely necessary.

"Did she go to the game on that Tuesday?"

"She did. And they won. Ronnie actually scored a basket, which didn't happen all that often."

I remembered Aaron Everton telling me Wednesday was a fun practice because they'd won the day before.

"Did Patricia ever mention any creepy people at the game?"

"No. They were in a good mood when they returned. As I said, they won and Ronnie scored."

"How about that previous weekend at the outlets? Did she mention any creeps?"

"No, and I'll stop you before you ask again. No one in our family ever mentioned any creeps or people taking an interest in Ronnie in the days or weeks before he went missing."

"Okay, I got it."

"I liked you better about three minutes ago," Grant said.

I smiled again. He'd brought his sense of humor and I was grateful for it. After our first meeting, I'd feared it had skipped a generation after Emmett.

It had me wondering if Ronnie would have been a funny adult. I tried to push it out of my mind. No good could come of imagining what he would have become.

"I'd like to say something, Grant. Even though I will be done with this case, it will never be done with me. Ronnie will always have a place in my heart. Just like I know he has a place in all of your hearts. In that regard, he's immortal."

Grant stood up from the couch, walked over, and hugged me. He'd now done so in both meetings.

"Thank you for that, Quint. It makes all the hard questions you've asked seem to fade away. I'm glad our little Ronnie has left a mark on you."

"Without question," I said as Grant sat back down on his end of the couch.

I saw him wipe a tear away.

There was nothing more to be gained from talking to Grant. I'd rather leave on a high note.

"I'm going to head out, Grant. I hope your family continues to slowly, but surely, get closer."

"Thank you, Quint. And thanks for all you've done for Emmett. And our entire family, really. This was a no-win case for you, but you handled it with class."

"That means a lot."

I stood up and we shook hands.

I exited the apartment and walked across the now immaculate patio and down the steps. It was one of the few encounters of the last week where I left happier than I'd felt coming in.

~

The sun was setting by the time I left Berkeley.

Like the sun was setting when Ronnie was abducted. Like the sun was setting for my time on this case.

As I drove, I tried to think if there was one last gasp effort I was overlooking. Nothing came to mind.

I drove back to Walnut Creek and by nine p.m., I'd fallen asleep on the couch. Part of the case files were sitting on my thighs and my chest when I nodded off.

I'd given my heart and soul to the case.

But nothing had come of it.

PART TWO: A THEORY EMERGES

CHAPTER 13

"How much would it cost to keep you on the case?"

I was sitting in my office, ten minutes from meeting with Emmett Fisk when I received a call from his granddaughter, Evelyn.

"Excuse me?"

"You heard me, Quint."

"I'm meeting with Emmett in ten minutes to finalize everything."

"Nope, not finalize. Think of it as a progress report instead."

"I'm not sure what's going on here," I said.

"It's not obvious? I'm trying to re-hire you. Or, more accurately, extend your current engagement for another week."

"Why?"

"Because I talked to Hank Tressel this morning. And he thinks you're doing extraordinary work."

"I haven't gotten anywhere."

"Those two aren't mutually exclusive. Especially not in a twenty-year-old case."

"You're right about that."

"So, I'll ask a third time. How much did my grandfather pay you?"

"I gave him a discount. Seven hundred for the week."

"What is your regular rate?"

I was reminded of Emmett's joke that with my lack of clients I couldn't possibly have a regular rate. Luckily, Evelyn did not make the same quip.

"A thousand dollars for a week."

"I'll gladly pay that. You're hired."

"Don't I have a say?" I asked, only somewhat tongue-in-cheek.

Evelyn laughed on her end.

"In all honesty, I don't think you want to stop. You're making progress and want to see it out. I can tell."

"I'm not sure there will be an end to see out."

"That's possible, but we certainly know that nothing will be brought to conclusion today. So why not give it one more week?"

I thought long and hard.

Did I want to keep going?

If I didn't get out now, would I ever get out?

It was going to be hard enough to forget this case after one week. Would another week just ensure this case would stay with me forever? Probably.

Nonetheless, Evelyn was right. I did want to see it out until the end, or at least until I'd exhausted every potential lead. I wasn't at that point yet.

Something Grant said popped into my mind.

I decided I had a favor of my own to ask.

"I can't believe I'm going to say this, but yes, I'll commit to one more week. Provided, you do something for me."

"What could you possibly want from me?"

"I want you to call your sister."

"You're kidding," Evelyn said.

"Not even a little bit."

If I couldn't catch their brother's killer, maybe I could get the two sisters talking again. You could make a convincing argument that would mean more in the end anyway.

"What made you think of this?"

"A talk I had with your father."

"Was this his idea?"

"No, he had nothing to do with it. This is all me."

"You're crazy."

"Maybe. Is that a yes?"

"And you're not going to continue with the case if I don't?"

"No," I said.

I was putting all my chips in the middle of the table. On a bluff, obviously, but she didn't know that.

"Fine, I'll call her. I can't guarantee what happens after that."

"Of course not."

"So, one phone call to my sister and you'll take the case again?"

"Yeah, with one more minor ask."

"What is it?"

"Can I start tomorrow? I need one day off. This case is suffocating."

"Sure. It will probably be good for you."

"No probably about it."

"What's the address at that firm of yours? I'll send you a check."

I gave it to her.

"I saw Gilly yesterday and told him I ran into you. We're going to meet up this weekend out this way. Do you want to come meet us?"

"If I'm not working."

"C'mon, it's not like you have to think about the case twenty-four hours a day."

"I may not have to, but it sure seems like I do."

"Good, then you could use the break. I'll call you later in the week."

"Alright. Now call your sister."

"You're a bulldog."

"I can be," I said.

"I've got to go. Thanks for this, Quint."

"Let's hope I don't regret it."

Evelyn hung up on her end.

I swiveled around in my executive chair, and as I did, I saw Emmett Fisk pulling into the parking lot.

This case was bonkers.

And I'd signed up for another week.

What the hell was wrong with me?

∼

"Nice to see you again, Quint," Emmett said as he stepped out of his car.

I walked outside to greet him.

He was parked in the same handicapped spot as when I'd met him a week earlier.

He didn't trip over the cement block this time.

"How are you, Emmett? Hope you're keeping your driving to a minimum."

He was wearing the same fedora and a different colored trench coat. He still looked like someone out of New York, circa the 1930s.

"Grocery stores and doctor's appointments are all done by a shuttle service. Unfortunately, they didn't know who the hell you were or where you were located, so I had to drive myself."

"You crack me up, Emmett."

"Well, thank you."

"Shall we go inside? I can't let anyone see me with a client and start getting a reputation as a working P.I."

Emmett laughed.

"You're a pretty funny dude yourself, Quint."

We walked inside and took the twenty steps to my office. I sat down behind my desk and Emmett took the seat across from me.

He laid his jacket and fedora on my lone table and I told myself I needed to invest in a coat and hat rack.

"I already know what you're going to say," Emmett said.

"Oh, yeah. What do you think that might be?"

"That even though the week is up, the mystery behind Ronnie's death has buried its claws in you and you've decided to keep working on the case. Pro Bono."

I smiled.

"You're not that far off."

"But the Pro Bono part was incorrect?"

I wasn't ready to tell him that Evelyn convinced me to stay on.

"You're right about one thing. Ronnie's death has buried its claws into me. I don't think a day will go by the rest of my life where I don't think about him, at least in passing."

"Welcome to the club."

"Can I ask you a serious question, Emmett?"

"Of course."

I thought back to our conversation when he joked about living longer than the doctors expected.

"Are you dying?"

"Yes. Then again, they've been saying the same thing for the last ten years."

"What is it?"

"My cancer has spread and they say I may only have a few months to live. I'm afraid they might be right this time."

I took a deep breath.

"I'm so sorry."

"Don't be. I've lived a long, great life. Ronnie's death will always be a horribly painful mark on that life, but it doesn't negate all the loving, eating, drinking, traveling, and everything else I've done in my ninety-two years."

"I like you, Emmett. I feel a bond with your family now. And I'm extremely sad about your prognosis. I really, really am."

"I sense a 'but' coming," he said.

"There was going to be one. I had planned on coming into this meeting and telling you how much your family - and Ronnie's case - meant to me. And then I was going to tell you that I couldn't continue with the case."

Emmett looked at me hopefully.

"Had planned?"

"That's right. Until I got a call from Evelyn this morning."

Emmett looked on excitedly.

"What?"

"She tried to convince me to take the case on for another week."

"And?"

"And she was successful."

Emmett jumped out of his chair with the vigor of someone forty years younger.

"Oh, that's such great news."

"I thought you'd be happy."

"Are you still giving me the discount?"

He sat back down.

"Do you remember when we first met and you said you didn't take any financial help from your granddaughters?"

"I remember."

"Well, this time you have no choice because Evelyn paid my salary for the next week."

He looked like he wanted to cry.

"She did that for me?"

"Technically, yes. I think she did it for your whole family. I'm going to be 100 percent honest right now, Emmett. I don't think I'm going to catch Ronnie's killer. I really don't. An extra seven days probably isn't going to change that. But you know what? Grant told me the other day that he's going to make a few positive changes in his life. And I'm thinking that as tough as my investigation has been on your family, that maybe it's bringing you closer."

This time, Emmett did wipe away a tear. I continued.

"Before I agreed to continue the case, I had Evelyn promise me one thing."

"I'm afraid to ask," Emmet said, through a cracking voice.

"I told her I'd only take the case if she reached out to Maddie."

"Oh, Quint."

"And she agreed to."

"That's fantastic. You're going above and beyond. This wasn't in your job description."

"No, it wasn't," I agreed.

"You've fallen for the Fisk family, haven't you?"

"Yeah, I guess I have. Maybe it's just guilt."

"Over what?"

"Over the fact that I don't think I'll accomplish your ultimate goal."

"If you bring my family closer together, that's probably more important than catching Ronnie's killer."

I nodded.

"I was thinking the same thing."

"After all, as everyone always likes to tell me, we can't bring Ronnie back. But maybe we can bring Evelyn and Maddie back together."

"Hopefully that call will be the first step."

Emmett wiped a few more tears aside.

"Look at me crying. I'm a regular old Kate Hepburn."

"The kids are going to love that reference."

Emmett laughed.

"Showing my age with that one?"

"Just a bit," I said.

"So what's next?"

"I told Evelyn I needed a day off. I'm exhausted. So today, I'm going to have a Quint day. Maybe have a drink. Maybe catch up on some Netflix. But I'm going to try, likely to no avail, not to think about Ronnie's case too much."

"You deserve it."

"And then tomorrow, I'll be back out there, looking for that proverbial needle in the haystack."

"Thank you, Quint."

"We should probably go over everything I've learned."

"Let's do it," Emmett said.

I spent the next thirty minutes describing the work I'd done over the previous week and the interviews I'd had with Grant, Patricia, Evelyn, and Maddie. Then I went through Ty Mulholland, Aaron Everton, the Finneys, the "gem" that was the daughter of Wanda Dixon's boyfriend. We discussed some of the assorted neighbors in Berkeley I'd talked to and my meetings with Hank Tressel.

Emmett sat there, almost in a daze. I don't think he realized just how much work I'd done nor how many people I'd actually talked to.

He never interrupted and only spoke when I had a few questions about Ty Mulholland and a few of their old neighbors, including Wanda Dixon.

"So that crazy old bird is dead?"

"Sounds like it. Although it didn't come from the most reputable source."

I still hadn't followed up on that.

"I wouldn't worry about it. She was nuts. Ed Finney was right in telling you that, but she didn't kill Ronnie. That woman was so frazzled, she'd have left a million clues. There's no way she could have gotten away with murder."

It made me think just how difficult this case truly was. While I'd had an interesting day meeting "Fucking Business, Nunya", in the end, it meant nothing, nor did it have anything to do with Ronnie's death.

There were so many interviews and police reports and hunches of mine that were never going to amount to anything. I'd already encountered many dead ends and there was surely more to come.

"What if the killer is dead?" I blurted out, not sure what Emmett could possibly say to satisfy me.

"It's better than the alternative," Emmett said.

And miraculously, he had found an answer I was content with.

"Indeed. Before I let you go, Emmett, is there anything that you've remembered over the last week that might help me out?"

"No, but I'm sure I've forgotten a few more things."

I laughed. I really hoped Emmett Fisk had more than a few months left on this planet. Although the case of Ronnie Fisk was a soul-crusher, Emmett had brought some humor and light to it.

"Don't ever change, Emmett."

"I'm too old for that."

"Is there anything else you want to know?" I asked.

"No, you were very thorough. Thanks."

"I think that about wraps things up for now."

I stood up and Emmett took the cue, slowly rising himself. I walked him out to his car and told him to drive safely.

He turned to me before he got in.

"Once again, Quint, thank you very much for everything you've done. For this case. And now, what you're doing for my family. You were only hired for the former, but I'm eternally grateful for the latter."

"You're welcome, Emmett. I'll see you soon."

"Yes, you will. I'm not going anywhere until you've finished your investigation."

His meaning was obvious.

CHAPTER 14

I went back to my apartment for lunch, knowing some leftover gumbo was in the fridge with my name on it.

As I was about to open my door, Rebecca began walking down the hallway. She was wearing jeans and a lime green, lightweight hoodie. She looked very pretty.

"Hey, Quint!"

"What's new, Rebecca?"

"Some friends and I are going to Happy Hour tonight at Stadium Pub to watch Monday Night Football. You want to join?"

A few drinks sounded like heaven. And it was my day off, after all.

"I'd love to. What time?"

"Around 5:30."

"I'll be there. Thanks."

～

I walked into my apartment, and against my better judgment, I started looking over the case file of the other fifteen children.

I was going to have some drinks tonight, so I was still getting my day off from the case. Sort of.

I sat on my couch, kicked my legs up on my coffee table, and started reading.

After what felt like twenty minutes, but was probably more like an hour, I noticed something for the first time.

The higher-aged boys, those who were fifteen or sixteen, had all been killed or went missing from either June to September of 2001 or from March to June of 2002. Only one kid who was fifteen or sixteen went missing between October and February. His name was Henry Penn and he'd been shot to death, which made it unlikely his death was related to Ronnie's. Not impossible, just less likely.

If I tossed that murder out, then all of the thirteen and fourteen-year-old boys went missing from October to February. And all the fifteen and sixteen-year-old kids went missing outside of those months.

Was this just a coincidence? Possibly, but it bolstered the possibility that Ronnie's murder wasn't a lone act.

It scared the shit out of me.

If he'd been murdered by a family member or friend, as bad as that was, at least it likely ended with Ronnie. My developing theory was much, much worse. I'd be opening a new can of worms if I went down this path.

Which I guess I'd already done with Officer Picker in San Ramon.

It's not like I had a choice. I was going to go wherever the evidence took me.

My mind was starting to feel overwhelmed again.

I vowed to stop, but I had to make one call first.

"Hello?" Hank said.

"I need a favor."

"Isn't today your day off?"

"Did Evelyn tell you?"

"I talked to her early this morning and she informed me of her plan to hire you back. Emmett called me about thirty minutes ago to confirm that you had accepted."

"I guess we'll be seeing more of each other," I said.

"I guess so."

"Listen, Hank, here's the reason I called. Can you get me a list of local missing or dead kids from June of 2002 to the end of that year?"

"I can probably do that. On such short notice, it won't be as thorough as the other fifteen. And there will probably be a few runaways thrown in."

"That's alright. I'll weed through them."

"Do you want to tell me what this is about?"

"I've got an idea brewing. I'll tell you about it next time we meet up."

"I'll do what I can and get back to you tomorrow. Now go enjoy your damn day off."

"I will."

The Stadium Pub was somewhere between a hundred and two hundred yards from my apartment. It was a sports bar with probably thirty T.V.s and tons of sports memorabilia on the walls, mostly signed jerseys, basketballs, footballs, and baseballs.

It had a dive feel to it which added to its charm. It was a good place to watch a ballgame.

They had some red and green streamers on the railings outside. It was a nice reminder that Christmas was only twelve days away. Something that was easy to overlook with how busy I'd been.

I saw Rebecca, who'd changed and was now wearing a yellow hoodie with white pants, sitting at a table near the bar. She had three girlfriends with her and one guy.

I told myself I was there to have a good time and have a few drinks. And that was it. My break-up with Cara was recent enough to where I wasn't looking for a rebound. Not yet, at least. Maybe I'd have a different perspective in a few months.

I'd begun to acknowledge that being a P.I. made it much more difficult to have a standard relationship. You're always out there, investigating, probing, potentially in harm's way. That can't be easy on a girlfriend and I know it wasn't on Cara.

Still, I wasn't ready to become a monk, so women were never far from my mind, even if a new relationship wasn't necessarily in the cards.

I approached their table.

Rebecca's friends were cute, but she was the best-looking of the bunch. They all appeared to be in their mid-thirties.

"Everybody, this is Quint, the guy who lives in my complex."

I said a quick hello to everyone as Rebecca ran down the names of each one. I'd never been good at remembering several names in a flash. Hopefully, once I heard their names a second time, they'd start to register.

"What do you want to drink, Quint?"

When I wanted it to be a mellow night, I'd usually drink beer. If I was looking to get a little buzz, I'd go with the following:

"I'll take a Moscow Mule," I said.

The petite redhead, whom I'm pretty sure had been introduced as Amber, quickly flagged down our server and asked for a Moscow Mule.

"Thanks," I said.

The drink arrived a minute later and when it did, we all raised and toasted our glasses. After we each had a sip, Rebecca turned to me.

"How's your week been going, Quint?" she asked.

There was a fine line with my new occupation. No one wanted to hear the grisly details of what I did on a day-to-day basis. I didn't want to be curt, either.

"Been really busy," I said.

"Quint is a private investigator," Rebecca said.

I could feel all the eyes on the table turn towards me. It was an interesting job, I had to admit.

"What's the case you're currently working on?" Amber asked.

"It's pretty brutal," I said. "Not sure it's a great Happy Hour topic of discussion."

Rebecca shook her head.

"Sorry, that's not going to work with this crew. Now we're just more interested."

The whole table nodded in unison.

I smiled.

"Alright, you asked for it. I'm investigating the death of a fourteen-year-old who was murdered twenty years ago."

There were a few audible gasps.

"Wow," Rebecca said. "No wonder you don't talk about your job that often."

"Not exactly the small talk our neighbors are looking for," I said.

"Have you made any progress?"

The lone blonde at the table joined the conversation. Her name hadn't registered.

"I've learned a lot about the case," I said. "But progress insofar as catching the killer? Not really."

"I imagine it's hard to catch a killer twenty years after the fact."

"You'd be right," I said.

"Do the police have a suspect? How about the family?"

"Everyone seems to have their own opinion."

"What do you think?"

"I think..." I said, pausing. "That this Moscow Mule tastes delicious."

A few people laughed.

From the corner of my eye, I saw Rebecca smile at me.

"Let's give Quint a break," she said. "It's probably not advisable for him to talk about his cases too much."

I nodded in Rebecca's direction.

"Thanks," I said.

"Did you used to be a newspaperman?" Amber asked. "There was a guy named Quint who wrote for *The Walnut Creek Times*."

"That was me," I said. "Not that many Quints out there."

"How cool is that? A reporter and now a P.I."

"Never a dull day," I said.

"I bet you've got some stories," she said.

It was a leading question, but I didn't take the bait.

"What do you do for work, Amber?" I asked, praying that it was indeed Amber.

"I'm a social media manager for Facebook."

"That sounds interesting," I said.

"It's not like going after bad guys every day," she said.

Amber had taken a liking to me. It was undeniable.

"I don't think it's quite as exciting as you think," I said.

I'd unsuccessfully tried to steer the conversation from my career. Rebecca saved me once again.

"Mark, tell everyone about what happened to you today."

While Mark told a story about running into a player from the Golden State Warriors, I nodded at Rebecca for getting the focus away from me.

I took another sip of my Moscow Mule and, despite the unwelcome questions about my job, I was happy to be out on the town.

One drink turned into two and then three.

One other woman had joined and we'd become a table of six. Four women, two men.

I was certain that Rebecca noticed Amber flirting with me. I couldn't tell if it bothered her or not, but she did change the subject a few times when Amber tried to make it a one-on-one conversation between the two of us.

At seven p.m. the first shot was ordered and I was officially buzzed a few minutes later. It was a fun-loving group and I'd managed to seamlessly fit in. That's not always easy to do.

By nine p.m., we were down to four of us. Amber, Mark, Rebecca, and myself.

"One more drink and I'm out of here," Mark said.

At 9:30, we were a party of three.

Amber was pretty drunk at this point, bordering on sloppy. Rebecca and I would swiftly glance at each other when she said or did something stupid.

"Amber, can I call you an Uber?" Rebecca asked.

She may have been drunk, but at least she realized it.

"Yeah, that would probably be best."

Ten minutes later, we were down to two, and a few minutes after that, Rebecca and I both closed out.

"I'd like to walk you home," I said.

"Wow, the generosity of men never ceases to amaze me."

"I won't just get you in the building, I'll walk you the twenty feet from my place to yours."

"You're a lifesaver," Rebecca joked.

We left Stadium Pub and started walking on North Main Street toward 1716 Lofts.

"I think Amber took a liking to you," Rebecca said.

"I'd say that's a safe bet."

"She's cute."

"Yeah, she is. Doesn't handle her booze all that well."

"She's usually good for two or three. After that, she can go downhill a bit. She's a good friend, though."

"I'm sure. Didn't mean to disparage her."

"I know."

"Were you mad she was flirting with me?" I asked, rather directly.

"Definitely not mad."

"Disappointed?"

"In what?"

"That she was flirting with a friend you brought?"

"You're not that handsome, Quint."

I laughed.

We arrived at 1716 Lofts and I used the fob to let us in. We got on the elevator and pressed the button to the 5th floor. We rode in silence.

The door opened and we took a left toward our respective apartments.

"Would you like to join us again?" Rebecca asked.

"Yeah, it was an entertaining group."

"Great. They liked you, and I don't just mean Amber."

We approached my apartment.

"Isn't this you?" Rebecca asked.

"I told you I'd get you to your door."

She laughed.

"What a gentleman."

We walked the extra twenty feet to her door.

"Thanks for tonight," I said.

She leaned against her door.

"You just broke up with a long-term girlfriend, didn't you?"

"A few months ago," I said.

"I'm not looking to be a rebound."

Rebecca then leaned in and kissed me. It was very sensuous and lasted for several seconds. She quickly opened her door and smiled.

"That's all you're getting," she said.

"Hey, I was just being a nice guy and getting you to your door."

"In that case, consider it a parting gift."

"It was a nice one."

"Nice kiss or nice parting gift?"

I laughed.

"Both."

"I'll see you around, Quint."

"Bye, Rebecca."

She shut the door and I headed back to my apartment, amused by what had just transpired.

CHAPTER 15

I headed to my office early the following morning.

The end of the night with Rebecca had crossed my mind a time or two. I wasn't worried. We were adults and I knew it wasn't going to be awkward.

Halfway through my walk, I received a call from Hank.

"I've got that information you wanted."

I was impressed with his expediency.

"That was quick."

"I still know a guy or two in law enforcement. Do you want to come and get it or have me fax what I've got?"

"I'll come see you," I said. "This afternoon fine?"

"Yup. I'm going to do some shopping this morning and then I'll be home all afternoon."

"Preparing for the storm?" I asked.

Meteorologists were predicting the storm would start sometime the following night. It was going to last three or four days and had alternately been called a "Bomb Cyclone" and an "Atmospheric River." We were told to expect a rain of "Biblical proportions."

"You know it. Not leaving the house after that."

"I'll see you this afternoon," I said and hung up.

Yes, drought-stricken California needed the rain, and this was a good thing. For me, however, this was going to be brutal. I was going to be zig-zagging the Bay Area dealing with rain that would have made Noah and his Ark blush.

~

To my surprise, there was a woman waiting outside my office when I arrived. She was in her forties, wearing some tight red yoga pants, and her hair was in a bun. She was either headed to or coming back from yoga or pilates or tai chi or barre or one of those other disciplines you'd never find me at.

"Are you Quint Adler?"

"I am."

"And you're a private investigator, right?"

"That's what the sign says," I said, being more sarcastic than was warranted.

"I think I'd like to hire you. My name is Marjorie."

We shook hands.

"Why don't we talk inside?"

"Sure."

I opened the door and was going to lie about the secretary running late, but there was no point. She'd find out soon enough it was just me.

We each took a seat once we arrived in my office.

"So, what do you need a P.I. for?" I asked her.

If I were a betting man, I'd have made some money on what she said next.

"I think my husband is cheating on me," she said.

"Why do you think that?" I asked.

"I found some panties that weren't mine."

"At your house?"

"Worse. In his car."

I had so many questions.

"Were you driving his car?"

"No. I walked by it and saw them, sitting there in the back seat, plain as day."

"It doesn't seem like a place where you'd casually leave your panties," I said.

"True, but maybe they were having a quickie in my husband's car."

I know beggars can't be choosers, and I was early on in my career, but I really didn't want too many 'my husband/wife is cheating on me' cases.

"And were you going to hire me to tail him?"

"You tell me. You're the P.I."

"Marjorie, I'd really like to take your case. However, I'm currently working on something and I pledged to work on it exclusively for two weeks. I just finished the first week. If you still want me to follow your husband in a week, then I'll gladly take your case."

"Haven't you ever heard of multi-tasking? All I'm asking is for you to follow him around for a few days. First, when he leaves for work in the morning. Then, at lunch. And finally, when he leaves work and comes home."

So, she did want me to tail him.

I couldn't decide. I could be the most selective P.I. around, but that wouldn't pay the bills. On the other hand, what kind of life was it to follow husbands and wives to seedy motels, trying to get a picture of them in sexually compromised positions?

Shit!

Marjorie was staring at me, waiting for a response.

In the future, I could be more discerning in which cases I'd take. As much as it pained me, I wasn't at that point in my career yet.

"Alright, I'll take your case, Marjorie. How long did you want to hire me for?"

"Let's start off with just this Thursday and Friday. I saw the panties on Friday night, so I'm thinking he might have his rendezvous later in the week," she said.

"Let's talk money," I said.

"Alright."

The pay rates of being a P.I. were kind of like the Wild West. You could charge whatever you thought you could get away with.

At least, the unscrupulous ones could. I was not one of them.

"I'll charge you $100 an hour. It may seem like a lot, but this might only be six hours of work and I'm not doing it for fifty bucks an hour. Keep in mind, I pay for my own gas or any pictures I might need to get developed," I said.

"It sounds more than fair. Cheap, some might say."

"So, I'll tail him for an hour each morning, at lunch, and on his way home on Thursday and Friday. Six hours total."

"That's perfect," she said. "Would you prefer cash, check, or a credit card?"

It appeared Marjorie really did have money. Not many people carried around $600 in cash. Especially these days, when everyone is so reliant on credit cards.

"Whatever is easiest for you."

"This cash is burning a hole in my pocket."

"Then cash it is," I said.

I wrote up a contract and had Marjorie sign it. Her last name was Ballard. At least for the time being.

We agreed to talk after the first two days and see if my job was indeed over.

After dotting the Is and crossing the Ts, she gave me all the details, starting with his name. Bruce Ballard. I'll be honest, my impression was that it was a very uppity, WASPy-sounding name. I had to remind myself to stop judging so quickly.

He founded an architectural firm and his office was only a few minutes from their family home. She gave me his work and their home address, along with Bruce's license plate number. Finally, she informed me of the approximate hours he arrived at work, left for lunch, and headed home from the office at night.

Marjorie told me they had no children together. I hated to consider that a blessing, but in this case, I did. She left a few minutes later and I'd secured my second new case at the new digs. I didn't go jumping up and down in celebration, I can assure you that.

~

As I headed to see Hank, I'd already regretted taking Marjorie Ballard's case.

Did it say something about my new occupation that I felt sleazy without having done anything wrong?

My rationale was that crappy cases like Marjorie Ballard's would allow me to pay the bills so I could take interesting, albeit painful, cases like Ronnie Fisk's. That doesn't mean I had to enjoy them.

It was like being a Hollywood actor. You do one for the studios and then find a passion project that you love.

I did manage to find a plus while beating myself up. If there was some downtime while following Bruce Ballard, I could continue my endless reading of the Ronnie Fisk case file.

The proverbial killing two birds with one stone.

I took the exit into Sausalito and looked skyward. The clouds were dark and ominous. Maybe the storm really wasn't kicking off until tomorrow night, but it looked like it could rain at any moment.

I parked in front of Hank's house and knocked on his door a few seconds later.

"Welcome back," he said.

"To the case or to your house?"

"Good point. You're a sharp one, Quint."

We walked into the house and once again, there was no way we'd be sitting on the deck.

We took our seats on the couch, the same ones we'd taken on my last visit.

"So, what did you discover?" I asked.

He handed me a piece of paper. I quickly scanned it, knowing I'd read it later. I noticed there were only four names.

"Almost nothing. Which made it interesting."

I knew what he meant.

"Not as many disappearances as the previous twelve months, right?" I asked.

"Not even close. And that's accounting for the fact that a few of these look like obvious runaways."

"That's kind of what I was expecting."

"I know you're up to something, but where exactly are you going with this, Quint?"

"Of the sixteen murders, which include Ronnie, only three occurred in the summer of 2001. I'm characterizing that as between June and September. That spiked to eleven murders from October to the end of February. Then, from March to June of 2002, only two more murders occurred."

"Alright. Still not sure what you're suggesting."

"Allow me a few liberties," I said.

"You have the floor."

"I'm going to put the eleven murders from October to February in the same category and combine the other two."

"For what reason?"

"There's a few. First off, I have my doubts that some of those warm-weather murders have any connection to Ronnie."

"Jesus, Quint. Does that mean you're saying the other eleven murders do?"

I stared at him.

"No offense, Hank, but you're not letting me lay out my theory.

"I'm sorry," he said. "I won't interrupt anymore."

"The reason I don't think the warmer weather murders can be related to Ronnie is twofold. One, they are predominantly older kids. Fifteen and sixteen-year-olds. Meaning they are in high school. Older and stronger than Ronnie or the missing middle schoolers. Second, several of these kids were stabbed or shot. While I'll concede that a murderer might kill in multiple ways, it still makes it less likely they are related to the murder of Ronnie."

Hank looked on, afraid to interrupt. I had the tough, former police officer on his heels. Not that it was my intention.

"Now, the murders that took place that winter were predominantly middle schoolers, aged thirteen and fourteen. Furthermore, most were either strangled or their bodies were never found. There were a few that were outliers. One was sixteen and one was shot. I don't think those murders were perpetrated by the same killer. And honestly, there are likely several others that also aren't related. I'm not saying that somebody killed eight or nine children that winter. But, and here's what you wanted to know, Hank. I do think, and yes, this is just my working theory, that several of the murders that winter were committed by the same man."

I saw Hank exhale.

"Fuck me!" he cried out.

"To be clear, Hank, I have no real evidence. No smoking gun. This is all circumstantial."

"Maybe, but it's still great work. I never bothered to separate the murders by age or, God forbid, by season. Probably because I never thought it was a serial killer. Maybe I still don't."

"I don't blame you. But it's where my investigation is now heading."

"Good. I've told you several times to listen to your gut."

"Which brings me to another hunch of mine."

"Let me have it," Hank said.

"If I'm right about winter, and that's still a huge if, then you have to ask yourself why he stopped killing middle school kids in the Bay Area after February. There are several possibilities. One, he died. Two, he was arrested for something else. Three, he moved and started killing some-where else. And four, he just decided to stop killing. I think four is extremely unlikely, considering all we know about serial killers. Maybe we got really fortunate and he dropped dead. I'm not counting on that. Which leaves options two and three."

"He was arrested or started killing somewhere else."

"Yup."

"What do you need from me?"

"First, if you could get a listing of people arrested in the East Bay around February or March of 2002. Obviously, that would be thousands of people. Maybe tens of thousands. I'm only interested in people who were up to no good with minors. Assault. Kidnapping. You can include sexual assault if you want, but none of the murders in the winter of 01/02 were sexual in nature. Thank God."

"If we limit it to arrests with minors that are not sexually motivated, the number won't be nearly as big as you think."

"Good. Let's go with that. The other possibility was that he started killing somewhere else. Could you get information on missing/dead kids from March to December of 2002, hopefully from San Francisco down to say, San Jose. And north of Walnut Creek as well? I want to find out if he started killing elsewhere in the Bay Area."

"San Francisco will be easy. I've still got a million connections on the force. I'll have to ask some favors for the South Bay and the far East Bay. The further we get from SF, the less pull I have with law enforcement. I know you think I was a well-known cop, but I was very San Francisco centric."

I smiled.

"You were a well-known cop, Hank. It's not just me who thinks it."

He nodded in appreciation.

"This may take a while, you know," Hank said.

"How long are you thinking?"

"I can probably get the San Francisco information in a day or two. The rest may take a few more."

"That's fine. Thank you."

"Call me tomorrow. And you don't have to keep coming all the way out here, you know."

"I'm heading to San Francisco after this, so this was no trouble."

"Alright, but next time you want to save time, I can just fax you the information."

"Do you have a fax in the house?"

"Sure do. Like I told you, I don't plan on leaving the house until this storm passes. I don't trust my seventy-five-year-old eyes to drive during a crazy storm."

"You might want to pass that information on to Emmett."

"That's a good idea. I'll tell him to keep off the roads."

I sensed the conversation was ending and stood up.

"So, this is really happening?" Hank asked. "We are going with the supposition that Ronnie was murdered by a serial killer."

"Yes. But I'm going to call it a theory. Supposition sounds too conceited."

Hank shook his head.

"You tend to find humor in the weirdest situations."

"I think that's when we need it most," I said.

"You may be right."

"I'll call you in a day or two and see what you've come up with. Thanks."

"You're welcome."

I turned to go but decided I should clear something up.

"Don't misunderstand my attempts at humor, Hank. I know how utterly tragic Ronnie's murder was to this family. I also know just how significant this leap I'm taking is."

"You didn't have to tell me that, Quint. Thank you, though."

"You got it. Talk soon," I said.

I walked out the door and was off to San Francisco to meet up with my favorite lawbreaker.

CHAPTER 16

Back when I was investigating the murder of my father, two unexpected people came to my aid when I needed it the most. First, Dennis McCarthy, who was certainly the biggest bookie in the history of the Bay Area, and possibly all of northern California. And second, Paddy Roark, his right-hand man, a tough guy's tough guy.

After a less than auspicious start, I'd come to trust both of them like members of my own family. It was pretty odd, considering these weren't Boy Scouts and had assuredly done some reprehensible things. They did have integrity, though. The old adage 'honor amongst thieves' came to mind.

I'd dealt almost exclusively with Paddy when setting up meetings, so I decided it would be wise to approach him first. It had always been at a San Francisco Irish-themed grocery store named Boyle's. I'd assumed it was a front for their bookmaking business.

With my prior two cases having been in Hollywood and Las Vegas, it had been a while since I'd seen these guys. I hoped they were still on team Quint.

~

Like clockwork, Paddy Roark made an appearance almost immediately upon me entering Boyle's.

He was wearing a flannel sweatshirt and looked more weathered than I remember. And Paddy was already weathered to begin with.

"Quint!" he yelled, approaching me with all the subtlety of a bull in a china shop.

Despite his rough exterior, he had always been polite and outgoing with me. I imagine he had the same vigor, for different reasons, with people who were on his bad side.

"How are you, Paddy?"

"I've been well. You've sure been busy."

A woman walked by us with some corned beef and Guinness in her cart. As if I needed any more confirmation this grocery story catered to the Irish.

"How did you know that?" I asked.

"We always keep an ear to the ground."

"You know about Hollywood?"

"We sure do."

"You know about Vegas?"

"We sure do."

He didn't have to specify who "we" was.

"Do you know what I'm currently working on?" I asked.

I'd have been shocked if he had.

Paddy looked on, surprised.

"No. Should we be taking an interest?"

"Only if you care about a bunch of dead kids."

"Follow me."

Ever since I'd known Paddy, we'd always walked to his office in the back to talk business. This time would be no different.

I accompanied Paddy back to the tiny, dingy office I was now well acquainted with. We both sat.

"A bunch of dead kids?" Paddy said, rhetorically.

"I don't know if you knew, but I started a P.I. firm."

"I did hear about that, yes."

"Well, I took my first case and it's a doozy."

"Let's hear it."

I gave Paddy the five-minute version of meeting Emmett, reading all of the case files that Hank had procured, and some of the investigating I'd done on Ronnie's death.

"Scary stuff," he said. "Let's hope this monster isn't still out there and finds you flipping over every unturned stone."

While I'd considered many times whether the killer was still alive or not, I'd never contemplated him coming after me.

"Thanks, Paddy. One more thing to worry about."

"Hey, what are friends for?"

"Sure am glad I walked in here today."

Paddy laughed.

"So, what do you want from us?"

"When we first met and it was apparent you had connections with multiple police departments, I asked you how. You told me that you had dozens of police officers who bet with you guys. Is that still true?"

"Maybe. What exactly did you have in mind?"

In this case, when Paddy said maybe, he really meant yes.

"The murder of children in the East Bay almost came to a halt around February of 2002. My fear is that he moved and started killing elsewhere."

Paddy looked at me. I hadn't convinced him yet, so I continued.

"Hank has plenty of connections in San Francisco and the rest of the Bay Area, but not much anywhere else. I know your's run up and down Northern California."

"That's a fact."

I'd danced around it enough and just decided to come out and say it.

"What I'd like from you, Paddy, is to ask your group of police officers, in as subtle a way as possible, if any of them heard of any clusters of missing kids from 2002 onward."

I saw Paddy thinking it over. He was never rushed on anything.

"I like you, Quint, so I'll ask the boss man if we can broach the subject. Missing children haven't exactly been our priority over the years. We try to stay out of things that don't involve us."

"I understand. It's only because I'm at a standstill, and naturally, I thought of you guys."

"Not sure if I should be worried or appreciative."

"Just trying to think outside of the box."

"We'd love to help get a monster off the streets."

"Maybe it's all for naught. It's been twenty years, and the guy could easily be dead."

"Is that what you believe?"

I only had to think about it for a split second.

"No."

"I didn't think so. You know, I bet Dennis would be willing to put out a tester for you. Whether any of the police officers bite is a different question entirely."

Dennis McCarthy was a well-known philanthropist in the Bay Area. He donated to hospitals and schools, among other things. It's certainly why many in law enforcement looked the other way. It was sports betting, after all. Of white-collar crime, it graded very low on the totem pole.

Especially when so many of their own were betting through Dennis.

"Thank you, Paddy. You have no idea how much this means to me."

He looked on with genuine compassion.

"This case has really gotten to you, hasn't it?"

"It's all I've thought about for the last nine days. Dead kids and grieving family members."

"Sounds terrible, Quint. Listen, we'll do what we can, but this sounds like a real long shot. The proverbial…"

"Don't say needle in the haystack," I said.

"That is what I was going with. I could change it up if you'd like. How about finding a polar bear in a snowstorm. An honest man in Congress. A virgin in a whorehouse."

I was reminded that when I first met Paddy, I thought he was merely a brute. Nothing more than an enforcer for Dennis. I was dead wrong. He was a smart, quick-witted individual who had a biting sense of humor as well.

"Good ones," I said. "You never fail to disappoint."

"I'll talk to Dennis as soon as I can. No guarantees, though. This is one of the more random requests you've brought our way."

"You're right. It's worth throwing a Hail Mary on this one. Think of the upside. As you said, there might still be a monster out there."

"I'll be in touch. You still have your main cell phone?"

"Yeah."

"Do you have a burner?"

"Not right now."

"Get one. C'mon, what kind of P.I. are you?"

I felt like a little boy being reprimanded by his father.

Paddy continued.

"If this case blows up and the police ever get the bright idea to see what's on that phone of yours, I don't want any evidence of our conversations on there. You dig?"

"Yeah, I dig."

"So get yourself a burner phone and contact me once you do. And then, if by some miracle I have some information, I'll give it to you."

"Thanks, Paddy."

"You got it, Quint. Let me know next time you're popping in. I'll make sure the big man is here. I'm sure he'd love to see you."

"And me, him. Alright, I'll let you know."

"Be safe out there. We like knowing you're out and about, alive and prospering."

It was a warning, but I smiled anyway.

"See you soon."

"Heed my warning."

"I will."

"You know how to show yourself out."

I did. And I did.

~

There was an accident on the Bay Bridge during my drive back to the East Bay. What should have taken thirty minutes took two hours.

I spent a lot of time in thought and by the time I arrived back in Walnut Creek, I was ready to double down on what I'd told Hank and Paddy. I no longer just thought it was just possible, I now thought it likely that Ronnie's murder was one of many.

It raised the stakes of my investigation to new heights. And maybe all the warnings to stay safe had not been in jest. I should take them seriously.

I spent most of the night reading about the case, but I did manage to go out and get the burner phone that Paddy had requested. I called him on his main cell and gave him my burner number. No reason to text him and leave a trail of the number. In turn, he gave me a new number to contact him on. I'd love to have known the number of phones Paddy had gone through over the years.

Hundreds? Thousands?

Those were the inane thoughts going through my head when I fell asleep that night.

CHAPTER 17

"Quint, how far are you from Tellus Coffee in Walnut Creek?"
It was 7:31 a.m. the following morning and Paddy had called my brand new burner phone.

"A quarter-mile tops."

"I need you to be there by eight."

"What's up, Paddy?"

"Dennis agreed to your request."

"And you got information this quickly?"

"Stop asking so many questions. Just go to Tellus Coffee and you'll find out."

"Alright. What does the guy look like?"

"He'll find you."

"Thank you for this, Paddy."

"Just another favor you owe us."

I was going to agree with him, but he'd already hung up on his end.

I took a three-minute shower and threw on some jeans, a t-shirt, and a warm jacket. The heart of the storm hadn't arrived yet, but the temperature on my phone told me it was a cold morning. Surely a sign of things to come.

Tellus Coffee had opened a few months before I'd moved into my new place. It was a coffee shop, obviously, but they also had a great menu and even served cocktails. The decor was all green and black and the back wall was about thirty feet high and filled with dozens of fresh plants.

At my previous apartment in Walnut Creek, I'd been a regular customer at the Starbucks downstairs. It had, in fact, played a major part in the case involving the death of my father. I wasn't quite a regular at Tellus yet, but I knew a few of the baristas.

One of them saw me walk in.

"A half-caff Americano, Quint?"

I had stuck with half-caffs for several years now. When you have as many coffees as me, I'd be bouncing off the walls with full caffeine.

"Please."

I looked around, but no one was staring back at me. 'He'll find you,' Paddy had told me.

Two minutes later, my Americano was ready.

"Order ready for Quint."

As I picked it up, I got a tap on my shoulder.

"Come meet me in the back," the man said.

He must have heard them announce my name.

There was a small, semi-secluded area at Tellus that supplied a little more privacy than the bustling front.

The man had the table in the corner and I joined him. He wasn't very old, several years younger than me, if I was to hazard a guess. The side of his hair was completely shaved and he had a makeshift mohawk on top.

"How long have you known, Paddy?" he asked.

"About three years," I said.

"Nine for me. Wish I'd never met him."

"Why's that?"

"Because it's too easy to bet the ponies these days. You can download an app and two minutes later you're betting a $20 exacta that has no shot of winning."

I smiled, knowing a little bit about horse racing myself.

"Not like the old days where you had to either go to the track itself or the OTB."

"You know your stuff, Quint. I'm Rick, by the way."

"Thanks for meeting with me, Rick."

"Should we get down to why we're here?"

He said it with an exuberance that didn't befit the subject matter.

"Sure," I said.

"I got a text from Paddy last night. Well, not me personally, but he sent it to a group of us. You see, my father is a former cop. He and a bunch of retired police officers bet through Dennis. Since they are all a little older, and not all that great with tech, apps, and betting online, I was nominated a few years back to put in their bets each week. So that's the reason I'm on this text thread. Anyway, Paddy asked all the cops if they knew of any cases with missing kids. Hold on, that's not exactly what he said. A cluster of missing kids, that's what he called it."

He paused as if adding to the drama.

"And?" I asked.

"And I thought of one right away. It was 2003 in Sacramento. I was graduating from high school. My father was working on the case. I called him right after I received the text from Paddy and asked him if it was alright to bring it to his attention. He said of course, so I called Paddy and told him what I knew."

"What can you tell me about the case?" I asked.

"Two little kids went missing in a matter of weeks and it got a lot of attention. Like I said, Sacramento 2003. One of the kids' names was Matt Greeson. I'll always remember that. It's weird how some things stick with you all these years later."

"How did the two kids die?"

"They were strangled. When I told Paddy that, he paid a little closer attention. That's when he told me about you and the dead kids in Berkeley."

I wanted to be mad at Paddy for telling other people, but how could I? He'd gotten me exactly the information that I'd asked.

"Do you know how old Matt Greeson was?"

"He was fourteen. In middle school."

I was dumbfounded. Fourteen and strangled. Two years after Ronnie's death. To say I was intrigued would have been a monster understatement.

"Do you remember the name of the other kid?"

"I hadn't, but I Googled it to refresh my memory. His name was Jeremy Stacks. Matt was killed first and then Jeremy a few weeks later."

"Was he the same age as Matt?"

"Yup. Fourteen also."

"Did they live close to each other?"

"I think it was about five miles, so yeah, pretty close."

"Did they go to the same school?"

"No, but considering it was only a few miles, I'm sure it was a rival middle school."

"And obviously, they never caught the killer?"

"Nope. Still irks my father to this day."

"Did any of the other cops respond to the text thread?" I asked.

"No. I don't think Paddy wanted the text thread to deteriorate into cops telling old war stories. So he said on the text to contact him directly. That's why, after talking to my father, I reached out and called him."

"Does your father live around here?"

"In the Bay Area, if that's what you mean."

I was hoping I could meet with him to discuss the case.

"Where?"

"In the South Bay. Mountain View."

That was down near where Evelyn lived and worked.

"Do you think he'd be willing to talk to me?"

"Yeah, probably."

"Thank you, Rick."

"You're welcome. I did a few things for you myself."

He reached into his pocket and grabbed a piece of paper.

"Here are the respective addresses of Matt Greeson and Jeremy Stacks. I've also listed their DOBs if that helps. I'm sure my father could get you some more information. This was kind of rushed, as you can guess, and I got it all from my Google search."

"This is very helpful."

"Paddy said you were worried some psycho is still out there."

This is not how I wanted the conversation to proceed. It was time to change the subject.

"Let's hope not. You must live close?"

"Yeah, I live in Walnut Creek. After we talked last night, Paddy called me this morning and said to pick a coffee shop and he'd have you meet me."

Rick sounded like he would do anything that Paddy said.

"Hard to say no to Paddy," I said.

He laughed.

"You can say that again. Do you think these deaths are related?"

He wouldn't give up.

"It's way too early to tell, Rick."

"Wouldn't that be crazy?"

As helpful as Rick had been, I didn't want to keep talking about the case.

"Sure would," I said. "I mentioned it earlier, but could I get your father's phone number?"

"It's 650-555-5295. And his name is Walter."

"Thanks."

"Do me a favor, though. Don't call him first. He's a pretty guarded man. Let me talk to him and I'll ask him to call you."

It's not what I wanted, but I chose to respect Rick's wishes.

"That's fine. Here's my number."

I pulled out the receipt for my burner phone and gave him that number, knowing Paddy would have preferred that. No reason to use my main phone for anything that sprouted from my initial conversation with Paddy.

"You'll be sure to tell Paddy if this helps your investigation."

"Of course."

"Maybe he'll let us slide on paying next week."

I gave him a courtesy laugh. Tying the murders to a gambling marker was hardly comedy gold, however.

"Listen, I have to run, Rick, but thanks again for all your help."

"You got it. Make sure to have Paddy tell us if anything comes of this."

This guy was resilient.

"I will," I said.

CHAPTER 18

W hen I originally took Emmett Fisk's case, a day trip to Sacramento was certainly not on my Bingo card.

I left Tellus Coffee at 8:15, went home, and loaded a backpack with a few things. My plan was to return to Walnut Creek later that day, but I came prepared in case a hotel was in my future.

Midway through my drive, I saw my burner phone light up as it sat on the passenger seat.

"Hello?" I answered.

"Is this Quint?"

"It is."

"My name is Walter Shard. My son Rick wanted me to call you."

"Thanks for calling, Walter. I'm actually headed up to Sacramento right now to look into Matt Greeson and the other murder."

I couldn't remember the name of the second victim.

"Is there anything you can tell me about them?" I asked.

The car in front of me slammed on his brakes. I saw it in time but reminded myself to keep attentive.

"Jeremy Stacks was the other victim. And they were both brutal cases, that's for sure. Two young kids, with bright futures ahead, taken well before their time."

"I can only imagine."

"It was extra tough since nothing came of it. If you work a case like that, and catch the killer in the end, at least you leave with some satisfaction. Not so on this case. We left with a rotten taste since we never found the guy responsible."

"Did you have any suspects? "

"No. We didn't have shit. Whoever this asshole was, he was no idiot. It felt like he was always a step ahead of us."

"And you're positive these two deaths were related?"

"Nothing is a hundred percent, but they were both fourteen, both strangled, lived a few minutes from each other, and both murders happened within a few weeks of each other."

"I get your point. I know you didn't have any suspects, but did you have a profile? White? Black? Hispanic? Young? Old? Rich? Poor?"

"We assumed it was a white male. Not that it was some ground-breaking take. The victims were white and they both lived in predominantly white areas. As for a female suspect, it's possible, but let's be honest, we always assume it's going to be a male when it's a case of strangulation."

"Is the case still open?"

"I retired over a decade ago. I honestly have no idea."

"Do you still have any connections with the Sacramento police?"

"Not really. I moved down to the Bay Area soon after I retired and didn't really keep in touch with anyone."

"Could you get ahold of the initial police report of the case?" I asked.

"I could probably tell them I'm a former cop and see if that carried any weight."

"That would be a great help to me."

"I have your number. I'll see what I can do and get back to you later."

"Thanks, Walter."

"Good luck in Sacramento," he said and hung up the phone abruptly.

I'd been hoping to ask a few more questions. So much for that.

There was some morning traffic as I approached Sac-town, as they call it, and I didn't arrive till after 10:00. All things considered, that was fine.

My first stop was going to be Pearson Way, the street on which Matt Greeson lived and went missing, only to be found dead a few days later. I had no idea if anybody still lived there from eighteen years ago. There was only one way to find out.

I parked my car at the beginning of the cul-de-sac. It was a tree-lined street, and the houses were nice, but the road itself was in dire need of an upgrade. I saw three potholes in only the first fifty yards of the street.

Halfway down, Pearson Way veered to the right, but you could see the end of the cul de sac where you were recycled back toward the front. There were approximately ten houses and I hoped I wouldn't have to hit them all. If necessary, I would.

The first house I approached was a modest blue-gray two-story home with a white picket fence. I'm not sure if there were 2.5 kids inside, but this looked like a prototypical American home.

I rang the doorbell and a few seconds later, a woman with gray hair who looked to be in her eighties answered the door.

"Can I help you?" she asked.

I'd decided on my drive-up that honesty was the best policy.

"Nice to meet you. I'm a private investigator and I was wondering if you lived here when Matt Greeson went missing?"

"I'm sorry, no. My son and his wife did, though. Can you hold on a second?"

"Sure."

She shut the door.

She was either visiting or her son and his wife had taken her in. It was so common these days with the price of senior assisted living going through the roof. My mother was still doing great at seventy-three, but I often thought about what I'd do if she started having issues.

The door opened again. This time a brunette woman in her fifties opened the door.

"My mother-in-law tells me you're a P.I."

"I am. Would you like to see my license?"

"Please."

I took it out of my wallet and showed it to her. I doubt very many people knew what a valid P.I. license looks like, but I was happy to do it.

"Quint, huh? Are you named after the character in *Jaws*?"

I usually got that about once a week, but it had been a while since I'd last heard it. I always liked it when people mentioned it. I imagined my father smiling down on me when he heard it.

"I am. You have good taste in movies."

She smiled.

"Thanks. So what brings you here?"

The door was still only open about halfway. I guess I couldn't blame her.

"I'm investigating the murder of a young boy in the Bay Area. And I'm trying to find if there is any connection to a few murders that occurred up here."

"Yeah, my mother-in-law said you asked about Matt Greeson."

"You were living here when he went missing?"

The woman opened the door and walked outside to join me.

"Sorry, I just had to make sure you were legitimate."

"No problem," I said.

"Yeah, we lived here. What a terrible time that was. For the Greesons most of all, but really, for anyone on this block. This is a very family-friendly street and I think everyone on the block had kids back then. You can imagine just how scary it was knowing that a child had been abducted and later found murdered. Especially when you have kids of your own. And we didn't know if the killer was still in the area, or God forbid, lived on this block."

"Were your kids around the same age as the Greeson boy?"

"A few years younger. Matt was thirteen or fourteen and our two kids were eleven and nine at the time."

"I know that no one was ever arrested for his murder, but did the people on this street have any suspicions?"

There were many things that I'd become tired of over the course of this case. Asking every Tom, Dick, or Mary if they had suspicions of their own was high on that list, but it had to be asked.

"I'm sure some people might have, but my husband and I didn't. We always assumed it was some random maniac. As I said, the alternative, thinking it was someone who lived on this block, was too frightening to consider."

"Certainly," I said. "Did you hear about any other child murders around Sacramento during that time?"

"There were two in the span of a few weeks. As I said, it was a very scary time."

Surely, she was talking about Jeremy Stacks.

"Did people think they were related?"

"The police never said it was the work of one guy, but yeah, I'd say most people thought they were probably related. Or, at the least, feared they were."

The woman standing in front of me, whose name I hadn't even learned, was being as helpful as she could. She wasn't going to help crack the case, but I appreciated the information.

"I'll let you go in a minute. Just a few more questions. Do the Greesons still live on this block?"

"No, they moved several years ago. They got divorced within a year or two of Matt's death."

Just like Grant and Patricia Fisk. I'd speculated the divorce numbers must be huge among married couples who lost a child.

"Which house was theirs?" I asked, choosing to ask her instead of looking at my notes.

"Do you see the house directly across from us?"

I turned around and looked.

"Yeah."

"It's on that side of the street, two houses up from that one. It's a light blue house."

"Do any of the Greesons' old neighbors still live next to them?"

"Yeah, the Osbournes live one house past the Greesons' old place. They've been here longer than we have. Those families were pretty close. The Osbournes had a son who was best friends with Matt."

"Thank you so much for your time," I said, with plans on heading up the street.

"You said this might be related to a child's murder in the Bay Area?"

"Possibly. That's what I'm trying to find out."

"What was the name of that kid?"

"Ronnie Fisk," I said. "I was hired by their family and now it's brought me to Sacramento."

"Good luck. And be safe. There's a lot of bad people out there."

I was tired of being told to be safe. Not that I was going to tell this helpful woman that.

"I will," I said.

"Take care," she said and walked back into her house.

I could hear the turn of the lock as I started to walk away.

～

"We're not buying anything."

That's how I was greeted when I knocked on the Osbournes' front door. They didn't even open it, just shouted from behind.

"I'm not selling anything," I responded.

"Then what are you here for?"

"I'm investigating the murder of Matt Greeson," I said.

"What are you, a cop?"

"A private investigator."

I could hear two people arguing.

The door opened and I saw what I presumed to be a husband and wife. They both had gray hair and looked similar to each other in the way that only older couples could.

Not that they were all that old. Mid-sixties I'd have guessed.

"What's your name?" the woman asked.

"Quint Adler," I said, and showed her my identification.

"Matt died a long time ago. What are you doing here now?"

"I'm investigating another child's murder and think they might be connected."

That got their attention.

"For real?"

"Yes."

The woman looked at her husband who shook his shoulders in defeat.

"Why don't you come inside?"

She appeared to be the more talkative and accepting of the two.

"Thanks," I said. "I won't take up too much of your time."

I followed them inside. They had me sit on a love seat and took the couch opposite me.

"You said your name was Quint?" the woman asked.

"Yes."

"I'm Mary Beth Osbourne and this is my husband Carl."

"Pleasure to meet you two."

"Where did this other murder take place? In Sacramento as well?"

"No, it took place in Berkeley."

"Really? That's pretty far away. Why do you think they might be related?"

I had been forthright with most people I interviewed, but I wasn't ready to talk about my current theory except with people I knew. So I avoided it.

"Just some similarities is all."

"When did this boy in Berkeley go missing?" Carl asked.

"In 2001. Two years before Matt Greeson was killed."

"Two years and a hundred miles apart. You sure the two are related?"

"To be honest, I'm not sure. That's what I'm here to find out. Are there any details you can tell me about Matt's murder that might help me?"

Mary Beth spoke this time.

"It's been a long time and we went over this with the police back then."

"I understand. I'm just wondering if there's anything you may look back on now as suspicious."

"Like what?"

"I don't know. Like the house was being painted when Matt went missing. Or, a creepy cousin happened to be living there at the time."

"No creepy cousins. No painters," Carl Osbourne said.

He wasn't too enthusiastic about my visit.

"I heard your son was close to Matt."

"Our son's name is Rob and they were best friends," Mary Beth said.

"Did Rob hang out with Matt on the day he went missing?"

I didn't have nearly the information that I did on Ronnie's case, only what Rick Shard had written down for me. So I had to probe.

"Well, they went to school together that day so I'm sure they hung out then. Plus, they were both on the basketball team."

My heart rate began to accelerate.

"Matt played basketball?"

The little information that Rick had written down hadn't mentioned that he'd played basketball. Not that he would have any idea that this held interest for me.

"That's what my wife just said. Are you hard of hearing, son?"

"Sorry. It's just that in the other murder I'm investigating, that kid played basketball too."

"Yeah, those two and twenty million other kids."

Carl was right. It was a tedious connection at best. And yet, basketball seemed to come up more often than it should have. Or, was that just my imagination running wild?

"What was the name of the school that Rob and Matt went to?"

"Will C. Wood Middle School," Mary Beth said.

"Is there anything else you can tell me?" I asked.

"Sorry, it's been so long. And to be honest, we didn't know much to begin with."

"I understand. Is there any way I could get your son's phone number?"

Carl spoke next and I knew I wasn't going to like it.

"How about you give us a business card and we'll let him decide if he wants to call you?"

"That's fine," I said.

I pulled a card out and set it on the table.

"I'll be going now. Thank you for your time."

"You're welcome," Mary Beth said.

A grunt was all that came from Carl's mouth.

I didn't see the point of going house to house anymore. The woman at the first house hadn't mentioned any other families that had lived on the street eighteen years ago.

And while Carl was right about millions of kids playing basketball, I couldn't just let that connection drop.

I put Will C. Wood Middle School in my GPS and started off in that direction.

I arrived eight minutes later, finding a spot in a tiny, almost empty, parking lot.

It's a dead giveaway that you're at a middle school and not a high school. Nobody can legally drive in middle school so the parking lots are always much smaller.

I started walking towards the front and saw a picture of a Spartan, the school's mascot. A student was walking by and I asked him where the main office was. He pointed me in the right direction.

A minute later I was standing outside, not sure exactly what I was going to say.

Hi, I'm investigating a murder from 18 years ago. What was your basketball coach's name?

Looked like I was going to be making things up on the fly. I was buzzed into the room and was greeted by a pig-tailed middle schooler sitting behind the main desk. She probably got some extra credit for working there.

"Can I help you?" she asked.

I came up with a quick idea.

"I was wondering if you guys carry old yearbooks here?"

She looked at me, perplexed.

"Hmmm, I'm not sure. Hold on a second."

An older - well, who wouldn't be - woman appeared a minute later.

"How are you?" she asked.

"Good, thanks. I was wondering if you have any old yearbooks I could look through?"

"Were you a student here?"

If there ever was a time for a white lie, it was at that moment. I certainly couldn't tell the truth.

"I was. Loved it here."

"What years?"

This was where my house of cards might fall apart. Matt Greeson went to school here in 2003, and if I pretended to be a student during that year, I'd be thirty-one or thirty-two years old. In real life, I was forty-two.

Here came the moment of truth.

"2003," I said.

She looked at me and didn't do an immediate double-take which I took as a good sign.

"Hold on a second. Let me call the library. I think they might carry all the old ones."

The older woman walked back to her office and the young middle schooler stared at me.

"So, you were here in 2003? That makes you, what thirty-one or so?"

"Yup. We can't all age gracefully."

She grinned at me like she was in on the joke.

"So who was your favorite teacher?" she asked.

"I liked so many of them."

"Name one."

I'd finally met my match. I was being confronted by the Nancy Drew of Will C. Wood Middle School.

"I liked Smith," I said.

"Surprised you didn't say, Jones," she retorted.

If this wasn't putting my entire plan at risk, I'd probably have enjoyed this little back and forth. The other woman returned and looked at us both as if she could sense something was amiss. Neither I nor the middle-schooler said anything.

"The library has every yearbook going back to when we opened."

"Great. Thanks so much."

"Do you need me to escort you there?" she asked.

"No, I'll find it. I appreciate your help."

"Actually, I was just being nice. We are required to do that now."

"Alright."

"I'll be outside in one minute. You can wait for me there," she said, walking back to her office.

The pig-tailed Nancy Drew looked at me one last time.

"You should pick up some anti-aging cream. Might make you look younger."

"You should become a detective when you grow up. Goodbye."

I left the office, laughing at my interaction with the young lady.

I felt like a child again, having to be escorted to the library. Schools sure had changed since I was a kid. I knew the reason why but didn't want to think about it.

We arrived at the library and she didn't leave my side until I stepped foot inside.

I approached the front desk, which was being helmed by a stereotypical librarian, an older woman with oversized, rectangular glasses. Some stereotypes were still true and I think older librarians often fit the bill.

"The main office sent me here. I wanted to look at an old yearbook," I said.

"No problem. What year?"

"2003."

"2003-2004 or 2002-2003?"

That hadn't crossed my mind. He was killed in November of 2003, so the yearbook I was looking for was 2003-2004.

"03/04," I said.

"Okay, I'll be right back."

She didn't do a double-take, which got me thinking. Maybe older people just knew I was young and couldn't tell if I was thirty-two or forty-two, while young people could tell there was no way I was in my early thirties.

The librarian returned with the yearbook a few minutes later.

"Thanks," I said. "I'll have this back to you in no time."

"No problem. You can sit at any of the desks you'd like."

I nodded at her and found a desk in the corner.

I started flipping through the yearbook, trying to find the section on sports. Once there, I made my way to the pages on basketball. There were four pages in total. Girls 7th grade, Girls 8th grade, Boys 7th grade, and Boys 8th grade.

It really made things hit home. These were boys, not men. Way, way, way too young to be taken from this earth.

I flipped to Boys 8th grade where there was a picture of around twelve kids and two adults who must have been the coaches. I looked down at the names and saw Matt Greeson.

He was in the front row on the far left and appeared to be the shortest boy on the team. I didn't know if it meant anything, but Ronnie Fisk had also been the smallest on his. This was another recurring theme. Several of the fifteen kids had been very small for their grade. Especially the middle schoolers.

I put that information away for a later date.

Next, I looked at the coach's names.

Under Assistant Coach, the name was Doug Bouman. Under Head Coach, it said Guy Polk.

Unlike Willard Middle School, they had two coaches.

Both were young men back then, probably in their mid-twenties.

I grabbed my phone and took a picture of the basketball team.

Before I returned the yearbook, I went to the index and looked if Matt Greeson was in any more pictures. There were only two more and he was, once again, the shortest in each of the pictures.

Could it be that the killer had a slight build and had to choose smaller 7th and 8th graders to ensure he'd prevail in any struggle?

Just another in my long line of unanswered questions.

I walked back to the front and returned the yearbook.

"Is that it?" the librarian asked.

"One quick question. I played basketball here back in the day. Do you happen to know who the coach is currently?"

"I'm sorry, I don't. But it seems like we have a new coach every year or two, so it's not going to be the same coach as when you were here."

"Got it. Thanks for your help," I said.

I walked out of the library and made my way to the parking lot.

～

It was only two p.m. and yet I felt like I'd already had a full day.

No rest for the wicked, however. I was only in Sacramento for one day and I didn't have any time to waste.

The other kid who was killed lived ten minutes from the school so I set my GPS to it.

His name had been Jeremy Stacks.

I pulled up to Atwater Street, the street he'd lived on. There were only four houses on the small little road. I hoped to find something that blew this case wide open.

～

Forty-five minutes later I was leaving Atwater Street dejected.

Unlike Matt Greeson's neighbors on Pearson Way, my questions about Jeremy Stacks did not prove beneficial.

The first neighbor I talked to was outwardly rude and wouldn't even tell me if anyone still lived on the block from when Jeremy Stacks died. The second neighbor was merely standoffish, and it took me five minutes to find out that he'd only moved to the street five years ago. The third neighbor had lived here for twenty-three years but refused to say much about Jeremy Stacks's murder. He did tell me that Jeremy Stacks's parents had moved years ago, which made knocking on their old home irrelevant.

He didn't remember if Jeremy played basketball.

I hadn't received a call back from Walter Shard, so I decided to head back to the Bay Area. If he put me in touch with someone from the Sacramento police, I could do that over the phone.

I couldn't decide if this trip had proved fruitful to my investigation.

I guess time would tell.

CHAPTER 19

The traffic leaving Sacramento was brutal.

Just as it had been in San Francisco the previous day.

The most intense part of the storm still hadn't arrived, but the freeways didn't know any better. Their oil loosened up after that first batch of rain which led to a few accidents that had me stuck in Sacramento for far too long.

Once I arrived back home, the sun had gone down and the streets were nasty. I wasn't going anywhere.

Or so I thought.

I looked at my phone and had missed a text from Hank on my drive home. He had the information I'd asked for and wanted to know where to send it. I texted him back with my office fax number, not having one at my apartment.

I could get my car from the parking garage and drive the quarter-mile or I could just say screw it, put on a jacket with a hood, and walk to the office.

I chose the latter, grabbing a satchel I had to ensure the papers Hank sent me wouldn't get wet.

A few minutes later, I was taking the elevator down to the ground floor and heading south on North Main Street.

~

When I arrived at the office, my gray puffy jacket was wet, but it had done its job of keeping me dry.

The fax from Hank, another in a long line of firsts at my new office, was sitting gently in the tray. The screen said that twenty-four pages had come through.

I tossed the cover page in the garbage and looked at the first page.

It was a typed note from Hank.

"Here you go, Quint. I was able to eliminate some of the cases that I received. I tossed anyone eleven years old and younger as well as anyone sixteen or older. I know you are the most suspicious of middle schoolers, aged thirteen and fourteen, but I included twelve and fifteen-year-olds just to be sure I didn't miss any. These are all the cases from San Francisco and most of the ones from the cities east of Walnut Creek, stopping at Fairfield. These go from March to December of 2002. There are a few cities I haven't been able to get to yet, but I'm working on it. Unfortunately, I have not been able to get the list of people arrested around March of 2002. Hopefully, those will come soon."

I flipped through the pages and was once again impressed by what Hank was able to procure.

I placed them in my satchel, locked the office behind me, and set back towards my apartment.

～

There was no question.

I'd never spent as much time "studying" for anything in my entire life as I had for Ronnie's case. Not the SAT. Not any college final. Not even my private investigator's license test.

There were very few things I'd ever known more about than the murder of Ronnie Fisk. And still, I hadn't learned the things that really mattered. Who? Why? How?

On my computer, I inputted all the information Hank had faxed me. I now had almost thirty-five cases of missing or deceased kids that occurred in the Bay Area from June 2001 to December 2002.

I started focusing on the new batch.

And none fit the MO of Ronnie's death. Not several. Not one or two. None.

There were some deaths by gunshot. A few by stabbings. A few they feared were gang-related. None were deaths by strangulation. And only one was found in a body of water, a death in which the coroner said it was likely a drowning.

I wasn't surprised and this wasn't a case of Hank gathering the wrong info.

Instead, it helped me confirm that the killer hadn't just moved to a different part of the Bay Area to continue murdering children.

The potential reason why was now staring me in the face. He may have moved on to Sacramento by then.

It's true, Ryan Greeson's death wasn't until 2003, but the killer easily could have been lying low after the murders of late 2001 and early 2002.

One by one, I started eliminating all the new cases Hank had found. I also took the step of officially ruling out the murders before September 2001 and after February 2002.

After reducing it down, I know had eight cases from October to February of the 01/02 winter, I also added the cases from 2003: Ryan Greeson and Jeremy Stacks.

That left me with ten cases that I felt were very similar to Ronnie's.

First and foremost, these were now all thirteen and fourteen-year-olds. None were shot and none were stabbed. Some were confirmed strangulations. Some causes of death were undetermined. Some were found in bodies of water. And some were never found.

I'm not saying my conclusions were perfect. A few of the ones remaining may not have had anything to do with Ronnie.

I was confident that I wouldn't come to regret the murders I'd excluded. I was as certain as certain could be that they were not done by the same man.

Besides the fact that they were in middle school, what connected all of these kids?

Was it basketball?

I'd found out earlier in the day that Ryan Greeson had played the sport. So had a few others who died in the winter of 2001 and 2002. And that was the time that middle school basketball was played. The season began in early November and went until late February or early March.

One problem with my theory was that many of the kids hadn't played basketball. Of the ten cases, five had been on their team. Fifty percent was a sizable number, but it was hardly 100%.

I started asking myself some follow-up questions as I was apt to do.

How many people play on a basketball team? Twelve.

How many students went to an average middle school? I was guessing, but let's say six hundred, three hundred or so of which were female. So that left three hundred boys. Twelve into three hundred was only one in every twenty-five kids.

That was four percent. For my cases, it was fifty percent. This was far from scientific, but a more than ten times difference couldn't be ignored. I had to spend more time following up this angle. There was no question about that.

My mind continued to wander and I shuddered at a terrifying scenario.

What if someone - a coach, a teacher, or another adult in the community - was attending basketball games in hopes of choosing their next victim.

If that were the case, it wouldn't just be the players who were at risk. Any middle schooler who attended the games could potentially be in harm's way.

I needed to find out if any of the other murdered kids had attended basketball games before they disappeared.

I couldn't tell if I was grasping at straws or was genuinely on to something.

One thing I did know is that a pit was starting to form in my stomach.

CHAPTER 20

When I awoke the next morning, the pit had not gone away. If anything, it had grown stronger.

I raised my blinds and saw the rain had picked up. It wasn't pouring just yet, more of a heavy drizzle, but in my mind, it served as an unpleasant foreboding.

I put a K-cup into my Keurig and was having my first cup of coffee a few minutes later. Oftentimes, I'd go to a local coffee shop for the first of the day, but the nasty weather convinced me to stay inside.

It was just before seven a.m. and too early to start on my plan for the day: Asking the loved ones of the missing kids if their sons attended basketball games before they went missing. An unenviable task if there ever was one.

I didn't want to arouse their suspicions, but I didn't know how else to get my information. What I didn't want is a rumor to start that someone involved in middle school basketball was now suspected in some long-ago murders.

I'd have to tread lightly and not give away too much info.

As I thought more about it, my plans began to change. Even if a relative knew that their murdered loved one had attended some basketball games, they'd never remember which teams they'd played against. It had been twenty years.

What I needed was to find some of the schedules. If I could get my hands on two or three of these, I could narrow down the teams that each of these middle schoolers played. And then focus on the teams in common.

The next half-hour or so was spent on the internet with nothing to show for it.

I wasn't surprised.

Even high school basketball schedules from twenty years ago would have been difficult to find. Discovering middle school schedules online would have been a minor miracle. And it wasn't to be.

That information would have to come from a family member.

I didn't like it, but I knew where I had to start.

"Hello?" the high-pitched voice of Patricia Fisk said.

"This is Quint again. I only have one quick question for you."

"What?"

If a word could be a snarl, I just got it.

"Did you happen to keep any of Ronnie's mementos? Specifically, I'm trying to find the schedule of his eighth grade basketball season."

"That's an odd request," she said. "Is there something I should know?"

I already knew this day was going to be full of white lies, so I guess starting now was as good a time as any.

"Nope, just following up on all possibilities and I want to see which teams Ronnie played that year."

"And then what? Go school by school and try to find students from twenty years ago and then contact them to find out if they went to a basketball game that there's no way they will remember, but still ask them if they saw someone suspicious talking to Ronnie?"

It belonged on the Mt. Rushmore of run-on sentences, but I couldn't tell Patricia that and alienate her further.

"I'm just trying to examine each and every avenue," I said.

"Maddie told me you were only doing this for a week. What changed?"

"Your other daughter hired me for a second week."

"I'm going to have a talk with Evelyn."

"I really only called for this one question. If you didn't save the schedules, I'll get out of your hair."

I heard her exhale and I think she realized she was being combative.

"I'm sorry, but we don't. We did save a few mementos, obviously, but a basketball schedule was not one of them."

I thought of something else. The Sacramento middle school yearbook didn't have the schedule of their 8th-grade basketball team. It doesn't mean that's true of every yearbook.

"How about yearbooks?"

"Yeah, we did save those."

"Do you know who would have them?"

"It would be Grant. When I moved, we kept all of Ronnie's belongings in Berkeley."

"I'll call him. Thanks for your time."

"Are you making progress?" Patricia asked, her voice having lost its earlier venom.

"I'm not sure," I said honestly. "Maybe."

"Sorry for being bitchy," she said. "If you really do discover something, will you please call me back?"

"I will. I promise."

"Thanks," she said and hung up.

I was about to call Grant.

SHIT!

I suddenly remembered what I had on the docket for this morning. Tailing Marjorie Ballard's husband.

How had I forgotten?

The answer was obvious. This potential philanderer was at the bottom of my priorities list.

There wasn't a single part of my being that wanted to follow this guy around, but I'd signed a contract. In a world of shady P.I.s, I wanted my word to count.

I was going to do what I'd agreed upon.

On the plus side, most of my day was already going to be spent making phone calls. There was no reason I couldn't do those while stuck in my car, waiting for Bruce Ballard.

That doesn't mean I had to like it.

I looked at my cell phone and it read 7:55 a.m.

My call to Grant would have to wait.

~

By 8:40 a.m., I was parked down the street from the Ballards' spectacular home. I knew he was an architect, but the home was truly breathtaking and I couldn't have imagined the price tag.

At 8:52 a.m., I saw a man leaving the house. I was a decent distance away, but the man looked to be around the same height and weight as myself. I looked back down at the information Marjorie had given me. Bruce Ballard was forty-four years old, six foot two and two hundred pounds. Almost identical to yours truly, except that I was a few years younger.

He was wearing a gray, fitted suit with a bright red tie.

I followed Ballard from his house at a great distance. I knew where his architecture firm was, so while I didn't want to lose him, it wasn't the end of the world if I did. Unless he was hitting up his mistress's house on his way to work. If that were the case and I lost him, I was inept at my new job.

I didn't lose him and arrived at the firm less than five minutes later.

As I pulled in, I was greeted with two signs. *"BALLARD ARCHITEC-TURE"* in big letters on top of the oval-shaped building. And right below that, *"BRUCE BALLARD, FOUNDER."* I parked a good deal away and watched him pull into one of the parking spots directly in front of the building.

The perks of being the founder.

Bruce got out of his car and walked straight into the office. I had nothing to be alarmed about thus far. He'd driven directly from his home to his work.

I changed parking spots so I was a little bit closer to the front entrance. I parked behind another car that was able to shield me.

And while I waited, I brought up an email that I'd sent to myself with some contact numbers.

It's almost like I was the one cheating on Marjorie Ballard, with the Ronnie Fisk case.

Before I called anyone from the list, I dialed Grant Fisk's phone number.

"Hey, Quint."

I wondered if everyone from the Fisk family now had my phone number saved.

"Grant, do you have Ronnie's yearbooks?"

"Yeah, I do."

A terrible thought came to mind. Would the Fisks have received a yearbook with Ronnie having died midway through the year?

"Hate to ask, but did you guys get an 8th-grade yearbook?"

"Yes, we did. Willard Middle made sure we got one. In fact, there was a page dedicated to Ronnie."

"That's nice to hear, Grant."

"That's not why you called, though."

"No, it's not. Can you check to see if they have the basketball schedule listed?"

I thought I'd get the fifth degree, but it wasn't to come.

"Sure," he said. "Give me a minute."

I looked towards the entrance to Ballard Architecture, but nothing was going on.

"You there, Quint?"

"I'm here."

"No schedule. A picture of the kids with the coach. And then a few in-game photos. That's it."

"Alright. Thanks, Grant."

"That's it?"

"For now, yeah. I'll be in touch soon."

"Take care," Grant said and hung up.

No luck thus far.

I looked back down at the first number on the email to myself.

Polly Williams. She was the mother of Adam Williams, who went missing on November 28th, 2001, from the city of Castro Valley. It was about twenty miles southeast of Berkeley. Adam had been found strangled and left in a river. Along with Todd Zobrist, these were the two cases with the most in common with Ronnie.

I dialed the number.

"Hello, this is Polly."

At that moment, it hit me just how difficult these phone calls were going to be.

"Hi, Polly. My name is Quint Adler and I'm a private investigator. I was hired by a client to look into his son's death twenty years ago. I've found some similarities between his death and your son Adam's. Can I ask you a few questions?"

There was a long pause.

"Yeah, I guess so."

"Thank you," I said, making sure to keep my eyes on the entrance, just in case Bruce Ballard was on the move. "Did Adam play basketball?"

"No, but he loved the sport. He tried out for the team but was the last cut. I think his being short finally caught up with him."

I knew from his file that Adam Williams was small, but hearing it from his mother helped it hit home. This had become more than just a recurring theme.

"Did he go to the games even though he didn't make the team?"

"Yes. I think he went to almost all of them."

Bingo.

Since Adam didn't play on the team, I would have had no knowledge that he went to the games. This was important information, without question.

"I know this will sound weird, Mrs. Williams, but is there any way you kept a schedule of the team?"

"Maybe if Adam had made the team, but obviously not since he wasn't on it."

"Of course not. I just thought I'd ask."

"What exactly is this about? Why would a basketball team that Adam wasn't even on have anything to do with his murder?"

While I'd already told myself that white lies were inevitable, there were times that telling the truth was the best course of action. Maybe, by being honest, I'd jar something loose in Polly Williams' memory.

"I've noticed that a few kids who went missing back then either played basketball or attended the games."

"That's unsettling, to say the least."

"I'm just trying to see if it's an angle to pursue."

"What angle, exactly?"

"Maybe these kids were picked out at basketball games."

"God forbid," she said.

"I may well be barking up the wrong tree."

"I kind of hope you are."

I understood her viewpoint. No one wanted to think their son was being observed, especially while innocently watching a sport he loved.

"Who's the boy you are investigating?" she asked.

"His name was Ronnie Fisk."

"I've never heard of him. You really think their deaths are related?"

"I think it's possible. I'm just investigating every loose end and that includes this basketball angle."

"You're scaring me."

Even though it wasn't intentional, I felt like an asshole.

"Don't be scared, Polly. It's probably nothing."

"If you say so."

"I'll be in touch, alright."

"Okay," she said meekly.

I could tell it was time to get off the phone.

"Take care," I said and hung up.

While I didn't get the schedule I desired, I did find out that another child was interested in basketball. And had attended most, if not all, of the games. While far from conclusive, my theory was gaining momentum.

The next two calls included being hung up on and a disconnected number. I had no idea how long it had been since Hank had updated these phone numbers. For all I knew, these were cell phone numbers from almost twenty years ago.

The reason I'd only called two more people was that Bruce Ballard had walked out of his office at one point. He sat there, alone, talking on his cell phone for several minutes. I had to keep my attention on him and didn't risk calling anyone.

At one point, his eyes darted in my direction, but I was blocked by the car in front of me. There was no way he'd been able to see my face.

It was a busy parking lot with people coming and going at all times. Still, I decided once he went back inside, I'd move to a different vantage point. There was no reason to take any chances.

I didn't want to read too much into his phone call, but it was spent smiling and laughing, a devious look on his face. If someone told me he was flirting, I wouldn't have been surprised.

Mercifully, he ended the call and went back inside.

I looked at my phone. I still had a good twenty minutes left on my morning shift. With Ballard back inside, I decided to call the next person on my list. Abigail Yount.

She was the mother of Christian Yount who went missing on January 9th. His body was never found. Christian was thirteen years old.

"Abigail Yount speaking."

"Hi, Mrs. Yount. My name is Quint Adler and I'm investigating the disappearance of a boy in Berkeley twenty years ago."

"If this is about Christian, I have nothing to say to you."

I blurted the first thing I could think of.

"I'm trying to catch a killer," I said.

"You're twenty years too late. You can't change the past."

And with that, I was hung up on for a second time.

I knew going in this wasn't going to be easy, but it was even harder than I'd expected. The first call with Polly Williams was the only one where I'd learned anything. After that, two hangups and a wrong number.

As I looked down at my list of names, deciding who to call next, my phone lit up with an incoming call.

I usually wouldn't answer if I didn't recognize the number, but when you're conducting an investigation, you never know who might be calling.

"Hello," I answered.

"Hey Quint, this is Officer Picker of the San Ramon PD."

"Thanks for calling."

"Are you free today?"

"I can be. What's up?"

"Can you come by the office?"

I pulled the phone back from my ear and looked at the time. It was 9:30 and I'd be done with my morning session in ten minutes.

"I can get there in thirty minutes."

"Great. I'll be here."

∼

Ten minutes passed and I couldn't decide if "following" Bruce Ballard was the easiest job ever or the most worthless. I settled on the fact that those two were not mutually exclusive.

At 9:40 a.m. sharp, my one-hour morning shift over, I pulled out of the parking lot of Ballard's architecture firm and headed off towards San Ramon, arriving at the now-familiar police station seventeen minutes later.

I walked in and saw Officer Fiona - I'd never caught her last name - and said hello.

"Is Officer Picker here?"

"He's in the back. He'll be out in a sec."

A minute later, he emerged from the lone door.

"Hey, Quint. Thanks for coming."

"Sure, what have you got for me?"

Part of me thought he might ask to talk somewhere else.

"Why don't you come back here?"

He meant the area behind the front desk, not the door he'd emerged from.

I walked through the small gate once again.

"Have a seat," he said.

I did. Fiona took a seat at Officer Picker's desk as well.

"Since I was on the case twenty years ago, I'll do the talking, but it was Fiona - Officer Trundle - who did the legwork."

The way he introduced Fiona by her first name made me wonder if they were more than just co-workers. I committed Officer Trundle to memory.

"Well, I'm a bit in the dark on what's going on, but thank you for your work, Officer Trundle," I said.

"You have the floor," Picker said to Trundle.

She turned to face me.

"Randall and I started looking over the case file for Todd Zobrist after you left. And I recalled that you were interested in whether Todd played basketball."

"I was."

"Why?"

"In several of the cases I've been looking at, the kids played basketball, as did Ronnie himself."

"What kind of numbers are we talking about?" she asked.

"Five out of the ten played for their basketball team. And at least one more attended games."

I saw their jaws drop and it had nothing to do with basketball.

"Jesus. You think it could be that many kids?"

"Potentially. Shit, there could be zero for all I know."

"But you don't think that."

"No. Not anymore."

"Then I think you'll be interested in what we found."

"What is it?"

"Todd Zobrist didn't play basketball, but he did go to every game. In fact, he attended a game a few days before he went missing."

"Wow. And this just now came to light?"

My words sounded accusatory, but they weren't meant that way.

"It's always been in the case file, but it probably didn't mean anything twenty years ago. A lot of kids went to those games. Having read it now, after you mentioned basketball? That's a different story."

"Makes sense," I said.

"That's when I followed up and gave Todd's mother a call," Officer Trundle said. "And she told me that he went to every game."

"Wow."

It's the only word I could muster. My little theory, which had just taken shape in the last few days, was gaining steam at a feverish pace.

"I asked his mother all the questions you'd expect. Did a stranger ever approach Todd at any of the games? Had Todd ever told her that he was scared of anyone? Things like that. She didn't remember anything like that."

"I'm just a P.I. and might be overstepping my bounds, but can I ask a favor?"

They looked at each other. Officer Picker spoke.

"That's why I invited you over. We're trying to help each other. I'd do anything to help solve a twenty-year-old case. Anything."

I took the second "anything" to mean he'd even work with a P.I.

"Could you get ahold of the schedule for the basketball team that year?"

"I'm sure there's a way," Officer Picker said. "I could go down to the school, find out who was on that team, And contact them or their parents. Someone's got to have it, right?"

"I wouldn't be so confident. I'm trying to do the same thing on my end. Judging by my lack of success, I don't think many people keep their basketball schedules from two decades ago."

"Not that surprising, I guess. What exactly are you going to do with the schedules?"

"My goal eventually is to triangulate them."

They looked on, a little confused.

"What do you mean exactly?" Picker asked.

"Alright, say I get a schedule from one of the teams. There will be twenty games on it or something like that. Not much you can do with that. If I get a second schedule, maybe we'll only have five or six mutual teams that they played. Maybe more, maybe less. I'm just guessing. But if I can get a third schedule, I'd bet we're only talking a few teams they all played."

They both nodded.

"Very smart, Quint, but you're forgetting one thing."

"What's that?"

"Depending on when the kids were killed, there might be quite a bit less than twenty games."

It was a great, albeit heartbreaking, point.

"You're right," I said. "The season lasts from November to February, give or take a few weeks. Ronnie was killed on December 5th. There might be as little as seven or eight games for him."

"This is morbid," Officer Trundle said.

"Sure is. This case is actually getting worse by the day," I said.

"I'm going to head down to Todd's old middle school today and see what I can find out," Officer Picker said.

"And I'll keep you posted from my end," I said.

"Anything else, Quint?"

I was about to overstep my bounds one more time.

"When you go down to the school, I'd keep it on the down-low. Maybe don't wear your blues if you don't have to."

This advice hadn't gone over as well. Officer Picker gave me a menacing stare.

"You don't lack for opinions, do you, Quint? Why exactly?" he asked.

"What if the killer was a coach, a teacher, a principal, or someone affiliated with the school? Rumor might spread quickly that the police were asking questions about a basketball team from twenty years ago. I just don't want to alert the wrong person. And yes, I know that's being overly cautious."

His stare turned into a grudging acceptance.

"I get your point. We'll be subtle. However, it's easier to convince people to do things when we are wearing our blues."

I smiled.

"I get your point also."

"We'll be in touch, Quint. Good luck on your end."

"I have one last question."

"What is it?"

"Are you going to alert any other police departments about this?"

"Not yet. No offense, but your theory is way too flimsy at this point. Maybe that will change. As of now, all we know is that a few of these kids played basketball or went to the games. That's not nearly enough. So, no, we will not be talking to anyone else for the time being."

"Good. I agree with you on every point you made."

"You can get out of here now. I'm tired of taking the advice of a newbie P.I."

I could tell he was half-kidding. Which meant he was also half-serious.

I smiled and exited the room seconds later.

CHAPTER 21

As I drove back towards Walnut Creek, not looking forward to my noon shift following Bruce Ballard around, an idea came to me. Truthfully, I should have thought of it earlier.

I dialed Aaron Everton's phone number as I drove.

"This is Aaron."

"Hey Aaron, this is Quint."

"How's the investigation coming?"

"I may be making some progress, actually."

"Really? I have to say I'm a bit surprised."

"So, I've got a weird question for you."

"Shoot."

"Is there any chance you have the schedule for your and Ronnie's basketball team back in 2001?"

"That is random."

"It's important or I wouldn't ask."

"The answer is no. I mean honestly, how many people keep a sports schedule from their middle school years?"

"Judging by my interactions thus far today, not many," I said.

"I'm sorry I can't help," Aaron said and sounded like he was about to get off the phone. "Wait."

"What is it?" I asked.

"I just thought of something. We had a teammate named Scott Shea and his mother videotaped all the games. Grade school. Middle school. Even High school. And yeah, I know Ronnie was gone by then."

My heart race accelerated slightly.

"Do you know how I can get ahold of Scott or his mother?"

"Well, because of the modern-day technology of Facebook, I know that Scott lives in San Francisco. I believe he's married with no kids. What I don't know is whether he - or his mother - still have the recordings of the games."

"Would you be able to get me his phone number?"

"Yeah, I could do that. I don't have it, but we have some mutual friends. Give me twenty minutes and I'll text it to you."

"Thank you so much, Aaron."

"I'd ask you for more information, but maybe I don't want to know."

"There's a chance your team's basketball games were connected to Ronnie's disappearance."

"Are you kidding?."

"No, I'm not. I've got nothing concrete yet, so please don't go telling anyone that."

"I won't. I'll text you soon with his number."

It was 11:15 when I arrived back in Walnut Creek and I was still forty-five minutes from my second shift watching Bruce Ballard.

I dropped by my office to see if there were any new messages. Fat chance.

I gave my strip mall neighbor, Starbucks, some business and bought a large coffee - sorry, a Venti - that would last me for the next hour.

At 11:50, I headed back towards Ballard's work, which was only five minutes away. As I pulled into the parking lot, I saw a message from Aaron Everton that included a phone number.

While Ronnie's case mattered infinitely more to me than Marjorie and Bruce Ballard, the phone call to Scott Shea would have to wait. I didn't want to be mid-call with him if he drove past me and I had to follow.

Which did happen a few minutes later.

I saw Ballard exit the office and enter his silver Bentley. He backed out and took a left. He'd be passing straight by me. I ducked as he approached, waiting a few seconds till I rose. I looked in my rearview mirror and saw that he was taking a right onto the main road.

I did a quick three-point turn and took the same right that he took.

He was a good hundred yards ahead of me and if I hit a red light, I'd never catch up.

Luckily, I caught a few green lights and was able to get close rather quickly.

After following Ballard at a safe distance for a mile longer, he exited into a little strip mall, very reminiscent of the one I'd just left at my office.

There was a Subway, another Starbucks, and a Kinkos. You couldn't have designed a more stereotypical American strip mall if you tried.

Ballard parked his Bentley in front of the Subway which was, in itself, quite amusing. I took a right and parked down by the Kinkos.

A few minutes later, Ballard emerged with a sandwich and a drink in hand. There were two tables with canopies, but the rain, although still sporadic, was enough to prevent anyone from eating outside, canopy or not.

Ballard took his food to his car and I expected him to head back to the office. Instead, he must have decided to eat it in his Bentley. If I had that car, I probably wouldn't have allowed anyone to eat in it. Certainly not a Subway sandwich that might spill everywhere. But hey, I wasn't a millionaire with an architecture firm and a Bentley. We probably thought differently on a great many things.

Fifteen minutes later, Ballard reemerged from his car and set the remnants of his sandwich and his drink into the garbage. He walked back to his car, reversed out, and got back on the road that brought him there.

I bided my time once again, running the risk of losing him. The alternative, getting caught, was much worse.

Once I got behind him, it was even further than last time. And this time I did hit a red light, causing me to lose him.

Once my light turned green, I accelerated quickly, but still couldn't see him ahead of me. I kept speeding up. Nothing.

I took the exit towards his architecture firm and pulled into the parking lot a minute later. Much to my relief, Ballard's car was parked in his spot and he was walking into the office.

My tailing/following/shadowing game was in need of a lot of work.

I looked at my phone. It was only 12:41. I considered calling Scott Shea, but I decided to wait until this shift was done.

The next nineteen minutes went by at glacial speed.

～

At one p.m., I headed back to the office, picking up a second coffee in the span of an hour.

I walked back to my office and took a seat in my executive chair.

I'd never met Scott Shea but if he was anything like me, he wasn't going to answer a call from a random number. So, I came up with a quick plan.

I texted him the following:

"Scott, my name is Quint Adler and I'm a private investigator. I'm about to call you right now. This is not spam, but it is very important. I hope you'll answer."

I dialed his number a minute later and sure enough, he picked up the phone.

"Is this Quint?"

My plan had worked.

"It is, thanks for answering."

"I think you might have just invented a new business model. The text before the call. And then you pull the old bait and switch once you have them on the line."

I laughed.

"No bait and switch here. What I said in the text was all true."

"I believe you. Are you the same Quint who had a couple of high-profile cases a couple of years back?"

"One and the same. That was before I was a P.I., however."

"Nice to meet a local celebrity."

"Hardly," I said.

"Now I'm curious what possible information you think I might have?"

"Do you remember the name, Ronnie Fisk?"

"How could I forget? You're investigating his murder?"

"I am."

"All these years later."

"Crazy, right?"

"How did that lead you to me?"

"It's complicated, but I talked to Aaron Everton earlier today and he mentioned that your mother videotaped all the basketball games for Willard Middle School in 2001?"

"She did. And you want to view them?"

"I do."

"I think you owe me a little better explanation before I agree to that."

"That's fair. I've found that some other kids who were killed around that time also played basketball. It's a long shot, but I'm trying to find out if basketball could possibly be a connecting point to all of them."

"And you want to watch all the game tapes and see if someone in the stands raises his hand and says, 'I'm the killer!'"

I paused before answering.

Scott beat me to it.

"I'm sorry, that was rude of me. I'll let you answer. What exactly are you trying to get from the videotapes?"

"I think I may have misled you. What I'm trying to find out is every team you guys played that year. I don't need to watch each and every video. In fact, if you happen to have a schedule lying around, I could bypass the videos altogether. Since I haven't been able to pin down a schedule, this seemed like the easiest way."

"Unfortunately, I don't have a schedule."

"You do have the videotapes though, correct?"

"Yeah. My mom gave them all to me a few years back."

"Are they labeled by the date and the team you played?"

"Some, but not all. They all had stickers on them at some point, signifying the date and team we were playing, but not anymore. A lot have fallen off. It's an old-school camcorder so you can see the date on the side of the video recording. Also, you should be able to see the opposing jerseys within seconds, so it wouldn't take too long."

"Do you remember how many games you played?"

"Somewhere between twenty and twenty-four, I'd say."

I was reminded of what Officer Picker had told me. I'd only need the games that Ronnie played in.

"Pains me to say this, but I'll only need the games when Ronnie was still on the team."

"I understand," Scott said somberly.

"And your mother recorded every game? I have to be sure I don't miss one."

"Every single game from eight years old to eighteen years old."

"Very nice of her."

"Yup, she was definitely my biggest fan."

"So, is this a yes? Will you let me watch the videos?"

"Sure."

"Aaron said you live in San Francisco?"

"I do. I'm working till six, though."

I had round three of watching Bruce Ballard from five to six. I'd be going against traffic at that point and could make it into the city pretty quickly.

"I could be out there by 6:30."

"Alright, my address is 747 Divisadero. Call this number when you get here and I'll come down and let you in."

"Thank you very much for this, Scott."

"I must be crazy," he said and hung up.

My five p.m. tail of Bruce Ballard proved as futile as the first two. He left his office at about 5:30 and went directly home. I actually saw Marjorie waiting for him outside of their house when he arrived.

I headed into San Francisco next and it's a good thing I got an early start. The rain was starting to pick up and conditions were ugly on the freeways. People were driving slow, riding their brakes, and it took longer than expected to get into the city. Traffic had been a recurring theme the last few days.

Once I arrived outside, I called Scott Shea. I was greeted by a guy who was at least 6'6", possibly taller, and in excellent shape. He looked like a great athlete. My guess was that basketball was more than just a hobby to him. I don't know if he played past high school, but it wouldn't have surprised me.

"You must be Quint."

"Thanks again for this, Scott."

"Let's go on up," he said.

We walked back up the stairs and I was briefly reminded of Grant Fisk's apartment. It was a bad comparison as Scott's apartment proved spacious with hardwood floors and vaulted ceilings. There were even a couple of jerseys hanging up on the walls.

"Did you play college ball?"

"Yeah. At UC Santa Barbara."

"Was your Mom still recording the games?"

"When she could get down there. Little tougher when you live three hundred miles away."

"Certainly," I said.

Scott was very hospitable. Not everyone who had a stranger in their apartment would have been as welcoming.

We passed a blown-up picture of his wedding.

"My wife. She works till eight. Probably for the best. She'd think I've lost it, letting a stranger in to watch old basketball games."

"Maybe she's right."

He laughed.

"Follow me," Scott said and led me into one of the two bedrooms.

On the ground was an adapter of some sort and there was an old school VCR lying on top of a T.V.

"Keep in mind, this was 2001," Scott said. "It was before everything went digital."

"My parents had a similar setup for my childhood home movies," I said. "I'm not a stranger to old-school camcorders."

"Those were the days," he said.

I looked down at the antiquated videotapes below me. It took me back to my high school days of going to a Blockbuster on a Friday night, wanting to rent a horror movie, but knowing my then-girlfriend would prefer a rom-com. She always won out.

Blockbuster was a big part of my childhood and I'd be lying if I said I didn't miss it.

"These are all the tapes?" I asked.

"Yeah, that should be every game. I counted and there's twenty-four of them."

"Were you able to figure out how many games you played before Ronnie was killed?"

"As you can see, only a few still have the stickers, so you're going to have to watch pretty much all of them anyway."

"No problem."

"I could probably guess. What day was Ronnie killed?"

"December 5th."

He thought about it.

"Probably only eight or nine games. I remember we took like a week or ten days off before we reconvened playing."

"I'm sorry."

"Rough times," he said.

"I'm going to get started," I said.

"Can I ask you one favor?" he asked. "It won't take very long."

"Sure," I said.

"I left some tiny post-it notes here. Can you just attach the date and team we are playing to the ones that don't have them?"

"Of course," I said. "I'm going to have a few questions about team mascots. If I see a Wildcats on the jersey, that won't tell me what school it is."

"Yeah, I get it. I'll be out in the family room if you have any questions."

Forty-five minutes later, I had all the information I'd come for.

I'd pop the videotape in the VCR and wait until I had a clear view of the opposing jerseys. The video was shot from the top of the bleachers and it would occasionally take a few minutes to make out the team mascot's name.

I'd then ask Scott what middle school was the Vikings, or the Dons, or the Cougars.

At one point, I asked him to show me, Ronnie. He had to fast forward to the end of a blowout game in order to find footage of him. It was almost unbearable. He looked tiny on the court and I couldn't help but mourn for the young life lost.

The one time I saw Ronnie shoot the ball, it hit the side of the backboard, nowhere near the rim. It would have been humorous for anyone looking back on old videotapes, something your friends would surely razz you about. Unfortunately, the opportunity to get old and laugh at yourself had been taken from Ronnie.

I'd never wanted to catch his killer more.

Ronnie had only played eight games before he was killed. If there was one positive that had come from this, we'd already eliminated two-thirds of the twenty-four games.

"Thanks, Scott. I appreciate all your help."

"You'll keep me updated on the investigation?"

I'd been asked that repeatedly the last few days. Not that I could blame anyone.

"Of course," I said.

"I hope these videotapes contribute somehow."

"Me too," I said.

A minute later, I walked out the door.

The rain had become worse. And we still weren't in the eye of the storm.

It's almost like the weather was mirroring my investigation.

By that logic, maybe we were getting closer to the truth.

I'm not sure whether that was a good thing or not.

CHAPTER 22

From 8:40 to 9:40 a.m. the following morning, I spent a meaningless hour following Bruce Ballard. In fairness, I was only following him from 8:45 to 8:50 and killed the next fifty minutes sitting in my car, looking out at Ballard Architecture.

I chose to focus on the bright side, happy that four of the six Ballard shifts were now in the bag.

At 9:54 a.m., as I was arriving home, I got an unexpected phone call.

"Hello?"

"Is this Quint Adler?"

"It is."

"My name is Rob Osbourne and I think you talked to my parents a few days back."

I'd met and talked to so many people that it took me a few seconds to place the name. His parents had been the standoffish ones who lived next to the Greesons.

"Yes, I did. You were close with Matt Greeson weren't you?"

"We were inseparable as kids."

"It must have been really tough on you."

"Not sure I've ever fully recovered."

I saw no reason to beat around the bush.

"I'm investigating a murder in the Bay Area and think it might be related to Matt's death."

"That's what my parents said, but they didn't tell me what led you to believe that."

"Both were strangled. Both ended up in bodies of water. Both were fourteen. Both were smaller in stature. And both played basketball."

"Wow. More than I would have expected. My parents insinuated you might be some crackpot."

"I'm not. But that begs the question. Why would you call me back if you thought I was some crackpot?"

"Because, like I said, Matt and I were inseparable. And I've always wondered why he was killed. So, if you were crazy, and I had to hang up, then, oh well. Now I know that won't be necessary."

I'd talked to Rob Osbourne for all of thirty seconds and already trusted him. It was hard to explain. It all was a bit surprising considering his father had been a pain in the ass. Maybe this apple did fall far from the tree.

"No, it won't be necessary," I said.

"I don't know if my parents told you, but I still live in Sacramento. And every day, as I walk by people on the streets, I wonder if maybe today was the day I walked by Matt's killer. Assuming he's still alive."

"I think he is."

"I figured you might," Rob said.

"Maybe investigating each day just makes it feel like he's alive."

"Or, maybe you're intuition is right and he is out there."

"Yup," I said.

That confirmation was all he needed.

"Is there something I could do?" Rob asked. "I'd do anything to increase the chances of catching Matt's killer."

I thought for a few moments.

"You played on the basketball team with Matt, didn't you?"

"Yes. That's twice you've mentioned hoops. Do you think this has something to do with basketball?"

I was so tired of explaining my reasoning to everyone. However, Rob genuinely seemed like he wanted to help. He deserved an explanation.

"I do. Half the kids played basketball. And a few of the others attended games regularly. It's too big a coincidence to overlook."

"I hate to ask, but how many kids are there?"

"As of now, there are ten I'm looking at."

"Fucking A. And you think they were all killed by the same guy?"

"I doubt all ten were, but I do think several might have been."

"My gosh. This is terrible."

"If I'm right..."

"So, what do you need? I don't want to ask a third time."

I thought of the games I'd got from the Scott Shea videos and the games that Officer Picker would hopefully have soon. Rob Osbourne might be able to supply the triangulation I had mentioned.

A team that played both Ronnie and Todd's teams wouldn't be all that surprising, considering they were twenty miles from each other. If it turned out a coach, parent, administrator, etc. also had gone to a game of Matt's in Sacramento two years later? That I'd have a hard time writing off as a coincidence.

"I'd love to know the teams that your basketball team played in 2003 before Matt's death."

"I've still got a few friends who live locally and played on that team with Matt. In fact, one of them still coaches middle schoolers and knows everyone involved around Sacramento."

"That would be great."

"I'll be in touch as soon as I find something."

∼

I called Officer Picker a few minutes before noon, but he had nothing new to share.

I followed Bruce Ballard at lunch and for the second straight day, he went to the same Subway. You had to hand it to this guy.

A $250,000 car and an eight-dollar sandwich.

He ate it in his car again and I kept my distance. I was starting to come around on this whole tailing thing. It had been easy as pie thus far.

Ballard exited his car, threw the wrappings and the drink in the trash, and headed back to work immediately thereafter.

∼

With several hours to kill until my final shift following Ballard, I had a few things to take care of. I went back to my office and noticed the law firm next to me was closed. With the skies getting darker and the rain starting to increase, I guess I couldn't blame them. The parking lot was starting to accumulate some water and would surely flood as it got worse.

The first thing I did was call Paddy Roark with my burner phone.

"Hello?"

"Paddy, it's Quint."

"How's my favorite P.I doing?"

"The information your friend passed on to me might prove invaluable."

"I'm glad to hear it."

"Just figured I'd ask if anyone else got back to you."

"One set of missing kids isn't enough?"

"You've got a point."

"To answer your question, no, nothing else. How's the investigation going?"

"I feel like I've made a lot of progress lately, and yet, not much is happening. Does that make any sense?"

"Stuck in quicksand?"

"A little bit. I'm waiting on some news, including from Sacramento. Then I'll know if I've gone down the wrong rabbit hole."

"And if you went down the right one?"

"Then there is a serial killer out there."

"When you phrase it that way, maybe it would be better if your theory is wrong."

"I've never wanted to be more wrong."

"And yet, part of you wants that professional satisfaction. Right?"

As usual, Paddy had me pegged.

"Yes," I admitted. "I've worked this case so freaking hard. I'd love to have something to show for it, and not just a paycheck."

"You're a P.I., not a miracle worker. Not every case you take on is going to end with wine, roses, and a victory parade."

I laughed.

"The other case I'm working on most certainly will not end that way."

"Wait, you've got a second case? Showoff."

"Hardly. I'm following around a guy whose wife thinks he's cheating on him."

"Sounds terrible."

"For the most part, it is. Although, I'm sure most people would say it's preferable to thinking about dead teenagers."

"I don't know how you do it."

"Because it's playing out like a true-crime podcast, which basically, it is. And I need to find out how it ends."

"Then why are you making small talk with me?"

"This is hardly small talk. Plus, as I said, I'm waiting on a bunch of information right now."

"I'm just giving you shit. I know how hard you are working."

"I'd like to see Dennis in the next few days and thank him personally."

"For what? I sent out that text to those cops. I put you in touch with Rick Shard."

"I'll be sure to let Dennis know that you deserve all the credit."

"Listen, if you're going to be out here, give me a call. I'll see if Dennis is around. Don't forget, you've got a damn big case you're working on. That should take precedence."

"Thanks, Captain Obvious," I said.

"I miss the Quint who was easy to boss around. You don't take my shit anymore."

"When I first met you, I thought you were a remorseless bully. Now I know you're just a big teddy bear."

"I'll let you get away with that."

"But not most people?"

"Something like that."

"Anything else, Quint?"

"No. Thanks again for the information on Sacramento."

"Good luck in the coming days."

"Talk soon, Paddy."

I hung up the phone and decided I owed Emmett Fisk a phone call. Let's hope he could hear me this time. Last time he'd mistaken my voice for a woman's.

"Hello?"

"Hi, Emmett."

"Is this Quint?"

"You can hear me this time. Good."

"Yup, the hearing aids are in."

"Has Hank been keeping you abreast of the investigation?"

"He has. But remember, Quint, I was the one who hired you."

"I know. And I apologize. I can promise you I've been working on Ronnie's case harder than anything I've ever worked on. That doesn't excuse me from forgetting to update you."

"It's okay. Just don't be a stranger from here on in."

"I won't. What exactly has Hank told you?"

"That you think a serial killer might have murdered Ronnie."

"Yes, I think that's a distinct possibility."

"And are you close to catching him?"

"No. I wouldn't say that. Not at all, actually. What I would say is that the next few days are crucial and I'll know more then."

"You're approaching the last few days of your second week. Paid for by my granddaughter."

Evelyn probably deserved a phone call as well.

"If my investigation spills over by a day or two, I'll do it for free. I have to find out where my current theory leads."

"Is that the whole basketball connection?"

"Yes."

"Sounds a little flimsy, but what do I know?"

I didn't like hearing comments like flimsy, but Emmett could say anything he wanted. He'd hired me after all, and more importantly, he'd dealt with this grief for twenty years. He wasn't going to hurt my feelings by doubting the direction of my investigation. I believed in the rationale that brought me to this point.

"We'll know soon," I said. "And maybe I'll have been way off."

"How's the weather in Walnut Creek?" he asked, changing the subject completely.

"Getting worse."

"I've taken your advice and I'll be staying off the roads until this ends."

"Good. I like having you around, Emmett."

"You're not so bad yourself. Now go get investigating."

"I'll call you once a day from here on in. I promise."

"I appreciate it."

"Goodbye, Emmett."

I kicked my legs up on my desk.

What the hell was I supposed to do next?

Yes, I was waiting on potentially game-changing information from Officer Picker and Rob Osbourne, but I didn't like just sitting around. I wanted to be out there, going door-to-door if need be.

But where? I'd already canvassed Ronnie's old neighborhood numerous times. I'd talked to all the neighbors who remained from twenty years ago.

As I debated what to do, my office phone rang. It was way too loud and startled me.

I'd almost forgotten I'd installed it.

"Quint Adler, P.I."

It sounded cheesy when I said it. Maybe I'd get used to it over time.

"This is Marjorie Ballard."

"Hello, Marjorie. What can I help you with?"

"Have you found anything out yet?"

"No, I have not. Your husband has driven from your house to work each morning, to and from lunch around noon, and straight home after work. There's been nothing to raise any suspicions," I said.

I remembered Bruce Ballard's phone call outside his office. Sure, I'd thought he might be talking to a woman, but I had zero evidence, only a sneaking suspicion. That wasn't enough to bring it up, so I said nothing.

"I think I made a mistake by having you follow him around during the workweek. Maybe I was wrong about when those panties found their way into his car. Would you be willing to follow him around this weekend?"

On the one hand, it was already Friday and I'd been looking forward to finishing this forgettable job. On the other hand, this work truly was a piece of cake and I was able to accomplish several things on the Ronnie Fisk front at the same time.

I reminded myself that I wasn't financially stable and couldn't pick and choose my cases just yet.

"I'll take it, Marjorie, on one condition."

"What's that?"

"If something comes up in my other case, that takes precedence."

"What could be more important than a marriage?"

I could have answered in a multitude of ways. How about the murder of a teenager that caused a divorce and ostensibly the ruination of a family? Would that have satisfied Marjorie? Maybe not, actually.

"I'm not going to discuss my other case," I said. "But I assure you that it's very consequential."

"Okay, I'm sorry. Plus, you had that case first so it should take precedence. I agree with your stipulation."

"Alright. We can deal with the finances next time I see you. Why don't you go ahead and text me the times, places he might go, etc."

"Okay. I don't think I got your cell number, though."

I looked down at my desk. Might as well get some more use out of my burner phone.

"It's 925-555-2052."

"I'll send you that information right now."

"And we'll talk on Monday."

"Yes."

I hung up the office phone and buried my head in my hands on my desk. I was tired of talking on the damn phone.

Which brought me back to what I'd been pondering earlier. How could I do more actual investigating?

"THINK!"

I quickly realized I'd yelled out loud what I'd been trying to internalize.

Think. Think. Think.

Finally, after several minutes of introspection, I knew what I had to do. There was something that had been bothering me about this case.

It was time to go ruffle some feathers.

And I was pretty sure Hank was going to hate me for it.

CHAPTER 23

The Berkeley Police Department was an oval-shaped structure located right in the middle of downtown Berkeley. There were long, rectangular glass windows that spiraled around the whole structure. It was oddly reminiscent of the Ballard Architecture building that I'd grown accustomed to over the last few days. I'm not sure Bruce Ballard would like his firm's architecture compared to that of a police department. Not that I cared.

I arrived at 3:00 p.m. There was a very good chance I'd be laughed out of the building - or thrown out - so getting back to Walnut Creek by 4:45 would not be a problem.

I walked through the front door and approached the desk, where no fewer than four police officers stood. This was not San Ramon, that's for sure. Berkeley saw its share of violence and was a fully staffed police department.

A muscular Asian police officer in his thirties asked me, "How can I help you?"

There were a few secretaries milling around, but I'd been approached by one of Berkeley's finest.

"I've got some information on a crime," I said.

His head jolted up, suddenly interested.

"What type of crime?"

"The type of crime that happened twenty years ago," I said.

I was being a bit snide. Sometimes, I couldn't help it.

"Is it a specific crime you are talking about?"

"Yes. The murder of Ronnie Fisk, which happened on December 5th, 2001."

He looked me over as if sizing up if I could have been the killer, here to confess to my crime.

"What information do you have?" he asked.

"This is where I have a request of my own."

"What might that be?"

"I'd like to talk to someone who worked the case. Not an officer who read the case file after the fact. A Berkeley police officer who was on the force in 2001."

"Hold on a minute," he said.

One minute turned into two which turned into five. Finally, a police officer who was obviously nearing retirement made his way towards the front.

"I'm Paul Piercy," he said. "I heard you're looking for a graybeard."

He was living up to his self-given nickname with gray hair that dominated his scalp and closely manicured stubble. There were a few brown specs thrown in, but gray held the big edge. He was probably around six feet with a slight pudge. Another thing, like the gray hair, that father time seemed to slowly add over the years.

"I'm Quint. Did you work the Ronnie Fisk case?"

"Yes, I did."

"So, you're a detective?"

"I was back then. I've been relegated to a regular old police officer in my old age."

I gave him a slight smile.

"Do you have somewhere we can talk?" I asked.

"We could arrange something."

He had the same distrustful expression as his fellow officer.

"Just so you know, this is not a confession. I didn't kill those kids."

His expression turned sober.

"Did you say, kids? As in plural?"

I saw a few officers looking over at us.

I'd told Officer Picker I thought we should try to keep this on the down-low. I'd also agreed we shouldn't involve any other police departments.

At this point, I was breaking both of those.

"Let's take a walk," I said. "I'd rather not talk in some interrogation room or out here where everyone can hear us."

I could tell he didn't know what to make of me and my odd request.

"Take it or leave it?" I asked.

"Fine. Let's go for a walk," Officer Piercy said.

We exited the front entrance and took a left down Martin Luther King Jr. Ave. We passed by a coffee shop.

"Would you prefer a coffee?" he asked.

"No, I'm trying to avoid having this conversation in front of others."

"What exactly is this conversation we're supposed to be having?"

It was time to get to the crux of why I was there. And I knew Officer/Detective Piercy wasn't going to like what I said next.

"I wanted to talk about how badly the Berkeley Police Department fucked up the Ronnie Fisk case."

I was expecting a reprimand. None came. In fact, his expression told me he agreed.

"Well, we never caught his killer, so it would be hard to disagree with you."

"It's not the end result that I'm referring to."

"What then?"

We took a left on a side street. Officer Piercy was a foot in front of me and I let him lead the way. We kept walking in silence as a group of four people passed us on the street.

"Many young boys went missing in the weeks and months both before and after Ronnie Fisk. And yet, the police reports rarely ever mentioned the possibility of a serial killer. That's the fuck up I'm talking about."

"Do you have some evidence that I'm not privy to?"

"I doubt it."

"Then what? A hunch? Surely, you must have something. If not, you got a lot of balls walking into a police department and throwing shade on an investigation."

It was time to throw my cards on the table.

"There were no less than fifteen young boys who went missing from June 2001 to June 2002. Now, I don't think all fifteen of those cases are related to Ronnie, but I do believe that six to eight might have been."

"That's a huge leap to make. I'll ask again. Do you have any evidence of this?"

"All circumstantial."

"Anything you'd like to share?"

I was not here to give away everything I'd learned. At least, not at this point in my investigation. I had to give him a little red meat, however.

"Have you heard the name Todd Zobrist? Or Adam Williams?"

"It's been twenty years. You'll have to remind me."

"They were both killed in the winter of 2001/2002. Adam was killed in November, a week before Ronnie. And Todd was killed in mid-January. Like Ronnie Fisk, they were both strangled. Also like Ronnie, their bodies were dumped into bodies of water."

I looked at Paul Piercy's face and it was hard to judge his reaction. He'd given me a lot more rope than I could have expected. For the time being, I considered him an ally.

"What did you come here for? To find out more information? To gloat?"

That last question hit me hard. Did it sound like I was gloating because I knew more information? Sure, I'd worked my ass off on this case, but my goal was to catch Ronnie's killer. Not to sound like a cocky asshole.

"I'm absolutely not here to gloat," I said. "I want to find out why none of these cases were followed up on?"

"But they were," he said.

It was not the response I was expecting.

"Excuse me?"

Officer Piercy looked at me intently for what seemed like the third time. I think he was trying to gauge if he could trust me.

"I'll get to your questions if you answer a few of mine first," Officer Piercy said.

"What do you want to know?"

"Why are you so interested in this case twenty years later?"

I let a young couple bypass us before answering his question.

"Ronnie Fisk's grandfather hired me to investigate the murder."

"I should have known," he said. "You're the guy who has been working with Hank Tressel?"

"Yes. Is it all over town?"

"No, I wouldn't say that. It's just that police officers have a way of hearing about things. No one has filed a complaint against you, so you're staying on the right side of the law. That isn't always easy when you are investigating a case that's two decades old."

"I've pissed a few people off," I said.

"Well, they haven't come to me."

Officer Piercy and I had a good back and forth. Maybe it was too early to say I could trust him, but it was trending in that direction.

"Who have you interviewed?"

"If they are a part of this case then I've interviewed them," I said.

"Ty Montgomery?"

"Yup. Not sure he liked me."

"I interviewed him way back when. He didn't like me either."

I tried to visualize the initial police reports. I seemed to remember an Officer Piercy in the notes. Or was my mind playing tricks on me again?

"I don't think he murdered Ronnie," I said.

"Neither do I. Some of the BPD did, though."

"Yeah, I know. I've read all those reports dozens of times."

"Sounds like a slight exaggeration."

"Very slight. Trust me, I've read them all many, many times."

"How is Hank Tressel?"

His tone gave him away. I could tell he loathed the man.

"You're not friendly with Hank?"

"No. He was an asshole."

"He's a good guy to have on your side," I said.

"That doesn't repudiate what I said."

I smiled for the first time.

"No, it doesn't."

We took another left turn, our third. My guess was that we'd be taking a fourth soon and ending up back in the vicinity of the police station.

"Now that you know who I am, would you mind telling me what you meant?"

"In regards to what?"

"You said the cases I mentioned were followed up on, Todd Zobrist and Adam Williams. I didn't see that in any of the police reports. In fact, the only way I knew about these other missing kids was because Hank himself had done some research."

Officer Piercy came to a halt. He leered at me, once again trying to get a read on whether he could trust me. He obviously had something to get off his chest.

"I consider myself a good judge of character," he said.

"I pride myself on the same trait."

He stood there for twenty seconds, not saying a word, obviously deep in thought.

"Do you promise what I'm about to tell you will stay between us?"

"Yes. I promise," I said. "Is that enough for you?"

He nodded.

"If I've pegged you correctly, then yes, it is."

"I'm a man of my word," I said.

Officer Piercy looked borderline excited to tell his story.

"Fuck it! Old Byron Grady is dead now, so I guess it's time it finally came to light."

The name rang a bell, but I couldn't place it offhand.

"What came to light?" I asked.

"First, I need a few more answers from you."

We were having our own little dance, each trying to get information from the other.

"Ask away," I said.

"Do you really think these other kids were killed by the same guy who killed Ronnie?"

"At this point, I think it's better than a 50/50 chance."

"My God," Officer Piercy said. "I really hope you're mistaken."

"So do I."

There was another extended silence as he absorbed my 50/50 comment.

"Who was Byron Grady, Officer Piercy? I know I've come across the name."

"If we are going to do this, you might as well call me Paul."

"Alright. Paul, it is."

"This is something I've wanted to talk about for twenty years. Maybe my impending retirement is giving me the balls to say it."

Paul Piercy exhaled and began talking again.

"Byron Grady was the sheriff of Alameda County in 2001, and he was running for re-election."

I had a bad feeling I knew where this was headed.

"Let me guess, he didn't want the public to know there was a serial killer out there?"

"That's a bit simplistic, but you're on the right track. We didn't know for certain that some madman was out there. Shit, it doesn't even sound like you're sure of it now."

"I'm not," I admitted.

"So, let's toss the phrase, serial killer, out for a bit. Sheriff Grady didn't want his county thinking that a bunch of young boys were being killed on his watch. Whether it was a serial killer or not wasn't all that relevant."

"How did he prevent it from becoming news?"

"He could never prevent it entirely. But the Chief of Police, Lou Preston, was a good friend of his. And probably, more importantly, Lou was scared of Sheriff Grady. Preston knew that Grady was running for reelection and these kids' deaths were to be kept on the down-low as much as possible. Grady was also friendly with several of the homicide detectives and they knew he could crush them like a bug."

"So, what, they didn't investigate?"

"No, nothing that egregious. Like I said earlier, we looked into the cases you mentioned. But remember, those murders didn't occur in Berkeley, so we didn't have carte blanche to do what we wanted. We were busy working our ass off trying to find Ronnie Fisk's killer."

"You make it sound like nothing was wrong."

"I didn't say that. What I'm saying is that we still did all we could to solve the murder in Berkeley. What we didn't do was state in police reports that we might have a potential serial killer on our hands. The Chief wouldn't have allowed that because he knew Sheriff Grady would tear him a new asshole."

I tried to remember some of the names and cities of the murdered kids.

"There was only the one murder in Berkeley. I'm trying to think of the other ones in Alameda. I know one kid, Jordan Ziele, went missing in Castro Valley."

"I remember that one. There was one in the Oakland Hills too. A rich white family."

"Yeah. Michael Yost, I believe."

"You're right, his name was Yost. Jeez, you really do know this case."

"How about the media?" I asked.

"In news conferences, a few local reporters suggested there were several missing kids. We would never directly answer their questions. And that wasn't just Lou and Byron Grady's influence. Officers, and more importantly, homicide detectives, had long been conditioned not to deal with the media except when necessary. Well, I guess not all. Your guy Hank Tressel certainly didn't subscribe to that, media whore that he is."

I smiled. Hank had become my friend, but Paul Piercy had a point.

"The internet was obviously a thing in 2001, but it was nothing like it is now," Paul continued. "In this day and age with all the true crime podcasts and the like, this never could have been kept under wraps. Back then, the internet was different. There wasn't social media. No Facebook or Twitter. Word didn't spread in a community as it does now. Nowadays, there would be a Facebook group of worried mothers. Byron Grady couldn't have kept it under wraps as he did back then."

"When was he up for reelection?"

"I don't remember exactly. I think somewhere in May or June of 2002. And by then, kids weren't going missing like they had been. Sure, there was a gang-style murder now and then. And maybe a kid would get killed in the wrong part of town from time to time. But no white kids were going missing in the middle of the suburbs."

I was livid.

I wanted to scream, but I had to keep my cool.

Paul could tell I was incensed.

Before I got even more fired up, I needed to change the subject.

"Would Hank Tressel have known the politics of the Berkeley Police Department?"

"He was kept in the dark. Sheriff Grady hated him. It goes back to my point about Hank being a media whore. Grady wanted all the attention that the media gave Hank. Byron Grady was a huge hypocrite in that sense. He was telling us not to deal with the media while secretly hoping they would fawn over him. And he knew that Hank had some pull. Maybe not in the BPD per se, but in Bay Area law enforcement as a whole. And Grady knew if Hank found out that there was a potential serial killer on the loose, it would be bad news for Grady. I know that Hank hated Grady as well, so he would have splashed that news everywhere. And you know what that means? No reelection for Byron Grady."

It took me a few seconds to digest all that Paul Piercy had told me.

"You chose Grady over Hank. I think you got that one wrong."

"That's fair," he said, surprising me. "But I think Hank is a jerk because he loves the camera. Not that he hasn't fought for Ronnie or the rest of these kids."

"I understand," I said.

Paul's explanation showed why Hank had never put much stock in the serial killer angle. The Berkeley Police Department, whom he'd considered friendly to him, had been holding back information, downplaying the threat of a serial killer. No wonder he, in turn, downplayed it to me.

"I hate to look a gift horse in the mouth, but why are you telling me all this?" I asked.

"Well, as I said, I'm nearing retirement. And you may think I'm an asshole, but I do have a moral compass. This has been driving me insane for years. In my defense, I did everything I could to catch Ronnie's killer. When I talked to homicide detectives in other cities, we discussed the possibility of a serial killer. It's just not something we included in our police reports or when we were forced to talk to the media. Some people, and not just Grady, thought it was the right thing to do. It's never good for a community to think there's a serial killer on the loose."

"It sounds like you're trying to absolve yourself of blame," I said.

Paul had told me more than I ever could have expected. He wasn't blameless, though. No, he didn't share the burden of Sheriff Grady or the Chief of Police, Lou Preston, but every homicide detective played a small part.

"I'm not trying to be absolved. I'm trying to explain and in my own way, apologize."

A guy on a huge unicycle rolled right past us. We were definitely in Berkeley.

"If it makes you feel any better, I realize you guys were in a tough spot," I said, the first time I'd been compassionate to his dilemma.

"If we went and told a member of the media there might be a serial killer, we'd be looking for a new job. What was I to do? I still investigated my ass off. I'm as pissed as anyone that Ronnie's killer was never found."

"I believe you," I said.

"And I'm not exactly a whistleblower," he said. "There's been numerous articles written about what a bad dude Byron Grady was."

"Did these articles mention that you guys muzzled information on the Ronnie Fisk case?"

"Probably not," Paul admitted. "The cops who retired in the years after 2001 knew how to keep their mouths shut. They were old school to the core. The younger guys like me, yes, I was young back then, had their future to think about. We mostly just kept our noses clean and pounded the pavement. Grady only died two years ago and believe me, he still had a lot of influence all the way up until he passed."

I could have told Paul that their noses were far from clean, but there was no reason to belabor my point.

"Is Lou Preston still alive?"

"He's in an old folks' home with severe Alzheimer's."

"This is all so sad. Ronnie Fisk deserved better."

"I don't blame you for thinking that."

My thoughts turned to Tom Butler, my old boss at *The Walnut Creek Times*. This would be a huge story for him and the paper. It was potentially so big, somewhere in the back of my mind, I'm sure I was considering coming out of writing retirement.

But it wasn't going to happen. I was a P.I. now.

I knew I couldn't go to Tom Butler right away. I needed some more time working on the Ronnie Fisk case. The last thing I wanted was an increased public awareness of the murders. If the killer was still out there, he'd crawl under a rock if the case gained renewed interest.

Plus, I couldn't just throw Paul Piercy under the bus. I'd promised him this conversation was between us. I wasn't going to break his trust.

However, I could at least extend the invitation.

"If, down the line, you want to tell the story of Sheriff Grady, I know some honest people in the media."

He looked at me, half hurt/half pissed.

"You gave me your word," he said.

"And I'm going to stick to it. This is only if you decide the public should hear the truth."

He said nothing.

"That's the last time I'll mention it," I said. "So, what happened after Grady won reelection? I'm assuming he did."

We took our fourth left and I saw the BPD precinct a few blocks down.

"Yeah, he did. It was close and I have no doubt he would have lost if the word had gotten out."

"And then the murders went away?"

"Yes. That doesn't mean we stopped working the Fisk case. It's just that, as I said, we weren't convinced it was a serial killer in the first place. So we were still investigating Ty Montgomery, the entire Fisk klan, and every weirdo in Berkeley."

I didn't like him mentioning that they investigated the Fisks. Obviously, he had just been doing his job, but it made me consider that I was overlooking them a little bit.

Doubts started creeping in.

Maybe I was wrong about the whole serial killer angle.

Maybe it had been someone close to Ronnie all along.

Maybe Evelyn and Ty planned this together.

Maybe Grant secretly hated his son.

SHUT THE FUCK UP, QUINT!

I'd kept that in my internal monologue, but Paul still looked up at me. He could tell something was amiss.

"Just running through everything in my head," I said.

"You've become close to the Fisks, haven't you? You didn't like when I mentioned them as suspects?"

It's almost like I had been thinking aloud.

"You're exactly right."

"It happens. We all get close to the people we deal with. I remember years ago a case in which a newlywed was killed. A beautiful, smart twenty-four-year-old woman. She was out shopping and got shot in her car outside of a Safeway. I was the lead detective and, of course, we interviewed her husband first. I fell for his sob story and didn't think he had anything to do with her murder. My second in command told me to distance myself, that these cases usually ended up being the husband. I told him he was crazy, you couldn't fake the emotions the husband was showing us. I became borderline friendly with the guy, always defending him in front of my fellow cops. And then, a few weeks later, on our fourth search of the house, deep underneath the floorboards, we found the gun he'd used to kill his wife."

I couldn't help but feel sympathetic.

"I don't know what to say," I said. "That must have been really tough."

"It was. And I'm not saying one of the Fisks murdered Ronnie. That wasn't the point of the story."

"Then what was?"

"Just because you currently think it's the work of a serial killer, don't overlook other suspects that pop up."

We were a few hundred yards from arriving at our starting point.

After Paul's little story and his subsequent advice, I was happy it was coming to a close.

"So, what's next?" I asked.

"Well, hopefully, you keep your mouth shut."

"I told you I will."

"And we keep in touch."

"I could present to you all the circumstantial evidence I have."

"Maybe in a day or two. I've got tomorrow off. And I plan on pouring myself a nice bottle of Cabernet and attempting to forgive myself for the sins I committed twenty years ago. Who knows, maybe it will turn into a second bottle."

"Don't be too hard on yourself, Paul."

"The booze will help."

I gave him my business card.

"I'll talk to you soon," I said.

"Thanks for allowing me to cleanse myself, Quint."

I didn't know what more I could say, so I merely shook his hand and walked in the direction of my car.

When I reached my car, I turned around and saw Paul Piercy slowly and deliberately saunter back into the Berkeley Police Department.

I wasn't the only guy with a lot on my mind.

The evening tail of Bruce Ballard produced nothing. Nor did my nightly reading of the case file.

My mind couldn't stop thinking about the entire conversation with Paul Piercy. There was so much to digest and I fully expected it to take a few days.

And yet, while I was disgusted by the BPD's deception, I'm not sure it affected my investigation in any meaningful way.

CHAPTER 24

By the following morning, the "atmospheric river" had arrived. The rain was coming down in sheets. It was as bad as I'd ever seen it in the Bay Area.

I looked down from my apartment in awe as I saw the ground below getting hammered.

It was almost surreal as I looked down from my bird's-eye view. The storm drains were losing the battle and pools of water were forming on the streets below.

I cursed myself for agreeing to follow around Bruce Ballard for the weekend.

∼

From seven to eight a.m., I printed out a makeshift map and added tacks to the locations of the teams that Willard Middle School had played. I then used a different color tack to add the locations where the other kids in question had been killed.

A few minutes after inserting the last tack, I got a text from Hank.

"I faxed you a few more pages. They could be important."

Shit!

Why I'd bought a home printer that didn't have the ability to fax was beyond me.

I looked down at my phone. It was 8:11 a.m.

I didn't have to start staking out Bruce Ballard's house until about 8:45, so I did have time.

"They could be important."

That last sentence by Hank ensured that I would, in fact, be going. I'd grab his fax and then head off to follow Ballard.

It doesn't mean I had to like it.

～

I put on a gray, rain-repellent tracksuit and double-checked to make sure it had a hood. This was definitely a casual Saturday.

My parking garage was on the second floor. Once I started my car, I immediately threw the heater on. Meteorologists often say the temperature is moderate in the worst of storms. I found that to be bullshit. It was cold as hell.

I exited 1716 lofts, took a left on North Main Street, and headed towards my office. I passed Stadium Pub and realized I hadn't run into Rebecca in a few days. I took a left on Cypress Street and was now only a block from my office.

I knew something was wrong as I approached. I couldn't yet see the police cars, but their lights radiated in the distance.

As I got closer, I just assumed something happened at the 7-11 on the corner. There wasn't much else there besides a Starbucks, but who causes trouble while getting coffee? There was the law firm, which wasn't even open yesterday. And then there was my tiny business stuck in the corner. Surely it couldn't have anything to do with me.

I was wrong.

Once I turned into the strip mall, I saw that four police cars and an ambulance all surrounded my minuscule office. They were parked next to the law firm as well, but I could distinctly see that they were gathered outside the entrance with the sign saying *"Quint Adler, P.I."*

What the hell had happened?

I parked my car in one of the 7-11 parking spots so as to not get too close and then started walking towards the commotion.

A police officer intercepted me thirty yards from my office. He was wearing a plastic raincoat and I couldn't make out his face.

"Can I help you?"

"That's my office at the end."

"What's your name?"

"Quint Adler."

"And you're the P.I. who owns the firm?"

"Yes, you can see my name on the outside of it."

"Let me see some form of identification."

I showed him my driver's and private investigator's license, water pelting them the second I removed them from my wallet.

"Here, follow me."

I had no idea what to expect as I walked the remaining feet to my office.

"Wait here," the officer said.

He walked twenty more feet and began talking to two of his fellow officers. One of them started walking in my direction.

"This is your business?"

"Yes. What is going on?"

"Follow us."

As I approached, I saw what the officers had been shielding. On the ground below them was a tarp. Judging by the shape, I was pretty sure it was covering a human body.

"What the fuck?" I said. "Was somebody killed?"

"Yes," one of the officers said.

My heart sank. Who the hell would have been killed or died outside of my office? I had no idea.

Don't be Emmett, I thought to myself. In this weather, he easily could have slipped and fallen on his head. No, he said he wasn't driving.

"Your name is Quint, right?"

Another officer had approached us.

"Yes, for the third time."

"Don't be a smart ass."

"Sorry. I'd just like to know what happened."

"A man was killed outside of your office. We've found a wallet on the deceased, but it could help us if you'd confirm it's him. Just to be sure, you know?"

Killed?

"What makes you think I'll know the guy?"

"Maybe you won't. But it happened right outside of your office."

He made a good point.

"Fine."

"Is that a yes?"

"Yes," I said.

The officer took my arm and led me towards the covered body. He bent over and lifted the tarp just far enough to where I could see the guy's face.

I glanced at the officers. They were all staring at me and I had the distinct impression they were judging my reaction.

I looked down.

I don't know what I was expecting, but it wasn't this. I moved a few inches closer just to be sure I'd seen it correctly.

I was looking at the corpse of Bruce Ballard.

CHAPTER 25

After a few seconds of disbelief, I told them his name was Bruce Ballard.

"Would you mind answering some questions for us?" one of the officers asked.

"No problem," I said, sobered by what I'd seen.

"Do you want to go down to the precinct?"

"Do we have to? I could open my office and we could talk in there."

The officers looked at each other and one nodded. The weather had worked to my benefit.

"That will be fine. Detective Wilcox will be joining you."

Detective Wilcox was the skinniest of his fellow officers. I'd guess he was in his thirties, but it was so hard to tell with the raincoat covering the majority of everyone's faces.

I opened the door to my business, with Bruce Ballard's body less than ten feet away. It was disturbing. Unpleasant. Frightening. And many other words that I couldn't think of at the moment.

Detective Wilcox followed me in and shut the door behind him.

"We can go to my office," I said.

"Right here will be fine," he retorted.

So we both sat on the couch in the front office.

"How do you know Bruce Ballard?" he asked.

"I've actually never met him. His wife hired me a few days ago, worried he was having an affair. Thursday was my first day on the case.

I've spent the last two days tailing him in the morning, at lunch, and when he got off work."

"Anything interesting happen?"

"Honestly, nothing."

"Nothing at all?"

"In the morning, he went straight from home to work. At lunch, he went to a Subway and ate in his car, then drove directly back to work. And at around 5:30, he left his office and went home. I saw his wife waiting for him."

"The woman who hired you?"

"Yes."

"And what is her name?"

"Marjorie Ballard."

"How would you describe her?"

"I only met her the one time, but I guess she was a little high strung. But that could have just been the circumstances."

"What circumstances?"

I was already tired of this officer's repetitive questions.

"That she thought her husband was cheating on her."

"But you found no evidence of that?"

"No. Like I said, nothing happened either day."

"How much longer were you supposed to follow him?"

"Originally, just Thursday and Friday. She called me yesterday and asked me if I'd follow him this weekend as well. I agreed to it. In fact, I was going to head over to his house after I left here."

"What were you doing here?"

"Someone had sent me a fax from a different case. I was just coming to pick it up."

Detective Wilcox seemed disinterested in my other case. Thankfully. The last thing I wanted to do was talk about Ronnie Fisk with him.

"Did this Marjorie woman seem like she wanted her husband dead?"

This was terrible. Did they suspect Marjorie already? I guess the husband or wife is always the first suspect. Especially if perceived infidelity is involved.

"No," I said. "She was worried he was having an affair, but never mentioned she wanted him dead."

"She never told you she wished he was dead?"

"That's honestly what I just said. You're reading my words back verbatim."

"Don't be a smart guy. We could do this at the station instead."

That's the last thing I wanted. I had an investigation of my own that I didn't want to derail.

I'd now been called a "smart guy" and a "smart-ass" in the span of three minutes. Maybe I should stand down a bit.

"I'm sorry," I said. "No, Marjorie Ballard never mentioned she wanted her husband dead."

"Do you have any idea why Bruce Ballard would come by your office this morning?"

"I have literally no idea."

"Literally? Is that more than no idea on its own?"

I was starting to hate the officer in front of me, but I told myself to behave.

"I was just trying to accentuate it. I don't have a clue as to why he was here."

"Maybe he found out you were following him?"

"That's possible," I conceded.

"And maybe you guys fought."

I couldn't believe my ears. Was I being accused of murder? It was three years ago all over again when Ray Kintner accused me of multiple murders. That was well before he realized his own mistake and we became very good friends. I missed Ray.

I'd been trying to hold my tongue. Some good it had done me.

"I don't know how I can state this any more unequivocally," I said. "I had absolutely nothing to do with this man's death. Do you think I killed him and then came back sometime later so I could be ambushed by the police? You've got to be kidding me!"

He tried to look at me with compassion. I wasn't buying it. He'd been a complete asshole. Unnecessarily.

"I understand your anger."

"I doubt you do," I said.

"Is there anything else you'd like to add?" Detective Wilcox asked.

"Just that I'm as surprised as you guys."

"Do you live locally?"

"Yeah, a few blocks away."

"No venturing or sauntering too far away today, you hear?"

"Yeah, I hear you."

"And do you have a phone number we can reach you at?"

I gave him a business card. He then stood up.

"Am I free to go?" I asked.

"For now, but as I said, don't wander far from Walnut Creek."

Don't venture. Don't saunter. Don't wander. This guy was too much.

I wanted to say a two-word phrase whose first word started with F and the second word was You. But I settled for a different two-word phrase ending with you.

"Thank you," I said instead.

I walked out with the officer a few seconds later.

I looked down in the direction of Bruce Ballard one last time. They'd put the tarp back over his face and I couldn't see anything.

I had a million questions.

Who had killed him? Why had he been at my office? Was Marjorie involved?

They'd secured yellow tape all around the front of my office so I took the long way to my car.

The officers were still looking at me. I saw Officer Wilcox getting admonished.

"Mr. Adler, please come back here," one of the officers said.

Pissed off, I did what he asked.

The man who had called me over obviously had seniority over the other officers. Wilcox looked like a puppy who'd been yelled at.

"Officer Wilcox was very generous in letting you go. We could take you down to headquarters right now.

"I answered everything he asked. And I can assure you, I had nothing to do with his death..."

"Be that as it may, we are likely not done questioning you. Where do you live?"

"1716 Lofts. A few blocks away."

"Alright, I'm going to let you go home for now. No leaving Walnut Creek. We may have you come back in for questioning later today."

"Okay," I said. "Can I ask you something?"

"Sure," the senior officer said.

"How was he killed?"

I could tell he was mulling it over.

"He was shot several times from behind. Through his back."

I hadn't seen a bullet hole through his forehead or face when they'd remove the tarp. Now I knew why.

"He was ambushed from behind?" I asked.

"It looks that way."

"I don't own a gun," I said suddenly.

"A big bad P.I. like you doesn't own a gun?" Detective Wilcox said sarcastically.

I thought back to the two-word phrase I'd wanted to use earlier, but there was no reason to dig myself a deeper grave.

"It's not that easy in California. And I've only just opened my business. Maybe eventually."

It was a long-winded answer, but I had to make it clear I didn't own a gun.

The officers looked like they believed me. Grudgingly.

"You're free to go," the boss said.

"Thank you."

"Answer your phone."

"I will."

He motioned that I could leave.

I walked back in the direction of my car, getting pelted by the rain, my jacket acting as a sounding board, and the drops ringing in my ears.

I could feel their gazes still on me.

A few seconds later I drove out of the parking lot/crime scene.

I arrived home and realized I hadn't picked up Hank's fax. In my defense, I'd had a few things on my mind.

I wasn't going back to get it anytime soon, that's for sure.

I sat down on my couch.

I was in disbelief.

My mind should have been on Ronnie Fisk, but instead, I was now caught up in another murder.

What the fuck?!

I wanted to call Marjorie Ballard. That was an impossibility for multiple reasons.

One, she'd soon be headed to the morgue to identify her husband. My ID seemed like it was for them to judge my reaction more than anything else.

Two, even though I was completely innocent, it wouldn't look good if I was calling the deceased's wife twenty minutes after finding out he was dead. I saw no reason to give the police an iota of reason to suspect me more than they already did.

And yet, I really wanted to talk to her. Why was Bruce at my office? Who the hell might have wanted him dead?

For all I knew, maybe Marjorie had killed him. I'm sure the detectives were going to have a lot more questions for her than they did for me.

There was no avoiding it, I was now involved in Bruce Ballard's murder. At the very least, peripherally. Hopefully, the police didn't see it as more than that.

I called Hank, needing someone to talk to.

"Hey, Quint."

"I had one hell of a morning."

I told him all that happened.

"Are you freaking kidding me?"

"I wish. Do you have any advice?"

"Not really. I imagine the police aren't done with you."

"Great," I said sarcastically.

"There's really not much to say. I'm sorry."

"Don't worry about it. I'll deal with whatever comes up. I didn't do anything so I should be okay."

His silence suggested that Hank had known innocent people who were, in fact, not okay.

"What did you think of the fax?"

I could tell Hank wanted to bring the attention back to Ronnie's case.

"Shit, I forgot to tell you. I couldn't pick it up. Well, I guess I could have, but I was being interrogated by the police and it didn't seem right."

"I don't blame you."

"Can you give me the CliffsNotes version?"

"First, I'd like a compliment."

"Okay," I said, not knowing where this was going.

"Have you been impressed with all of the information I've collected on Ronnie's case?"

"Yes, a thousand times over," I said. "You know that."

"Thanks. I just wanted to hear that before I tell you about some mistakes I've made, which were by no means intentional, but important all the same."

"I have no idea what you are talking about, Hank."

"I've updated every section of the case file with regularity, with the exception of one area. The other missing children."

"What do you mean exactly?"

"Well, for those first two years I made notes of my own. None of what you've read came from the Berkeley Police Department. It was all me. But while I amended all new information throughout the rest of the case file, I rarely updated the section I'd labeled the addendum. No, that's not fair. I never updated that section."

"I know you are getting to something, but I'm not sure what exactly."

"The information I gave you was wrong."

"How so?"

"At least four of those cases, and likely more, should never have been included in that case file. They had absolutely nothing to do with Ronnie's death."

"I've thought that about many of those other cases, Hank, but what makes you so positive?"

"Because I've spent the last few days doing my own investigating. Take Nolan Rose. He went missing in June of 2002 and was fifteen years old. Well, guess what? He was found two years later. Alive. He had been a runaway. And because I never tried to edit the addendum, I didn't know that. Here's another one. Jacob Hosmer, aged sixteen and killed in June of 2001. In 2012, DNA concluded that he'd been killed by his uncle. He was convicted and died in jail in 2018."

"No offense, Hank, but if it's just the kids who are fifteen or older, then I'm not surprised. I've told you that I've basically already eliminated them from consideration."

"Let me finish, Quint."

"I'm sorry. Go ahead."

"Stephen Snider, aged 14. Went missing on February 20th, 2002. He was in middle school and went missing during the winter months. He was on your list, correct?"

He meant my list of kids who might have also been killed by Ronnie's assailant.

"Yes."

"Well, he's alive."

"What?"

"He was kidnapped by his father who had lost visitation rights. He fled with the kid to Canada where authorities caught up to them five years later. There was an article in a Canadian online magazine in 2007. I even found a follow-up article from last year by the same magazine. Stephen Snider is still alive and living in Ottawa."

"My gosh. I'm sorry to have interrupted you. That's enormous news."

"I'm not done. Henry Penn, aged 14. Went missing on January 18th, 2002. His body was never found. Was he on your list?"

"Yes."

"He was killed by a neighbor. The man gave a confession on his deathbed. It took me hours and hours of research to discover that."

"I don't know what to say, Hank. You deserve a lot of credit."

"So, let's go through the six remaining."

He was done with my compliments and all business now. He spoke before I could interject.

"Ronnie Fisk. Todd Zobrist. Adam Williams. Billy Warren. Christian Yount. Eddie Young. All of them are still in play."

"Along with Matt Greeson and Jeremy Stacks."

"Yes, of course. I was only including the East Bay kids."

"There's something I have to tell you, Hank."

"What is it?"

"It's not your fault you never believed in the serial killer angle."

"What do you mean?"

"Do you remember the name, Byron Grady?"

"That old jerkoff. Of course."

"Well, he screwed you over because he had an election to win."

"You're being a little vague, Quint."

"Grady was up for reelection and thought if the voters of Alameda County knew there might be a serial killer on the loose, he'd lose for sure. So, he and the Chief of Police of Berkeley intentionally downplayed that possibility. Homicide detectives were told not to include it in official police reports and they never mentioned it to the media or in press conferences."

"I'm dumbfounded," Hank said.

"It gets worse."

"I'm listening."

"Grady didn't like you because of your stature in law enforcement. He knew if you found out it could be a serial killer, word would get out and his reelection would be in serious jeopardy. So he told the BPD detectives not to relay that information to you."

Hank didn't react for a few seconds.

"Is that all?"

"Pretty much. I met an old detective named Paul Piercy who'd wanted to spill his guts for twenty years. I just happened to walk in at the right time."

"So they knew all along it was a serial killer?"

"Not exactly. Shit, I don't even know if it is."

Paul's words about investigating the Fisks entered my mind.

"But they suspected?"

"They realized it was feasible. I'll put it that way. And Grady knew he'd probably lose his reelection if it came out, so he used all the intimidation at his disposal. Not to defend this guy Paul Piercy, but he said anyone who spoke up would have been unemployed soon thereafter."

"He's probably right. Byron Grady was a menace and very influential. Actually, authoritative would probably be a better word."

"Do you know why I told you all this?" I asked.

"Because we are working a case together and it's the right thing to do?"

I laughed.

"Yes to all that, but do you know why else?"

"No."

"Because I don't want you to beat yourself up about the serial killer angle. In fact, it just proves how thorough you were. Despite them not feeding you this information, you still went out on your own and researched missing kids in the Bay Area."

"Not hard enough if I'm finding some of them alive twenty years later."

"Stop, Hank. You're being unnecessarily hard on yourself."

"Maybe you're right," he said.

"I am right. And the information you told me earlier is monumental. I'm not just saying that."

I could hear Hank choking up on the other end.

"Even a seventy-five-year-old curmudgeon like me appreciates words like that. Thanks, Quint."

"I'll tell you in person sometime soon."

"That can wait. There's no reason to travel in weather like this. Plus, you might be getting a call from the Walnut Creek police."

The death of Bruce Ballard and my meeting with Paul Piercy had been so front and center to our conversation, I'd forgotten something important.

"I met with someone named Scott Shea last night. Do you recognize his name?"

"It rings a bell, but I can't place it."

"He played on the basketball team with Ronnie."

"Okay. And…"

"And his mother videotaped every game they played that season. I met with him and wrote down each team they played along with the date."

"So we still think basketball is the common thread?"

"I think it's very likely. Do you remember how I told you I talked to a San Ramon cop?"

"Yeah. About the Todd Zobrist case, correct?"

"That's right. Anyway, I had originally asked him if Todd had played basketball and he correctly answered in the negative. Dead end, right? Wrong. He called me back yesterday and told me that Todd went to all the basketball games."

"Jeez."

I thought of something else I'd overlooked.

"Hold on a second."

"Alright."

I looked at my notes.

"Stephen Snider and Henry Penn were two of the three kids in which I couldn't find a connection to basketball."

"Fucking A!" Hank exclaimed.

"Yeah, I'd say that's warranted."

"Who is the other one?"

I looked back at my notes.

"Eddie Young."

We paused a few seconds as his name hung in the air.

"Maybe his was a random murder," Hank said.

"Yeah, could be."

"If I now accept your basketball theory, do you think it's a coach, a parent, an administrator?"

"It's way too early to harbor a guess. Could be none of the above."

"True."

"I've asked Officer Picker in San Ramon to try and find a schedule for Todd's school's basketball team. Now that I have a list of Ronnie's school's games, I'm hoping to find teams that they both played."

"This is phenomenal work."

"It's nothing on the information you gave me earlier."

"Let's stop with this mutual admiration bullshit," he said.

The curmudgeonly Hank had returned.

"The East Bay is kind of a small area, all things considered," I said. "It's likely that Willard Middle School and San Ramon might have played quite a few of the same teams. So my next order of business was to try and find the basketball schedule for one of these other kids who was killed. And I've currently got someone who played basketball with one of the Sacramento kids looking into that."

"If there's a connection between the Bay and Sacramento, that would a lot to overlook."

"That's what I've been thinking," I said.

"So what happens if you get all three schedules?"

"I'm afraid to get that far ahead of myself. Start knocking on doors, I guess."

"I never expected this when I recommended investigating the other dead children."

"Well, now we know why."

"Fuck Byron Grady," Hank yelled.

"He's dead, you know?"

"Fuck him, anyway."

"Good to have you back, Hank."

I heard him laugh.

"So, what's next for you today?"

"Unfortunately, it's probably this freaking Bruce Ballard case," I said.

"You could volunteer to go in."

"Do people do that?"

"Innocent people do," he said.

"Let me think about it. I'd like to be able to investigate Ronnie's case without fear of being called in."

"Precisely."

"I hate to be an inconsiderate jerk, but the timing of Bruce Ballard's death couldn't be worse. Today, of all days."

There was a long silence. I knew something was wrong without knowing why exactly.

"Hmmm," Hank said.

And then he took a deep breath on his end. It was ominous and I didn't like the sound of it.

"What?" I asked.

"Listen, Quint. I hate to bring this up, especially after all we've discussed on this phone call, but there's something I have to ask."

"What is it?"

"How far was Bruce Ballard from your office when he was killed?"

"The body was probably ten feet from my front door."

"And how old was this Ballard guy?"

"Around my age."

"How about his build?"

"Around my height and weight."

I now knew where he was going with this. And a shiver went up my spine.

"And we both know the weather isn't very good over there in Walnut Creek, is it?"

"No, it's not."

"People wearing raincoats that kind of cover their faces?"

"Yes. Why don't you just come out and say it, Hank?"

"I hope with all my heart that I'm wrong. But if there ever was going to be a murder of mistaken identity, these would be the circumstances. What if you were the intended victim?"

It took me several seconds to respond. And by the time I did, my mouth had gone dry and I could barely get the words out.

"Holy shit," I said.

CHAPTER 26

I couldn't go to the cops.

While Hank's words scared the shit out of me, I had zero evidence that I was the intended target. Zilch. Nothing. Nada.

Furthermore, the last thing I wanted to do was to conflate these two cases. I needed to keep them separate.

At least for now.

While I wouldn't be going to the cops, one thing was for certain. My head was going to be on a swivel from this point forward. Hank had made sure of that.

I wanted to talk to Marjorie Ballard earlier. Now, I felt it was a necessity.

Maybe she could allay my fears, tell me that Bruce had pissed off some business partners over the years, or that she thought it was a jealous husband.

It still wouldn't explain why he was killed outside of my office. The only way that made any sense is if someone followed Bruce from his house and then ambushed him when he arrived at my work. It was possible, I guess.

I hated to admit it, but what seemed more likely was that someone was scoping out my office, waiting to kill me, and had mistakenly killed Bruce Ballard instead. After all, we were right around the same age, height, and weight. Plus, it was raining and impossible to see anyone clearly.

This was insane!

I was agreeing with Hank.

Twenty minutes later, on a day that was inexplicably still only 9:45 in the morning, Officer Picker called.

"Tell me you've got some good news," I answered.

"I got the information. I know every team that Iron Horse Middle School played up until Todd Zobrist went missing."

I think it was the first time I'd heard the name of Todd's middle school. For some reason, it stung. Maybe I was just imagining my own carefree time in middle school. In some respects, it's the best part of your childhood. It comes after the frivolity of grade school and before the machismo and bullying that become more prevalent in high school.

At least, I believe that was the case twenty years ago.

I'm guessing grade school isn't so frivolous these days.

I felt my mind wandering and now wasn't the time.

"That's great," I said. "Was it difficult?"

"It was. But Fiona and I took it as a challenge. We reached out to as many former players as we could find. And somehow, someway, one of those kids had saved their win/loss record from that year and it listed all the teams they'd played."

"Should we compare the two teams right now?" I asked.

This was a monumental point in my investigation and yet, I had so many things on my mind, I was finding it hard to appreciate it.

"I'll be honest. I think we should do this in person."

He was right, of course. No, the weather wasn't ideal, but this case was starting to take shape. A little rain wasn't going to stop me. Or, an atmospheric river.

Plus, San Ramon was close enough to Walnut Creek that if the police called, I could hurry back.

"It's Saturday," I said. "Are you at the office?"

"I am on this Saturday," he said, alluding to how important this was.

"Alright, I'll be over there in twenty."

I exited my apartment three minutes later and looked both ways as I did. When I entered the elevator, I half-expected someone to be standing there with a gun. When I made my way to the parking garage, I thought every shadow was a killer waiting to shoot me dead.

This was no way to live.

I made it out of the parking garage in one piece and headed towards

San Ramon. With Hank's revelation that I was potentially the intended target, it felt like I was now on the defensive.

On my drive over, I spent a few minutes thinking about Bruce Ballard. I didn't know the man, and maybe he was a philanderer. That didn't matter to me.

This was a human being who'd lost his life in the most cowardly way imaginable. Someone shot him several times in the back. No one deserved that.

There was also the elephant in the room. There was a decent chance he'd lost his life because the bullets were meant for me.

I had never been a very religious guy, but I said a quick prayer for Bruce Ballard.

~

I arrived at the San Ramon Police Department.

Officer Picker was waiting outside.

"There's some newbie in the office right now. I'd rather not have him listening to what I have to tell you. Not yet, anyway."

"No problem. What did you have in mind?"

"We'll talk in my squad car."

I followed him to the back of the police station where he clicked on the fob to open the doors to his police car. It was a sharp, sleet-looking blue on blue. I was pretty sure it was a Dodge Charger.

"Will Officer Trundle be joining us?" I asked.

"No, she's out on a case. She was very integral to this, however."

"Thank her for me," I said.

We entered the police car. Hopefully, it was the only police car I'd be entering that day. We'll see what the Walnut Creek PD had to say about that.

Officer Picker pulled out a manila envelope with printed, typed pages.

I took out my cell phone, having saved the schools in the Notes section of my iPhone.

I felt like a student who was woefully underprepared for a test.

"Sorry, I haven't had time to print these out yet," I said.

"No problem. The info is what matters."

"Alright, how do you want to do this?" I asked.

He pondered my question.

"How about you read off your list and I'll see which ones match on my end. You told me you only have eight or so games. Iron Horse played eighteen before Todd went missing, so it's easier for you to read your teams off."

"Okay," I said.

I took a deep breath. I may have been distracted, but I wanted to spend a few seconds soaking in the moment. I'd come a long way from the day Emmett Fisk walked into my office.

"Alright, their first game was Stanley Middle School out of Lafayette."

Picker scanned his sheet of paper for a good fifteen seconds. He had eighteen teams to go through so it was understandable.

"No match," he said.

"Next is Pleasanton Middle School."

Another fifteen seconds.

"No match."

"Antioch Middle School."

This time there was a quick response and I knew what was coming.

"That's a match. Iron Horse played them on December 29th, about three weeks before Todd went missing."

"Willard Middle School played them on November 15th. Also about three weeks before Ronnie went missing."

"Okay, let's both mark Antioch Middle School down. What's next?"

I entered the info into my cell phone.

"Joaquin Moraga Intermediate School."

"Ah, they went fancier than Middle School."

I smiled, in spite of myself.

Officer Picker took a while, so I knew what to expect.

"No match."

"Next is West Oakland Middle School."

The requisite fifteen seconds passed.

"No match."

"Three left," I said. "How about Francisco Middle School?"

Picker scanned his list.

"No match."

"Two left. Redwood Middle School out of Hayward."

A quick response.

"That's a match. Played Iron Horse on January 8th. Eight days before Todd went missing."

"They played Willard on November 29th, a week before Ronnie went missing."

We both looked at each other.

"Don't overreact," Officer Picker said. "We have no idea what this guy's timeline was."

"Let's finish up," I said. "One more. Creekside Middle School in Castro Valley."

I saw his eyes go up and down as he scanned his list twice. Probably because it was the last one.

"No match," he said.

"Alright, let's review then. Two matches. The first is Antioch Middle School. They played Willard on November 15th, roughly three weeks before Ronnie went missing. Antioch later played Iron Horse on December 29th, also about three weeks before Todd went missing. The second match is Redwood Middle School in Hayward. They played Willard on November 29th, a week before Ronnie went missing. And Redwood played Iron Horse on January 8th, eight days before Todd went missing."

"So, what are you thinking?" Officer Picker asked.

"They both have similarities. The Antioch Middle School games were both about three weeks from when Ronnie and Todd were killed. And the Redwood games were only a week before."

"I think we both instinctively were suspicious of the one-week break. But who the fuck knows? Maybe this psycho, assuming we are on the right track in the first place, stalked these kids for a few weeks and the three-week scenario was more likely."

"Agreed. We can't jump to conclusions on either," I said.

Officer Picker looked at his notes and then over at me.

"This is madness," he said.

"I was going to go with lunacy."

"That works too."

"So, what's next?" I asked. "I mean on our end. Obviously, if I hear back from my friend in Sacramento, you'll be the first to know."

"Why don't we both pick a school? In fact, I'll pick for us. I'm closer to Hayward so I'll go check out Redwood. And you go to Antioch Middle school."

I was going to be venturing further from Walnut Creek than I should be, but I didn't mention it.

"Yeah, that works."

"Try to find out who the basketball coach was and maybe who the principal was as well."

"That will be easy enough," I said. "In fact, when I went to the middle school in Sacramento, they had a yearbook in the library. You may want to try that."

"I will."

"Bring a little less attention to ourselves as well."

I said that fully knowing I might have already come to the attention of the killer.

"What's going to be difficult is where we go from there," Officer Picker said. "What if it was the stats guy? Or the scoreboard monitor? Or the father of a player? The further we get away from the actual team, the harder it's going to be to get information."

"True," I said. "But if we have the coach and the principal, we can pursue those other leads off of them."

"Good point. And who knows, maybe it will be the coach himself and this will be easy."

"One can hope."

Picker opened his door.

"We can walk back now," he said.

I got out of the police car and shut the door. I looked over the hood at Officer Picker and realized I had to do what was right.

"Since I pride myself on honesty, I have to tell you something," I said.

"I don't like the sound of this."

"I talked to another police department about this. Berkeley Police Department, actually. I met with a homicide detective who worked the case twenty years ago and he said they kept the serial killer angle under wraps."

"One, thanks for telling me. And two, I'm not surprised. That's what police departments do. They don't want to panic the general public."

"That may be true, but this was more sinister than that. A guy was trying to win an election."

"Let me think back. 2001 in Berkeley, which is Alameda County. I'd guess Sheriff Byron Grady?"

"Impressive," I said.

"I've heard a lot of stories about the guy. None good."

"They might have missed a chance to connect Ronnie and Todd back then."

"Don't dwell on it. We can't go backward," he said.

I had another admission.

"They aren't the only police force I've talked to in the last twenty-four hours."

"C'mon, Quint. You're testing my patience."

"This one is different," I said and proceeded to explain everything about the death of Bruce Ballard.

When I finished, I asked, "So what do you think?"

"Actually, I'm afraid that Hank could be right. If you weren't the target, it's a huge coincidence that this guy was killed directly outside your office."

"I was afraid you might say that."

"Are you going to tell the Walnut Creek PD?" Picker asked.

"Not unless I can prove I was the intended target. I don't want to involve them in what we are doing."

"I concur. Maybe I'm breaking some sort of police department code, but as you said, we don't conclusively know you were targeted."

"I'd prefer to think that I wasn't."

"Clearly."

"That doesn't mean I'm not scared," I admitted.

"You wouldn't be human if you weren't. Is your home address publicly listed?"

"I honestly don't know. My P.I. business is, so it makes sense the killer would go there. Also, my apartment complex has a fob system, so it's not easy for some random to get in."

"If we are assuming this guy killed a bunch of kids and was never caught, I don't think a fob would prevent him from getting into an apartment complex."

I felt like an idiot. He was right. The fear was starting to ratchet up.

"I'll be careful," I said. "If I was the intended target, then obviously someone feels us closing in. "

"Which would make him extremely dangerous."

"A wounded animal?"

"Exactly. And whatever we discover, it isn't going to be pleasant."

"I'm willing to take that risk. Not knowing who killed Ronnie is worse. So is being worried the killer might be waiting around the next corner."

"Why don't you hire another P.I. to follow you around?"

It wasn't a bad idea.

"I'll consider it."

"I'd seriously consider it if I were you. Shit, if I worked in Walnut Creek, I'd have a cop car patrolling your work and apartment. But as you said, you don't want to involve them."

"Not yet, anyway. Let's see what happens when we get the information from Sacramento."

"I won't bring it up again, just keep it in mind. Let's talk later today once we've been to the respective middle schools."

"Great. I'll be in touch," I said."

"Be careful, Quint."

It was probably the fifth time I'd heard that phrase since taking the case. And, for the first time, I actually took it to heart.

CHAPTER 27

I was five minutes outside of San Ramon when I got a call from an unknown number. It was a 925 number. Walnut Creek's area code.

I knew what was coming next.

And if I was right, Antioch Middle School was not going to be my next destination.

"Hello?"

"Is this Quint Adler?"

"Yes.

"This is Detective Youman with the Walnut Creek Police Department. Do you mind coming in for a few questions?"

I could act pissed. I could be combative. What was the point? A man had been killed outside of my office. If I were a cop, I'd want to talk to me as well.

"I can be there in ten minutes," I said.

"See you then."

～

The Walnut Creek Police Department was somewhere between the size of the San Ramon PD and the Berkeley PD.

It was a long, rectangular red and white building that took up half a city block. Of course, it wasn't just the police station. It was the home of the City Hall as well.

I entered the building, suddenly realizing this was the third police station I'd been at in the last eighteen hours or so. No, I technically didn't enter the San Ramon PD earlier that morning, but I was counting it.

Three police departments were three too many if you asked me.

I told myself to settle down. This interview was very important.

One, I had to try and discover if I was the intended target. Two, I had to manage to keep the Ronnie Fisk case from them.

And, oh yeah, not become a suspect in the murder of Bruce Ballard.

I approached the front desk.

"How can I help you?"

"Quint Adler here to see Detective Youman."

A minute later, he approached.

Detective Youman was a tough-looking guy, probably in his late-thirties. He did not look like a barrel of laughs.

It was hard to tell, but I don't think he was one of the detectives at the crime scene. They likely wanted to start fresh since I hadn't exactly hit it off with the other officers.

"Mr. Adler?"

"Yes."

"Nice to meet you. I'm Detective Youman, do you mind if we talk?"

"That's why I'm here," I said.

I'd said it in a non-combative way even though I probably could have chosen a better use of words.

"Great, follow me."

We walked along the front desk, him on one side and me on the other, until we met at the end. He opened the door and we went back into what I assumed would be their interrogation rooms.

He led the way and while I did see some interrogation rooms, he took me to a desk and had me sit. He pulled up a chair and sat across from me.

There were other WCPD officers on the other side of the room, but I already knew they wouldn't be approaching us. This was a coordinated effort to make the room feel homely.

"We don't consider you a suspect just yet, so I figured we could avoid the stuffy interrogation rooms."

It was a nice gesture if he'd truly meant it. My guess was that this was to try and gain my trust and hope I'd make a mistake. Not that it would make any difference. I had nothing to do with Bruce Ballard's death.

"Thanks," I said, seeing no reason to make my feelings known.

"First off, I apologize if you already went over this with Detective Wilcox at the crime scene."

"It's okay."

"Let's begin. How did you know Bruce Ballard?"

"I didn't."

"How did you know of him?"

I spent the next ten minutes repeating the information I'd gone through earlier that morning.

"Have you talked to Marjorie Ballard since finding out Bruce was dead?"

"No. I kind of figured you guys would be."

"We have."

"How is she taking it?" I asked.

I wanted to ask if they considered her a suspect, but I had to be subtle and work my way into the conversation.

"Not well, as you'd imagine."

"Has to be tough," I said. "Especially since she thought he was cheating on her."

"Wouldn't that technically make it easier?"

"I don't think so. Now she's probably wondering if some furious husband did it. Or a scorned lover."

"Or a P.I. paid to follow him around."

I'd been courteous the whole time, but that was over. I couldn't let a comment like that stand.

"You tell me I'm not a suspect and don't question me in one of the interrogation rooms. You pretend to be my friend. But it was all bullshit and your comment proves it. I'll say it again for the cheap seats. I had nothing to do with Bruce Ballard's death."

"So you say."

I really didn't want to lose my cell phone, but I had an idea.

I pulled my iPhone out of my pants and set it on the table.

As I did, I saw a text had come through from a 916 area code. That was Sacramento. I quickly looked down and saw what it said: "*Quint, this is Rob. I have that information you asked for.*"

"What is the point of putting your iPhone on the table?" Detective Youman asked.

I could call Rob with my burner if necessary. I tried to memorize the number in front of me.

"I arrived at my office around 8:20 or 8:30 and Bruce Ballard was already dead."

"I'm listening."

"Well, can't you guys run a GPS trace on cell phones? I was at my apartment all morning."

"You could have left your cell phone at your apartment, walked to your office, killed Ballard, and then walked back to your apartment, knowing you could rely on the GPS for your alibi."

I felt like I'd been hit with a two-by-four. Here I was, thinking I'd been so smart, and the detective had body-slammed my alibi.

"That didn't turn out as you wanted?" He said and then laughed.

I had the detective from hell sitting across from me.

There was one lifeline I hadn't used.

I rarely liked to talk about my previous exploits, but now was the time.

"Did you follow the whole Bay Area Butcher case?" I asked.

"Sure. Didn't everybody?"

"Did you know that I was the one who prevented him from killing all those young kids?"

He looked at me in disbelief.

"That wasn't you. It was some crime reporter."

"One and the same. I've only been a P.I. for a short time. Plus, how many Quint's do you know?"

He stared at me, slowly realizing I was telling the truth.

"I'm not bringing it up for recognition's sake," I said. "I'm simply asking you this question. Do you think I'd go through all of that only to take some woman's money and kill her cheating husband? Of course not."

He still didn't respond.

"And that I'd do it right outside my office where I'd obviously come under suspicion? Once again, of course not."

"I've met a lot of dumb criminals," he said, but I'd taken some of the wind out of his sails.

"I'm not trying to be an asshole, Detective Youman. I'm just telling you, I had nothing to do with this."

"I never said you were a suspect."

I subtly put my iPhone back in my pocket. I didn't want him to look over and see what Rob Osbourne had texted. It surely would have led to a new round of questioning.

"No? I think you alluded to a P.I. who might have killed him. I'm going out on a limb and saying that P.I. was me."

I was walking a fine line. I think he was starting to doubt that I was involved. But if I continued to ridicule him I could easily piss him off and turn him back against me. I couldn't let that happen.

"Once again, I'm sorry for acting defensive," I said. "I just want to reiterate that I had nothing to do with Ballard's death. I went to pick up a fax and was greeted with the worst surprise imaginable, a dead guy outside of my office."

I could tell that mentioning the Bay Area Butcher had thrown him for a loop. I'd received almost universal approval for my actions that day. And now, unbeknownst to him, he had been besmirching that guy.

"We have to investigate wherever the leads take us," he said.

It was the most vanilla line imaginable. If this was a prizefight, I had him on the ropes.

"I understand," I said.

I saw a small opening.

"Have the leads led anywhere besides me?" I asked.

"As I said, we interrogated Marjorie Ballard."

He chose the word interrogated over interviewed.

Interrogated implied they were suspicious. Interviewed brought to mind a more carefree, back and forth exchange. At least, that was my take.

"And?"

I knew once I said it, I'd gone too far.

"And...I don't care if you prevented the Bay Area Butcher's massacre. I'm still the detective on this case and I'm not going to tell you how it went with Mrs. Ballard."

"Fair enough," I said. "I'm just trying to determine why a guy was killed outside of my office."

He gave me the stare that I'd encountered so many times in the last few days.

"I'm supposed to be interviewing you. Not vice versa."

I could have feigned disgust. Instead, I smiled.

"I was once accused of a crime I didn't commit. I couldn't let it happen again, so I'm trying to present my case to you."

"You're quite a character, Quint. And you're probably not a murderer."

"I'm assuredly not one, but I'll take probably for now."

"Is there anything you can add to our investigation?"

It's a question I'd asked many times.

"I'm going to assume the cameras from 7-11 or Starbucks don't extend to my little business in the corner."

"C'mon, you're better than that. You know we checked that."

"You're right. I'm sorry."

"Anything else?"

I didn't want to alert the WCPD to my worries, but I wouldn't mind a little police presence around my office.

"Maybe it was just some random occurrence. A crazy man from the street. I know there are very few in Walnut Creek, but it's not unheard of."

"You've seen some by your office?"

It was white lie time.

"A few."

We'd see whether my ploy to increase the police presence around my office would work.

"Why do I feel like I'm not doing the interviewing anymore?"

"You asked me if I had anything," I said. "Just trying to help."

He gave me a half-smile. I was officially winning him over.

"I think you've helped enough."

"Understood."

"You can go now, Quint. I don't consider you a suspect at the moment, but you're also inextricably tied to this case."

I could have lived without "at the moment", but all in all, this was ending on a positive note.

"I get it," I said.

"I don't know if we'll call again, but answer us if we do."

"I will."

We both stood up and exchanged handshakes. It was another in a long line of up and down conversations over the last two weeks.

I'd accomplished my goal. While Bruce Ballard's death wasn't leaving my psyche any time soon, I could now go back to concentrating on Ronnie Fisk's murder without fear of the Walnut Creek Police Department.

CHAPTER 28

I was still going to hit Antioch Middle School, but I needed to decompress for a few minutes. I had the weight of the world on my shoulders.

The streets were so flooded that when you approached a curb, you could shoot the water fifteen or twenty feet onto the said curb. Twenty-one-year-old me probably would have looked for some pedestrians to hit.

Luckily, I was no longer an immature young man. Instead, I was a guy in his early forties who might have a serial killer after him. I was wrong. I'd have been lucky to be that carefree young man again.

I arrived home, still wary of the shadows in the garage and the unknown of a slowly opening elevator.

I called Rob Osbourne upon entering my apartment.

"Hey, Quint."

"What did you find?"

"I got all the information you wanted."

"So quick?"

"I reached out to that friend I told you about. His name is Rudy Swatek and he's still involved in Sacramento basketball."

"'He knew all the coaches?"

"If he didn't know them offhand, he knew some of the old-timers who would."

"Great work. I obviously can't drive to Sacramento."

"I can fax them to you," he said.

"If it's just the middle school names and the coach's names, can't you just text it to me?"

"We did more than that, Quint. Rudy printed out a picture of each team with the coach and the players' names listed at the bottom."

"You went above the call, Rob."

"Rudy deserves the credit, but thank you. I guess I could take a picture of each team and then text you, but the resolution is going to be pretty small. I really think I should fax the printouts to you."

I was not looking forward to going back to my office, but Rob was right. If I was going to be looking at people's faces, I'd much rather have an eight and a half by eleven than an iPhone photo I had to pinch to zoom in.

I gave him my office fax number.

"I'll send it right now," he said.

"How many are there?" I asked.

"Matt only played in ten games before he was killed. It's why Rudy and I were able to get this done so quickly."

"You can tell yourself that, but you've accomplished a lot. Down here, we're going school by school and it's taking forever."

"Might have helped if you knew someone involved in basketball."

"Certainly."

"I just hope it helps catch Matt's killer."

"Me too, Rob."

With that, our call ended.

It made me realize just how long a net a serial killer could cast. There are the victims themselves, obviously, and then anyone in their immediate family. Finally, there were all the friends and classmates affected, which could number in the hundreds.

It was apparent that Rob Osbourne had never gotten over his friend's death. How many other people could say the same?

I looked down at my phone. It read 12:15 p.m.

The never-ending day continued.

∾

I called Officer Picker.

"Any news?" he asked.

"Yup. Rob, the guy from Sacramento, came through."

"Excellent."

"Have you made it to that Hayward Middle School yet?" I asked.

"No. I'm leaving in a minute. Are you already done in Antioch?"

"No. The WCPD called me in."

"Oh, shit. How did it go?"

I realized I'd never mentioned the Bay Area Butcher case to him. I didn't feel like getting into it now.

"I charmed the detective so thoroughly that he longer suspects me."

"I honestly can't tell if that's the truth or some fiction you grabbed out of thin air."

"Somewhere in the middle," I said.

I heard him quietly laugh.

"Alright, I'm headed to Hayward."

"And I'm off to Antioch."

"Good. Why don't we plan on talking at say, two o'clock?"

"Sure. And don't you dare tell me to be safe."

I hung up the phone before he had a chance to sarcastically say it.

～

Antioch was a town of 100,000 or so, but I doubt its population was near that high back in 2001.

As the prices of homes near San Francisco soared in the early 2000s, many people moved to the outer stretches of the Bay Area. Antioch was one of those cities.

It could still be charming, but there were areas where you could get in trouble as well.

It was only twenty miles from Walnut Creek, but it felt like an altogether different world.

～

I arrived at Antioch Middle School and it was pretty depressing from the outside. A red brick wall ran around the perimeter. The classrooms were "painted" blue but in dire need of retouching. Each classroom had those old school windows that looked like they'd shatter in a rough wind.

It was Saturday and I couldn't be sure that the library would be open. These days, with all the extracurricular things that schools had to deal with, I imagined it would be open. Sunday, probably not.

There was a booth at the front gate that I imagined was manned during the week. On this day, I was able to walk through undisturbed.

There weren't many people kicking around, but I found two girls talking to each other.

"Do you know where the library is?" I asked.

They pointed me in the right direction.

I arrived out front and the library looked much nicer than the school itself.

A white man in his early thirties walked out of the library. He was wearing a name tag and was obviously an employee.

"Are you guys open?" I asked.

"I'm closing up right now. We're only open till 1:00 p.m. on Saturdays."

"Can you please give me five minutes? It's very important."

"You're obviously not a student here. What could be so important about entering our library?"

Think, Quint!

"We're having a reunion for our old basketball team. And we can't find a few of the kids on Facebook."

"I'm not sure I follow."

"All I'm trying to do is see the names of the 2001 8th grade basketball team."

He looked at me dubiously.

"You went here in 2001?"

He wasn't quite Nancy Drew at Will C. Wood in Sacramento, but he was close.

"That's right. I did. And this means a lot to me."

"I don't know. It's already five minutes after 1:00."

"I'll tell you what. I'll give you twenty bucks for your time and I promise I won't be more than two minutes. You have old yearbooks, right?"

He shrugged his shoulders.

"Yeah, we do."

"Well, point me in that direction and I'll be done in no time."

I could tell he was waffling.

"Ok, fine. But two minutes only."

"I'll take a picture of the team and then I'm outta here."

The library door was still open since he hadn't had a chance to lock it.

"C'mon in," he said.

I followed him into the library. The lights were out and it was dark. He pressed a button that lit up a small section in the corner. He obviously knew the lighting system well.

"The yearbooks are in that corner that I just lit up. You have two minutes."

I briskly walked in that direction and saw the yearbook section on the bookshelves. I removed the 2001 8th grade yearbook from the shelf.

I found a small table to set the yearbook on, but I remained standing. I scrolled the pages until I found basketball. Specifically, the 8th-grade boys' team.

I took about three pictures from my phone and then quickly allowed myself a few seconds to look at the team. Half the team was white and the other half was Hispanic.

The coach's name was Mateo Perez. He was around thirty years old, wore glasses, didn't look at all athletic, and had a dorky, fun-loving smile. When you think of hard-nosed basketball coaches, this wasn't what you thought of.

I wasn't ready to rule out suspects, but I'd have been shocked if Mateo Perez was the killer.

"It's time to go," the man said.

I remembered to get the principal's name as well.

I scrolled to the front of the yearbook. And on page two, below 'Antioch Middle School Spartans 2002', it read, *Joaquin Martin, Principal.*

I took a picture of that as well.

At this point, the library employee was walking over.

"I'm done," I said. "Putting the yearbook back right now."

"Fine," he said.

I walked back to the front, he turned off the corner lights, and we exited the library together.

"Thank you very much," I said.

"You're welcome," he said. "Now, how about that twenty?"

I grabbed a twenty from my wallet and paid the man. A promise is a promise.

I got to my car and was about to head back to Walnut Creek. It was only 1:20, so I'd wait to call Officer Picker. San Ramon to Hayward and Walnut Creek to Antioch was just about equidistant. And I'd been in and out of the library so quickly, I couldn't imagine he'd be done yet.

As I stopped at the red light to exit the school, I quickly scrolled through my iPhone to get to my pictures. I looked at Mateo Perez again. I was hoping to find something sinister in his eyes, anything to make me suspicious of him.

I found nothing. He looked like a happy-go-lucky guy. No, his potbelly didn't look like your average basketball coach, but what did that matter? Maybe he was a teacher and no one else wanted the job.

Coaches were only a small part of the puzzle, anyway. Principals, administrators, teachers, scorekeepers, parents. They would all have to be considered.

As I arrived back in Walnut Creek, I wanted to take a nap more than anything. Not that I would have been able to fall asleep. I had too much adrenaline running through my veins.

Plus, it was time to pick up Rob Osbourne's fax. Hank's would still be there as well.

I approached the parking lot and was happy to see there was no more police presence. Yellow tape still surrounded my office, however, and I'm sure the neighboring businesses were curious as to what had happened, if the news hadn't already spread. Or, worse yet, they'd seen the tarp covering the dead body.

My mind turned to Marjorie Ballard once again. Bruce might have been cheating before she hired me, but at least he was alive. That was not the case anymore. Did she hold me responsible?

And what if Bruce was dead because someone was trying to kill me? No, that didn't make me culpable, but it still meant he'd died because Marjorie had hired me.

There was some elderly man hovering outside of the 7-11, but was the only person I saw. No one was walking in or out of Starbucks, which was rare. I'm sure the yellow police tape didn't help. Who wants to worry about a crime scene when you are ordering a double frappuccino macchiato. If that's even a thing.

As I walked up to my office, I intentionally didn't look down at where Bruce had been killed. I kept my eyes focused on the lock.

I opened the door and quickly shut it.

My mind was moving at warp speed and I didn't like it. I wanted to get the faxes and get the hell out of there.

Which I did as expeditiously as I could.

Arriving home, I took a seat on my couch and set the Ronnie Fisk case file on the table in front of me.

I quickly reviewed the information that Hank had sent.

We'd gone over it on the phone so I didn't need to spend too much time on it. His evidence was incontrovertible. He'd even included death certificates on the two boys. How he got those I have no idea. And I wasn't going to ask. He had connections, there was no doubt about that.

Next, I took a look at Rob's set of faxes. There was one page that listed each of the respective schools along with their head coach. And then, a picture of each team. Just as he had promised.

I decided to check if Mateo Perez was one of the Sacramento coaches. I'd have been shocked if he was. I looked at all ten of the team photos and

Mateo Perez was, unsurprisingly, not one of the coaches. Eight of the ten coaches were white and the other two were black. No Hispanic coaches.

This didn't eliminate Antioch Middle School as a potential connection to Sacramento, but it did all but remove their head coach as a suspect.

Without Officer Picker's information, I couldn't compare Redwood Middle School just yet.

I started to wonder if this had been a wild goose chase all along. Even if I was correct about basketball connecting these dead kids, how exactly was I supposed to find the killer through old team photos? That was assuming it wasn't the coach and we got an easy match.

How was I going to find out the name of the scoreboard operator? Or the guy who wrote down the stats?

Sure, I could contact each coach and hope to amass a list of people who regularly attended the games. And cross-reference the Sacramento list with the two schools from the Bay Area. But this happened twenty years ago. People moved on. Was a coach going to remember the name of the guy who kept the stats? I doubt it.

I tried to tell myself to stay on point. Acknowledging this was a long shot wasn't helping matters.

I spent a few minutes looking at each Sacramento team. I looked at the coaches' faces like I'd done with Mateo Perez. It was true that I was a good judge of character. Unfortunately, identifying serial killers based on a still picture was not in my wheelhouse, nor in any other human being's.

I read over the players' names. Was there any chance a middle schooler could have been killing his fellow teenagers?

Stop being ridiculous, I told myself.

These murders weren't committed by a pimply-skinned eighth-grader. They were the victims.

I continued looking over each team picture. Rob had supplied a picture of Will C. Wood's team as well. I'd taken a picture from their yearbook when I'd gone up to Sacramento, but that was unnecessary now.

I looked over the printout, finding Matt Greeson. I'd seen this picture in the Will C. Wood library, but I looked more closely now.

He was seated on a bench at the end of the front row. The taller kids were standing behind the bench. It's how so many young basketball team pictures were taken. Weirdly, once they got to high school or college, it was usually just everyone standing in a semicircle.

Matt had an awkward smile and was probably still growing into himself. That seemed to often be the case with smaller kids, even those on the basketball team.

The majority of my time had been spent on Ronnie's case, for obvious reasons, but for the last several days I'd been thinking a lot about Todd

Zobrist, Adam Williams, and Matt Greeson. I grieved for all of them - and their families - just like I did for Ronnie and his.

After finishing up with Matt's team, I set all the pictures on the desk next to Ronnie's case files. I looked at my phone. It was now 2:45 and I expected to hear from Officer Picker soon.

I walked over to my window and looked at the streets below. The rain hadn't relented and the streets were getting worse.

My eyes focused on the only two people out in the rain. A mother was inexplicably out there with her four or five-year-old son. I could see the young boy kicking his feet in the pools of water, and while I couldn't see his facial expression, I'm sure he was having the time of his life.

It's probably something that Ronnie, or Todd, or Adam, or Matt would have done when they were that age. And if their lives hadn't been stolen from them, maybe they'd be enjoying being out in the rain with their own four or five-year-old.

Looking at the kid suddenly made me sad.

I moved away from the window.

CHAPTER 29

O fficer Picker finally called at 3:30.
"I've got the information, Quint."
"Great. I've got ten printouts from Sacramento and a picture I took at Antioch Middle School."

"Let me guess. The coach from Antioch was not one of the coaches in Sacramento."

"No."

"Well, let's try the coach from Redwood Middle School. Have you got those printouts handy?"

I grabbed them from the neighboring desk.

"Got em."

"My guy's name is Andre Dimmock."

I already knew that wasn't one of the coaches in Sacramento. Still, I went over each printout one by one just to be thorough.

"No match," I said.

"It was never going to be this easy, Quint."

"I know, but it's still frustrating."

"I believe in the work you've done. These murders took place twenty and eighteen years ago. They've been investigated by dozens of great detectives and they've never caught the killer. You probably weren't going to solve this in two weeks. That being said, I do think we are getting closer. Why don't we meet up and start contacting some of these coaches tomorrow? Maybe they'll remember someone affiliated with the team who was more than a little creepy. Or maybe we'll ask the Antioch and Hayward coaches if they knew anyone associated with the team who later moved to Sacramento?"

"I like that last angle, Officer Picker."

It was odd. Hank was a former police officer and he insisted on me calling him by his first name. I'd known Paul Piercy for all of ten minutes when he asked me to do the same. But Randall Picker was just fine with me calling him Officer Picker. Who knows the reason, but it always seemed so formal when we talked to each other.

"Yeah, me too. Let's meet after this atmospheric river bullshit ends. We both drove enough today."

"Alright, I'll call you tomorrow. Can you text me the picture of the Redwood team?"

"Of course. I'll do it right now. Send me the one from Antioch Middle School as well."

"I will."

~

I received the text from Officer Picker a few seconds after we got off the phone.

It was now 3:37 p.m. and although I hated taking late afternoon naps, I was exhausted and needed to make an exception.

I set my alarm for 4:45 p.m., not wanting to sleep too long. I made sure I hadn't accidentally clicked Silent Mode on. I didn't want to miss an important call and my ringer always woke me up.

I decided to give Officer Picker's picture a quick look before I laid my head down.

I could see the faces of the Redwood basketball team, but they weren't very clear. This was an iPhone picture of a twenty-year-old photo. There were thirteen people in the picture, fighting for space. And the lighting wasn't all that good, to begin with.

I persevered, looking at each player, although I'm not sure what exactly was to be gained. Curiosity, I guess.

The last thing to do was to read the names of the players which ran along the bottom of the photo. Compared to the faces, the writing was relatively easy to see.

Allen Wood. Timmy Revere. Gavin Rolle. Jeff Scully.

Something felt familiar.

I read the four names aloud, hoping that might make a difference.

I stopped at the third name.

Gavin Rolle.

I briskly jumped out of bed and grabbed the photocopies. I knew I had seen that name.

I scrolled through four teams until I found the name I was looking for.

Gregory Rolle. A player for George Washington Middle School in Sacramento.

I held the phone up to the printout and pinched the photo of Gavin Rolle to enlarge it.

Were they brothers? They certainly looked similar, but it would never be conclusive with the two old pictures I had to work with.

I didn't care. My adrenaline was at an all-time high.

Should I call Officer Picker or Hank first?

I didn't call either.

I opened my laptop, hoping to find more information. With a unique last name like Rolle, it was a distinct possibility.

After waiting a few seconds for my computer to boot up, I typed "*Gregory Gavin Rolle*" into Google.

The results shocked me to my core.

I clicked on the first article.

The Sacramento Bee. August 12th, 2004.

"Leonard Rolle was convicted yesterday of second-degree murder in the murders of his two children, Gregory and Gavin. In a trial that received plenty of local attention over the last few months, the jury returned its guilty verdict against Rolle, aged forty-six. Gavin, seventeen at the time of his death, and Gregory, fifteen, went out fishing with their father on the Sacramento-San Joaquin Delta on March 29th, 2003. They never returned and were both found a day later floating in the Delta. Leonard Rolle was arrested the following day.

Gavin had been hit repeatedly with what prosecutors determined to be a baseball bat. He died of blunt force trauma. Gregory was determined to have drowned to death despite having been hit several times as well.

In their defense of Leonard Rolle, his lawyers claimed that Gregory and Gavin got in a fight and Gregory hit his brother several times with an oar. They allege that Leonard was driving the boat while this occurred and when he came to confront Gregory, they got into their own fight. Leonard was able to secure the bat from Gregory and hit him a few times before pushing Gregory into the Delta.

Both sides stipulated that Gregory Rolle was not a very good swimmer.

The prosecution argued that Leonard killed his older son Gavin first and then hit Gregory a few times before pushing him into the Delta, knowing with his injuries, the current, and his lack of swimming skills, he'd surely drown.

The defense claimed that Leonard was just trying to save his own life from the deranged, unstable Gregory and pushed him into the Delta as a means of self-defense.

The prosecution called several witnesses who all testified that Leonard Rolle was an evil man who treated his children terribly. The defense didn't call a single witness to speak of Leonard's character.

Many experts thought that was the difference.

Sentencing will be carried out in approximately one month."

At the end of the article, there was a link to another one. I clicked on it.

The Sacramento Bee. September 17th, 2004.

"Leonard Rolle was sentenced today to almost eighteen years in jail. After factoring in the time he has already served, Rolle will be released from prison on November 26th, 2021. He will be transferred to Folsom County Prison and will serve out his time there.

Many in the Sacramento community thought the sentence was too light.

Reached for comment, Raul Diaz, the District Attorney of Sacramento, said the following: "We are happy with the sentence of eighteen years. He was convicted of second-degree murder, not first. For this reason, we thought eighteen years was punitive, but fair. Mr. Rolle will be in prison for a long time and will pay dearly for his crimes."

Rolle was convicted last month in the murders of his sons, Gavin and Gregory."

There was only one picture of Leonard Rolle and it was in the text of the first story. It was his mugshot.

He was an odd-looking man, anyone would have agreed with that. He had small, beady eyes that were too close together. He had a huge forehead and what little hair he had left was parted downward. A poor attempt at a combover.

And while it was only a mugshot, and you couldn't see his whole body, my impression was that he was short but squat, and probably quite strong. His neck was huge.

His expression was one of disdain.

This wasn't a guy you wanted to meet in a dark alley.

∼

I leaned back on my couch.

I was in shock but tried to keep my mind focused.

I didn't want to overreact so I asked myself the most logical question there was.

Is Leonard Rolle the guy?

Obviously, I couldn't be certain.

There was now a whole lot of circumstantial evidence, but nothing I could hang my hat on.

A few factors that contributed to me thinking it was him.

One, his eldest son, Gavin, played against both Ronnie Fisk and Todd Zobrist's teams in basketball. Two, his younger son Gregory, played against Matt Greeson's team in Sacramento. What are the odds that a guy has sons who played against murdered kids ninety miles away from each other? While alarming, other things were more damning.

The killings of middle schoolers ended in the eastern Bay Area after the basketball season of 2001/2002. The two murders in Sacramento occurred during the basketball season of 2003. And it was a safe assumption that Leonard Rolle lived in the Bay Area for the first set of killings and lived in Sacramento when Ryan Greeson and Jeremy Stacks were killed.

Furthermore, there were no more middle school murders in Sacramento after Jeremy Stacks. The fact that Leonard Rolle was arrested soon thereafter could very well have been the reason.

The fact that he was a convicted murderer only solidified my opinion.

I was assuming we'd find out soon that Redwood Middle School, where his eldest son Gavin played, had played the other teams of the murdered Bay Area kids.

Was it a slam dunk?

Probably not, but for me, there were just too many coincidences.

I think we had our man.

My excitement turned to horror when I remembered something.

Leonard Rolle was set to be released on November 26th, 2021.

FUCK!

This scumbag murderer had been back out on the streets for over three weeks.

I tried to find something on the internet about his release but was unsuccessful.

I'd read a lot about serial killers over the years and the thing most oft-repeated was that they don't stop killing. If that were the case, Leonard Rolle was out there, probably planning his next murder.

If he hadn't committed one already.

I was on information overload.

I picked up the phone, still unsure of who to call first.

I was going to need a few seconds.
My hands were shaking and I couldn't hold on to the phone.
I looked at Leonard Rolle's mugshot one more time.
Are you a child murderer, Leonard?
I was certain the answer was yes.

PART THREE: LEONARD ROLLE

CHAPTER 30

The elation didn't last.

My original knee-jerk reaction was to call everyone I'd met working on the case, rejoice in the discovery of a suspect, and soak in all of the compliments coming my way.

As the minutes passed, I decided that might not be the best idea.

Shouldn't you wait until you're positive this is the guy?

I was starting to second-guess myself.

I had a strong circumstantial case, but that's all it was.

My mood started to sour a bit.

～

There were a few phone calls I couldn't avoid making.

Officer Picker being one of them.

I told him what I'd found with regards to Leonard Rolle. He sounded excited but hardly exuberant. We'd been working together for a few days now and I'd expected more of a reaction.

It knocked my confidence down another notch.

Picker said he'd make some calls and try to set up a meeting with the Berkeley Police Department the following morning.

I wanted to ask why they wouldn't be storming Rolle's home tonight, but the reason was clear-cut. Picker didn't think this was as open and shut as me. He'd have to sell the Berkeley police on the name of Leonard Rolle.

I almost asked him why San Ramon didn't just take over, but I knew the answer to that as well. Their police department wasn't equipped for something like that.

He told me to expect a call in the morning detailing where and when the meeting would take place.

"What's the earliest it would be?" I asked.

"Why, you have something more important to be at?"

I prided myself on my sarcasm, but his comment seemed downright rude.

"I'm going to try and meet with the Fisks."

Picker promised me the meeting wouldn't be before ten, and since it was a Sunday, likely later.

Not only wouldn't they be breaking down doors, they also couldn't be bothered with an early morning meeting.

Picker was being a bit more standoffish than usual, but I told myself to wait until the meeting tomorrow to pass any judgment.

I started a group text with Emmett, Grant, and Evelyn. I asked them if they could meet at my office tomorrow morning at nine a.m.

Evelyn confirmed within a minute. Grant a few minutes later. And fifteen minutes later, Emmett was the last to confirm.

～

The sun was now setting and the rain below was finally starting to subside, albeit, only slightly.

I considered calling Scott Shea and Rob Osbourne.

I resisted.

Let's wait until the officers confirm he's formally a suspect, I told myself.

These people had waited twenty and eighteen years, respectively. They could wait one more day.

～

I didn't text Maddie or Patricia Fisk either.

This wasn't a case of getting gun shy, I just knew their family members would relay it to them after our meeting.

That would be followed by another meeting, this one with the Berkeley Police Department. At that point, I'd know whether I could shout the name Leonard Rolle to the heavens. Actually, hell would be more appropriate.

～

The other call I had to make was to Hank.

We talked for ten minutes and I updated him on everything since we'd last talked.

Like Officer Picker, he was intrigued, but not wholly convinced of Leonard Rolle's guilt.

I told him I was meeting with the Fisks the following morning and I'd be in touch throughout the day.

Before I knew it, eight p.m. had rolled around.

It had been one of the longest days of my life and it was going to be an early night. I'd certainly earned it.

If Hank was correct, that long day could have very easily been the shortest day of my life. And the last.

I bowed my head one more time for Bruce Ballard. One minute you're here and the next minute you're gone. Life could be so brutal. And fickle.

And if the bullets were indeed meant for me, that meant Leonard Rolle was not only out of jail, but somewhere close, and a real threat to my life.

A short, brutal, nightmare caused me to violently jolt awake at four a.m.

The balding, enormous forehead of Leonard Rolle was repeatedly slamming into my face. My legs and hands were tied and I could do nothing to stop the recurrent head butts.

At one point, I tried to say stop, but the blood in my mouth prevented me.

"You should have left well enough alone!" Leonard Rolle said.

I tried to respond again to no avail.

His voice was gravelly and there was no sense of life in his eyes.

He said the phrase each and every time he brought his head down onto mine.

"You should have left well enough alone!"

"You should have left well enough alone!"

"You should have left well enough alone!"

Finally, he head-butted me so hard that I knew I was either going to die or pass out.

That's when I jolted awake.

It took me several minutes to get my bearings straight.

CHAPTER 31

I awoke in a better state of mind a few hours later.

It was now Sunday, December 19th.

It had undoubtedly been the least Christmassy December of my life. And that was unlikely to change over the next six days.

Was I going to be chasing a serial killer on Christmas Day? I had no idea, but it was certainly possible.

My mother and I had a party on Christmas Eve every year. It was with her sister and her husband and their four rugrats. I wouldn't miss that. No, I couldn't miss that.

I needed to call my mother. I'd been a lousy son over the last few weeks, barely keeping in touch. The reason was obvious. I didn't want to burden her with the details of the Fisk case.

Still, she deserved more from me.

I vowed to call her before the day was over.

～

Officer Picker called and said there were some logistics they were dealing with. He'd text me when they'd nailed down a time.

I was fine with that.

It would give me more time after my meeting with the Fisks.

I hated to think of the Fisks as a dry run, but I might be making the same speech twice in the next few hours. Maybe not a speech, per se. More of a closing argument to convince everyone that Leonard Rolle was the likely killer.

Before I knew it, the meeting with the Fisks was ten minutes away.

After a quick shower, I threw on some khakis, a crisp blue dress shirt, and my nicest tan jacket. It was sprinkling below, but the weather was immeasurably better than the last few days. I generally wore jeans in winter, but with two meetings over the next few hours, I'd decide to dress the part.

My trip to the parking garage was uneventful. That doesn't mean I wasn't on guard and looking over both shoulders.

As I made my way out onto North Main Street, I couldn't decide whether I should tell the Fisks about the murder of Bruce Ballard. So far, only Hank and Officer Picker knew. I guess it depended if the police tape was still up. It would be hard to play dumb if it were.

I arrived a minute later and there was no yellow tape. I'm sure Starbucks and 7-11 were happy to see it gone.

I parked a few spots away so the Fisks could take the ones directly out front. Hopefully, Emmett would arrive safely and park in his handicapped spot. Or better yet, his son or granddaughter picked him up and kept him off the road.

A few minutes later, Evelyn arrived. She was wearing jeans and a heavy, dark brown raincoat. You couldn't blame her. Even though it was only tepid rain, the air was brisk. The news that morning had reported several power outages and downed trees. The storm was becoming milder, but it wasn't over.

"Thanks for coming, Evelyn."

"You're welcome. This must be important if you're having all of us out here."

I'd told them very little in the text message, wanting to wait until I had them all in person.

"It is. I can promise you that."

"I want to ask if you've found the guy, but I guess I'll know in a few minutes."

"You will. And I'm sorry I haven't given you many updates over the last five or six days. I promise you it's been a whirlwind."

"I understand," she said. "I just put up the money. It's Emmett and Hank who deserve the updates. And my father."

I didn't tell her that I'd already updated Hank last night.

"Do you want to come inside?" I asked Evelyn.

I was fully aware that she was feet from where Bruce Ballard had been killed.

"Sure. Thanks."

I opened the door and had Evelyn sit on the couch in the waiting room. The couch would have been a tight fit for four people so I'd probably be sitting in the executive chair that was meant for my non-existent secretary.

I raised the blinds so we could see the parking lot.

Grant Fisk was next to arrive, and I was pleasantly surprised when Emmett Fisk exited the passenger side door.

Evelyn and I walked outside to greet them.

"I know, I know, don't fall over the cement block again," Emmett said.

He was irascible as ever.

I shook Grant's hand.

"Thanks for coming and for driving this guy. Can't you get him off the road?"

"Oh, phooey," Emmet said.

"We hired a service for the grocery store and doctor visits. That's a good first step," Grant said.

I brought them into the office and asked the three of them to sit on the couch. It was even snug for three.

I decided that sitting in the executive chair was too informal, so I sat on the desk itself.

All three sets of eyes focused on me and had to be wondering why I'd brought them here.

"First off, thank you all for coming. Evelyn, I know it's a far drive and these conditions certainly are not ideal. I wouldn't have set this up if it wasn't important. I promise to describe how I got to this endpoint, but I'm just going to come out and say it first. I think I know who killed Ronnie."

There were gasps or audible noises from all three. I heard a 'Dear God' from Emmett. A sigh by Evelyn, followed by her covering her face. And a groan from Grant. I couldn't get a read on it, but I construed it as anger.

"His name is Leonard Rolle. He had two sons, Gavin and Gregory Rolle. Do any of those names ring a bell?"

They all shook their heads.

"I will try to make this as painless and quick as I can, but here's how I've come to that conclusion."

"Don't hold back," Emmett said. "We should know everything. Even if it's going to hurt."

I nodded.

"For the first five or six days of my investigation, I focused on your family, neighbors, and some other assorted suspects. That included Ty Mulholland, who was the closest the police had come to labeling a suspect. While there were people who thought Ronnie was killed by someone close to him, I wasn't one of them, but I wouldn't have been doing my job if I hadn't given it my due diligence. Sure, some of the neighbors weren't savory characters. I concede that. I just didn't think any were killers. So around Friday or Saturday of last week, I started considering the idea that Ronnie had been taken by a stranger or someone he barely knew. I leaned towards it being someone he partially knew because if it was a total stranger, Ronnie would have put up a fight and people would have heard. But as you all know, nobody saw or heard anything that night."

I looked at the three faces. They were transfixed, as you'd expect.

"So I started looking at Hank's list of other kids who had gone missing. I was able to eliminate many of them over the coming days, most of them being fifteen and older. I stayed focused on the missing or dead middle school kids. Those were the murders and disappearances that felt most similar to Ronnie's. A recurring theme that kept coming up was basketball. Three of the kids played for their middle school team and as I dug deeper, I found that two of the other kids attended their school's games. Five of the six in the eastern Bay Area had ties to eighth-grade basketball. This led me down a long, deep rabbit hole of trying to find out the schedules of these basketball teams. I got help from several people, including an old teammate of Ronnie's named Scott Shea."

I got one reaction.

"I remember him," Grant said.

"He was very helpful. I'd also come to suspect that a few murders in Sacramento might be related. One of these kids, Matt Greeson, played for his basketball team as well. I acquired a schedule as well as the team picture."

I paused for a moment, remembering I'd left Todd out.

"I left something out. Todd Zobrist was an 8th grader who was killed in San Ramon a few months after Ronnie He wasn't on the basketball team, but attended games. That's the other schedule from the Bay Area that we were able to get. There were two middle schools that played both Willard and Iron Horse Middle School in San Ramon. Antioch Middle School and Redwood Middle School in Hayward. I was hoping it was going to be easy as one of those two coaches had also coached in Sacramento. It wasn't to be. Next, I started looking at the team pictures we'd gathered. We had Antioch, Redwood, and the Sacramento schools. And that's when, last night, I saw a very uncommon last name on both the Redwood team and one of the Sacramento teams. Gavin Rolle had played for the Redwood team that played Ronnie's team. And Gregory Rolle had played for George Washington Middle School, a team that played Matt Greeson's."

I felt like I was rambling, but the Fisks' attention hadn't wavered.

"I decided to Google the names of Gavin and Gregory Rolle. I hoped to find them on Facebook or something. Instead, I discovered they both met with a tragic ending. Their father, the aforementioned Leonard Rolle, killed the pair of them out on the Delta back in 2004. Now, the fact that he's a convicted murderer doesn't mean he's guilty of the crimes I'm investigating, but it doesn't hurt. The fact that his sons were at games attended by Ronnie, Todd, and Matt is a huge coincidence."

Grant spoke up.

"First off, it's amazing just how much work you've done, Quint. I'm sure I speak for all three of us when I say that. But, and don't take this the wrong way, I'm not sure that would hold up in a court of law."

It wasn't the reaction I was expecting. Or hoping for. But I'd become used to it since discovering who Leonard Rolle was.

"I left a few things out. Hank and I had looked for information on clusters of murdered kids around the eastern Bay Area. After the winter of 2002, these murders ended. I reached out to a friend of mine who is close with a bunch of old cops. The only cluster any of them could remember was the two kids killed in Sacramento. Now, Leonard Rolle left the Bay Area sometime between the end of the 2002 winter and the fall of 2003. And that's the point where the murders stop here. And when they begin in Sacramento."

Emmet spoke up next.

"That should have been your opening. That feels like stronger evidence than that flimsy basketball connection."

Even in a serious moment, Emmett had an irreverence about him.

"The basketball connection is what led me to everything else. And just wait. I'm meeting with the Berkeley PD in a few hours. I'm sure they've already started doing their homework on Leonard Rolle. And I'd bet he attended some of the other missing kids' basketball games."

"What does Hank think?" Evelyn asked. "He rarely mentioned the potential of a serial killer to us."

"There's a reason. It's a bit complicated, but the Berkeley Police Department wasn't exactly forthcoming with all the information they had."

"What?" Grant was pissed.

For a guy who had come across as pretty mellow, he'd been fired up. Maybe the fact that I'd mentioned an actual suspect's name had hit home with Grant.

"It was political with an old Alameda DA trying to win reelection," I said.

"Byron Grady?" Emmett asked.

"That's right. He didn't want Alameda County in general - or Berkeley, specifically - to think there was a serial killer on the loose."

"I always hated that mother fucker!" Emmett said.

"Grandfather!" Evelyn exclaimed.

"What, we're talking about dead kids and I can't use the phrase mother fucker?"

"Just a little surprising coming from a ninety-year-old."

"Ninety-two," he said.

"Let's get back to the issue at hand," Grant said. "So this DA held back info to win an election?"

"Basically, yes," I said. "They still investigated Ronnie's death. They just didn't mention the phrase, serial killer, to the media or in police reports. Do you guys remember a detective named Paul Piercy?"

"I do," Grant said.

"He's the one who broke all this news to me. He worked on Ronnie's case. I think he still feels very guilty about it."

"As he freaking should," Grant said, and his two other family members nodded in unison.

"It wouldn't surprise me if, in a few months, he caves and starts talking about Ronnie's murder investigation and the corners that were cut."

"I'll believe it when I see it," Emmett said.

"So, what's next, Quint?" Grant asked. "Will the police go interview Leonard Rolle in prison?"

I realized I'd made one other big mistake.

"I'm sorry. I forgot to tell you. Leonard Rolle got out a few weeks ago."

"What the hell?"

"How is that possible?"

The questions came rapid-fire.

"Well, he was only convicted of second-degree murder and eighteen years was agreed upon."

"So this guy, who may have killed Ronnie, is out there running free?" Grant asked.

If I was going to bring up Bruce Ballard, this would have been the time. I resisted, not wanting to turn this into a discussion about me.

"Yes, but as I said, I'm meeting with the Berkeley police in a few hours. I think they'll be confronting Mr. Rolle very soon."

This information garnered a few nods.

"When I hired you, Quint, the phrase needle in a haystack was mentioned. I can't believe you've come this far. I really can't."

"Thanks, Emmett. And just so you guys know, I will be seeing this to its conclusion. You can pay me if you want, but I don't really care. There's nothing in the world that would keep me from finishing this case."

"We appreciate everything," Evelyn said.

"Any other questions?" I asked.

No one responded.

"You were pretty thorough," Emmett said.

"Now there's an understatement," Grant said.

I heard my phone ringing. I pulled it out and saw it was Officer Picker.

"Guys, I have to take this call. Hang tight."

I walked outside my office and shut the door.

"Officer Picker, any news?"

"I've got some good news and some bad news, Quint."

"Hit me with the good first," I said.

"I contacted the current principal of Redwood Middle School last night. I told him I needed him to pull any strings he needed to in order to get the schedule of the 2001 8th grade basketball team. He called me back with that information this morning. You have a better knowledge of the missing kids than I, so I'll let you see which of the other dead kids Redwood had played against."

"That's great. Can you text me that schedule?"

"I did right before I called you."

"Sorry, I didn't see it. I'm in a meeting with Ronnie's family."

"How are they taking it?"

"Pretty well, all things considered. So what's the bad news?"

"You're not going to like it."

"Just tell me," I said.

"You're not going to be coming to the meeting with the Berkeley PD."

I was crushed.

"Why not?"

"Since this is predominately based on Ronnie Fisk's murder, the Berkeley Police Department have closed ranks and are trying to keep this for themselves. They were trying to keep me out of it and only acquiesced when I told them I'd worked the Todd Zobrist case from the beginning."

"Is this because I'm a P.I. and not a cop?"

"It certainly doesn't help."

"This is such bullshit. I've spent more time on this than anyone."

"More than Hank? More than detectives who have been on this case from the beginning?"

He had a point, but I didn't want to hear it. Not now.

"I'm talking about the last two weeks."

"Isn't the most important thing to catch Leonard Rolle?"

"Of course."

"And if we do, you'll have been a huge part of it, Quint."

"Do they know where he lives yet?"

"I will probably learn all that information today. While you, and to a lesser extent, me, think he's the killer, we don't exactly have a slam dunk case. Hopefully, I can do some convincing this morning."

The 'lesser extent' comment stung.

"I should be there," I lamented.

"True. But it's not going to happen, so stop dwelling on it."

"Will you call me after the meeting is over? I deserve that."

"Yes, you do. And yes, I will."

"I guess there's nothing more to say."

"Take care, Quint."

And just like that, I was no longer an integral part of this investigation.

I walked back inside, the wind having been taken from my sails.

"What is it?" Evelyn asked.

My poker face must have been terrible.

"The goddamn cops aren't allowing me into their meeting of the minds."

"I'm sorry, Quint. I can't say I'm surprised," Grant said.

He was probably right. I shouldn't have been so shocked.

"Don't worry, I'll still be investigating on my own."

"Who needs them? You've done more in two weeks than they've done in twenty years."

"Thanks, Emmett."

"Is there anything else?" he asked.

"No, I think we've covered everything. I will text all of you once I hear how the meeting went."

"Good. Hopefully, they go arrest this piece of human garbage."

"Agreed."

I shook hands with all three.

Grant and Emmett walked out first and they got in their car and drove off.

Evelyn approached hers.

"Evelyn," I called. "Did you call Maddie?"

She swiveled around.

"I did."

"And?"

"And there's a lot of old wounds we have to get through. It was a good start, though."

My heart warmed a bit.

"I'm glad to hear it."

"Thanks for making me do that, Quint."

Evelyn got in her car before I had time to respond.

She exited the parking lot and I was there by myself.

I looked down and realized I was standing on the spot where Bruce Ballard had been killed.

$\sim$

Ten minutes later, I was at my apartment looking over Redwood Middle School's basketball schedule for 2001/2002.

I had Hank's notes open and was cross-referencing each game to see if they matched with one of the murdered kids' middle schools.

And to my delight - or was it dismay - three of the schools matched up.

Delight, because this just helped cement my opinion. Six kids were killed that winter in the Bay Area and Leonard Rolle was in contact with five of them. Sure, other parents may have been at every Redwood Middle school game, but none of them then moved to Sacramento and attended a Matt Greeson game as well.

I made a note to myself to look more into Eddie Young's murder. He was the only child who didn't go to basketball games and San Leandro Middle School, where he attended, was not on Redwood Middle School's schedule. Maybe Eddie's murder wasn't related, but he did die by strangulation. I wasn't ready to rule it out just because there was no basketball connection.

There was dismay as well, imagining Leonard Rolle scoping out these 8th-grade basketball games, looking for his next target.

The thought disgusted me.

Randall Picker called a few hours later.

"How did it go?" I asked.

"I've got another good news and bad news scenario."

"I'm tired of this," I said.

"The good news is that the Berkeley PD are looking at Leonard Rolle as a suspect. I thought I made a convincing argument that he was involved. They aren't ready to drop the guillotine, but he is now on their radar."

I was starting to realize why Officer Picker had been behind a desk in San Ramon. He wasn't a very good cop.

He'd said, "I *thought I made a convincing argument.*"

I was calling bullshit.

"That's lukewarm good news, at best," I said, bluntly. "I thought they'd be raiding his house by now."

"That brings me to the bad news. Leonard Rolle has not been seen or heard from since he was released from jail."

"Doesn't he have to report to a parole officer?" I asked.

Right away, I realized my mistake.

"He wasn't paroled. His sentence was done."

"He has to have gone somewhere," I said, stating the obvious.

"We talked about that. The Berkeley PD is currently looking at relatives."

"Was he married? The articles didn't mention it."

"He was widowed."

"Did he kill her too?"

"That's what I feared," Officer Picker said. "But no, cancer got her."

"Was the Walnut Creek Police Department present?"

"No, just me and the BPD."

"So Bruce Ballard's murder didn't come up?"

"Not during the meeting."

"You don't think it was relevant that Leonard Rolle might be out there trying to kill the P.I. investigating him?" I asked.

I could feel my blood starting to boil. How had I ever gone into "business" with Randall Picker?

"I only had the floor for a few minutes, Quint. I'm on the outside looking in and mainly talked about Leonard Rolle."

"What else was discussed? Do you have a timeline of Leonard Rolle before he went to jail?"

"I have his addresses in Hayward and Sacramento. He moved out of Hayward and up to Sac in April of 2002."

"Just as I'd assumed. The murders of middle school kids in the East Bay had stopped after March of 2002."

"I know, Quint. It's not me you have to convince."

"That means he moved in the middle of the school year," I said.

"True."

"I'll bet he feared the police were closing in on him. He was wrong, obviously."

It was an intentional shot at Officer Picker. I didn't care. He didn't respond.

"Can you send me those addresses?" I asked.

"Yes."

"How does someone just vanish after they get out of jail?"

"I'll bet that's a lot more common than you think."

"You're probably right," I conceded.

"And with no immediate family, he's not going to be easy to find."

"Then I'll go knock on his old neighbors' doors. I'll find something. I have to."

I'd said I or I'll in three straight sentences. It was no longer we when it came to Picker and me.

"Listen, we all want to catch this guy. It's not just about you."

He'd obviously picked up on my first-person trifecta.

"No offense, but I don't have that much faith in the San Ramon and Berkeley Police Department," I asked.

I was going full scorched earth policy.

"Listen, Quint."

"Don't tell me to listen. I'm not a child. I'm listening."

"As I said, the Berkeley PD is looking into Leonard Rolle. They'll soon be coordinating with other East Bay police departments. They aren't going to have much time for a P.I."

"I brought you into this," I said.

"You did. But this is now beyond my control."

I was glad I'd never gotten on a first-name basis with Officer Picker. He was selling me down the river.

"Are you going to send me updates?" I asked.

"I don't think the Berkeley Police Department wants me dealing with an outsider."

"First off, stop mentioning police departments every two seconds. It makes you sound like a damn fraternity. Second, I'm not an outsider. I'm as entrenched in this case as anyone."

"Maybe you should start bouncing your ideas off of Hank."

I was pissed. I wanted to tell him off, but I needed to get all the information he'd learned at the meeting first.

"Did the BPD specifically tell you to stop talking to me?"

There was a pause that gave away his upcoming answer.

"Yes."

"What a joke!"

"I'm sorry, Quint. This is beyond my control."

"You already fucking said that."

I hung up the phone, the proverbial steam coming out of my ears.

Now what?

CHAPTER 32

Monday passed without much happening.

I went to interview people on the street where Leonard Rolle lived in Hayward. Only one couple remained.

They told me that Rolle was a jerk, not that it came as any big surprise. He would yell at anybody who came near his property. Rumor had it that one time, he almost swerved into a bunch of kids on their bikes, steering his car away from them at the last second.

The couple said you could never predict someone would kill their kids, but they hadn't been completely shocked. It was a stunning admission.

Rolle was a blue-collar guy who worked as a plumber, pipefitter, and often in construction.

They had no idea where he might have gone upon being released from jail.

And when I brought up the local murders of 2001 and 2002, they got very skittish. Not because they had something to hide. It was just an extremely awkward thing to talk about.

I left a few minutes after that.

I also reached out to a few more family members of the murdered kids. I didn't mention the name, Leonard Rolle. Word like that would spread like wildfire, and even though I hated the local police right now, I had to give them a few days.

I still hadn't been able to find a basketball connection with Eddie Young. I'd talked to his brother who was adamant that Eddie never attended the games.

Basketball had tied several of these murders together, but it didn't have to be the sole way that Leonard Rolle picked his victims. Still, Eddie Young's case stood out like a sore thumb.

If my list was correct, he was also the first kid who went missing.

Maybe that meant something.

It was impossible to know at this point.

~

I had seen no media coverage of the case.

Not that I'd expected to.

They certainly weren't going to name a suspect before the police. That was a lawsuit waiting to happen. And to be honest, they probably hadn't even heard the name Leonard Rolle yet. Not with the BPD's history of not taking to the media.

I was starting to feel like I was alone on an island.

~

To make matters worse, it appeared Randall Picker was officially done with me.

Not that I was surprised.

I had ended our phone call with an F-bomb, after all.

~

I went to sleep on Monday night depressed as hell.

My big discovery, the culmination of two weeks of exhausting work, hadn't amounted to jack shit.

CHAPTER 33

I called Hank early on Tuesday morning. An idea had been percolating since I'd woken up.

"Hey, Quint."

"I figured I should come to see you."

"Thought you'd never ask. What time?"

"How about ten a.m.?"

"See you then."

～

The atmospheric river was now a memory and the sun was out in full force. As much as it can be for December, anyway.

The drive to Hank's was easy and I arrived in near record-setting time.

I knocked on the door and he answered soon thereafter.

"Do you want to sit on the deck today?" he asked.

"Thought you'd never ask."

Hank poured us each a cup of coffee and we took our respective seats on the deck. The water below was as calm as I'd ever seen the Bay.

"Everything alright, Quint? You seem to be at a standstill of sorts."

"That's a fair assessment. You'd have thought finding a suspect would have pushed this thing forward. Instead, I feel like I'm hamstrung."

"From what you've told me, you can blame that on the BPD."

"Partially. I need to be better as well."

"Do you have a plan?"

"I've had an idea marinating this morning."

"I'd like to hear it."

"It involves you cashing in on every last unused favor you have."

"I've still got a few people who owe me things. What do you need?"

I could tell Hank what a big ask this was for me. How I knew how slim the odds were. Or, I could just come out and say what I wanted.

"I want to talk to Leonard Rolle's last cellmate."

I was expecting a reprimand, but none came.

"That's not going to be easy."

"You didn't say impossible."

"No, I didn't. He was at Folsom County Prison, right?"

"Yeah."

"Do you like Johnny Cash, Quint?"

"Sure, I like his music," I said, not knowing where this was going.

"Then you've heard of *At Folsom Prison*, his famous live album?"

"Of course. It's a classic."

"Cash recorded that in 1968. There was a young prison guard who worked at Folsom Prison at the time. His name was Bob Oxford. He was only twenty-three years old. He'd later tell me it was the best live album ever released. Nothing could ever match the intensity of performing live at a prison, he'd argue."

"He probably has a point," I said.

I didn't bother telling Hank I had no idea where he was headed with this. He would arrive at his destination when he was good and ready.

"Bob said the roars within the jail when Cash sang *Folsom Prison Blues*, which he opened with on both nights, could have registered on the Richter scale."

"I can only imagine," I said, now fully playing along.

"Cash proceeded to sing several songs about prison, including "Green, Green Grass of Home," "The Wall," and "25 Minutes to Go." He also played classics like "The Long Black Veil" and "Give My Love to Rose.""

"I wish I could have been there."

"Me too. Luckily, Bob Oxford would remind me through the years of just how great it was. You see, I grew up with Bob. When I joined the police force, he started as a prison guard. You might think that's not as prestigious as being a police officer, but Bob had no plans on staying a guard. He was going to rise fast. And he did. By the time 1985 hit, Bob, still just forty years old, had become the warden of Folsom County Prison."

I liked where this was headed.

"And you guys stayed in touch?" I asked.

"We sure did. Remember, we were friends since we were kids. Now, we didn't have all that much professional overlap. Most of my collars went to

San Quentin, being a lot closer to San Francisco. But there were times I'd venture up to Folsom. Usually, it would be to interview a guy in jail, trying to get information on a suspect. And like clockwork, every time I went up there, I'd meet with Bob. Sometimes, we'd be able to sneak away for lunch, but usually, we'd just talk at the prison."

Bob Oxford would be in his mid-seventies. He couldn't still be the warden, could he?

"And he'd regale you with stories of Johnny Cash playing live?"

Hank smiled as bright as I'd ever seen.

"That's exactly right, Quint. He'd always bring it back to Johnny Cash and that memorable concert."

"So where is Bob Oxford now?" I asked.

"Oh, he retired as warden about fifteen years back. But you know what?"

"What?"

Hank smiled again, this time a lot more deviously.

"I seem to remember that he hand-selected the next warden. And I imagine that guy would do anything for Bob."

It was my turn to smile.

"This has been well worth the build-up, Hank."

"I thought so."

"So you really think Bob will ask the warden for a favor?"

"That's not even a question. Bob will do anything for me. What is up for debate is whether the current warden can make this happen. And my money is on yes."

I didn't know what to say.

"Cat got your tongue, Quint?"

"Five minutes ago, I was writing you off as having Alzheimer's and rambling about Johnny Cash. Now I know why you are a legend."

Hank laughed.

"Those last two sentences are perfection."

"Thanks. What exactly can the warden do?"

"Not sure exactly. Promise the prisoner more days in the sun? A steak now and then? A few extra bucks in his commissary? Don't you worry yourself with that. Just be prepared to drive to Folsom in the next day or so."

"You're serious?"

"As a heart attack. I'm going to call Bob Oxford as soon as you leave here."

"I don't know how to thank you."

"Get some information that will lead you to Leonard Rolle. That'll do."

"Do you have any advice in dealing with inmates?"

"Be yourself. Be upfront. Tell them the truth about why you are there. In my experience, they're either going to help you or they're not. The rest is decoration. But it can't hurt to be the real you."

"Thanks."

"You'll do fine. You have a good rapport with people."

"I'm not sure everyone would agree with that."

"Pissing a few people off lately?"

I nodded.

"From what you've told me, it sounds like the BPD is just following protocol."

"They are going to regret it when I'm proved right about Leonard Rolle."

"Time will tell," Hank said. "If I was going to defend them, I'd say most of your case is still circumstantial."

"Every time Leonard Rolle leaves a city, young boys stop dying. Whether it be Hayward or Sacramento."

"And that's why I keep telling you that I believe you. However, what you've just told me is not holding up in a court of law. And I know police officers aren't lawyers, but if they are going to arrest a guy, they like to make sure it's something the District Attorney can convict on."

Even though Hank was defending the police departments, it raised my spirits. He was saying the police were more worried about potential court cases and things like the burden of proof. Not me. I had one goal. Trying to catch a serial killer.

"No offense, but screw cops," I said.

"I'll let that slide since I know you're attempting humor. Poorly, I might add."

"Present company excluded, of course."

"Don't make my seventy-five-year-old body kick your ass."

We both smiled and simultaneously looked down towards the water below.

It was still relatively placid.

"They always talk about the calm before the storm," I said. "This is more like the calm after the storm," I said.

"In meteorological terms, yes."

"What other terms would we be talking about?"

"If we were referring to Leonard Rolle, maybe this is the calm before the storm."

"It's a stretch, but I get your point," I said.

Hank stood up, signifying the meeting was over.

~

To my shock, Hank called me back less than two hours later.

After we said our greetings, he said, "Are you ready to hit up Folsom County Prison?"

"When? Today?"

"That's right. I told you it might come soon."

"You're a miracle worker. What time?"

"Four."

I looked down at my phone. It was 12:15 p.m. Folsom, CA was about ninety minutes from me.

"I'll be there. What do I have to know or bring?"

"Just bring your driver's license and your P.I.'s license. Don't worry, they won't give you much grief. It's the warden who OK'd this, after all."

"You've done a lot for me, Hank. This may be the cherry on top."

"Well, with my fellow cops stuck in the mud, you may be our best chance. God save us all."

He was busting my balls and I responded with a quick laugh.

"I'll call you on my way back."

"Yes. You will."

I was about to hang up the phone when Hank said one last thing.

"And the prisoner's name is Cole Townes."

CHAPTER 34

Folsom County Prison is the second oldest prison in California. The cell blocks were originally built in 1878 and it was the first prison in the country to have electric lights.

These were a few of the fun facts I learned reading up on Folsom before my ride up there.

For the first forty years, there were no walls surrounding the prison. A different time for sure. The granite walls they eventually built were now the signature look of Folsom Prison.

Some of its famous inmates included Charles Manson, Suge Knight, Erik Melendez, and Danny Trejo, who later became a well-known actor.

There were many references online to Johnny Cash's concert. No mention of a young prison guard named Bob Oxford, but I was grateful to the man.

The current warden's name was Anthony Lahr.

I also tried a quick google search of Cole Townes. There was a brief article that mentioned a Cole Townes who killed a Brinks security officer in the course of a robbery. This happened in Sacramento, and I was pretty sure this had to be the guy.

If I was correct, Cole Townes wasn't necessarily an irredeemable monster like some in prison. There's a chance he just made one terrible life decision. I wasn't excusing his actions, but I was happy I wasn't meeting with a child abuser or a family annihilator.

Maybe I was just trying to conjure up a little empathy for the guy I was about to interview.

~

I arrived at Folsom County Prison around 3:45. The granite walls I'd read about were very prominent. Out front, they rose to form what almost looked like a mini-lighthouse. I'm sure it was to have a bird's eye view of the prisoners below. It had a green, triangular rooftop that stood out among the gray granite walls.

I parked my car in visitor parking. I was wearing jeans with a dress shirt. I wasn't a lawyer and thought wearing a suit would have been too much. Like Hank had said, be yourself. And I was not a suit-and-tie guy.

To my surprise - or maybe it wasn't one at all - I was greeted by Anthony Lahr outside of the front gates.

"You must be Quint Adler. I'm Warden Lahr."

He smiled at me and my initial impression was that he was a very civil, measured man. Not always what you'd expect from a warden. He looked to be in his mid-fifties and still had a full head of hair that gave off a youthful vibe.

"I am. Thanks so much for this, Warden Lahr."

"You can thank my predecessor, Bob Oxford. Sounds like you have a friend who's pretty tight with Bob."

"I do. And he regaled me with stories of Johnny Cash and Bob as a young man at his Folsom concert."

The warden smiled.

"I've heard those stories myself."

"I enjoyed them."

"I didn't ask much, but I heard you're suspicious that a former tenant of mine, Leonard Rolle, may have been murdering more than just his own kids."

"That's what I'm trying to find out, but yes, I do believe that and it's the reason I'm here."

"A few words about Cole Townes. He's been in here for fifteen years for killing a Brinks security guard. He got a life sentence. He's a hardened inmate, but he's not the worst of the worst. He's got a giving soul and he'll expose it from time to time if you let him. And none of the prison guards have ever had a problem with him. I don't expect you will, either."

This was surreal, talking to the warden of Folsom County Prison outside the gate.

"Thanks for all of that," I said.

"Shall we go inside?"

"Sure."

Warden Lahr motioned to someone and a gate opened. We walked in.

"I'll try to see you on your way out. Stay here and someone will help you do the paperwork you must complete to interview one of our tenants."

I was mildly amused by him referring to the inmates as tenants. Not that I was going to tell him that.

"Thank you for everything."

"You're welcome. Good luck."

And with that, he walked away.

A prison guard approached me and asked for identification. I gave him my driver's and P.I. license and told him who I was there to see.

A few minutes later, he was walking me down the corridor of Folsom County Prison. I wouldn't have believed it myself if I hadn't been there.

~

We entered a room that wasn't what I'd imagined.

I'd been expecting a row of prisoners on one side with their loved ones on the other, both talking on phones through the reinforced glass.

Instead, I was going to be having an actual one-on-one talk, devoid of people all around me.

I don't know if this was all Bob Oxford and Warden Lahr's doing or if lawyers, police officers, and P.I.s were treated differently than family members. I'm sure as my career moved forward, I'd become more acquainted with the protocol of prisons.

The prison guard hadn't said a word since I'd finished filling out the paperwork.

"I will be right on the other side of the glass," he finally said. "I can almost guarantee you that Mr. Townes won't try anything, but I'm here just in case."

"Thanks," I said.

I was both excited and uncomfortable.

The guard led me into the all-white room. There was a long rectangular table in the middle and a chair on each side of it.

On the other side of the table was a man in his forties with slicked-back brown hair. He had tattoos all over his arms, but mercifully, none on his face. He wasn't a big guy but looked wiry-strong.

He was wearing an orange jumpsuit.

What he was not wearing were any handcuffs. This was surely intentional. An inmate would be more likely to talk if they were unchained.

The prison guard closed the door, but didn't lock it, and took his seat at a table directly outside of the room.

I felt both safe and vulnerable all at once. This whole experience was a clash of perspectives.

"Nice to meet you, Mr. Townes. My name is Quint Adler and I'm a private investigator."

"How do you do?" he said, taking me by surprise with his accent.

It most certainly wasn't from Sacramento. Or California.

"Where are you from? I don't get to hear many accents like that."

"Louisville, Kentucky. Known for basketball and thoroughbreds."

"That football team has been pretty good lately, too," I said.

"I reckon so. Lamar Jackson put us back on the map."

I had no idea the conversation would start this way, but I was pleasantly surprised.

"Won a Heisman Trophy for you guys."

"That he did."

"I've always wanted to hit the Kentucky Derby," I said. "Sports bucket list for me."

"It's the biggest party of them all. Better than Mardi Gras if you ask me. The infield is full of gorgeous women. Some of them even take their tops off, Mardi Gras style. I had the pleasure of attending four Kentucky Derbys before I came out west and started my life of crime."

Sure, he was a felon who'd murdered someone, but I couldn't help but have sympathy for the guy in front of me.

I wasn't sure if more small talk was necessary or would come off as fake. Being as I was new to jailhouse interviews and all.

"Did anyone tell you why I was here?" I asked.

"Warden Lahr came and saw me himself. Told me it was regarding my old cellmate. That's all I know."

"That's right. And I could sugarcoat it and dance around the issue, but I'll just come out and say it. I think you deserve that. I believe Leonard Rolle murdered several teenage boys."

"You don't say."

"You don't seem all that surprised."

"Well, he already killed two boys, right?"

"That's a little different. Those were his sons."

"Shouldn't they be harder to kill? If you can kill your own kin, you can pretty much kill anything. At least, that would be my guess."

I doubted that Cole Townes had much of a formal education, but he was no dummy. His comment was very insightful.

"You may be right," I said. "I hadn't thought of it that way."

"Count yourself lucky not having to share a cell with that guy for eight years."

"I'm sorry."

"Yeah, me too. I was so dang happy when he got released a few weeks back."

The fact they didn't get along was a blessing to me. I assumed Cole would be more willing to talk ill of Leonard Rolle.

"What pissed you off about him?"

"Where do I start? Pretty much everything, I reckon. To start, he was the most impolite SOB I ever met. If we're going to be cellmates, is it that fucking hard to say please and thank you?"

Out of the corner of my eyes, I could see the prison guard switch positions. I was expecting him to admonish Cole Townes for swearing, but it never came.

"I don't blame you. That's the least he could have done."

"Plus, I'll be honest, I was a little scared of him. I'm tough, but I ain't big. With those arms and that neck, he could have killed me if he wanted."

"Did he get angry easily?"

"It wasn't like that. He was like, I guess you'd call it permanently mad. It wasn't some switch that went off."

"I get your point."

"We used to call them sourpusses in the South, but obviously, for old Leonard, that wasn't going far enough."

"Did he ever talk about killing his kids?"

"Rarely. No, never. I mean, I knew what he was in for obviously, but we never talked about the actual day he killed his kids."

"It's probably something you don't want to discuss."

"You wouldn't think so. But we got a lot of inmates in Folsom who won't shut their yappers about what they done. If there's one good thing I could say about Leonard, it's that he didn't talk much."

I nodded.

"So, I'll just come right out and ask this, even though I'm afraid I already know the answer."

"Ask anyway."

"Did Leonard ever mention killing any other kids?"

"No. Nothing like that."

"I had to ask."

Cole Townes looked at me oddly.

"We did have one weird conversation a few weeks before they released him."

"I'd love to hear it."

"It was late and we were about to hit the hay. We almost never talked, but for some reason, he wanted to talk that night. I'd assumed it was because he was getting out soon. We talked about our childhoods and how that was the best time of our lives. He asked me about Louisville which came as a shock. One thing Leonard wasn't was a question asker. He didn't give a shit about expanding his mind. But I'll give him credit. For one night, he cared. Or, pretended to anyway. Our talk went on like that for a little while. I knew he was getting out in a bit so I asked him what he was going to do. He said, 'Not be so easy on kids this time.' I said something like, 'You weren't easy on your kids, because that's what I thought he was talking about. Then he just laughed and said, 'Not those ones.' Our conversation ended a few minutes later, but I remember that clear as day."

I didn't want to overreact. This was a conversation between two convicts, after all. And it was obvious that Cole Townes hated Leonard Rolle. But fuck, if it didn't sound like an admission of some sort by Rolle.

No, I was wrong. This was worse. It wasn't an admission. It was a look into his future.

"Did you tell anyone this?" I asked, knowing I wouldn't like the answer.

"No, I didn't tell no one. I thought the old crackpot was just trying to sound tough. Plus, it was, what's the word? Vague, that's it. It's not like he told me something specific."

"Probably not a good thing to go ratting on your cellmates."

"No. I wouldn't have wanted to share a cell with old Leonard those last few weeks if he'd known I talked. Now that he's gone, I don't give a fuck."

I could feel the prison guard look up from his desk. Still, no warning from him. I wondered if Warden Lahr had told him to give us some rope.

"Now that you mention kids' deaths," Cole said. "Maybe he did mean something by it."

"Did Leonard tell you where he was going when he got out?"

I saw Cole thinking about it.

"Nah. I don't think he had no family left either. Obviously, his sons were dead. And they were his only kids. His wife had died well before then. And he never mentioned no cousins or uncles or anything like that."

Cole's double negatives were oddly endearing.

"Do you know if he had any money for when he got out?"

"I don't. I'll never have that issue being a lifer. Ain't that some bullshit? The guy kills his two kids and gets out. Meanwhile, I make one horrible decision in my twenties and have to rot here for the rest of my life."

"I'm so sorry. Yeah, that's fucked up," I said.

"Well, what I said ain't exactly true. I made a lot more mistakes than just that one. But that was the unforgivable one."

This was tough. I genuinely felt bad for Cole Townes.

"Maybe you catch old Leonard and they give me credit for time served and get me outta here."

We both smiled, knowing that would never happen.

"I'll put in a good word," I said.

Cole laughed again.

"You can put money in my commissary so I can buy shit in here. How about that?"

"I will," I said. "I promise."

"You're a good guy. Quint, right?"

"Yeah. Thanks."

"So, any more questions?"

"I'm trying to find out where Leonard might have gone."

"Wish I could help you. If you had no family, where would you go?"

"I'm not sure."

"Maybe somewhere you knew well," Cole said. "Where it felt like family."

Was he making the case that he'd go back to the Bay Area? I can't imagine he'd move back to Sacramento.

"Wouldn't someone want a fresh start?" I asked. "Not have everyone know your crimes?"

"I'm not saying he'd go back to Sacramento. They'd have drawn and quartered him if he'd done that."

We'd agreed on that point, with his conclusion being a little more graphic.

"Did he talk about his time in the Bay Area at all?"

"No, but that was no different than Sac. He never talked about that either. That's why this one conversation we had was so weird."

"And nothing else that night stood out?"

"Nothing important. That line about the kids was what stood out."

Was Leonard Rolle out there right now, looking for his next victim? And did 'Not being so easy on kids' mean what it sounded like? Was he going to do worse than strangling them? Draw out their murder longer? I was revulsed.

"Was he friendlier with any other people in prison?"

"Nah. He kept his distance. Plus, everyone knew Leonard was a vile old cuss. No one wanted nothing to do with him."

I was trying to rack my brain for more questions to ask. Nothing came to mind.

I decided to go with the old faithful. The question I'd asked almost everyone.

"Is there anything else you can add? Something that only you might know?"

"I wish I did. I'd love to lock up that old cuss again. Just promise you won't send him back here. I'd be a dead man."

"He won't be coming back here," I said.

"Yeah, probably not."

I could feel the conversation coming to a close.

"Thanks for talking to me."

"You may be surprised to hear this, but I enjoyed it, Quint. Now you be sure to deposit some money in that commissary for me."

"I told you I will, Cole. And I'm a man of my word."

"Thanks," he said. "Be a nice Christmas present for me."

I smiled.

The most Christmas spirit I'd felt in two weeks was from a convicted murderer. To say this interview had been odd would have been underplaying it.

I turned around and gave the prison guard a thumbs up.

"Thanks again, Cole."

"I like how you call me by my first name. Don't happen much in here."

I smiled.

"Check your commissary before Christmas."

"Oh, they'll let me know."

The prison guard entered the room. I turned one last time to Cole.

"You take care of yourself," I said.

"Will do. Now go bring down Leonard, that old cuss."

We both gave a slight nod to each other.

I was going to remember this for a long time.

Five minutes later, the door to the Folsom County Prison was opened for me.

Sadly, it would never be opened for Cole Townes.

Maybe I'd appear at his next parole hearing. Who knew?

Warden Lahr was not waiting for me when I walked outside. I drifted around for a few minutes, but when he didn't show, I figured it was time to go.

I walked back to my car and started my drive back to the Bay Area.

CHAPTER 35

I bypassed Walnut Creek and drove straight to the Berkeley Police Department. On the drive, I'd become increasingly livid that I'd been left out of the investigation. I'd done more in fifteen days than the BPD had done in twenty years.

"I'd like to talk to Detective Paul Piercy," I said upon arrival.

"Give me a minute. Your name?"

"Quint Adler."

The officer gave me a look that signified he knew my name.

Two minutes later, Detective Piercy appeared. He'd wanted me to call him Paul, but I felt misled by him. Like Picker, he didn't deserve to have his first name used. Funny that I'd been complimented by a felon for using his first name.

"What can I do for you, Quint?" He didn't look happy to see me.

"Why aren't you guys investigating Leonard Rolle?"

"Why don't we take a walk again?"

"No, thanks. I'm not going to be here very long."

"What do you want?

"I want to know why you're not investigating Leonard Rolle?"

"Maybe we are."

"Maybe we are, like maybe you were investigating the murder of Ronnie Fisk?"

Several cops looked in my direction. I didn't care. Let them hear what I had to say.

"To be honest, Quint, we're not as confident as you that Leonard Rolle is a killer."

"Is that coming from you or your superiors?" I asked. "Who is the new Sheriff Byron Grady of 2021?"

He looked genuinely hurt. I didn't care. I was trying to save lives.

"That's completely unfair," he said.

"Why wasn't I allowed to be part of this?"

"Higher-ups than me."

"Take a stand," I said.

Detective Piercy looked around.

"I think it's time for you to go, Quint."

He wasn't the brave whistleblower I'd first believed him to be. He was the same coward now as he was twenty years ago.

"You know I just talked to Rolle's cellmate? Leonard said he's not going to go as easy on kids this time."

"What are you talking about? How did you get to meet with his cellmate?"

"Are you serious? I tell you that Leonard might kill again and you ask me about protocol?"

A few officers moved in my direction. The last thing I needed was to get arrested.

"I'll go now," I said. "You have my number if you ever want to do what's right."

He had a pained expression on him as I turned around to go.

More than anything else, I spent that night thinking.

I'd read and reread the case files so many times that it was becoming the law of diminishing returns. I was hoping that just sitting back and thinking about the case might bring something to mind.

After a few hours spent mostly in thought, one thing kept coming back to me.

The fact that Eddie Young had never gone to basketball games. It was the one case that stood out from the others and it begged the obvious question. Where did Leonard Rolle find Eddie Young? The Mall? Church? A random restaurant?

I didn't know, but it wasn't at a basketball game.

I looked at my notes.

Eddie Young went missing in San Leandro, a city that bordered Hayward. Eddie was the victim who lived the closest to Leonard Rolle. The rest of his victims had lived a good distance from Hayward. And

Eddie was the first child who went missing. That suddenly seemed very important.

I looked back at my notes.

It had been Eddie's brother, Kyle Young, that I'd talked to. I remember him being adamant that Eddie never went to any basketball games. I also recall him mentioning that his mother was in an old folks' home and having memory issues.

I hadn't pushed it then, but I wanted to talk to her now.

I looked down at my notes a third time and dialed Kyle's number.

"Hello."

"Kyle, this is Quint Adler again."

"How's the investigation going?"

I didn't want to mention Leonard Rolle . My hope was to get a meeting with his mother, but if Kyle knew we'd be talking about potential suspects, he might have nixed it.

"I'm making some progress."

"That's good to hear. What did you want from me?"

"I just wanted to confirm. Eddie never attended basketball games, correct?"

"Never. Not one. Our family, myself included, were not sports fans in the slightest. Plus, I was only two years younger than Eddie. I'd have known if he went to any of those games."

"Just verifying. Thanks. And you said your mother was in an old folks' home?"

"Yeah. She's only about eighty percent there if you know what I mean."

"I'm sorry to hear that."

"The tough part is she's only sixty-seven. It's happening too early."

"Way too young," I said. "What's her name again?"

"Lena. Why do you ask?" he said suspiciously.

It was now or never.

"Is she here in the Bay Area?"

"Yes."

"I'd like to meet with her. With your permission, of course. I understand that her memory probably won't be great, or maybe not even good, but this is very important to me."

He waited a few seconds, clearly thinking it over.

"What if I was there with her?" he asked.

"That would be fine."

"She'd feel safer. And truthfully, she might be more apt to answer your questions."

"Perfect. When can we do this?"

"How about tomorrow afternoon? I get off work at four and can meet you there at 4:30."

"Great. What's the name of the home?"

"Senior Living of San Leandro."

For some reason, I was happy to know she was still in San Leandro. Maybe I thought it more likely she'd remember things about her son.

"I'll be there. Thanks, Kyle."

Next, I made the call I should have been making more often, to my mother.

"Hello, Quint," she said. "This is you, right? Or maybe it's the guy who hijacked his phone the last few weeks."

"Love you too, Mom!"

"Oh, you know I love you. Even though you haven't called much lately."

"I'm sorry. I really am. I've been in the middle of a complicated case."

I wanted to say as little as I could about it.

"I figured. I'm proud of your new job, but you don't seem to be very good at keeping in touch with dear old Mom when you're working."

She was referring to Hollywood and Las Vegas as well. I hadn't been great about touching base with her then, either.

"That will change, I promise. It's just tough working my first case up here and trying to get the business off the ground."

I certainly wasn't going to mention the second case and where Bruce Ballard was killed.

"Do you want to tell me about the case?"

"Not now. Sorry, Mom. But maybe at our Christmas Eve dinner."

"I thought you forgot. Are you coming to Ginny's?"

With the death of my father and me being an only son, our Christmases were not big occasions. My mother's sister, Ginny, lived in the Bay Area, however, and they had four kids, so we usually ate with them on Christmas Eve.

"Of course I am," I said

"Good. We can catch up then."

I was happy to be talking to her but bummed I couldn't tell her more. The alternative was worse. She'd worry about me 24/7.

"I love you, Mom. I'm sorry this is such a short call, but I promise I'll make it up to you on…"

I blanked.

"On Friday," she said. "Christmas Eve is on Friday."

"See you then, Mom."

I should have known what was coming next.

"Be safe, Quint. I can tell from your voice that what you're doing is a little more dangerous than getting a cat out of the tree."

I laughed.

"Ever so slightly."

"I love you," she said.

"I love you too, and I'll see you soon."

CHAPTER 36

Not much was accomplished on Wednesday morning.
Nor early that afternoon.

I didn't want to admit I'd put all of my Wednesday eggs in the Lena Young basket, but honestly, I had.

At three p.m. I took my first shower of the day and headed off towards San Leandro.

I arrived ten minutes before four and headed towards the entrance to 'Senior Living of San Leandro'. It was a long, green, one-story building. Did most old folks' homes try to limit the number of floors? That would make sense.

There was a guy who looked to be around thirty waiting right out front. I assumed it was Kyle Young. If so, it was the second time in twenty-four hours someone was waiting outside for me.

The difference was this wasn't a prison. At least, not one with bars.

Maybe people losing their memories would say that's a prison of its own.

"You must be Quint," he said.

Kyle Young had dark brown hair that was parted with authority. You could definitely see the scalp between the two sides of the part.

From the photos I'd seen of Eddie Young, it looked like a grown-up version of him. I imagine the brothers had looked very similar in their youth.

"I am," I said. "Kyle?"

"It would be weird if I wasn't."

I laughed and we shook hands.

"Come on in," he said.

I followed him and we checked in at the front desk. They asked for our driver's licenses and we signed the ledger, specifying what guest we were there to see.

The receptionist was friendly with Kyle. I assume he visited his mother a lot, which had me feeling guilty, despite calling my mother the previous night.

"It's this way," Kyle said.

His mother was in her own room about thirty feet down on the left. The wallpaper was littered with flowers and babies.

I had no idea just how far gone Lena Young was, but I'd soon find out.

She had a full set of white hair that made her look older than her sixty-seven years. The old-fashioned haircut didn't help. She was wearing a loose-fitting, lavender, fleece sweatsuit.

"Hi, Mom."

I waited by the door.

"Hello, Kyle. I didn't know you were coming today."

"It's a surprise day. I brought a friend too."

He motioned me to walk over.

I extended my hand and she took it.

"This is Quint."

"Nice to meet you, Quint."

Not knowing what to call her, I said, "Thanks, Mrs. Young."

"How are you friends with my boy?"

I wasn't sure what to say. Luckily, Kyle came to my rescue.

"He's investigating what happened to Eddie."

"Really? That was almost fifty years ago."

That was the first indication she wasn't all there.

"It was only twenty years ago, Mom. And Quint might be making some progress, so I hoped you might answer a few of his questions."

"Sure, but there's no catching the boogie man."

"Why don't we sit?" Kyle asked.

There was a pair of small two-seat couches in her family room. There was a door that remained locked that surely was her bedroom.

They sat together on one couch and I sat opposite them.

Kyle motioned his hand, telling me to proceed.

"Do you remember the day Eddie went missing, Mrs. Young?"

"I don't remember yesterday. And you think I'm going to remember fifty years ago?"

This was going to be even tougher than I'd expected.

Kyle didn't correct his mother a second time.

"I bet Eddie was the best little kid," I said.

Maybe trying to remember the good times would jar her memory.

"He was the greatest. I just wish God hadn't called him home so early."

"I'm so sorry," I said.

"At least I have another kid who I love dearly," she said.

Kyle leaned in and hugged her. It was obvious they had a nice relationship. It had probably been bolstered by their shared grief.

"Is there anything you remember from back then that might help me?" I asked.

It was the twentieth time I'd asked the question and the least likely I was to get a helpful response.

"I got nothing for you. I'm sorry. I wish I remembered more."

Despite having made the mistake of saying fifty years twice, Lena Young wasn't all gone. In fact, I bet she and Kyle had some very nice visits. Hopefully, her inevitable decline would be slow.

I could ask her a hundred more questions about her son, but it would be of no use.

I might as well ask the question I'd come here for.

"Do you remember the name, Leonard Rolle?"

Kyle Young let out a noticeable flinch. Lena Young stared at me with disdain.

"Why are you here?" she asked. "Who sent you?"

I looked at Kyle, but he looked as pissed as his mother.

"What did I do?" I asked.

"Get him out of here," Lena Young screamed. "Now!"

I wouldn't have thought a woman that frail could have screamed so loud. It pierced the room.

I stood up to go. This wasn't going to end well if I stayed.

"Wait for me outside," Kyle said.

His eyes were as piercing as his mother's scream.

I walked out of the room, down the hall, and exited the building.

I had no idea why they'd acted so violently to Leonard Rolle's name.

A few minutes later, Kyle Young stormed out. He got within a few feet of me and for a second, I thought he was going to throw a punch.

Instead, he pointed in the direction of the end of the parking lot. We walked there. He obviously didn't want to have this conversation in front of the building.

"What the hell was that?" he asked. "Are you intentionally trying to hurt an old lady?"

"No, of course not."

"Then why the hell did you say that godforsaken name?"

"I don't know what's going on. Honestly. I think I need an explanation," I said.

"You first. How the hell did you know that name?"

I took a deep breath.

"In my investigation, Leonard Rolle has come up as a potential suspect in the death of your brother."

Kyle Young looked at me, stupefied.

"You're joking?"

"Not even a little bit."

It took him a few seconds to get his bearings. So I spoke again.

"What did he do to your mother?" I asked. "And please, believe me, I had no intention of bringing up something that would trigger her."

"They had an affair," Kyle said. It obviously hurt him greatly. "Which led to things far worse."

I had so many questions.

"When Eddie went missing, did you ever consider Rolle a suspect?"

"I was only twelve years old, so I suspected both nobody and everybody at the same time. If that makes sense. But no, I don't think he was ever a suspect. Their affair had been several years previous. And for all I know, she hadn't seen him in years."

"I'm very sorry your mother had to hear that. Please apologize for me."

Kyle looked at me with a new understanding. If a face could do a 180, his had just done one.

"I'm going back inside after we're done talking. My mother and I will discuss something else, and hopefully, she'll forget it. Jeez, I can't believe I'm saying that, but for once, it will be good for her to forget."

I just nodded in compassion. There was nothing I could add.

"Why is Rolle a suspect?" Kyle asked.

I had more questions for him, but it was only fair I answered some of his first.

"As I told you on the phone during our first call, several kids were killed in the Bay Area in 2001 and 2002. All five of the other kids either played for the basketball team or went to their middle school games. Leonard Rolle's oldest son was on a team that played against every other missing kid."

"That's why you were asking about basketball?"

"Yes. Eddie was the only child where I couldn't find that connection."

"So you thought maybe it was personal?"

"I'm not sure if I'd thought that far ahead. I just knew that this case was a little different. He was the first to go missing and had no basketball connection"

"Okay."

"And since you were so young when your brother went missing, I wanted to talk to your mother."

He nodded.

"How long did they have an affair?" I asked.

"Only a few months. It was less the affair and more my father's reaction to it. He was livid. And very old school. To him, being cheated on was a fate worse than death. Remember earlier when I said the affair led to things far worse?"

"Yes."

"Well, my father ate his gun several months after finding out. He just couldn't get over it, apparently."

"I'm so sorry, Kyle."

He looked like he wanted to cry. How could you blame him? A guy that had an affair with your mother which led to your father's suicide could now be guilty of murdering your brother? It was unimaginable.

"Thank you. Sorry for jumping on you earlier."

"No need to apologize. I was completely in the dark regarding your family's history with Leonard Rolle."

"Where is he now?"

"He just got out of jail."

"He was in jail?"

I looked at his surprised expression, which told me that he really didn't know.

"He killed his two children. 2004 in Sacramento. He was released late last month."

"You're kidding me?"

"I guess I just thought you would have known."

I'd never heard of the Leonard Rolle case before I researched it. Maybe it was a big deal in Sacramento but hadn't matriculated down to the Bay Area. It made sense he wouldn't have known.

"After the affair and then my father's suicide, we never mentioned the name Leonard Rolle in our home."

"And no neighbors told you guys what happened to him?"

"Rolle didn't live near us. He lived in Hayward. They would rendezvous in dirty motels. I doubt a single neighbor of ours knew about the affair. We certainly didn't tell anyone why our father took his own life."

"Of course not."

"And once Eddie died, my mother was never quite the same. The last thing she was ever going to do was try and find out what happened to Leonard Rolle. She blamed him for her family falling apart and wanted nothing to do with him."

"Did she finally talk to you about him? You seem to know a little bit."

"About three years ago, when her mind was starting to falter, she sat me down and told me all of it. There were parts I already knew. When she finished, we agreed to never say the name Leonard Rolle again. It never even crossed my mind to Google the guy. Nor did I ever think he might have killed Eddie. This was a brief affair from what my mother tells me. Why would he go and kill Eddie?"

"I don't have an answer to that. I don't know if it was revenge or if he got infatuated with your older brother."

"But you think he killed Eddie?"

"I thought that before I came here today. This only solidifies it."

"You said he's out of jail. Is he going to be rearrested? Are the police at least monitoring him?"

"No. The police aren't as convinced as I am."

"This keeps getting worse," Kyle said.

"I know. Maybe this information will finally have them see the light."

I'd already decided I was going back to the Berkeley Police Department when I was finished here. I didn't care if Paul Piercy hated me. They'd have to listen now.

"Do me a favor," Kyle said.

"Sure," I said.

"If you're right and Rolle did kill my brother, please don't contact my mother. Can you imagine the guilt?"

I couldn't.

"I won't contact her. I promise. And I'll tell the cops the same. If they have any heart, they'll honor my request."

"Okay. Thanks."

"Did your mother tell you anything else about Leonard?"

"I know his wife died. And I knew he had those two kids. And my mother thought he was shacking up with another woman."

"What made her think that?"

"When my mother cut it off with him, he apparently said he was going back to this one woman."

"Do you remember her name?" I asked.

Kyle looked deep in thought.

"It was a total old lady name. Give me a second."

I waited, knowing how frustrating it was to have something on the tip of your tongue.

After fifteen seconds, he blurted the name out.

"Betty Jean Clifton."

"That would certainly suffice as an old lady name."

I was trying to bring any sort of levity to this brutal conversation.

"It was weird. My mother said that whenever Rolle mentioned her name he'd say all three names. 'I'm going to visit Betty Jean Clifton.' 'If you leave me, I'll just go back to Betty Jean Clifton.' Things like that."

"Very odd," I said.

"Sure was. Kind of freaked my mother out."

"Do you know where she lived?"

"I don't. From what I gathered from my mother, she was older. And I'm not just saying that because of the name."

It was time to find out more information on Betty Jean Clifton.

"Thanks for all your help, Kyle."

"Are you going to talk to his woman?"

"If she's still alive, yes."

"And you'll let me know what happens with Leonard Rolle?"

"Of course. Once again, I'm sorry your mother had to hear that."

"Don't worry about it. I understand now."

I shook his hand and watched him head back into the old folks' home to comfort his mother.

I couldn't handle much more of this case.

I got back to my car and googled the name '*Betty Jean Clifton*.'

A few names popped up.

I amended my search to include 'home', 'address', and 'Bay Area.'

Nothing came up.

I called Hank.

"What's up, Quint?"

"I need another favor."

"Getting you into Folsom County wasn't enough?"

"This will be easier, I hope. I need to know if a woman named Betty Jean Clifton is still alive. I think she'd be an old lady at this point. She probably lived close to Hayward in 2001. I have no idea where she is now. But if she's alive and still in the Bay Area, I'd really appreciate an address."

"How soon do you need this?"

"As quick as you can."

"Hold tight," he said and hung up.

I was going to wait until I heard back from Hank. There was no use driving back to Walnut Creek if Betty Jean Clifton still lived near Hayward or San Leandro.

After Hank didn't respond for fifteen minutes, I began to reconsider my stance. It was starting to get dark and the last thing I wanted to do was sit in an old folks home parking lot waiting for a text that might never come.

I hadn't seen Kyle walk back out. I hoped he was able to make his mother feel better. I felt terrible for what had happened. Not that I could have known.

I looked down at my watch.

Wednesday, December 22nd, 2021. 5:14 p.m.

I told myself I'd give Hank until 5:30. I was driving home if I hadn't heard back by then.

At 5:26, with only minutes to spare, Hank called back.

"Give it to me, Hank."

"She's still alive at eighty-four years young. 2962 Rocking Horse Way in Union City."

"Thanks."

"Dare I ask what you're doing now?"

"Eddie Young's mother had an affair with Leonard Rolle."

"You're fucking kidding me?"

"Nope."

"This has to be the nail in his coffin. Way, way too many coincidences. This should be enough even for the inept Berkeley Police Department."

"I was thinking about dropping by there tonight. Not to exult, but to convince them they need to take this seriously."

"With this info, they'll take it more than seriously. They'll put out an APB out on the monster."

"I hope you're right."

"So, how does this Betty Jean lady fit in?"

"It sounds like Leonard Rolle was also having an affair with her."

"And just maybe she knows where he'd go after getting out of jail?"

"You'll make a good cop yet, Hank."

I heard him laugh.

"Why don't you call me when you're done with her. Maybe I'll meet you at the BPD."

"Yeah?"

"Yeah, why not? After twenty years, I think I've earned the right to spike the ball."

He was right. Hank deserved it more than anyone.

"I'll text you when I'm done with old Betty Jean."

I sounded like Cole Townes, putting old before somebody's name.

"I got Grant calling on the other line," Hank said. "Talk soon."

And with that, he hung up.

CHAPTER 37

My GPS said that Union City, and specifically 2962 Rocking Horse Way, was thirteen miles and twenty-eight minutes away.

I was getting low on gas and there was a Chevron right across the street, so I decided to fill up before heading that way.

My eyes looked up at the crescent-shaped moon. The sky was now dark. It had only taken minutes.

I got back in my car and merged onto the freeway.

It was now rush hour and Interstate 880 South was no picnic at this time of night.

With Christmas Eve only two days away, I imagined this would be the last day that some people would go to work.

I slowly made my way down Interstate 880 until I found my exit. My GPS said I was still five minutes away. I took a left, two rights, and another left.

I was now one minute away from Betty Jean Clifton's home.

In five hundred yards, I was to take a right on Rocking Horse Way.

The homes I drove past were a little run down and it probably wasn't the most desirable area. That being said, it still felt like the suburbs where kids played in the street and you watched your family grow up.

I took the right on Rocking Horse Way and looked out upon the street. My immediate hope was that Betty Jean Clifton was not the house on the end.

There were two houses on the left and two houses on the right. They were all fairly close to each other. Then, at the end of the Cul-de-sac was an old Victorian house that was very different from the other homes on the block. And not just because it was a Victorian on a street full of nameless, average-looking homes.

It looked like it had trees growing out of its roof. I'm sure they were actually behind the house, but with the moon lighting them up, and the shadows it created, they looked as one.

I looked down at my GPS. Just my luck.

The Victorian was the 2962 address.

I could already tell Betty Jean Clifton was going to be a peach.

~

I parked my car to the right of the home.

There were two sets of steps to get to the front door and I thought it would be odd to park at the base of them.

I opened my door and took in the house from street level. If anything, it had become even creepier.

A small part of me wanted to call the cops, but that was never going to happen.

What was I going to tell them?

"Hi, I'm scared of an eighty-four-year-old lady and her macabre-looking home."

I'd come this far alone. I'd interview Betty Jean and then I'd go to the Berkeley Police with the connection between Lena Young and Leonard Rolle.

I walked from my car to the bottom of the steps. I looked up and saw the home with all the trees behind it. I'm sure it was lovely during the day. Not so much at night.

I started walking up the steps, one by one.

I got to the break between the two sets of steps where it leveled off for a few feet. I then started up on the second set of steps. A few seconds later, I was standing in front of a large front door. It had an old-school knocker, but I chose to use the doorbell.

~

The door was answered by a woman who looked to be over a hundred years old.

I'm not kidding.

The skin around her cheeks and jawbone had become so emaciated that she looked more like a skeleton than a living human being.

Her hair was a mixture of white and gray. Not elegant gray, but dirty gray, as if she hadn't washed her hair in weeks.

She was wearing a long gown that was littered with food stains. She stared me down, a menacing growl on her sunken face.

"What the hell do you want?"

She let out a loud whooping cough.

"Are you Betty Jean Clifton?"

"What's it to ya?"

I didn't like the woman in front of me or the way this had started. Something told me I shouldn't bring up Leonard Rolle.

I didn't want to expose my hand to this woman. I sensed evil.

"Just had a few questions, is all."

She slammed her feet on the ground in front of her. She was still inside the house and hadn't joined me on the steps. Nor did I think she would be.

I looked down at her feet. They were filthy and what parts of skin you could see were nothing but varicose veins.

Half of me still wanted to get the hell out of there. The other half knew something was going on and needed to find out what it was.

Her feet hit the ground again.

Betty Jean Clifton was nervous about something and I hadn't even brought up Leonard Rolle.

I considered the possibility that maybe she was just an old, nervous lady. But I didn't believe that.

There was something more sinister at work.

"What kind of questions?" she asked.

Every few seconds felt like a minute. It was hard to describe, but a lot was going on.

I looked at her feet one more time. She was moving them back and forth and could not keep still.

"Oh, the questions are from a long time ago. How's your memory, Betty Jean?"

If I was wrong about this and she was just a scared old lady, I'd owe her a big apology.

"I'm eighty-four years old. What do you freaking think?"

She let out another vicious cough, staring at me the whole time

I could no longer lie to myself. It was time to go. My anxiety was through the roof along and I had a huge vibe of uneasiness.

But I had to know one thing before I left.

I was going to say Leonard Rolle's name and judge her reaction. If she reacted suspiciously, I wasn't going to wait for the BPD, but call the police immediately.

She stomped on the floor one more time.

For the first time, I considered that maybe she wasn't nervous, but trying to alert someone.

FUCK!

It was time to ask my question and get the hell out of there.

"Do you know a man named Leonard Rolle?" I asked.

And just as I finished saying his name, the real-life Leonard Rolle appeared. He emerged in a split second from behind the front door. He was holding what I first feared to be a gun, but I quickly realized was a Taser. I turned to run as he pointed it towards me and pulled the trigger.

∼

The first tase sent me to the ground.

The second came immediately thereafter.

And a split second later, Leonard Rolle was grabbing me by my feet and dragging me into their house.

Barely conscious, I looked at the houses down the block. It had all happened so quickly, there's no way any of them saw. And it wouldn't have been loud enough to hear. I was sure that's why Rolle hadn't used a gun.

I tried to thrash around, but he gave me a third tase, and I was done fighting back.

Once my body was completely in the house, he quickly shut the door. Betty Jean Clifton was now ten feet from us, standing over what looked to be a downward-headed staircase. It was dark in the house, but I could make that much out.

My spasms from the taser came to an end, but I was in no shape to fight back.

"You're supposed to be dead," Leonard Rolle said to me. "But I'm going to relish this second chance."

I saw him go and lock two huge deadbolts, one for getting out and one for getting in. Vacating this house was not going to be easy.

"Going to take your time this time?" I asked.

"That's right."

"That's exactly what you told Cole Townes you'd do to kids once you got out."

I was trying to say anything to get him riled up. If I wasn't moving physically, I had to at least be moving our conversation along. If not, he'd surely grab his gun and kill me.

"Fuck. You get around, don't you?"

"Cole says you were a disgusting piece of human garbage. Even amongst the filth at Folsom Prison."

I looked up and Rolle had a sly smile on the side of his lips.

Betty Jean Clifton stood back in the shadows and didn't say a word.

"You got balls, I'll give you that," he said.

I took in the figure in front of me.

He'd lost the bad combover from his mugshot and was now completely bald.

His neck was gigantic.

His eyes were vacant.

And none of that mattered because I didn't have a plan.

Keep talking!

"He told me a lot of things. Said you only killed middle-schoolers because once they got to high school, you wouldn't be able to restrain them. Said you cut off their hair and would make dolls out of it. Said you'd have dreams at Folsom where you and the dead kids were playing house together."

I was making all of this shit up. Anything to rile him up and keep his eyes off the prize, which was me.

"He didn't tell you any of that, you lying scumbag."

"I'm the scumbag? Look in the mirror you freaking monster."

I was starting to get a little strength back but wasn't sure what I could do. He was three feet away and pointing a taser at me.

"Betty Jean, go downstairs and get my gun. You hear?"

She looked like a zombie as she walked to the top of the stairs and disappeared down them.

"Why don't you try to strangle me?" I asked. "Can't deal with a grown man?"

Truth was, Leonard Rolle was built like a linebacker.

I was just attempting anything that might get him to lower his guard.

I heard some noises coming from downstairs. I hoped it was only Betty Jean.

God forbid, don't let there be a child down there.

I racked my brain for any course of action.

It better happen swiftly.

Once the gun arrived back up, I was a dead man.

I looked out at the stairs beyond Leonard Rolle.

I had a long-shot idea, but what wasn't at this point?

I was still on the ground and Leonard Rolle was approximately three feet from me. He had to stay relatively close for the taser to work properly.

There were another four or five feet between him and the top of the stairs. If I was able to fling my body into his at just the right time, maybe he'd fall back into Betty Jean Clifton and they'd both fall down the stairs.

It was worth a chance. The alternative was being shot to death.

I heard more rustling downstairs.

How long did it take to find a gun?

"What's taking so fucking long?" Leonard Rolle yelled.

"I found it. Coming up."

It was almost a miracle that this eighty-four-year-old woman could get up the stairs.

My plan was to send her back down them. Violently.

I had no qualms about it.

She was part of this. There was no question. Going to get the gun only cemented it.

I heard her take the first step.

My heart rate, already off the charts, accelerated even further.

It took a few seconds until I heard her move again.

Maybe she'd have a heart attack on her way up.

I'd take my chances against a taser as opposed to a gun.

Judging by the sounds below, she was now about a third of the way up.

There was going to be no heart attack.

She took a few more steps and was now closer to the top than the bottom.

Leonard Rolle looked down at me.

I tried to put on the most pathetic face possible. One more tase and my plan would be futile. I'd be twitching in pain when she arrived at the top.

My hope was that Rolle would either turn around or possibly extend his hand to her. In the process, turning his back on me.

I saw the disgusting hair of Betty Jean Clifton appear. I couldn't see the rest of her body yet, but I knew she was only a few steps from the top.

I knew I'd never have time to get to my feet. I'd be tased well before then. The same would be true if I pushed off my feet and lunged at him.

There was only one chance.

To push off my butt and propel my legs in Rolle's direction. I didn't know if my legs would reach him, but it was my one shot.

The top of Betty Jean Clifton's shoulders appeared.

Rolle turned around for the briefest of moments, but it was too early. I needed to wait until she was at the top to ensure they'd collide.

"Two more steps," Rolle said.

He then looked directly at me and said, "I think we'll give you one more tase for good measure."

I no longer had any time to waste. It was now or never.

I used my hands and my butt to propel my legs forward and I launched them at Leonard Rolle.

They were going to fall short. I knew it.

And they probably would have if Leonard Rolle had taken even a single step back. Instead, he saw what I was doing, and was adjusting the taser to make sure it was pointed directly at me. It was a mistake on his part.

My feet somehow connected with his chest, and he wasn't able to pull the trigger until he started falling back.

That made all the difference.

I felt a quick shock, but nothing like I'd dealt with earlier.

My eyes remained focused on Rolle. He continued to flail backward and it looked inevitable that he was going to connect with Betty Jean.

He'd managed to swivel around so he was now facing her, but he couldn't stop his momentum.

The "skeleton" at the top of the steps couldn't have weighed more than ninety pounds and I knew even the slightest connection would send her tumbling down the stairs. And, quite possibly, to her death.

Leonard Rolle did indeed make contact with her. It wasn't much, but it was enough. The gun dropped from her hands, but to my disgust, it fell forward and onto the ground above the top step.

It felt like everything was happening in slow-motion. After dropping the gun, Betty Jean's arms went up in the air and Leonard Rolle realized she was going down the stairs. It was now a foregone conclusion.

He hadn't hit her straight on, so he was able to allow his body to fall down above the stairs.

Betty Jean was now leaning back at an almost unthinkable angle. It couldn't last. Gravity was about to win out.

A split second later, it did.

She fell backward, which was followed by a loud thump, surely her back hitting the stairs. Next, I heard the sound of her somersaulting down the stairs. The last sound was her body hitting a wall down below.

There was a deafening silence for a few seconds.

Until Leonard Rolle screamed.

And the word he yelled shocked me to my core.

"Mother!"

CHAPTER 38

The gun was still on the ground next to Leonard Rolle.
He stood up and was bending over to pick it up.

I quickly went through my options.

One, I could rush him, but he was now ten feet away from me. I wouldn't make it.

Two, I could try to open the door. I'd seen how long it took to shut that deadbolt. That was a worse option than rushing him.

The third option wasn't exactly optimal, but at least it gave me a fighting chance.

I looked over and Leonard Rolle was now raising the gun.

I had no time.

I quickly rose to my feet, took one step, and hurled myself over the railing and onto the stairs below.

～

I landed on my back, probably about a quarter of the way down the stairs, proceeding to somersault the rest of the way down.

The body of Betty Jean Clifton softened my blow. I didn't have time to look whether she was dead or not. She wasn't the one I was worried about.

I was probably more injured than I realized, but I couldn't stop moving. That would be a death sentence. As I was about to jump in the hallway, I allowed my eyes a quick glance up the stairs.

Leonard Rolle was pointing his gun at me.

I heard two gunshots go off as I leaped towards the hallway.

I landed and quickly realized he'd missed me altogether. I looked back to the base of the stairs.

It no longer mattered if Betty Jean Clifton had died coming down the stairs. She was dead now, shot through the heart.

I heard Leonard Rolle scream from the top of the stairs.

"You're going to pay for this!" he yelled.

And I heard him take the first step.

I looked to the left and right. It was dark, but I could tell the right was a dead-end that ended with a room of some sort.

I'd be a sitting duck if I went that way.

"Not many places to go," Rolle said. "And by not many, I mean none."

He let out a horrific, manic laugh.

I took a step to the left but didn't commit to going down the hall. I considered waiting there and attacking him when he arrived at the bottom of the stairs.

He likely foresaw my plan and that's why he was taking his time.

I yelled as loud as I could. I was trying anything to get him to move too fast. The more methodical he was, the less chance I had.

"Nice try. The neighbors can't hear that," Rolle said.

I heard him take another step, but he was still on the upper half of the stairs.

"Yeah, but maybe they heard those gunshots," I said. "Especially that one that killed your mother. She was alive before that, you know?"

I continued to try anything to get him rattled.

"Don't you speak about my mother!" he yelled.

"I know you didn't call her that. Lena Young told me you always called her Betty Jean Clifton. What kind of psycho calls his mother by her full name?"

"You don't understand."

I had him reeling. I was cornered, and without a weapon, but I was winning the mental battle.

"Is this your bedroom down here? Were you not allowed on the main level like normal people?"

"I said stop!" he yelled and I heard him take another step or two.

He was silent for several seconds.

And then I heard him take a few more steps.

"How did you find Lena Young?" he asked.

Although it was a logical question, it felt forced.

He was furious at my last few questions. Why would he change the subject and try to talk amicably?

I was afraid I knew what he was doing. He was now far enough down the stairs where he could fire through the wall and hit me.

And I thought the question might be to establish where I was standing.

I slowly, quietly took several steps backward.

A few seconds later, two gunshots blasted the area where I'd just been standing. I was a few feet - and a few seconds - from being dead.

"Did I hit you, Quint? Must have been one straight to the heart because I didn't hear you scream in pain. Maybe you got lucky and it just killed you instantly."

I was done talking.

For the obvious reason that he'd then fire in my direction. Also, him thinking I could possibly be dead might work to my advantage. I wasn't sure how, but the less information he had, the better.

I looked to see what was next to me, careful to be silent as humanly possible.

I saw a bathroom a few feet ahead and quickly formulated a plan.

A bathroom would be the worst hiding spot imaginable, but that's not what I needed it for.

It was dark, but I saw something on the tile. A glass of some sort.

I moved closer.

It was a glass with two toothbrushes in it.

I grabbed the glass and left the toothbrushes.

I heard Rolle take another step and he was now nearing the bottom of the stairs. He was likely staring at the lifeless eyes of his mother and wanting to disembowel me. I wasn't going to let that happen.

I had an ingenious plan. If it didn't get me killed.

To my count, Rolle had fired four shots from his gun. Two towards me when I landed at the bottom of the stairs. And two more when he tried to shoot me through the wall.

I'd gotten a brief look at the gun. It had been a revolver, and while they varied, most of them carried six bullets.

If I could get him to fire twice more, there was a good chance he'd have emptied the chamber.

My plan was to throw the glass against the door on the other side of the hall. My hope was that Rolle would instinctively fire in that direction. The problem, and where my life would be at immediate risk, is if he realized his mistake and quickly fired in the opposite direction.

To combat this, as soon as the glass hit the door, I'd jump into the bathroom. I figured that extra door would supply me with the protection I needed.

My heart felt like it was about to go through my chest.

Better that than one of Rolle's bullets.

I took a step forward in the hallway so I could have a clear throw. The glass would shatter when it hit the door. I just hope he fired the gun.

Here goes nothing!

I couldn't duck into the bathroom until the glass struck the door. If I went too soon, he'd hear my footsteps.

I cradled the glass in my right hand and knew the time was now.

I threw it hard, directly at the door.

I saw it shatter and quickly ducked into the bathroom.

Within a second of the glass shattering against the door, a gunshot echoed through the downstairs area.

I kept hoping I'd hear another one and praying it wouldn't hit me.

But a second gunshot didn't go off.

"Was that the glass from the bathroom? Very, very smart, Quint."

His voice sounded like he was now off the stairs and likely a step or two from the hallway.

I stepped back out into the hallway. I was at risk again, but I didn't think he'd fire his last bullet unless I was in clear view.

"You were probably hoping I'd fire off that last round too, " Rolle said.

There was nothing to be gained by talking anymore. I'd just narrow down my location for him.

My plan had worked to a degree. He was now down to one bullet.

But what now?

There was the bathroom. And one door on each side.

He'd likely be stepping into the hallway at any moment. And if I was standing in the middle of it, I'd be a dead man.

Door one on the left or door two on the left?

There was no rhyme or reason.

And whichever one I entered, I'd have to stay there.

I saw that they both had push-button locks that locked from the outside. I was afraid to know why.

I quickly pushed down the button, locking the door on the right.

I then did the same with the one on the left, but not before walking in.

It was pitch black and I couldn't tell what type of room I was in. And obviously, there would be no looking for a light switch.

I extended my hand to the right and it touched the end of the room. I did the same with my left hand. It touched the other end.

I was either in the smallest room ever or I'd walked into a closet.

FUCK!

For the first time, I started hearing footsteps in the hall itself. Rolle was probably examining the broken glass and realizing I'd thrown it from the other side of the hall. He'd be heading down this way soon.

Worse yet, I was stuck. I couldn't risk moving rooms.

Rolle was moving slowly down the hall.

And that's when I heard another sound.

Oncoming police cars.

They were nearby, without question. A few streets away, maybe closer. They'd be here in no time.

Rolle surely heard them as well.

If he was going to try and escape, now was the time.

"You get a stay of execution," he yelled. "But don't think I won't be back. Might visit that office of yours again."

He started running back towards the stairs.

I might just get out of this alive!

A second later, I heard a booming sound, followed by several voices screaming, "Police!"

They had broken down the front door.

And then, the footsteps returned to my side of the hall. Leonard Rolle was back.

I was very much in harm's way once again.

"Which room are you in, Quint?"

I didn't answer and focused on not moving a muscle.

"Left or right? Right or left?"

I said nothing.

I heard him inch closer.

"Ah, you locked both doors? Smart of you. You may have noticed, they lock from the outside. I had been planning on doing some entertaining."

I was sickened by the man on the other side of the door.

"I'll be honest, Quint. You're not much of a conversationalist. That's alright, I'll do the talking. So it looks like my time is coming to an end here on earth. No, I won't be going back to jail. They'd throw away the key this time. So I think it's best I vacate this world today. But, you see, I don't want to leave this godforsaken place alone. So why don't you just tell me which room it is, Quint?"

And then, to my shock, I heard him start singing, "Eenie Meenie Miney Mo."

The meaning was obvious. He was going to fire his last bullet into one of the two rooms.

As he progressed through the song, I heard a loud voice from upstairs.

"Oh shit! Look at this!"

A second later you could hear the police making their way down the stairs, surely walking towards the corpse of Betty Jean Clifton. They'd be in the hallway in a matter of seconds.

Rolle was still singing.

I tried to think of any sort of plan.

He'd likely shoot around eye level.

I couldn't fall to the ground because he'd inevitably hear me.

But I could do something.

He was nearing the end of the song.

"My mother told me to pick the very best one…"

As quietly as I could, I lowered my head and my chest towards my knees, trying to get as compact as I could. The less body space I occupied, the less likely a bullet was to find me.

"And you are not it…"

He finished singing the song.

"Goodbye, Quint."

And a split second later, a gunshot rang out.

It had entered the room I was in.

I couldn't be sure, but scrunching down may well have saved my life.

The police heard the gunshot and were moving towards us in a frenzy.

"Police!"

"Police! Come out with your hands up."

They were now in the hallway, fast approaching us.

"Police! Say your name and drop your weapon if you don't want to be shot."

That's the moment I realized I wasn't out of the woods. Far from it.

If the police started firing at Leonard Rolle, I'd likely be hit in the crossfire. The hallway was all of three feet wide and the room/closet was just as narrow.

Leonard Rolle must have been thinking the same thing.

"Suicide by cop it is," he said, for my benefit. "Although, in reality, I'd be murdering you."

He laughed. A reprehensible sound.

I couldn't let Leonard Rolle have the last word.

"You're a scumbag murderer. You had the taser and the gun and you knew the house. And still, I outthought you. You're pathetic. And I'm glad your gruesome mother will be your final kill. On the bright side, you're about to join her in hell."

"Fuck you," he said, but he was obviously rattled.

"Police! Show yourself!"

The cops were feet from us.

Light flooded the hallway. A little crept into my room.

"Put the gun down," an officer yelled.

I couldn't be Leonard Rolle's last victim.

"Don't shoot!" I yelled. "He's out of bullets. You'll kill me in the crossfire."

"Fuck you all!" Leonard Rolle yelled.

He wasn't going to let me talk with them.

I knew what was coming next. He was likely raising his empty gun towards the police.

And right on cue, the hallway erupted in gunfire.

I covered my ears and fell to the ground.

It lasted for what seemed like ten seconds but was probably only a second or two.

It was followed by a bizarre silence.

That was broken by a voice coming over one of the walkie-talkies.

"What the hell? Are you guys okay down there?"

"We're alright. The suspect has been taken out."

The suspect was taken out. And I hadn't been shot.

Even though I was still petrified - and probably in shock - those two things registered.

I was going to live.

A few seconds later, I heard a voice.

"Can you hear me?"

"Yes," I answered.

"Who are you?"

"My name is Quint Adler and I'm a private investigator."

They had no way of knowing the magnitude of what they'd been called to.

"You're in the room on the left side, correct?"

"Yes."

"I want you to get on your knees and put your hands behind your head. Can you do that?"

"Yes. Done."

"Now, I'm going to open the door. Do not make a move. Do you understand?"

"Yes."

"And I'm going to place handcuffs on you. Is that understood?"

"Yes.

A few seconds later, they entered the tiny room and put the handcuffs on me.

"Thank you for not shooting in my direction," I said.

I received no response.

They backed me out of the room.

I looked down at Leonard Rolle.

His eyes were wide open. There were two prominent bullet holes through his forehead and who knew how many more in his chest.

I wanted to spit on his corpse.

He'd killed ten young boys. His sons and eight other innocent victims. He'd also killed Bruce Ballard.

He'd caused immeasurable harm to all of their families. People like the Fisks had their lives forever altered by this monster below me.

I took one last look down at him.

"I'm glad the last words you heard were mine," I said.

Technically, it was the cops warning him to put the gun down.

Regardless, I was glad he heard my voice and choice words before he was blown away.

The officers continued backing me through the hallway and then eventually up the stairs, where a fellow officer was examining the body of Betty Jean Clifton.

We walked right through the broken-down front door and, once outside, made our way down the sets of steps.

The two officers hadn't said one word since putting me in the handcuffs.

That changed when we arrived at the waiting police car.

The younger of the two asked, "What the hell did we walk into?"

The older officer gave him a dirty look. His partner had surely broken protocol.

"Why don't we wait until you get me to the station," I said. "You're not going to believe it."

The younger officer shook his head, not buying what I'd said.

He'd know the truth soon enough.

I looked up at the old Victorian.

This should have been a moment of triumph for me.

Violent? Yes. Horrific? Yes.

But still, triumphant.

Leonard Rolle was dead.

And yet, I felt oddly vacant.

I knew why.

While this case had been about catching Ronnie's killer, my relationship with his family had become a huge aspect of it.

And I couldn't soak in the moment without them here with me.

"Watch your head," the younger officer said and slowly pushed me into the police car.

I knew I had a long night of interviews ahead.

Instead of focusing on that, I imagined what Emmett, Hank, Grant, Evelyn, and everyone else would have to say when I next saw them.

I'd done the impossible.

I found that proverbial needle in the haystack.

CHAPTER 39

By Thursday afternoon, there was no doubt.
Leonard Rolle had killed eleven people in total.
The police had found a journal at the house in Union City.
He outlined each and every murder.

∼

A bunch of information had leaked out on Betty Jean Clifton as well.

She had been born Betty Jean Withers and then became Betty Jean Rolle when, at nineteen years old, she married a man named Stan Rolle. This marriage brought Leonard Rolle, her only child, into this world.

Stan Rolle died when Leonard was just two years old.

Betty Jean Rolle then met Mason Clifton, a doctor, and she took his name for the rest of her life.

When Mason died, Betty Jean inherited a decent sum and moved back to the Bay Area where Leonard had settled.

She bought a plot of land in Union City, only a few miles from her son, and against her neighbors' wishes, built a Victorian-style house at the end of the block.

The house had set her back more than expected and Betty Jean had to get a job. She worked for the DMV from 1995 to 2009, retiring at the ripe old age of seventy-two.

∼

I slowly learned this information over the course of Wednesday night and into Thursday.

After being escorted from the crime scene, I was driven to the Union City police station and interviewed for three hours.

Finally, word started to get out.

Officer Picker and Hank Tressel called the Union City police, telling them I was the hero, not the bad guy.

The Union City PD eventually got the picture and released me.

In their defense, they never treated me like a suspect. They were just fascinated by my entire investigation that led to the house on Rocking Horse.

I didn't get home till past ten p.m. and fell asleep before I was able to start making any phone calls.

~

That following morning, I spent two hours at the Berkeley Police Department.

From there, I went to the Walnut Creek PD and answered a few final questions about Bruce Ballard's murder. They now knew I was the intended target.

Marjorie Ballard admitted that she told her husband she'd paid a P.I. to follow him. She says Bruce Ballard came to my office that morning to fire me.

Another senseless death at the hands of Leonard Rolle.

~

At each of the stops, the detectives were willing to give me information of their own. They knew I'd helped bring down a monster. So they kissed my ass.

I also periodically talked to Hank who'd learned a lot of information as well.

Among the things I'd found out:

Eddie Young was, in fact, Rolle's first murder. It was not a murder of revenge for Lena Young breaking up with him. Leonard Rolle had long wanted to kill and sadly, he'd become infatuated with young Eddie. And his murder awoke the monster in Rolle.

After the murder of Eddie Young, Rolle realized he needed to distance himself from his victims.

He started selecting his victims from basketball games in which his son Gavin played, making sure the team in question was a safe distance from

Hayward.

Over the course of a game, he'd become fixated on one of the kids on the team - or, in the stands - and decide then and there, he would be his next victim.

An officer told me the way Rolle described it in his journal, it was like he turned into a werewolf during the course of the game. Or a monster. He was not the same person as the one who'd entered the gym and whatever teenager he'd chosen was now on borrowed time.

He'd find out where the kid lived and spend the next week or two stalking them. And finding out their patterns, routes home, etc.

He never approached them.

He was afraid they'd mention it to their parents and they'd relay that information to the police after their child was murdered.

So Rolle followed from afar.

Watching. Probing. Calculating.

It was something that I tried to avoid thinking about.

How could anyone stalk a teenager for a week?

And then strangle them to death?

I knew I would never understand.

Rolle was more wicked than I'd ever thought possible.

One police officer asked me the following:

"How did Rolle find out where these kids lived? It would be easy enough to get their names, but it's not like he could follow them home. He had to drive his own son home."

I responded by stating what I'd thought was obvious.

"I was told his mother worked at the DMV."

Which begged the question of just how much Betty Jean Clifton knew.

I don't think she took part in the killings but was probably in on everything else.

The connection to the DMV was impossible to overlook.

More than that, I'd met her. She was wicked to the core.

She wasn't some old lady who had been blindsided by my visit.

Plus, she went to grab the gun for her son.

There was no question she was in on it.

I hoped she rotted in hell too.

The way Leonard Rolle said her full name brought some incestual questions to mind, but I decided not to entertain them.

~

Apparently, Rolle never wrote about committing the murders themselves.

If I was going to play armchair psychologist, I'd guess that stalking them for a week and imagining them dead was more enjoyable than the final act of killing them.

He'd get them close to his car by mentioning the recent basketball game. He also had a taser if things didn't work out as planned.

This was tough to hear after what I'd been through.

I couldn't imagine what a taser would do to a fourteen-year-old body.

A few detectives told me they were working on finding a motive.

It almost seemed unimportant to me.

He was a madman. A psychopath. A nutjob.

All those things and worse.

Sure, he'd had a lunatic mother and probably an atypical childhood.

I didn't care.

Leonard Rolle wasn't going to get any compassion. Not from me.

He was a murderer, plain and simple. And worse yet, a murderer of children.

The journal did offer a closer look into the murder of his two sons. It was one of only two journal entries since returning to the Bay Area after prison.

In it, Rolle mentioned that his sons were starting to suspect he was a murderer. After two kids in Sacramento went missing, that seemed to steel their resolve.

Rolle planned the trip on the Delta to quell their fears and deny he was a killer. His sons loved fishing and he hoped they'd be more likely to listen to him. It didn't work out that way. Things went wrong from the beginning. His two sons didn't fall for his bullshit. Worse yet for Rolle, they said they'd tell the cops when they got back to land.

Leonard Rolle decided he had no choice.

He bludgeoned his older son, Gavin, to death with a baseball bat. Gregory tried to protect his brother, but Leonard Rolle hit him twice in succession on the head and then pushed him into the Delta. He looked unconscious after the blows and wasn't much of a swimmer anyway. Leonard Rolle knew he was as good as dead.

Knowing he wasn't going to be able to make this look like an accident, he shoved Gavin's body over as well.

Rolle hadn't planned these murders and wasn't sure what to do. His initial idea was to tell the police they'd gone out fishing by themselves. Hopefully, they'd think it was some random maniac who'd killed his sons.

He knew they wouldn't buy that. Leonard Rolle had rented the boat and several witnesses saw the three of them head off the dock together.

Fleeing was his only chance. He packed a bag the next morning, but the cops arrested him before he had a chance to go anywhere.

The second entry discussed the murder of Bruce Ballard. As Hank had guessed, Rolle thought he was killing me, but in the torrential downpour, he shot the wrong man.

I'd been wondering how he'd found me.

The truth was unnerving.

When Rolle got out of jail, he'd occasionally type the names of his victims into Facebook or Twitter. The sadistic asshole enjoyed seeing the families still grieving around birthdays and the holidays.

It was disgusting.

And what led him to me.

A neighbor of the Fisk's had posted that some guy named Quint was asking questions about the twenty-year-old murder of Ronnie.

Ronnie Fisk's name came up during Leonard Rolle's search.

And so did mine.

Had Rolle been out there following me around?

I hated thinking about it, even with him gone forever.

I arrived home Thursday night and had my first moment of free time since I'd left to interview Lena Young on Wednesday afternoon.

By this point, I'd talked to everyone affiliated with the case. All the Fisks, including Patricia and Maddie. Scott Shea. Rob Osbourne.

Three different police departments. Probably ten police officers in total.

And maybe the number I was most proud of.

Zero members of the media.

I didn't dare bother turning on the T.V. I imagined it was getting wall-to-wall coverage and I preferred not to see it. I'd lived it, after all.

I hoped the media had chosen to keep my name out of it.

I wasn't holding my breath.

Grant called me Thursday night and told me they were planning a makeshift event for the following day, Christmas Eve.

The time was noon to two p.m. so people could make their other Christmas Eve obligations.

"Can you make it?" he asked.

"C'mon, Grant. Of course, I'll be there," I said.

CHAPTER 40

G rant called me back the following morning and informed me they were attempting to make it a festive occasion.

Obviously, tears would be shed on Ronnie's behalf, but Grant didn't want it to turn into a solemn event.

It was Christmas Eve and Ronnie's killer was gone forever. There were a few things to be happy about.

"I'll see you in a few hours," I said.

I hung up the phone before he could thank me for all I'd done. I knew there would be plenty of that at the party itself.

$\sim$

I decided there was someone I should include.

"Quint, I hope you're not calling to say you can't make it tonight."

"No, Mom. We are going to your sister's. I'm also taking you somewhere else beforehand."

"Really?"

"Can you be ready in forty-five minutes?"

"Where are we going?"

"You'll find that out on the way. Will you be ready?"

"I guess."

"Great, I'll pick you up at 11:30."

$\sim$

The next call was to the Folsom County Prison. I put two hundred dollars in the commissary of Cole Townes and was going to ask the Fisks to match me.

～

"Quint!"

I was about to enter the elevator when I heard a voice from behind.

It was Rebecca, who I hadn't seen since our night drinking at the Stadium Pub.

"It's been a while," I said.

"I thought you might be avoiding me."

I smiled.

"But now I know why," she said.

She was bringing her phone towards me and I could see the mugshot of Leonard Rolle with the headline, "Serial Killer?"

"I'm sorry Rebecca, but I really don't want to see that."

She was respectful and put her phone back in her pocket.

"I didn't mean anything by it," she said.

"I know. I'm just not ready."

"No problem. Hey listen, my friends and I are going out on New Year's Eve eve next Thursday. Do you want to join?"

"New Year's Eve eve?" I asked.

"Yup. Since New Year's Eve is amateur night, we are doing it the day before."

I laughed.

"I like it," I said.

"I'll come knock on your door once we've picked a time."

"Maybe I'll let you in," I said, alluding to the last time I'd seen her.

She laughed and walked away.

～

I arrived at my mother's place. It was out of the way for me, but I didn't mind being her chauffeur for the day.

She was wearing a tan dress and was probably overdressed. Not that I was going to mention it.

On the drive over to Grant's apartment, she was alternately frightened, alarmed, horrified, and finally, proud of her only child.

We arrived, twenty minutes after it had begun. As I exited the car, I was pleasantly surprised to see dozens of people.

They'd made a communal area down on the street level and had brought in several large park benches for people to eat on. There were two huge trash cans filled with paper plates and plastic utensils.

They had a few upright collages filled with photos of Ronnie that definitely tugged at the heartstrings.

I looked up at Grant's deck and there were another ten or twelve people up there, drinks in hand.

His deck had come a long way from that first day.

The first person who saw me crossing the street was Evelyn.

"Hi, Quint."

"Hello, Evelyn. This is my mother. We're heading to a Christmas Eve event after this so I brought her along."

They shook hands.

"I'm glad you brought her," she said, looking in my mother's direction. "None of this would be possible if it weren't for your son."

I could see my mother beaming.

"I'll show her around, but there's someone I'd like you to meet," Evelyn said.

I had no idea who it would be.

"Maddie! Come over here."

Among the crowd of people, Maddie Fisk started walking in our direction. For a moment, I thought I might get emotional.

She had curly auburn hair and was wearing jeans and a red, Christmassy sweater.

Finding Ronnie's killer was the reason I'd been hired. Partway through my investigation, I'd come to think that reconciling this family - as much as I could - was a goal as well.

I couldn't believe that Maddie had flown in from New York. And more importantly, that she and Evelyn seemed very friendly. Sisterly, I might go so far as to say.

They hugged when Maddie arrived. Evelyn whisked my mother away.

"Thank you, Quint," Maddie said. "Thank you for everything."

She leaned in and hugged me for a good twenty seconds. When she let go, I saw tears in her eyes.

"You're welcome," I said.

"You did more than just catch Ronnie's killer. You brought our family back together."

"Thanks, but you guys had to take those first steps. Not me."

"Did you know our mother is here?"

Patricia Fisk had come too. She'd probably been the toughest on me of the whole family, but I was still thrilled she was here.

"I didn't. Can't wait to meet her."

"She said she owes you a few apologies."

"Absolutely not. I would have hated me in her situation."

"Well, not anymore. You're the toast of this family."

I was getting uncomfortable with all the praise.

"Should we join the party?" I asked.

We were still standing on the sidewalk, fifty yards from the party. And yes, it did look like an actual party.

"Sure," she said. "I'm sure you've got a lot of people to talk to. I just wanted you to know that I appreciate everything."

She hugged me again.

"You're welcome, Maddie. Don't let this be a one-off. Keep this momentum going."

"I will. There will be growing pains, but we'll get through it. These last few weeks have brought us back together."

"That makes me very happy," I said.

I led us towards the party.

I saw Hank talking to a woman that I recognized from old pictures. It was the just mentioned Patricia Fisk. Grant was on the deck and appeared to be grilling. Not something you saw every Christmas Eve.

I saw Ed and Lenore Finney, the first neighbors I'd interviewed. They managed to still be shabbily dressed, even on Christmas Eve.

It made me happy that some old neighbors were going to be here. It might help give them a little closure as well.

Someone tapped me on the shoulder from behind.

"Ready to let bygones be bygones?"

It was Randall Picker.

We shook hands.

"All is well that ends well, right?" I said. "And thanks for calling the Union City police on my behalf."

He nodded.

"I spent yesterday breaking the news to the family of Todd Zobrist."

"How did it go?"

"It was a less joyous occasion than this."

"Not surprised," I said.

"But they were still happy to have closure. And I tell you this Quint because it's not just Ronnie Fisk's family that you've provided that closure for. There are several other families as well."

"Thanks, Officer Picker."

"Shit, you might as well call me Randall at this point," he said.

I laughed.

"I wanted to call you something very different a few days ago."

He laughed.

"Yeah, I know."

"But Randall it is from here on in," I said.

We shook hands.

~

I didn't see Paul Piercy.

Considering he'd worked on the initial Ronnie Fisk investigation, he probably would have been Persona non grata. I hoped down the line he'd reach out to me and consider talking to Tom Butler. Time would tell.

~

I spent the next thirty minutes making the rounds, feeling insecure with all the praise being heaped on me.

And yet, I did feel a little prideful.

It was me who had brought all these people together. It was me who had spearheaded this investigation for the last two weeks. It was me who had stared into the eye of the devil and taken him down. With a little help from the Union City police, obviously.

Patricia Fisk and I talked for five minutes or so. It ended with her giving me the hug to end all hugs.

"Thank you for all you've done for Ronnie."

I was close to tearing up but was able to remain stoic.

~

Hank and I only talked for a few minutes. We were now friends and we'd surely be having a coffee on his deck soon, so it felt superfluous to spend too much time with him.

As soon as I walked away from Hank, Emmett Fisk approached me.

"You been avoiding me?" he asked. "This is ageism, you know."

I laughed, as I had so many times in my dealings with Emmett Fisk.

Once my investigation had started, I'd dealt with several people more often than Emmett.

And yet, he was the one who had brought me the case. Without Emmett, none of this would have been possible.

"I didn't see you," I said. "Thought maybe you'd scooted off to the local Bingo Hall."

Emmett laughed.

"Shit, I'm even too old for that."

I decided to be serious for a moment.

"Emmett, thank you for this. Thanks for coming to me. Thanks for trusting me. And thanks for letting me be a part of your family for the last few weeks."

"Are you kidding me? It's me who should be thanking you."

"It goes both ways. I've been rewarded in numerous ways."

"My family is back together. Believe me, I get the best end of this deal."

"I'm happy for you."

"Don't take what I'm about to say the wrong way, Quint, because this is a great, great day."

"What is it, Emmett?"

"If and when I die, I will do so a happy man. And a big part of that is what you've done for this family."

I didn't know whether I wanted to cry or tell him to stop.

"Thank you, Emmett. That makes it all worthwhile."

He leaned in and hugged me.

It was the third hug and the third time I'd almost cried.

"Now, where is that eighteen-year-old Scotch?" he said and walked away.

Emmett was a man who always liked to get the last word in. And I was more than happy to let him have it.

~

I met Grant up on the deck as he turned a few hot dogs.

"Hot Dogs. The cornerstone of any good Christmas Eve celebration," I said.

He laughed.

"Ronnie loved hot dogs. I thought it was apropos."

"I'm so happy to see your family together," I said.

"It's supposed to be me thanking you for that," Grant replied.

"I know. That's why I beat you to it."

He laughed.

"You are always a part of the Fisk family going forward. You can pop into any family occasion you want."

"Thanks, Grant. How about one of those dogs?"

He threw one on a paper plate and added some sautéed onions.

I went to the corner of the deck and ate it in three or four quick bites.

I'd seen my mother talking with several of the gathered people. She'd also been in Vegas for a similar celebration.

I decided that's the way it would be going forward. I'd invite her to something like this, but keep her in the dark during the investigation. It was best for both of us.

I was also happy that she was having a Christmas Eve with dozens of people. With the death of my father, we'd become an even smaller family. And her sister's annual Christmas Eve party wasn't exactly a barnburner. So this meant a lot to me.

∼

Grant had told me to invite anyone who had contributed to the investigation.

There were two people I was almost positive wouldn't show.

I was wrong.

I saw Paddy Roark and Dennis McCarthy walking up the steps of the deck as I finished my hot dog.

They walked over to greet me.

"Now, this is a shocker," I said.

Dennis stepped towards me.

"You've done well, Quint," he said.

"Thank you, Dennis."

We shook hands.

"Your help was critical."

"That was all Paddy."

"Where is he?" I joked as he stood behind Dennis.

"Right here, smart guy," Paddy said.

Instead of shaking my hand, he hugged me.

"Boss is right. You've done well."

I saw Hank approaching us, a curious look on his face.

"Are these the guys who helped with Sacramento?" he asked.

I had no idea how he'd guessed that.

"Yeah, this is…"

Before I could finish, he was shaking the hand of Dennis McCarthy.

"So, you guys are now doing good for the community?" Hank asked.

It was tense for a few moments.

And then Dennis smiled.

"I used to do battle with your friend Hank here."

I should have known. A famous San Francisco cop and the biggest bookie the city has ever seen.

"He's exaggerating," Hank said. "We crossed paths a few times, but I was trying to nab real bad guys."

Dennis patted him on the back.

"I always respected that about you."

"Thanks for your help, Dennis."

"I'm just glad that Quint was able to take down that monster. Hank, this is Paddy, a friend of mine," Dennis said.

"Paddy Roark, right," Hank said. "I know the name."

"We met once. Under less joyful circumstances."

"Ah, I remember. The Irish grocery story, correct?"

"That's right. Good memory."

I was enjoying this more than I should have.

It was time I spoke.

"A bunch of supposed tough guys getting all mushy and sentimental."

They all laughed.

Dennis looked down at my plate.

"I'd love one of those hot dogs."

"Perfect. I'd like to introduce you to Ronnie's father and he's manning the grill."

We walked the ten feet towards the grill.

Hank had a huge smile on his face as I passed by him.

I'd find out his history with Dennis next time I visited Sausalito.

I introduced Grant to Dennis and Paddy.

I then receded to a corner and looked out on all the gathered guests.

I took it all in.

~

A few minutes later when I was back downstairs, I heard my phone ring.

With all that was going on, I'd gotten into the habit of answering calls from unknown numbers.

This time was no different.

"Hello?" I said.

"Is this Quint Adler?"

"Yes, it is."

"My name is Gene Bowman. You are the man who brought down Leonard Rolle?"

It sounded like a member of the media. I shouldn't have answered.

"I did my part, yes. How can I help you, Mr. Bowman?"

"I've got your next case."

Well, it wasn't the media.

"Darn, and here I thought I'd have a say in the matter," I said.

"I'm sorry. That came across wrong. I've got a case that I think would interest you greatly."

"With all due respect, sir, it's Christmas Eve and I'm with friends."

And it was true. These people were now my friends.

"Can I describe the case?"

"You've got five seconds."

"I'll give it to you in two."

He paused.

"Alright...go," I said.

"A knife through the heart."

"That's it?"

"I'll give you the rest when we meet."

"Call me next week," I said.

He hung up.

A knife through the heart?

The visual had my attention, I'll admit that much.

I had no idea if that was going to be my next case.

What I did know was that the Fisk case had been all too real. And I was at their party, so that's where my mind should be.

I walked back upstairs and found Grant.

"What do you think about getting a photo of everyone?" I asked.

"It's a great idea. Let me finish these last few hot dogs and I'll get everyone to go downstairs. Not enough space up here for all the people."

"Shows how beloved Ronnie was."

"Thanks for that, Quint."

"I'd also like to get one with just me and your family," I said.

A photo with me and the Fisks - a family that had been at odds for twenty years - would mean the world to me.

After we took a few minutes of photos - including one where we all yelled 'This is for you, Ronnie' - I started recollecting the last hour.

It had been something to treasure.

And I was happy the name Leonard Rolle had been mentioned so infrequently. Going forward, I wanted everyone to think about Ronnie Fisk instead. Along with Todd Zobrist, Matt Greeson, Eddie Young, and the others.

Their lives mattered and shouldn't have to be linked to that monster.

I hoped the families could properly grieve now, knowing Rolle was gone.

And just like that, I vowed not to mention his name ever again.

Or, as close to that as I could.

I started saying my goodbyes.

I'd be keeping in touch with many of them, including Hank and hopefully, the entire Fisk family.

I'd never thought this case could have a happy ending.

I was wrong.

No, Ronnie wasn't coming back, but Patricia had come back. So had Maddie.

The Fisk family itself had come back.

And I was grateful for it all.

~

As I turned to leave the party, I saw that Emmett, Grant, Patricia, Evelyn, and Maddie had all gathered together on the deck.

I looked up.

They all waved goodbye or gave me a salute of some sort.

I'd helped bring this family together and it was all culminating in this moment.

Several times I'd become emotional, but had been able to resist shedding tears.

I was no longer strong enough.

The waterworks began.

ALSO BY BRIAN O'SULLIVAN

First off, a huge thank you for finishing **Quint Adler, P.I.** I hope you enjoyed reading it as much as I did writing it. I'd be honored if you left a review. Thanks!

I'm currently working on my 6th Quint novel, **A Knife Through The Heart**, if you'd like to pre-order now!

If you've been reading them out of order, here you go:

Book 1: *Revenge at Sea*

Book 2: *The Bay Area Butcher*

Book 3: *Hollywood Murder Mystery*

Book 4: *Nine Days in Vegas*

Please don't forget my personal favorite, the enthralling, multi-narrative nail-biter, *The Bartender*!

And if you like political thrillers, you'll love my first two novels, *The Puppeteer* and *The Patsy*!

Finally, I'd like to thank you for giving me a chance. It means more than you'll ever know. Cheers! And I hope you'll tell a friend or twenty about these books :)

Sincerely,

Brian O'Sullivan

Printed in Great Britain
by Amazon

44941837R00179